KERRY J DONOVAN

ON THE TRAIL

BOOKS

The Ryan Kaine Series by Kerry J Donovan

On The Run

On The Rocks

On The Defensive

On The Attack

On The Money

On The Edge

On The Wing

On The Hunt

On The Outside

On The Lookout

On The Brink

On The Offensive

On The Charge

On The Trail

To Margaret, a wonderful sounding board who helps me find my way through life's confusion.

Vinci Books

vinci-books.com

Published by Vinci Books Ltd in 2025

1

A CIP catalogue record for this book is available from the British Library.

Paperback ISBN: 9781036710194

Chapter One

Mike's Farm, Long Buckby, Northants, England

Something touched Ryan Kaine's naked shoulder. A hand. Warm, the grip firm.

"Ryan, wake up."

Lara. Distress hung heavy in the three short words.

Wide awake in an instant, Kaine sat up in bed, wiping the sleep from his eyes. Lara, fully dressed, stood over him, her expression grave.

"What's wrong?"

"It's Mike." Tears filled her hazel eyes. "He's asking for you. It's close."

Kaine reached out, held her hand, squeezed gently. They'd been expecting this moment, preparing for it, for

1

weeks. Months. He and Lara shared a brief glance before she broke his grip and turned away.

"I'll be right there," he said.

She left their shared bedroom.

He dressed in a hurry, jogged down the stairs to Mike's old office, and knocked before entering what he and the guys had turned into a fully equipped sickbay. It smelled not of death, but of freshly cut lavender.

The half-drawn curtains allowed in a channel of watery sunshine, but a shadow fell across the bed, making Mike difficult to see. An oxygen cylinder released a gentle hiss of gas through the transparent, plastic mask strapped to Mike's face. The jagged line of the heart rate monitor stuttered across the screen, the numbers showed a fast beat and rapid breathing. Behind the mask, Mike's open mouth gasped for breath, his chest rising and falling in sharp jerks.

Close. Close to the end.

Kaine's breath caught in his throat.

As he approached the bed, Lara—who'd been adjusting the levels on the machine that delivered pain meds—smiled down at Mike and rested a hand on his wasted shoulder. She backed away and stood near the door, watching. Clearly distraught.

Mike reached up a hand and pulled down the mask. He gasped something but the words didn't carry over the oxygen cylinder's hissing.

Kaine edged closer to the head of the bed and bent lower.

"What was that, Mike?"

"I … said … thanks for … for coming," he repeated, the words punched out between gasps.

Sweat burst out on Mike's forehead. The effort to speak must have been enormous.

"What else am I going to do when you call?" Kaine said, gently, and forced a smile onto an unwilling face. "But save your breath, Mike."

Kaine took a damp cloth from a dish on the bedside table and dabbed Mike's gaunt, grey face. The sunken cheeks and hollow eyes told a desperate tale. Close to the end but hanging on for no reason other than his innate stubbornness.

Mike grabbed the hand holding the cloth and tugged it away. Kaine let him. Mike's eyelids fluttered and closed.

"It wasn't … your … fault," he said, straining out the words through dry, chapped lips.

"I know, Mike," Kaine said, knowing exactly what he meant, but not believing a word of it.

"It wasn't … your … fault," Mike repeated with all the strength he could muster. His watery eyes opened and locked on Kaine's. "It wasn't. … Forgive yourself."

"I have, Mike," Kaine lied.

The dying chief petty officer shook his head. "You haven't, but you … you must. It … It will … eat you up. What you're doing … for The 83, is a good thing, but you need to leave time … time for yourself. Time for … Lara."

A rock formed in Kaine's throat. Hard. Choking. Mist blurred his vision. He couldn't blink it clear.

"I will, Mike. I promise."

"When … I'm … gone," he said, "stay away. It's too … dangerous. People will … come. Many people. Stay … away."

"I know, Mike. Don't worry. Rest yourself."

Mike squeezed Kaine's hand tighter.

"Closer," he whispered. "Come … closer."

Kaine bent lower, pushed his ear towards Mike's mouth.

"I … I love … you, son. Be … be kinder to yourself."

"Love you, too, old man," Kaine gasped, the words driven through a restricted throat.

Mike's thin lips stretched into the ghost of a smile. His eyes closed, his grip loosened, and the hand fell away.

"Mike?"

Kaine straightened. He snapped a look at Lara.

The jagged line on the heart rate monitor flattened and screeched a raucous warning. Lara stepped closer, reached out, and pressed a button on the machine. The alarm fell silent.

"Do something!" Kaine shouted.

Teary-eyed, Lara shook her head.

"Do something," he repeated, the words broken. Shattered.

"No," she said. "It's time."

"But—"

"Ryan, it's time. Let him go."

Kaine knew. Deep down, he knew.

He stood straight, pulled back his shoulders, and breathed deep and slow. He stared down at the once-vital form of his oldest friend, who lay in his bed, almost unrecognisable. He reached out but pulled his hand away.

He'd seen plenty of dead bodies in his time, but few had died peacefully, in their beds. Kaine hadn't been there when his mother passed. He'd been away, fighting in some Godawful, half-forgotten backwater. But at least he'd held Mike's hand at the end. Mike, who'd been a near-constant presence in Kaine's life since long before his dad passed away. A second father. They'd served together, Mike and Kaine's dad. Briefly.

Kaine rested a hand on Mike's immobile chest.

"Goodbye, Mike," Kaine gasped. "It was an … honour

to know you." Kaine couldn't believe how well his voice held up to the emotion.

Lara put her arm around his waist and rested her head on his shoulder.

"Go, Ryan," she said. "Make us a cuppa. Let me look after him."

Kaine stiffened. Pulled away.

"Sorry, what?"

"Tea," she said and added a gentle nod. "I'll look after him."

"Oh, yes. I see." He nodded and again tried to blink away the mist. "Two teas coming up."

"Better make four," she said. "Connor and Dele are already up and about."

"Are they?"

She nodded. "Have been for a while."

Kaine read the time from his diver's watch. 09:31. He'd been asleep for ten hours straight. He frowned.

"And before you complain about not being woken," she said, "you've been stretching yourself too much lately. I decided you needed your rest. Turned off the alarm."

"Oh you did, did you?" he said, only partly annoyed.

"I did. Now tea." She snapped out an arm and pointed towards the door.

"Doctor's orders?"

"You'd better believe it, Marine."

Kaine cast Mike a sad, parting look, nodded to him, and left the sickbay. Since Mike had asked for a closed coffin, Kaine would never see his friend again.

Chapter Two

Saturday 3rd July - Morning

Mike's Farm, Long Buckby, Northants, England

Kaine sat brooding over his untouched cuppa.

"Why did he tell you to stay away?" Lara asked. She cradled her mug in both hands, but, like Kaine, had yet to take a sip. "And what are you supposed to stay away from?"

"The funeral," Kaine answered. He tried to think of the good times long gone, but with Mike's hollow and lifeless body lying in the room along the corridor, none came easily to mind.

A good man, Mike had been part of Kaine's life for decades. God, he'd miss the curmudgeonly, old sailor. As staunch a friend as anyone could ask for. And the way he'd taken to Lara … treated her like a daughter. Such a terrible loss. Taken too soon. Far too bloody soon.

"Why can't you go to the funeral?"

Kaine shook his head sadly. "You know why. The service will be full of old crewmates. I can't take the risk. Someone's bound to recognise me, and I wouldn't want Mike's funeral to degenerate into a circus. I'll have to stay clear."

The boot room door opened, and Connor Blake pushed through into the kitchen. Dele Hunter followed close behind.

"Funeral?" Connor asked, looking from Kaine to Lara. "Mike's …" he trailed off unable to complete the question.

Lara nodded.

Connor made the sign of the cross and stepped further into the kitchen. "Me Mum woulda called it a 'Blessed Release'. Never really knew what she meant 'til now. At least the poor guy ain't suffering no more."

"Amen to that, bro," Hunter said, head lowered.

Connor fired Hunter a sideways glance and nodded. When they'd first met, Connor would have shot the man down for being so familiar as to call him "brother", but a grudging respect had developed between them, if not an actual friendship. In that regard, Kaine's decision to have them work together, securing the farm, had worked out well enough.

Being the newest recruit to Kaine's unofficial and volunteer troop, Hunter had only known Mike for a short time, but he'd seen what the retired CPO had meant to Kaine and the rest of the men. He busied himself with the coffee machine.

"You gonna make yourself scarce, boss?" Connor asked Kaine.

"For the funeral and the memorial service, but I can hang around for a while."

"What about Nigel?" Hunter asked, referring to the nurse Kaine had contracted to help Lara with Mike's care. "Want me to call and cancel his visit?"

"No," Lara said. "I'll need him to help me prep the body."

Kaine stared at her. "I thought you'd already done that."

"No," she answered, her hazel eyes liquid. "I was saying goodbye. And I told him I'd take care of Dynamite and Lexie, and look after the farm. Like I promised."

"Oh, I see." Kaine nodded. "It's just that you were in with him for a while. I thought you were … you know."

"I also phoned Mike's GP." She lowered her eyes, stared at her tea, and finally took a sip. "It took me ages to get through."

"What a surprise," Hunter said, his voice heavy with irony.

He handed Connor a mug of black coffee sweetened with three sugars.

"He'll be here within the next hour," she added.

"When's Nigel due?" Connor asked.

"Any time now," she said.

As if Nigel had overheard the conversation, a car horn blared twice to announce his arrival in the time-honoured way.

Connor set his mug down on the counter. "I'll go meet 'im. Give 'im the sad news."

"Go easy on him, Connor," Lara said. "He's known Mike quite a while."

On his way through the door, Connor cast her a

doubtful look that made her hold up her hand in apology. Hunter snorted and shook his head.

Kaine stood and carried his tea to the window with a view to the courtyard at the rear of the farmhouse. Nigel's car—a three-year-old Range Rover Discovery that Kaine had given him as a reward for helping to look after Mike for so long—pulled into his spot in the courtyard. The stockily built man in his starched, white tunic climbed out of his car and smiled as Connor approached. He stood, looking up at the slightly taller man, listening intently. Nigel's tight expression told of sad but expected news. Connor dropped a gentle hand on the nurse's broad shoulder. They stood still for a moment before Nigel straightened and tugged invisible creases out of his immaculate tunic. Connor removed his paw, and they headed to the back door.

Kaine had seen enough. More than enough. He turned away from the window, lowered his full mug to the kitchen table, and fixed Lara with heavy eyes.

"Do you need me for anything?"

"Not for now," she answered. "Why?"

"I need to go out. Be on my own for a while."

She nodded her understanding.

"Thanks."

Kaine spun and hurried from the kitchen, ahead of Connor and Nigel's entrance, feeling like a coward. He raced up the stairs, dived into his and Lara's bedroom, and changed into fresh running kit. In the absence of a nearby open water source, his landlocked therapy beckoned—a ten-mile run over the fields and along farm tracks. He doubted it would do any good but could think of no better alternative. Exercise would dull his mind and stress his body. For a few short moments, it would ease the pain of loss.

Chapter Three

Saturday 3rd July - Early Evening

Mike's Farm, Long Buckby, Northants, England

Kaine picked at his meal, for once struggling to eat. Connor had drawn the short straw and prepared the food with great care. Although a half-decent cook, nobody had much of an appetite to do his chicken chowder full justice. No one but Hunter, who packed it away as though he hadn't eaten all day. Which he hadn't.

While Kaine had raced through the rolling, Northamptonshire hills on his extended run, the GP had arrived, ninety minutes later than promised. After all, there was no rush. Mike wasn't going anywhere, and he was hardly in a position to complain. Kaine had deliberately kept away from the farm, leaving Lara to carry the responsibility for the legal requirements. A cowardly act, and one he didn't feel good about, but Lara understood. It came jointly from the need for Kaine to keep his head down and also to hide his emotions from the men. Mike's death had hit home much worse than he'd anticipated. Although he'd been desperately and terminally ill for months, Mike's passing had struck hard, gutting, taking him back to the deaths of others he'd known and loved.

Death and destruction. Kaine had flirted with the twin disasters all his adult life. When would it end? When would it bloody end?

The family doctor—who'd known Mike for years and had also treated his wife, Ellie—determined the cause of death as complications stemming from prostate cancer. He'd completed and signed the death certificate and left after the briefest of stays. A busy man.

After he'd gone and with Kaine returned from hiding, Lara called the undertakers, who'd been prepped for weeks and arrived within the hour. Two soberly dressed men took Mike away while Kaine, Lara, and the guys stood on either side of the private ambulance—an unmarked, black, panel van—as an impromptu guard of honour.

The funeral arrangements had been long planned and with military precision. Lara and Connor had divided up the list and spent most of the afternoon notifying the interested parties—the Royal Naval Association, Mike's solicitors, his closest friends and neighbours. Meanwhile, Kaine called the absent members of his troop.

To give anyone wishing to attend the time to make travel arrangements, the funeral service would take place at the local crematorium two weeks after Mike's passing—the 17th July. Although Mike couldn't have been much more popular, he had no surviving family members. Lara would inherit the farm. As agreed with Mike, she would run it as a horse sanctuary, in the guise of Loren Verger, a veterinary surgeon from Bristol who happened to be Mike and Ellie's long-lost niece. Corky had been working on her new legend for weeks and he'd proudly proclaimed it to be the best and most detailed he'd ever built—only he used more self-aggrandising turns of phrase. For her part, Lara had so fully immersed herself in her new legend over the previous days that she refused to answer to any names but "Loren" and "Doc".

As he played with his chowder, Kaine recalled his parting conversation with Nigel.

"Would you like to stay?" Kaine had asked. "Join us for a meal?"

"Thanks, Mr Jeffries," Nigel answered, "but I'd best be off. Leave you to your grieving. Or are you 'John Stones' today, sir?" He eased out a knowing smile.

During their first meeting, Kaine had introduced himself as the fictitious "John Stones" and subsequently explained that, from time to time, he needed to work undercover for The Trust. He added that when he immersed himself in a false character, it would occasionally stick. He'd laughed it off as a side-effect of "method acting".

"No, no," Kaine answered. "Today, I'm myself … Arnold Jeffries."

Nigel nodded. "That's good to know."

Kaine nodded and then allowed his gaze to drift towards the office they'd turned into the sickbay. "Thanks for all you've done, Nigel. It's really appreciated."

The nurse lowered his head. "It's what I do, sir."

"No," Kaine said, shaking his head. "You went above and beyond."

"Thanks, sir. Mr Procter was a decent man. I just tried to make him as comfortable as I could."

Kaine accompanied him through the kitchen and the boot room, and out the back door. They stood for a moment in silence, absorbing the hot, midday sunshine.

"Any immediate plans?" Kaine asked.

Nigel breathed deep and released the breath in an extended sigh.

"Nothing much. I'll probably spend a couple of weeks with my parents, decompressing."

"Where do they live?" Kaine asked as though he had no idea. Before contracting the nurse as day carer for Mike, Corky had run a full-press, background search, and had produced his usual, detailed report. Kaine knew everything about the nurse, from where he lived and where he'd trained, to his shoe size and the football team he supported —Manchester United. Nobody was perfect.

"Cornwall," Nigel answered, smiling. "They retired to St Ives five years back."

"St Ives?" Kaine said, adding a thoughtful smile. "Lovely place, St Ives. I've been there a few times."

"It is beautiful." Nigel nodded. "They have a lovely house overlooking the beach. I visit as often as I can. The perfect place to unwind."

Kaine nodded. He already knew that.

Dynamite, the black stallion, whinnied, kicked his rear legs, and galloped out of sight behind the stable block. A powerful beast, all bulging muscle and chomping teeth. Kaine had no idea how Lara managed to control the horse enough to saddle him up, let alone ride him along the Northants bridleways. Every time she mounted the steed, Kaine shuddered. Worried to death.

"And after St Ives?" he asked.

Nigel shrugged. "I'll go back to my old job with the palliative care team. I took an unpaid leave of absence to look after Mike full time, but the NHS position is still open."

"Good," Kaine said, smiling and holding out his hand. "The NHS needs as many good people as it can find."

As they shook hands warmly, Lara emerged from the boot room. She approached Nigel, threw her arms around him, and they hugged tight. Then Kaine and Lara walked him to his car.

"Thanks again for all you've done, Nigel," Lara said, teary-eyed.

The nurse nodded his acceptance, climbed into his car, and rolled away. He drove as slowly and carefully as always.

"A good man," Kaine said.

"And a damn fine nurse," Lara agreed. "I couldn't have managed without him these past few weeks."

Kaine draped a gentle arm around her shoulders and squeezed.

"And the next time he checks his bank balance," Kaine whispered, "Nurse Nigel Cathcart is going to find a healthy severance bonus, courtesy of my personal retirement fund."

Lara smiled and hugged his waist. "That's a nice gesture."

"He deserves it."

She'd rested her head on his shoulder, and they watched Dynamite and the slightly smaller, brown horse, Lexie, blissfully unaware of the recent loss of their owner, poke their heads over the paddock fence, hoping for some attention. At least, Lara watched the horses. Kaine didn't. He'd had other things on his mind. Things like wondering how Lara would cope with her new responsibility, and how she'd manage to ease herself back into the real world.

Kaine pushed his food away, unfinished, and leaned back.

"I did my best, boss," Connor said, staring into Kaine's bowl.

"Nothing wrong with the rations, Sergeant," Kaine said. "In fact it's very tasty, but I can't claim to have much of an appetite this evening."

"Yeah," Hunter said, spooning up another mouthful. "Good grub, bro." If anyone could challenge Larry Kovaks for the troop's competitive eating crown, Dele Hunter would be in the frame to give it a go. He'd lose, but he'd go down fighting.

In a rare show of affection in front of the men, Lara reached for Kaine's hand. He let her hold it for the briefest moment before standing and heading for Mike's drinks cabinet in the lounge area. He grabbed a bottle of rum and four shot glasses and carried them to the table. He poured, passed them out, and held his up.

"To Mike," he said, still standing. "The best of us all." He almost choked on the words.

"To Mike," they repeated. The men knocked back the fiery toast. Lara only sipped hers.

Kaine lowered his empty glass to the table and sat.

"Now would be the time to tell some Mike-related war stories, but …" He sighed. "I can't really think of any."

"It's too soon," Lara said. "Too raw."

Connor nodded.

"Never saw the guy in 'is prime, but 'e were a real gent. Salt of the earth."

"Too right," Hunter agreed, eyeing the bottle. "Never heard him complain. Not once. Never felt sorry for himself either. Any chance of a top up, Captain?" He pointed to the bottle and pushed out his glass.

"Help yourself," Kaine answered.

Hunter grabbed the bottle, pulled the cork, and offered Kaine the next pour. Kaine covered his glass with his hand and shook his head.

"Not for me but feel free. Mike wouldn't want it to go to waste."

"You sure, boss?" Connor asked.

"Go for it."

Hunter poured himself and Connor a second tot. This time, they drank more slowly.

"In his prime, he could be one tough SOB, though," Kaine announced, unable to tell where the sentiment came from. "Mess up a drill or arrive on duty unprepared and he could scream so hard he'd peel the paint off a bulkhead. But he was fair. Supportive. Not a bully like some of them." Kaine stared into the middle distance and saw nothing but memories. "At least, that's what my old man told me." He turned his eyes to Lara. "Mike served with my father for a time. Did I tell you?"

"No. You didn't." She leaned closer, attentive, fiddling with her nearly full glass.

Kaine shrugged when he should have apologised. He'd do that later—in private. Hunter and Connor listened, intent on learning more. Kaine rarely opened up to his men, but he couldn't think of a more suitable occasion.

"The Med, the South Atlantic, the Gulf … all over," Kaine continued. "I remember Dad telling me about this lieutenant on his first posting. Bloody useless, he was. Or so my dad said. Threw up on the main deck on the second day at sea even though it was millpond-calm. Mike could have savaged the poor kid. He could have made his life a living hell. But he didn't. Took him under his wing. Looked after him for the rest of the tour. Taught him the ropes. Helped him through …" Kaine snatched up his empty glass and held it out for Hunter to refill. "The lieutenant quickly made captain. Broke all peacetime records doing it, too. And when the Admiralty gave him his own ship, Mike signed on as his CPO."

Kaine knocked back a healthy swig. It scorched his throat on the way down, but he refused to grimace. Mike would have called him a southern softie.

"You'll never guess who that captain turned out to be."

"Your Dad?" Lara asked, taking another dainty sip of her rum.

"Nah," Kaine answered, shaking his head. "It was some other captain. Dad couldn't stand the man. Said he was an arrogant piece of work who deserved Mike as his CPO."

When Lara jerked back in shock, Kaine winked.

"Kidding."

Connor's eyes widened, clearly unable to believe his ears. Hunter laughed. Lara smiled at the poor joke, and Kaine's phone vibrated on the table. He snatched it up, read the caller ID, and accepted the call.

"Hi, Cough," Kaine said. "Where are you?"

"Heading south on the M1. Be with you in thirty-five. Unless we hit more traffic." The roar of Cough's classic Audi Avant all but drowned out his words.

"Stefan with you?"

"Oh yes," Cough answered, "Dumpster's here alright. We're gutted about Mike, boss. A really sad day."

"You didn't need to rush. Funeral won't be for another two weeks."

"Nothing better to do, boss," Stefan said, speaking up over the roar of the Avant combined with motorway traffic.

"Besides," Cough added, "you'll need help setting up for

the wake. And there's bound to be a few reprobates hanging around in need of restraint."

"Yes," Kaine said, smiling almost for the first time that day, "and two more will be arriving in thirty-five minutes."

"Thirty-three now, boss," Cough said, a grin in his voice. "See you soon."

He rang off, and Kaine lowered the phone to the table.

Lara slid her unfinished glass towards Kaine and stood. Kaine shot her a questioning look.

"Dynamite and Lexie can't groom or feed themselves."

"Need a hand?"

She scoffed. "No, thanks. I don't want to spook them. They can smell fear, you know."

"Fear?" Kaine said, throwing a hand to his chest. "Scared of half a tonne of savage horseflesh and all those vicious teeth and hooves? *Moi?* The very idea. Take the lads with you." He pointed to Connor and Hunter—two men even less comfortable around horses than Kaine. "They'll be happy to muck out the stables for you. Won't you, men?"

"Shovel shi—manure, boss?" Connor grunted. "Might as well be back in the bleeding army."

Lara held up her hand.

"No," she said. "I'd rather do it myself. It'll take my mind off … things." She threw a hurried glance to Mike's sickbay, rushed to the boot room, and let herself out.

Kaine thought about following, but Connor shook his head.

"Best leave 'er to it, boss," he said, nursing his third neat rum. "She's potty 'bout them 'orses. Taking care of 'em will do 'er nothing but good."

Kaine nodded and leaned against the back of his dining chair.

"You're right, of course," Kaine said. "I'll give her time. Any more rum in that bottle?"

Chapter Four

Saturday 3rd July - Early Evening

Mike's Farm, Long Buckby, Northants, England

Half an hour later, and with three small tots of rum inside him, and no more, Kaine stood.

"Where you going, boss?" Connor asked.

They'd moved to the upholstered chairs in the lounge that were gathered around the unlit fireplace. Before his illness, winter or summer, Mike would rarely allow the fire to burn itself out during the day. He seemed to possess an inexhaustible supply of firewood, a mixture of oak, chestnut, and willow—which burned fiercest of all and threw out a decent level of heat. The radiator in Mike's sickroom did the same job, but without the work or the dirt, and with none of the romance of a real fire.

Kaine scratched at his beard. It needed a trim. If things panned out with the upcoming general election and a new government took over, he might finally earn exoneration and, as a result, be able to shave the bloody thing off. Kaine's police friend, DCI Jones, had approached the opposition leadership and had received encouraging mood music for his pains. On top of which, Kaine had the backing of their new "inside man", Sir Ernest Hartington. The head of the National Counter Terrorism Agency, Hartington owed Kaine his life and had promised to exert his influence over the incoming government, no matter which side of the political divide it straddled. Hopefully, a new broom would sweep through the dusty corridors of power and remove all the crud. All in all, Mike's passing aside, Kaine had reason for cautious optimism.

"We've killed that one," Kaine said, nodding to the empty bottle standing on the coffee table between them. "Mike has—*had*"—he clenched his fists—"a supply somewhere. Thought I'd try finding it for you."

Hunter raised a lazy arm and waved it towards the cabinet standing against the wall opposite the fireplace.

"In the sideboard," he said, speaking clearly despite having knocked back the better part of half a bottle of Captain Morgan's finest. Kaine didn't know how he managed. "On the right, behind the sealed bottle of Courvoisier and the near-empty Glenfiddich. Mike had damn fine taste in the hard stuff." His eyelids drooped slightly, in the first outward signs of intoxication.

"Can I?" Connor asked. Without waiting for a response, he jumped up and crossed the room. "I'll replace it in the morning and get a load more booze in. We'll need to stock up before the rest of the guys get 'ere. Provisions are running low, and there's the wake to think about. That's gonna be a blast, by the way. Mike deserves a good send-off."

"Help yourselves," Kaine said. "I'm done."

A moment later, three sharp blasts of the Audi Avant's two-tone horn made Kaine smile.

"That'll be Cough and Stefan," he announced. "I'll go let them in. Don't want them startling the nags."

"Oh dear," Connor said, squatting in front of the drinks cabinet, shaking his head. "Don't let the doc 'ear you call 'em nags, boss. She'll go ballistic."

Kaine's heart lurched. Mike had said a similar thing not so long ago in response to the same, ill-judged slight. He hurried through to the kitchen, leaving Connor to break the seal on the new bottle.

He greeted the newcomers with a wave, watched them grab a backpack each from the back of the classic car, and carry them towards him. The angular Cough looked sombre, and even Stefan had dialled down his natural ebullience.

"Cough, Stefan," Kaine said, shaking hands with each in turn. "Connor and Hunter have raided Mike's store of booze. Go help them out." He stood aside and waved them to the back door.

Cough handed his pack to Stefan and let him pass.

"Stow the gear in the boot room for now, Stefan," Kaine said. "We'll sort out the billeting later."

"No problem, boss," the youngster said and dived through the back door. Seconds later, the raucous greeting, "Dumpster!", announced his arrival in the lounge. Few people in the team were more popular than Stefan Stankovic, especially since he'd survived being knocked down by a runaway rubbish bin during the mission in Southampton.

"Afternoon, Cough," Kaine said, leaning against the garden wall. "You made good time."

"Traffic was lighter than we expected, and Norwich isn't exactly the other side of the world."

"How's Angela?" Kaine asked, reaching out and gently touching Cough's arm.

The former army sergeant lowered his head.

"Holding up, boss. She strong. Gutted about Mike, of course."

"Aren't we all."

"She sends her commiserations. As does Bobbie. They both know how much Mike meant to you ... to the whole team."

Kaine broke eye contact and nodded.

"How's Bobbie holding up?"

"She's ... coping. Burying herself in her studies. At least she's finally started talking about Danny."

"That's a good sign. She's been through the mill, but she's young. She'll pull through," Kaine said and shook his head to draw a line under it. "So, what have you been up to?"

Cough hiked his left shoulder, raising it above its natural resting state.

"Not a lot. Keeping a weather eye on a certain loan shark. Can't give Max Campese a free ride. Wouldn't want him bouncing back from his little challenges."

Cough winced as a loud cheer erupted from deep inside the stone farmhouse. "Want me to tell them to keep it down?"

"No. Leave them to it. Things have been tense around here lately, and Mike wouldn't have minded. Go join them. Help yourself to anything you find in the kitchen. There isn't much. I'll be asking for volunteers to go on a provision run in the morning. Connor and Stefan will do."

Cough grinned at Kaine's loose interpretation of the concept of volunteering.

"Fair enough. Are you off anywhere?"

"The stables," he said, looking across the courtyard. "The doc's been in there a while, and I wanted to make sure she's okay. It's been a challenging day."

"Good idea," Cough said, and another roar exploded from the house. "I'll go instil some discipline into the rabble." He headed towards the open back door but stopped short and turned to face Kaine. "Before I forget to ask, how's Rollo doing?"

Kaine took his turn to wince.

"Says he's on the mend, but Marie-Odile tells it like it is. He's not listening to the physio's advice. Pushing himself too hard and too fast."

Cough curled his thin lips. "Doesn't surprise me. They'll make it to the memorial service and the official wake, though. Right?"

"They will."

"Good. I'm sure you'll be able to put him right about the need to follow his medic's orders." He dipped his head in salute and carried on into the house.

Kaine crossed the immaculate, weed-free courtyard, which showed a second benefit of having access to military people with time on their hands—the first being the protection they offered—and quietly sidestepped through the part-open stable door. He didn't want to startle the horses and risk Lara an injury.

It took Kaine a little while to spot her in the unfamiliar, dark, and pungent interior. He found it difficult to understand how two horses could create so much … mess.

Lara stood in a stall with her back to him, arm draped around Dynamite's sleekly muscled neck. The black monster whickered as though enjoying the experience, but Lara's shoulders quaked. Kaine cleared his throat softly. Lara jerked her head up. Dynamite rotated his ears, raised his head, and whickered again. Lara soothed the horse with gentle words, a firm hand on his neck, and turned. Her eyes streamed, and tears ran down her cheeks.

Kaine rushed forwards, stopped well short of the stall, and waited with his arms outstretched. She left the big, black thoroughbred and ran to him.

"Mike's gone," she whispered through her distress. "I thought I could cope but I ..."

She buried her face into his shoulder and let the tears fall. He'd rarely seen her so emotional.

With his vision watering, the stereophonic snorting and breathing of Dynamite and Lexie in the background, and his sense of smell slowly adapting to the ripe tang of horse-flesh and their droppings, Kaine held Lara until her sobbing eased.

Eventually, after what seemed like an age, Lara pulled away and broke his hold. She dragged a tissue from the pocket of her jeans, wiped her eyes, and blew her nose.

"Sorry about that," she said, back to business. "It just hit me. Overwhelming."

"He was a good man," Kaine said, unable to come up with anything more profound.

"Yes. And now I have the farm to run."

"You could always sell up."

"And break my promise?" She shook her head forcefully. "Not a chance."

He smiled and squeezed her hand. "I know."

"I have plans for this place."

"I know," he repeated. "A horse sanctuary."

"It's going to take up a lot of my time."

He nodded. "Yep."

"And quite a bit of cash."

"You don't have to worry about money. I'll see you right."

Again, she shook her head. "No need. Mike had quite a bit saved up. It'll help me start, and I've been doing well since joining the team. You've seen to that."

"Like I said." He leaned closer. "I'll see you right."

"And don't think you're going to see the end of me, *mister*. I'll still be here for you. I mean, I'll be hiring staff to free up some time. After all, someone has to run the comms room. We can't leave the whole system to Connor."

He leaned even closer, kissed her, and said, "That's my girl. Mike would be so proud."

A brief shadow fell across her eyes but soon vanished. Before he could apologise, his phone rang out—three short, three long, three short bleeps. Corky's SOS.

Hell.

Kaine's heart lurched.

"Control," he said into the phone.

"Whatcha, Mr K. How you diddling?"

Kaine met Lara's eye and winced.

"Not having the best of days, as you can imagine."

"Yeah, Corky's upset, too. Wishes he could be there for the wake and the memorial service, but … you know. It ain't possible."

Kaine hit the speaker icon.

"I've put you on speaker."

"Right, okay. Who else is listening in?"

"The doc."

"Oh hi, Doc," he said, his delivery more muted than normal. "Corky and Frodo send our condolences."

"Frodo does?" she asked. "Really?"

"Sure he does, Doc. Being an orphan, the poor bloke understands the concept of loss. He just don't express himself the same way as the rest of the world."

Lara arched an eyebrow at Kaine, clearly seeing the irony in Corky's words.

"You used the SOS number, Corky," Kaine said. "Who's in trouble?"

"Toby Fabien."

Kaine's heart fell to his boots.

"Did he hit the emergency button?"

"Nah, Mr K. This is what you might call Corky's pre-emptive strike."

"Damn."

That made it even more worrying. Corky never over-reacted.

"How long will it take you to reach the comms room?" Corky asked.

"About sixty seconds."

"Good. Corky'll wait for you to boot up the system."

"It's always booted up, Corky."

"Corky knows that, Mr K." He chuckled but it sounded a little hollow. A little forced.

Corky cut the call and Kaine slipped the phone back into his pocket. Lara moved towards the exit. Kaine hesitated.

"Where are you going?" he asked.

"To the comms room with you."

"Are you finished in here?" He followed her to the open doors.

"Yes. They're fed, watered, and bedded down for the night. You might need my help with the system. Judging by the noise I can hear coming out of the farmhouse, Connor won't be of much use."

"Good point," Kaine said, frowning. "Let's go find out what happened."

Seven Days Earlier

Chapter Five

New Mill Road, Featherstone, Staffordshire, England

Tobias "Toby" Fabien, grandfather of the two beautiful kids who sat on booster seats in the back, stared hard through the rain-plastered windscreen, trying to pierce the gathering gloom. Perhaps it hadn't been such a good idea to leave home after all. Too late to change his mind now, though. Everyone was looking forward to the meal. They'd booked the table weeks earlier and the twins deserved a reward for being so ... stoic. An early evening meal at the Rose & Crown would be the highlight of everyone's week.

Toby and Melissa had been dining there since moving to

Featherstone before Robert was born. They loved the food, and the ambience, and they always received a warm welcome. The children's menu far surpassed those of most restaurants, and as far as he could tell, the twins loved eating there, too.

Melissa sat in the front passenger's seat, her pale blue eyes glued to the view through the windscreen, adding her concentration to his. She drove every mile, every turn, and spotted every junction with him. Helping him negotiate the terrors of the heavy traffic on modern roads.

"Roundabout," she said, pointing straight ahead.

"I see it," Toby answered.

Yes, he could see it. Blooming thing was lit up like a Ferris wheel.

Two minutes later, she called out, "Watch that van," meaning the bright, yellow truck approaching from the left, looking as though it might plough straight through the fast-approaching T-junction.

"No problem, love. I see it."

Toby lifted his foot from the accelerator and hovered it over the brake. The yellow truck's front end dipped as it stopped sharply at the give way sign—leaving it until the last possible moment.

Although he'd been driving for forty-seven years and could boast the proud ownership of an unblemished driving record, he both appreciated and resented the need for her assistance. He hated sitting behind the wheel these days. The joys of the open road had long since disappeared. Overly aggressive drivers in a desperate rush to reach the next set of traffic lights or the next holdup were a blight, as were the countless tailgaters and the sheer volume of traffic. Potholes that turned main roads into obstacle courses only added to the challenge. They all made driving a total nightmare. And these days, he had more responsibility than just himself and Melissa. He had the twins. God bless them. His precious, precious cargo.

He smiled and glanced in the rear-view mirror. Olivia, head down, read from her tablet computer, calm and quiet. A pale-faced Rupert, prone to car sickness, stared through the side window at the rain-soaked view beyond, trying to relax and breathe normally.

The rain continued to hammer down. The automated wipers swept faster but struggled to cope effectively with the deluge. Huge puddles had formed at the sides of the road, adding to the spray thrown up by the cars ahead and further reducing visibility. Outside, beyond the overwhelmed windscreen, an early darkness had fallen. Red tail lights stretched out ahead, sprinkling dappled blooms over the rain-deluged windscreen. In return, head on, white headlights flared, some set to angry full beam. Dazzling. They made his dry eyes water.

Selfish so-and-sos.

He had half a mind to give up and turn for home, but giving up was not in Toby's nature. He'd made the twins a promise and would honour it. Besides, Melissa deserved an evening off from cooking. The meal out would do her, do them all, the world of good.

Toby yawned and rubbed his eyes. He had no reason to be so tired. They had been to the park that afternoon and bumped into the Kendalls. Kenneth and Lucinda Kendall, and their kids Emily—Olivia's best friend from school—and young Arthur. Toby smiled at the memory.

He and Kenny ended up kicking a football around with an overexcited Arthur and a less-enthusiastic Rupert.

Melissa and Lucy had walked the perimeter in pleasant conversation, while five paces back, Olivia and Emily giggled and laughed behind their hands. They'd had cake and drinks in the café and even the quiet and reserved Rupert seemed to enjoy the occasion.

Well, maybe Toby did have good reason to be tired, after all. Already his legs were stiff and cramping, and his lower back ached with the aftereffects of chasing a football around the park. Such a stupid thing to do at his age. He wouldn't see sixty-four again. Toby tried to remember the last time he'd played footie in the park. With Robert and an even younger Rupert, probably. Two years ago. No, three.

Robert.

Moisture welled in Toby's eyes and a solid lump formed in his throat. He coughed to clear the constriction and blinked to rid his eyes of the tears.

Don't go there, Toby. Do not go there.

After all these months, the pain still burned deep. The depression of loss never fully left him.

The road curved sharply to the right. The nearside tyres touched the rumble strip, and the angry throbbing vibrated up the steering column. Toby over-reacted. He yanked down on the steering wheel, and the Toyota swerved to the right. The car's lane departure warning system bleeped, and the dashboard icon winked aggressively. He twitched the steering wheel and centred the car in the lane. Behind, headlights flashed. Toby raised a hand in apology but doubted the driver could see it through the flooded rear window. Melissa turned her head and frowned but said nothing.

Wake up, man. Concentrate.

Minutes later, the rain's furious assault eased, and the

windscreen cleared. Toby relaxed his shoulders and breathed more easily.

Behind them, bright headlights flashed, flooding the inside of the car—an aggressive tailgater trying to hurry him along.

No chance, mate. That's not happening.

He would not be rushed. Plummeting headlong into danger was not Tobias Fabien's way. Especially not with the twins sitting in the back. He shot another rapid glance in the rear-view mirror and caught Olivia's eye.

"Are we nearly there yet, Granddad?" she sang, unaware of the cliché she was inadvertently perpetuating.

"Not long now, love," Toby answered. "A couple of miles, no more. Five minutes."

"Five minutes?" she moaned, staring up into the rear-view at him. "You said that five minutes ago." Olivia frowned and shook her head in exaggerated patience. In doing so, she looked the image of her mother, and of Melissa, when the mood took her. The golf-ball-sized lump returned to constrict Toby's throat.

Golf. When had he last played a round? When would he play another? These days, he couldn't even spare the time for a bucket of balls on the driving range. How things had changed over the previous nine months.

Lights from an articulated lorry travelling too close to their rear bumper flared, flooding their car with a dimpled field of dazzling brightness.

"We want the next left, Toby," Melissa announced, her voice firm.

"Thanks, Mel. I've got it."

Toby flicked the indicator stalk down and slowed to make the turn. The truck behind drew closer, close enough to make Melissa gasp, and its lights flashed again.

Bloody driver. Why so aggressive?

Toby made the turn. The driver blared his horn and roared past, throwing up a huge spray of dirty water in the process. In times past, Toby would have yelled an irritated curse or two, but those days were long gone. He had to show a better example to the twins. At their age, they soaked up knowledge like dry sponges.

Half a mile later, Toby turned into the gravelled car park of the Rose & Crown Inn. They parked in one of the many available spots.

"Uh-oh," Toby said.

"What's wrong?" Melissa asked.

"The car park's usually packed."

"We're early."

Toby read the time from the dashboard clock.

"Not that early and look"—he pointed towards the sign above the gastro pub's front door—"the porch lights are off."

"Oh dear," Melissa said. "Power cut? The weather's been so awful."

"I hope not. Stay in the car. I'll go check."

He opened his door, climbed out, smiled at the twins, and picked his way around the puddles. The front door stood slightly ajar. Inside, the foyer glowed dark and gloomy.

"Hello?" he called, stepping out of the driving rain and wiping the rain from his hair. "Anyone here?"

"Be right with you," a woman's voice called from deep inside the pub.

Footsteps clattered on bare boards. The door behind the bar opened. Torchlight led the way and Alison Goodman stepped through the opening. Toby recognised a harried face when he saw one.

"Alison," he said. "Everything okay?"

Silly question. It clearly wasn't.

Alison clicked off the torch, lowered it to the counter, and pressed the freed hand to her large chest.

"Mr Fabien, Toby," she said, panting. "I'm so sorry. We tried calling to let you know, but you didn't answer your phone. We did leave a message, though."

Toby grimaced. "We've been out all afternoon, and I never could figure out how the message system works. What's happened?"

"Power's out," Alison said. "Has been since about two o'clock this afternoon. Apparently, a substation at the bottom of the road blew a gasket or something. Staffs Electricity are working on it, but …" She sighed. "As you can see, they haven't fixed it yet."

Toby offered her his most sympathetic smile. "I'm so sorry to hear that. The twins have been looking forward to their meal all day."

She winced. "And we've been looking forward to seeing them again, the poor, little mites. How are they settling in at their new school?"

Toby hesitated but went with the partial truth. The whole truth would take too long and be too painful.

"Very well, thanks. Olivia's already moved to the top reading grade for her age."

"And Rupert?"

More hesitation. Toby glanced away but didn't want to make a big thing of it. A lovely woman, Alison meant well, but she could be a bit of a gossip, and the twins needed their privacy. They'd been through enough emotional trauma recently.

"As usual," he said, "Rupert's … taking longer to settle. Always has been a quiet lad. Still waters, you know? He sits there, taking it all in, moving at his own pace, but ... Olivia looks after him. As big sisters do." He took a breath and deliberately changed the subject. "So, the kitchen's closed, and we're going hungry?"

"Afraid so, Toby. Brian's given the staff the evening off. He's in the kitchen, getting rid of all the fresh food we prepped for the night—doing it by torchlight. Luckily the freezer will keep the food frozen for a while longer."

"Anything we can do to help?"

"Oh bless you," she said, removing her hand from her bosom. "Thank you so much for the offer, but everything's in hand. We're just finishing off here. After that, we'll head to my sister's for supper."

With nothing more to say, Toby wished her all the best, accepted Alison's second copious apology and good wishes, and took his leave. He dodged the easing rain, retreated to the car, and delivered the bad news.

"Poor Alison and Brian," Melissa said. "It's such a shame. What are we going to do? I'm due to go food shopping on Monday, and there's nothing in the house. I suppose I could open a few cans of soup and rustle up some sandwiches, but—"

"I've had an idea," Toby interrupted, turning to face the twins.

"Yes, Granddad?" Olivia and Rupert asked as one. They had an uncanny ability to do that very thing—speak in stereo.

"Anyone fancy a burger?"

"Oh Granddad!" Olivia said, frowning and shaking her head. "Shame on you!"

"Yes, please," Rupert said, for once, keenness itself.

"I don't eat meat!" Olivia snapped, folding her arms.

"Of course you don't, dear," Melissa said, throwing Toby a mock scowl.

"Not all burgers are meat," Toby announced, winking at the overly serious, nine-year-old girl. He stood on the brake, pressed the ignition button, and waited for the engine to purr. "Seatbelts on?"

"Yes, Granddad," the twins answered, again in stereo.

"Where are we going?" Melissa asked.

"It's a surprise."

"Tell us, Toby," Melissa demanded.

"Yes, Granddad," Rupert said, eyes wide. "Tell us."

"We're going where there's a whole world of food to choose from." Again, Toby winked into the rear-view mirror.

He reversed out of his parking spot, threw a U-turn, and waited at the exit. Instead of turning left to head for home, he indicated right.

"Toby," Melissa said. "You're not serious."

Toby turned his head and grinned at her.

"Yep. Why ever not?"

"You know why not."

"It has a well-stocked food hall." He smiled. "Plenty of choice."

"But it's miles out of our way. We'd have to backtrack for ages."

"Ordinarily, but we know a little short cut." He arched his eyebrows.

"Toby," Melissa warned, her brows creasing. "You're not supposed to—"

He flapped his hand to interrupt her.

"Everyone does it," he said. "At least, every local in the area with an ounce of common sense. And anyway, those no-entry signs are advisory."

"No, they're not," Melissa said, and folded her arms to indicate an end to the conversation, which suited Toby no end.

He checked both ways carefully before pulling out and turning right into the empty, but waterlogged, Hilton Lane.

Half a mile later, Toby indicated again and braked sharply. He negotiated the tight, right turn and crawled along the twisting, treelined road. A road without a name. Three quarters of a mile later, the road ended at a T-junction, and emerged in the middle of the Hilton Motorway Services, adjacent to the petrol station.

"And here we are," Toby announced. "That didn't take long, did it?"

The twins cheered. Melissa shook her head slowly and sighed.

"The food court."

"Exactly. It's never closed," Toby answered. "And I did promise you a world of choice."

Melissa nodded.

"I'll give you that," she said. "There is plenty of choice." She sighed and twisted in her seat to smile at the twins. "It's not the Rose & Crown, but beggars can't be choosers, I suppose."

"And there's an added bonus," Toby said.

"Which is?"

"The petrol station's open. We can fill up on the way home."

He paused in expectation and didn't have to wait long.

"Granddad?" Olivia asked.

"Yes, Olivia?"

Here it comes.

"What fuel does Charlie take?"

And there it was. Toby grinned.

"Petrol," Toby answered, pulling away from the T-junction, making another right turn, and heading towards the parking bays in front of the food hall and shopping area.

"Not diesel?" Olivia asked, giggling.

"No," Toby said. "Dear me. It was an honest mistake. Nobody told me your … Nobody told me the Audi was a diesel." He just managed to stop himself saying, "Nobody told me *your dad's* car took diesel not petrol." He didn't want to risk bringing back the pain, not that pain ever truly left any of them. It might ease over time, but it would never leave.

"Honestly," he said, "I make one little mistake. … I put petrol in a diesel car and have to call out the mechanic, and nobody ever lets me forget it."

His simple mistake had cost them a fortune in lost petrol, another fortune in replacement diesel, and a two-hour wait at the petrol station for the recovery service to drain the tank. And the trauma had been compounded by the fact that Toby and Melissa had only just collected the twins from the social worker after the plane crash that turned them into orphans.

"Poor Granddad," Melissa said, without a jot of sympathy.

"Yes," the twins said together as though they could read each other's minds. "Poor Granddad."

Toby growled at them in the rear-view mirror and shared their laughter. After a short search, he found a three-car gap with a clear view of the food hall's eating area and parked in the middle space. There was plenty of room all around. It seemed safe enough.

"And now, *mes enfants*," he said. "*On y va.*"

"*On y va*, Granddad?" Rupert, who'd chosen French as his language option at school, said. "That's new."

"It means," Melissa said, "'Here we go.'"

"*On y va,*" Rupert repeated, trying the phrase on for size. "I like it."

"Okay," Toby said. "Let's go find something to eat. I'm starving."

Again, the twins cheered.

Chapter Six

Saturday 26th June - Tobias Fabien

Hilton Services, Hilton Lane, Staffordshire, England

The Fabien family rushed the short distance through the heavy drizzle. Toby took the lead, holding Olivia's hand the whole way. Melissa kept close to Rupert who steadfastly refused to hold hands because, "I'm a boy!", and brought up the rear. Laughing the whole way, they dodged the puddles and dived through the automatic doors. Shaking the rain from their clothes and hair, they headed straight for the food hall and joined the back of a short line.

"What would you like, Olivia?" Melissa asked after they'd reached the counter.

"A garlic hummus and salad wrap, please."

Toby smiled. The first time Olivia had asked for vegetarian food, he'd been gobsmacked. As a lifelong carnivore, he had no idea his older grandchild—older by a whole eighteen minutes—had chosen to shun meat from the tender age of six.

"And you, Rupert?"

The lad carefully studied the offerings on display behind the glass and raised a finger to his lips. He frowned in concentration as though unable to make up his mind, but everyone knew he'd choose the same as his sister—his benign leader.

He lowered his digit and nodded.

"Same, please," he said, quietly.

"Of course," Toby said, mussing the lad's dark hair which desperately needed the attentions of a barber. "And, ooh look." He nodded to one of the signs above the counter. "All day breakfasts."

"Toby," Melissa warned, "don't you dare!"

"Just this once, love."

"What did the doctor say?"

"Oh, pleeeeease?" Toby begged. He winked at the kids, who giggled at his childishness.

Melissa sighed and shook her head in forced patience.

"Okay, it's your own arteries you're clogging." She gave their order to the bored-looking server in the red-and-white-striped apron, the cardboard hat, and the blue plastic gloves. "A Full English breakfast for the gannet but hold off on the black pudding. And I'll have a goat's cheese salad and a pot of tea for two, please."

As a special treat, Melissa added two chocolate brownies to the list and the server piled the order onto two trays. The kids' drink of choice, diet colas, had somehow morphed into unsweetened fruit juice—pineapple for Olivia, blackcurrant for Rupert.

Rupert offered to carry one of the trays, but Toby shook his head.

"Thanks, lad," he said, picking up the heavier tray while Melissa swiped her bank card over the reader, "but we can manage."

Toby had learned from experience the dangers of accepting Rupert's generous offer of assistance. Unfortunately, what the boy had in terms of good manners and helpfulness, far exceeded his abilities in terms of strength and coordination.

"*Suivez-moi, troupe*," Toby said, and led them through the seating area towards the wall of glass overlooking the car park. He had to slalom between the closely packed tables and chairs, most of which stood empty. The kids took the seats with their backs to the window, and Toby set his tray down in front of them. He unpeeled the cellophane from the hummus wraps, cut each in half, and placed the plates in front of the kids.

Melissa arrived with the drinks and served the kids first. Toby remained standing until she'd taken her seat and then sat beside her keeping an eye on "Charlie" through the rain-and-grime-splattered windows. Rupert had come up with the car's name, based on her make and model, a Toyota C-HR. He could be quite a deep thinker when he chose to be.

Although eight years old, one year younger than the twins, Charlie was perfect. Absolutely mint. Not a mark on her gleaming, black bodywork. Without doubt, Toby's pride and joy. He hated parking in public spaces where any idiot could open a door too wide and damage the paintwork. He lived in constant fear of it picking up a ding or a scratch and hated letting her out of his sight. Silly really. With their recent influx of capital and The 83 Trust's continuing financial support, they could afford to splash out on a new car any time they wished. A new car each if the fancy took them, but neither Toby nor Melissa were profligate. Charlie would suffice for the time being. Nothing wrong with her. A beautiful and reliable beast.

"Nobody's going to hurt Charlie, Granddad," Olivia said, always the observant one.

"I know, little one," he said, shooting her a gentle smile. "It doesn't stop me worrying about her though. After all, she is part of the family."

Melissa removed the plastic cover from her salad, picked up her knife and fork, and started eating.

Toby said, "*Bon appétit, mes chéris,*" and tucked in while his food was still hot. As expected, the bacon hit the spot. These days, he rarely had the chance to indulge in fried food, but once in a blue moon wouldn't hurt. Probably.

As one, Rupert and Olivia frowned, said, "*Merci*, Granddad," picked up the first half of their wraps and started munching. They always cringed when he broke into French in public, and he loved embarrassing them—one of the many perks of being a fulltime grandparent.

For a few minutes, they ate in silence.

"Nice?" Melissa asked, after swallowing a mouthful of green stuff.

The kids nodded, but Olivia answered for them.

"Yes, thank you, Granny."

Toby dipped a piece of sausage into the yolk of his fried egg, popped the delicious morsel into his mouth, and chewed. He looked up. Through the steaming window, a fast-moving mass of bright green caught his eye.

Uh-oh!

The green mass transformed into a massive, Ford,

pickup truck. Front windows down, music blaring, the ridiculously aggressive, "look at me" pickup raced through the car park at a speed more suitable to the adjacent motorway. Wincing, Toby followed its progress as it darted into a narrow opening five spaces away from Charlie and slammed to a stop. Its shiny, bull-bar-covered nose dipped as its monstrous front tyres bumped the kerbstone. Seconds later, the beat-heavy music cut off, the side windows rolled up, and the front doors flew open. The driver's door missed the neighbouring car's front wing by a whisker. Two individuals climbed out—a large, heavily tattooed man in blue jeans and a tight, black T-shirt, and a slender, ink-free woman in ripped jeans and a strapless, black top. The driver, well over six feet tall and almost as wide, stomped forwards and joined his blue-spiky-haired partner at the walkway. Toby winced when the tattooed man rudely brushed straight past her and marched towards the entrance. The woman struggled to keep up—her three-inch stilettos impeding her progress.

The automatic doors split apart. The tattooed driver ploughed through the opening without waiting for his partner and headed straight for the food hall's counter.

"Keep up, *Chardonnay*," he growled. "We don't got all day."

"Coming, Babe."

Again, Toby winced. The ill-mannered, tattooed yob looked less like a "Babe" than any creature he'd ever seen. Toby glanced down at the kids. Fortunately, they were concentrating on their wraps and had failed to notice the newcomers.

At the tail of a small queue, "Babe" shot out his hand and snapped his fingers.

The blue-haired Chardonnay skipped forwards, digging

through her tan-leather shoulder bag. Her hand emerged with a man's black wallet, which she held out to him. Babe snatched it from her, opened it, and leafed through the contents. Slowly, the small queue shuffled closer to the counter.

Babe turned to face the woman for the first time. He looked down, fixing her with a dark-eyed glare.

"There's forty-five quid missing," he said, his voice deep and loud. Intimidating. Aggressive. "What you done with it?"

Chardonnay shrank under his accusatory glare.

"We just filled up with petrol, Babe," she said, rushing her answer.

Head tilted to one side, Babe paused for a heavy moment before nodding, his eyes never leaving hers.

"Yeah," he said at length. "I remember. Just checking."

The queue dispersed, and Babe shouted his order—a large espresso and one slice of chocolate cake. The subdued Chardonnay ordered a small cappuccino and paid in cash taken from her purse. Babe waited for the server to fulfil the order, scowling and tapping an impatient right foot the whole time.

Olivia frowned, lowered her part-eaten wrap to her plate, and looked up at Toby.

"Granddad?" she asked.

"Yes, sweetie?"

"Why's that man being so nasty to that woman?"

"I don't know, angel," Toby answered. "He's being very rude, isn't he?"

Olivia nodded.

"Don't like him," Rupert said, keeping his voice low.

"Me neither," Olivia added.

"Me neither," Melissa agreed. "Try not to stare at them,

darlings. Eat up. I'd like to be home before it gets dark." She smiled at Toby who nodded his wholehearted agreement.

Toby took another piece of sausage but no longer enjoyed the taste. Watching Babe browbeat his diminutive partner had ruined his appetite. He tried to avert his eyes, but they refused to obey his instructions, and he followed the couple's progress.

Babe turned away from the counter and headed towards the tables, leaving the overworked and bullied Chardonnay to carry the tray.

You nasty piece of … work.

Toby lowered the knife and fork to his plate. He picked up his teacup and held it to his lips, trying not to grind his teeth.

Babe chose a chair three tables away, took a phone from the back pocket of his faded jeans, and plonked himself down, back to the window. He checked the screen, tapped in a number, and raised the phone to his ear.

"Baz?" he bellowed after a short pause, "it's me, Dylan. … How you doing, geezer?"

Chardonnay arrived, lowered the tray to the table, and sat.

"Just a sec," Babe, Dylan, said. He pulled the phone away from his ear and covered the mouthpiece with his free hand. "Where's my fork?" he demanded. "You expect me to eat with my fucking hands?"

Olivia's mouth dropped open. Rupert, eyes wide, stared at the foul-mouthed oaf.

"Sorry, Babe. I-I forgot," Chardonnay said, rushing her words. "Won't be long."

She jumped up and scurried away to the serving counter, tottering on the ridiculous heels.

"Fucking idiot. … No, not you, Baz," Dylan said to the

phone, still speaking loudly, a few decibels lower than a shout. "Stupid bitch forgot summat. Woman's a bloody liability. Needs trading in for a better model." He laughed. "So, how's tricks your end, man?"

"Dear Lord," Melissa muttered under her breath. She hated bad language as much as Toby did. More even.

"Olivia, Rupert," Toby said, "try not to listen."

He tried to catch the lout's eye and embarrass him into silence, but the man sat, leaning back, phone raised, and his face in profile.

"It's hard, Granddad," Rupert said, turning his head away from the aggressive nightmare and looking up at Toby. "He's talking so loud."

"I know, lad. But try tuning him out. How was your wrap?"

"Very nice, thank you," he said, lowering the dry crust to his plate alongside the first. "May I have my brownie now, please?"

"Of course."

"Don't forget to use your fork," Olivia said, quietly, adding a mischievous grin.

She could be quite the little rascal when she put her mind to it.

"As if," Rupert countered quietly.

"Olivia," Melissa said, raising a finger in warning. "That's enough."

"Sorry, Granny." Olivia turned her cheeky grin into a sweet smile. "I've finished my wrap, too. May *I* have my brownie now, please?"

"Yes, dear."

The precocious, little girl picked up her fork, showed it to Rupert, and pulled the plate containing her brownie closer.

Three tables away, Dylan kept talking, every fourth word an expletive—each one driving a dagger through Toby's heart.

"Dear Lord," Toby said. "This really is too much."

He lowered his teacup to the table and leaned forwards, preparing to stand. Melissa dropped a firm hand on his forearm and shook her head.

"Don't say or do anything, Toby," she whispered.

Toby shot her an inquiring look.

"He's the sort that carries a knife in public," she added even more quietly.

"Oh for pity's sake," Toby said, dismissing her warning. "Paranoid much?"

"Toby," she said. "Please?" She glanced at the kids, worry in her expression and in her hushed voice.

Toby hated to see her so distressed, and he huffed out a sigh.

"Okay, okay. We'll do it your way."

Toby relaxed back into his chair and retrieved his cup. Scowling at the foul-mouthed man with the ugly, black-vine tats, he held the teacup to his lips but didn't drink.

The beleaguered Chardonnay returned to the table brandishing a fork. She placed it on Dylan's plate, sat, and picked up her coffee. Her hands trembled. Dylan refused to acknowledge her presence and continued his expletive-laden telephone conversation. After taking her first sip, the woman turned towards Toby, and looked at him, blank-faced. Toby half-expected a grimace or an unspoken apology, but she must have been too browbeaten to understand her situation.

"Yeah, yeah," Dylan said into his mobile. "Too fucking right, we will. See you there in an hour, man. We'll order a curry, play some poker. ... Yeah, too right. Massive. See ya! Wouldn't want to be ya!"

Dylan laughed as he ended the call and lowered the mobile to the table. He picked up his drink and slurped it loudly. A loathsome creature, he did everything noisily and seemed to delight in drawing attention to himself—as amply demonstrated by the lime-green Ford. The other customers scattered around the dining area appeared as upset as Toby, but none seemed willing to complain.

A young couple—late teens, early twenties—sitting on high stools near the serving counter crouched closer, shooting occasional unhappy, frowning glances in Dylan's direction. A single man, wearing a white T-shirt beneath a dark jacket, read a folded newspaper and drank from a large, insulated cup. He studiously avoided looking at the man seated across the aisle from him and making too much noise. A pair of grey-haired women sitting in the comfy seats in the corner glowered at Dylan, shook their heads, and spoke to each other behind their hands. Another couple who sat with their backs to Toby stared straight ahead, lowered their drinks, stood, and left the seating area without a backwards glance. They hurried to the exit and slipped out of sight around a corner.

In the middle distance, standing near the unused video games and gambling cubby hole, a wide-bodied security guard stood with his back to the food hall, chatting to a slender cleaner wearing a dark green tunic. The smiling cleaner didn't seem to mind the guard's attention, or the interruption to her working day.

"We're going to Baz's tonight," Dylan announced, talking to Chardonnay, but not caring who overheard.

"But I thought ..." the poor woman said and allowed her voice to fade under his withering glare.

"But what?"

"I-I thought we were seeing Trudy."

"Fuck Trudy," he snapped. "We're going to Baz's place. We're having a curry."

"But she's expecting us. You promised."

"Changed my mind, didn't I! Shut your fucking whining, woman. I've had enough."

"Oh for pity's sake," Toby said. It spurted out, louder than he expected.

Dylan lowered his coffee mug and twisted in his chair, turning to face Toby.

"What you say, Granddad?" he growled through a sneer.

Toby met his eye and, despite the wave of fear coursing through his system, refused to back down or look away. He couldn't lose face in front of his family.

"Don't answer him," Melissa whispered. "Don't rise to it. Please."

Toby ground his teeth. "I can't just sit here and say nothing."

Chardonnay stretched her hand out to the tattooed thug.

"Babe," she said, "he's just an old man. He isn't worth your time."

"Shut the fuck up, woman," Dylan snapped. "I'll decide what's worth my time. Not you."

"Don't be like that, Babe," she said, voice catching. "I-I was only—"

"Shut up, bitch!" Dylan flicked the back of a hand at her. His fingers caught her bare upper arm. She flinched and her eyes watered.

"That's enough!" Toby called, jumping to his feet, anger momentarily overriding the fear. He simply couldn't back down in front of the twins. They needed to learn right from wrong—to learn from Toby's example.

"What?" Dylan shouted. "What d'you say?"

"You heard me, Dylan," Toby said, lowering his voice to stop it quaking. "I said, 'That's enough'. You swear too much and there are children present. And how … how *dare* you hit a woman!"

Toby shot a glance at Chardonnay, who, eyes wide, shook her head in warning.

The ruffian jumped up, quivering with rage. He towered a full head taller than Toby, who quailed under his threatening glare. Toby tried to remember the last time he'd raised his voice in anger, or the last time he faced down a bully. Tried and failed. School, maybe? He swallowed down the bolus of fear.

He'd never won a fight in his life.

You idiot, Toby! What are you doing?

Chapter Seven

Saturday 26th June - Tobias Fabien

Hilton Services, Hilton Lane, Staffordshire, England

Dylan's brows knitted together in confusion.

"D'you know me, Granddad?"

"No. I don't."

Thank goodness.

"You know my name."

"The whole place knows your name," Toby said, surprised at how steady his voice sounded. Pity it was nothing but pure bluster.

Away to his right, the security guard turned his head to face the ruckus. Toby relaxed a little. Support would soon be on its way.

Fists formed, Dylan approached, closing the three-table gap between them. Menacing and aggressive.

A hush fell over the food hall. All eyes turned to their little corner.

Rupert started sniffling. Olivia whimpered and her lower lip trembled.

Dylan glowered at the twins and snorted. Such a bully.

Anger built within Toby. He glanced to his right. The security guard had vanished.

Oh dear.

Toby's stomach lurched. He swallowed hard, forcing the part-digested sausage back down before it made an unwanted, return appearance. Melissa stood and gathered the crying, terrified children into her arms.

Dylan snorted, placed his hands on his hips, and half-turned towards the downtrodden Chardonnay.

"Yeah," he said. "You're right. He ain't fucking worth it. Hate cry-babies, me. Listen to 'em wailing. Fucking pitiful."

Toby stood taller and found the strength to say, "Mind your language."

"What?"

"I said, 'Mind your language'. There are children present."

The tattooed man roared with forced laughter. Chardonnay approached and stopped at his side. Abruptly, Dylan stopped laughing and leaned even closer to Toby.

"Don't tell me what to do, Granddad." With his right hand raised, he emphasised every word by jabbing his index finger at Toby. Each jab edged a little closer to connecting with Toby's chest. "No one tells me what to do. Got it?"

To Toby's right, the man in the dark jacket slapped his paper onto the table, stood, and approached their little group. Maintaining a neutral expression and saying nothing, he stopped alongside Toby, making it clear whose side he was taking. He stood as tall as Dylan and didn't seem the least bit daunted by the idea of facing down a mouthy thug. Slight scarring over his left eye and a nose that had been broken at least once suggested he'd been on the receiving end of a thrown fist or two in his life. He carried himself like a boxer—or a nightclub bouncer. Toby breathed again and swallowed past a dry throat.

"What the fuck d'you want?" Dylan demanded of the new arrival. His voice lifted half an octave higher than before.

The boxer didn't respond. He simply stared and stretched out a slow, confident smile.

Chardonnay edged closer to her man.

"Watch him, Babe," she said. "He looks hard."

"Fuck off, Chardonnay," Dylan snarled, flapping a backhand at her, but keeping his eyes on the tough-looking man in the dark jacket. "I asked you a question, dickhead!"

"I think you owe this gentleman and his family an apology," Boxer said quietly. Still smiling, he met Dylan's glare with steady eyes. He exuded confidence.

Dylan stiffened. "Say what?"

"Didn't I make myself clear, son?" Boxer asked, his flat, Yorkshire inflection pushing to the surface.

"No, you didn't."

"Must be my accent. Please forgive me. I'll speak up for thee. What I said was, 'You owe this gentleman and his family an apology.'" He repeated the sentence slowly and clearly, and with a little more volume.

"What the fuck for?"

Boxer dropped the smile and mirrored Dylan's actions by leaning slightly forwards at the hip and canting his head to one side.

"Well now, lad. Let me see," he said, lightly. "'Ow about apologising for your aggression, for your foul language, for hitting your girlfriend, and … for scaring the children." He nodded at Rupert and Olivia.

Melissa had straightened and stood with her arm draped over Olivia's shoulders. Standing at Melissa's other side, Rupert wiped his eyes with his fists. Like his sister, his lower lip trembled.

Dylan stared hard at Boxer, no doubt trying to determine the strength of his opposition and to decide his next move.

"And what happens if I don't?" he said, chin jutted out, issuing it as a challenge.

Boxer shook his head.

"Nothing," he said, mildly. "It might just make you feel good."

Dylan snorted.

"I feel pretty good, already," he said.

"Go on," Boxer said, stretching out an encouraging grin. "Try it. See 'ow much better it makes you feel."

Dylan hesitated for a moment, then he seemed to deflate. He sneered at Toby, shot a sideways glance at Chardonnay, but kept his attention on the tough man with the Yorkshire accent.

"Fuck this," Dylan said. "You're right, Babe. The old bugger ain't worth the hassle. We're done here. Grab your bag."

He backed away but before turning, he glowered at Toby and jabbed his finger at him again.

"Watch yourself, Granddad," he snarled. "Nobody fucks with me and gets away with it. I ain't finished with you yet."

He dropped his hand and turned his back on them. Ignoring Chardonnay, he stomped away.

"And me, lad?" Yorkshireman called after him. "What about me?"

Dylan ignored the question and carried on walking. Chardonnay looked at Toby and winced in embarrassment.

"Sorry," she said, shooting a despairing glance at the departing Dylan. "He gets carried away sometimes." She snatched her bag from their table and hurried after the aggressive idiot with the ugly tats.

Toby's stomach flipped. Nausea returned along with a real sense of having escaped a thumping. He looked at the Yorkshireman and pushed out a grateful hand. "Thank you, Mr ...?"

"Barraclough," he said, giving Toby's hand a gentle squeeze. "Jerry Barraclough."

"Thank you, Mr Barraclough," Toby said, retrieving his hand from a giant, calloused paw. "My name's Fabien. Toby Fabien. I don't know what I'd have done without you."

Barraclough curled his upper lip and shook his head.

"Nowt would've 'appened, Toby," he said, his voice calm. "I've seen 'is sort before. A bully and a coward. All mouth and no boll—er, trousers." He corrected himself after glancing down and showing the twins a warm smile. "He might 'ave 'uffed and puffed a bit, but that's all. And besides"—he pointed high up at the wall behind Toby—"the place is full of surveillance cameras. If 'e'd started a rumble, 'e'd 'ave ended up in all sorts of bother."

Olivia ducked out of Melissa's grasp and ran to Toby. She hugged him tight around the waist, and he hugged her back. Rupert stayed with Melissa, who shook her head at Toby. He was going to be on the receiving end of an angry but restrained earbashing the moment they'd tucked the kids into bed for the night. Although he didn't look forward to it, Melissa's bark usually ended up far worse than her bite. After facing up to Dylan, Melissa wouldn't present a problem. Well, not so much of a problem.

"Granddad," Olivia said, looking up through tear-soaked, blue eyes. "You were so brave. I thought that man was going to duff you up."

"Duff me up?" he said, grinning down at her. "I don't think so, little one. We were just talking. And Mr Barraclough stepped in to help."

Olivia peeled herself away from Toby and turned to face Barraclough. She tilted her head back to look up at him.

"Thank you, Mr Barraclough."

"You're welcome, lass," he said, offering his large paw to Olivia.

Before taking it, she looked at Toby for permission. On receiving it, she shook hands formally. Barraclough's fist engulfed hers, his shake gentle and brief.

"Aye up," the big man said, nodding towards the wall of glass. "There they go."

Toby and his little family watched Dylan and his acolyte exit the building and head for their bright, green pickup. A fast-marching Dylan stretched out far ahead of the tottering Chardonnay. He reached the Ford first, yanked open his door, and it thumped into the front wing of the neighbouring car—a white Hyundai. He climbed into the cab, fired up the engine, and revved it hard. Dark blue fumes exploded from the exhaust in a large, carcinogenic cloud. Chardonnay arrived and reached up for the handle. She shot an apologetic glance at the food hall window, struggled to open the passenger door, and took her time to climb inside.

The big Ford reversed out of the parking spot at warp speed, and narrowly avoided colliding with an approaching, silver Lexus. The drivers exchanged car horn blasts, but the blonde woman behind the wheel of the Lexus gave way. She reversed her car far enough to allow the belligerent Dylan room to clear the narrow confines of the car park and make his angry escape. The Ford exited stage left and the Lexus drove into its parking space at a far more sedate speed than its predecessor had arrived and departed.

Toby released another long breath.

"Good riddance to bad rubbish," Olivia said, breaking the spell.

"Amen to that, lass," Barraclough said. "And now, I'd best be off. I've a long drive ahead of me afore I'm done for t'night."

"Where are you going?" Melissa asked.

"London. I've a job interview first thing Monday morning, which gives me tomorrow to look around t'city. I've 'eard its worth a visit once in your life."

Toby wondered what job he'd applied for—nightclub bouncer or bodyguard—but wouldn't dare ask for fear of embarrassing their knight in shining armour. Or rather, their knight in a dark jacket and white T-shirt.

"Are you a boxer?" Rupert asked, excitement lifting his voice. "A cage fighter?"

Barraclough turned his dark brown eyes on Rupert and graced him with a wide smile.

"A cage fighter? Are you looking at my broken nose, lad?"

"And your bad eye."

"Rupert!" Melissa said, her voice stern. "You're being rude."

Barraclough flapped an open hand at her.

"That's okay, Mrs Fabien. Not rude, just observant. No,

lad. I'm no cage fighter. In fact, I'm no sort of fighter. These injuries," he said waving the hand in front of his face, "are from a car accident way back when. But you'd be surprised at 'ow often looking this ugly 'as given people the wrong impression. It's got me out of trouble more times than I care to remember."

"I apologise for Rupert's … frankness, Mr Barraclough," Melissa said, dropping a hand on the boy's shoulder. "And I'd call you distinguished, not ugly."

"Thank you, Mrs—"

"Melissa," she interrupted, her blue eyes shining with gratitude. "Call me Melissa."

Again, Barraclough's smile lit up and softened his face.

"Thank you, Melissa, but I'm afraid you're being kind." He turned to face Toby again. "'Ere, let me give you this. In case you need me for anything."

Barraclough dug a hand into the pocket of his jeans, pulled out a black, leather wallet, and flipped it open. He removed a business card and handed it across.

"And on that note, I'll be off," he said and waved to the kids. "Cheery bye."

"Drive safely," Melissa said. "And good luck with your interview."

"Thank you," he said and added, "but there's no luck involved. If I want the job, I'm a shoo-in. They 'ead 'unted me. Monday's a face-to-face to negotiate terms." He leaned in closer and lowered his voice. "To be 'onest, they'll 'ave to up their offer quite a bit if they want to entice me down south. I'm only taking advantage of a free 'otel in London for a couple o' nights."

Again, he gave them all a warm smile, turned, and strolled towards the toilets. He ignored the newspaper he'd left on his table.

Toby waited for him to drop out of sight before reading the business card. He grinned.

"Well," he said. "I didn't expect that."

"What does it say, Granddad?" Olivia and Rupert asked simultaneously. They had such an unnerving habit of doing that. Uncanny, it was.

Toby handed the card to Melissa.

"You'll never guess what Mr Jethro Barraclough does for a living," he said.

"Tell us, Granddad," Rupert begged.

"He's a robotics engineer, specialising in packaging. Not a cage fighter at all."

"Robotics?" the lad asked, excited. "We've done robotics in school. It's really cool. Almost as cool as cage fighting."

"Perhaps he fights cages in the evenings," Toby suggested. He frowned and said, "Although I can't see what sort of a fight you can have with a cage. Cages can't throw punches since they don't have any arms or fists."

Olivia shook her head.

"Oh Granddad," she said, groaning, "you're *so* not funny. Men and women fight each other *in* cages, silly."

"Ah," Toby answered, "I see. Thanks for making it clear. Perhaps Mr Barraclough fights *in* cages in the evenings."

"Like a hobby, you mean?" Rupert asked.

"Yes," Toby agreed. "Like a hobby."

"Robotics and cage fighting," Rupert said. "That's so cool."

Toby smiled and ruffled the lad's mop of hair. Their mood had lifted quickly. He wanted nothing more than to draw a line under the incident. Allowing them to dream of having been saved by a robotics engineer who moonlighted as a cage fighter—which could legitimately be the very definition of a superhero—was as good a way as any. Although a man with the name "Jethro Barraclough" would never have passed muster as the alter ego of any regular superhero.

Jed Barrow, maybe.

Toby smiled and raised his hands to silence the ongoing discussions.

"Okay, okay. That's enough excitement for one evening. Are we all finished here and ready to head for home?"

"Yes, please, Granddad," the twins said.

"I'll second that," Melissa said, reaching for her coat.

Toby glanced through the wall of glass. A low sun had broken through the rolling bank of grey clouds, but the rain still sprinkled the large windows.

"Okay, let's go."

"Don't forget to fill the car," Rupert said.

"Thanks for reminding me. Can anyone remember what fuel Charlie uses?"

"Petrol, Granddad," Olivia piped up.

"Yes, Granddad," Rupert added, excited amusement filling his words. "Petrol."

Toby led them from the food hall.

"Are you certain it isn't diesel?" he asked.

"Yes, Granddad," Olivia said through a giggle. "It's petrol."

As they strolled through the food hall, they passed the uniformed security guard, who'd returned to his original position outside the gamblers' kiosk. He didn't even have the good grace to lower his eyes in embarrassment.

"Thanks for all your help," Toby said, shooting the man an accusatory glare.

"You're welcome, sir," the guard replied, as brazen as he was useless.

Rupert poked his tongue at the man and hurriedly caught hold of Toby's hand.

"Anyone need the bathroom?" Melissa asked, but no one did, and they strolled straight past the toilets.

At the exit, the automatic doors slid apart, and the fresh, evening air greeted them along with the welcome warmth of the bright sun. Miraculously, the rain chose that very moment to stop.

Things were looking up.

Chapter Eight

Saturday 26th June - Tobias Fabien

Hilton Services, Hilton Lane, Staffordshire, England

At the pumps, in the time-honoured way of all family jokes, Toby deliberately reached for the diesel pistol and waited for Olivia and Rupert to yell, "No, Grandad. Petrol!" Even though this particular family favourite had only been in existence for a matter of months, being their first, it would run and run. Eventually, Toby filled the tank with Premium 98 petrol, winking at the kids as the electronic numbers climbed up and up. Long gone were the days when he could fill a tank from empty with premium unleaded and still have change from a tenner. He sighed. Distant times. Times when Robert was the same age as the twins. If only he hadn't insisted on flying with Helen to Amsterdam on that midweek break. If only he'd chosen a different day, a different flight.

No, Toby. Don't start that again.

After narrowly surviving a confrontation with the thuggish Dylan, what would be the point in wondering what could have been? That way only led to depression and pain.

Toby paid for the fuel, bought a daily paper and a packet of boiled sweets, and returned to the car.

"Everyone okay?" he asked, handing Melissa the paper and sweets, which would remain unopened in the car until the next long trip.

"Yes, thank you, Granddad," Olivia said, speaking for both her and Rupert. Things were returning to normal. A very good thing.

"Then let's go."

"*On y va*, Granddad?" Rupert asked.

"That's right, lad. *On y va.*"

Toby belted up, confirmed the twins were still strapped in, and pushed the ignition button. He selected drive and pulled away. At the T-junction, he made a semi-legal, left turn and crawled slowly along the narrow, treelined road.

"That's a 'no entry' sign, Granddad," Olivia piped up.

"It is?" He glanced up through the rear-view mirror and grinned at the little route guardian.

"Yes, Granddad."

"I know," he said. "It's a special shortcut known only by granddads—and locals."

Ignoring the red signs, and the one below them that read, "Except Lodge Guests," Toby kept going. They wound their way through dark, rain-dripping woods. Half a mile later, they reached another T-junction.

"And here we are," Toby announced. "That saved us a twenty-five-minute detour. Aren't I a clever, old granddad?"

"Did you just break the law, Granddad?"

"Not really. I've been a 'Lodge Guest' in the past, and by doing so I've earned a lifetime exemption."

Ignoring Melissa's derisive snort, Toby turned left onto Hilton Lane and powered up through the gears. Trees and hedges on either side threw a shuttered light over the narrow road, making the driving tricky. Toby slowed to a modest forty and took it even easier while negotiating a sharp, right-hand curve. Fortunately, only locals used Hilton Lane. Traffic was light, even so early in the evening, and the surface was relatively free of potholes. After the next left bend, the road straightened. Toby added a little more pressure to the accelerator, and the speed crept up towards forty-five. Plenty fast enough for the conditions.

Hilton Park Arena & Stables, where Melissa took Olivia riding most Sunday mornings, rolled past on their right.

"Granny?" Olivia asked.

"Yes, love?"

"Are we still going riding tomorrow?" Olivia asked, keen as hot mustard.

"Of course," Melissa answered, twisting in her seat to face her granddaughter. "Unless you'd rather we didn't."

"Why wouldn't I?"

"Oh I don't know," Melissa said. "I just wondered whether you'd become bored with riding. If you prefer, we could go swimming with Rupert and Granddad instead."

From the corner of his eye, Toby could make out Melissa's wicked grin.

"Oh Granny!" the little girl groaned. "Please stop teasing. You know how much I love riding. And I'm learning to groom the horses. And … you promised to buy me a pony when I'm old enough to look after her properly."

They passed the Hilton Hall Business Centre on the right and the lane arced into a gentle, right curve before straightening again. Trapped by the road camber, large puddles gathered on the outside of the bend and Toby edged towards the centre of the road.

"A pony?" Melissa said. "When did I ever promise you a pony?"

"Didn't you, Granny?" Olivia said, wide-eyed innocence itself. "I'm sure you did. Didn't she, Rupert."

She turned to face her brother, who did what he often did when Olivia asked him a "yes or no" question. He nodded and said, "Yes."

"Told you, Granny," Olivia said. "You *did* promise."

For her part, Melissa responded with her own tried and tested, "We'll see," and with that, settled the discussion.

Deep puddles lined the outside of most of the bends and, watching carefully for oncoming vehicles, Toby kept Charlie straddling the dashed, centre line. Fortunately, Hilton Lane remained traffic free.

Two miles later, he slowed, indicated left, and turned into the ominously named Doom Lane. The lane narrowed into the familiar, single-track with passing places every few hundred yards. Rolling fields stretched out on the right, trees and hedges crowded in on the left, held in check by a moss-covered, wooden fence. The deep, black waters of Rook Pond lay beyond the fence and beyond a thin line of trees. Toby had once promised to take Rupert fishing in Rook Pond but had somehow never found the time. Maybe during the upcoming, summer holidays … once he'd dug out Robert's old rod and tackle. Wherever they were. Loft? Garage? Lord alone knew.

A glare of headlights flashed in the rear-view. A large shape appeared, growing larger as the gap between them closed rapidly. The shape coalesced into a bright, green, Ford pickup, its shiny, chromium bull bar festooned with spotlights. Headlights flashed in anger.

Dear God.

Toby stamped on the accelerator. Engine screaming, Charlie roared ahead.

"Toby!" Melissa said, urgency in her voice. "What are you doing?"

"Dylan!" Toby muttered, keeping his voice down to avoid scaring the twins.

Melissa twisted in her seat.

The gap between them closed. Quickly. Scarily.

Oh God! Surely not?

On the dashboard, warning lights flashed, and Charlie's rear, collision alarm chimed.

Melissa screamed, "Toby!"

The Ford's bull bar slammed into Charlie's rear end. She lurched. The rear wheels lost grip, bounced. Charlie slid sideways. Melissa and the kids screamed. Toby fought the bucking steering wheel, righting the car. He stamped harder on the accelerator. The front tyres squealed, bit, and Charlie leaped forwards. In the rear-view, a gap reappeared between the Toyota and the Ford. The pickup's headlights blazed twice, flooding Charlie's cabin with a brilliant, white glare.

Engines roared, screamed.

The Ford closed again. Rammed Charlie again.

Metal crunched.

The Toyota lurched.

Toby's world burst into a spinning, swirling, twisting frenzy.

Doom Lane spun sharply to the right. Charlie continued straight ahead. Smashed through the moss-covered fence. A solid, lime green mass streaked behind them. The pickup roared away, blaring its two-tone horn. Mocking.

Again, Melissa screamed. The twins shrieked.

Bushes parted. Trees raced past on either side. Branches snapped. Scored metalwork. Leaves whipped by. The land dropped away. A crack ran down the windscreen.

A wide, black chasm opened up below them. Charlie plunged towards the night-black water. Toby's stomach lurched into his throat.

Charlie spun. The darkly mottled trunk of an oak tree reared up out of nowhere. Huge and solid.

Charlie slammed sideways into the oak in a jarring, shuddering stop.

Airbags exploded. White mushrooms bloomed in a smothering, suffocating cloud of hot silk.

A dark curtain descended, and crinkling silence fell. A sharp, deathly silence.

Chapter Nine

Sunday 27th June - Dylan Bentley

Bentley House, Brocton Village, Staffordshire, England

Harsh sunlight shone through Dylan Bentley's closed lids, searing into his consciousness. Blasted him awake.

Fuck!

He groaned. Head throbbed. Pounded. Hammered. A furry tongue stuck to the roof of his mouth. Felt and tasted like the floor of a budgie's cage.

Jesus fucking wept.

He'd done it again. Too much booze. Too much weed. Too much … everything.

Why? Why put yourself through it? Moron.

Long night. So many lagers and whisky chasers he'd lost

count. Liquid lungs made him cough. Head exploded. Split right open like someone had taken a hatchet to the bastard. Spread his brains out over the pillow. Bile rushed up a gnarly throat. Dylan swallowed it back. Nasty stuff.

Never again. Never, ever again.

He turned onto his back, dropped his arm to Chardonnay's side of the bed. Cold. Empty. Where the fuck she go? Woman should be by his side, ready to service him. What else was the fucking point of her?

Dylan opened his eyes. The sun slammed through the wide gap between the curtains, slicing his head apart again. Shitty thing. Too bright. Crashing, splitting headache. Couldn't cope with it.

Christ, it hurt.

Alarm clock read eight-forty-something. Way too shitting early.

Dylan turned away from the window, grabbed her pillow, covered his head. Farted long and hard. All but followed through. Leaned back and searched for sleep.

———

BANGING.

Hammering.

Fat of the hand slapping on his bedroom door.

"Dylan!"

Christ sakes. Leave me alone, will ya?

"Dylan, you lazy bugger. Are you gettin' up today?" Gravel-voiced. Dad. Always pushing. Always shouting. What the hell was wrong with the old geezer? What rattled his cage this time?

Braving the sunlight, Dylan slid the pillow off his head, threw it to the floor. Cool air sluiced his face. Made him shiver. Bloody freezing. Why didn't he put the fucking heating on? It wasn't like they couldn't afford it.

"Coffee," he called. Throat dry. Sore. Voice rasping.

"Get your own shittin' coffee," Dad shouted, halfway down the stairs, heading away. Voice growing more distant. "I ain't your chuffin' servant."

No. You're my fucking jailor.

Dylan flipped onto his back. Groaned. Stared at the ceiling for ages. Then tried to sit up. The room swirled and swam in front of his eyes. Falling back against the pillows, Dylan closed his lids. Queasiness flowed up from his guts. Took a slow, deep breath. Settled his stomach.

Coffee. Needed coffee.

He sat upright. The room swam again. Dylan clasped his head in both hands, holding it together. Stopping it from splitting apart. Breathed deep. Filled his lungs. The room settled.

"What's wrong with Doreen?" Dylan yelled, risking another head shock.

"Weekend off," Dad shouted up from downstairs. "We're on our own. Get your arse down here. You've got questions to answer."

"Fuck," Dylan muttered. "What's wrong now?"

Dylan sat up straighter. Studied himself in the big mirror on the wall opposite. Admired what he saw reflected back. Smiled. Satisfied. Bounced his pecs in time to the banging tune running through his throbbing head. The vine tats rippled and swayed across and back. Left and right.

Yeah, man.

If he didn't look the dog's bollocks, no one ever would.

He leaned against the pillows for a while, staring hard, breathing deep and slow. Eventually, his headache eased, and his stomach settled. About pigging time.

"Coffee's up, Dylan," Dad called. "Get your arse out of bed. Now!"

Dylan eased out another smile. Good, old Dad. Never let him down. Looked after him since Mum buggered off somewhere never to be seen or heard of again. Ten-something years past. Not so much as a birthday card.

Bitch.

Dylan threw back the covers. Climbed out of bed. Swayed a little then steadied. Scratched his left bollock. Admired the way he looked in the mirror again.

He grabbed the dressing gown from the stool where he'd thrown it. Stepped into his slippers. Spilled through the bedroom door. Hit the staircase. Steadied himself by grabbing hold of the handrail on the way down. Wouldn't want to fall down the stairs and end up going arse over tit. Not cool at all. Painful, too. Probably.

He snorted. Swallowed sticky spit. Kept descending the stairs. He'd have preferred to stay in bed, but Dad's summons wasn't something Dylan could ignore. Not when Dylan wanted something. Had his hand out. All needy.

He reached the kitchen and smelled the strong coffee. Loved it. One thing about Dad. The old bloke couldn't half put together a decent cup of the brown stuff.

Nice one.

Dylan schlepped over to the counter and poured himself a large mug from the carafe. Grabbed a jug of cream from the fridge, added it to cool the coffee. Stirred in two heaped spoons of brown sugar and slurped. Yep. Hit the spot. Medicine for the head. Cured the migraine. He topped up the mug. Added more cream and another sugar. Going strong on the sweet stuff.

"Thanks, Dad. Where you at?"

"In here."

The shout came from the front room the old man liked to call "the salon" since he'd struck it rich. Sounded right poncy to Dylan, not that he'd ever tell Dad. What was wrong with "front room" or "lounge", for fuck's sake?

He took another deep sip and sloped through the hall into "the salon". Sun bright, dazzling. Not so lethal since the medicinal coffee, but still harsh enough to scorch his eyeballs and make him squint.

Dad stood, mug in hand, staring through the French doors. Curtains drawn back wide. Doors closed.

"What the shit happened last night, boy?" he demanded, pointing with his mug. "What'd you hit?"

"Huh?"

Taking another slurp, Dylan closed on Dad. Stopped right up behind him. Looked over Dad's shoulder, through the glass. Saw the way he'd parked the Raptor. Skewed on the gravel drive. Front end pointing at the house. Left-hand side of the shiny, chrome bull bar was bent and buckled. One of the four spot lamps missing. The one next to the gap bent back, the lens smashed.

Fuck!

Memories flooded back. The service station food hall. Granddad dissing him. Sneering at him. Looking down his nose at Dylan. Old man telling him to stop swearing. Ignorant bastard. Backed up by the mean-looking fucker with the busted nose and the damaged eye. Threatening. Dylan turned on Granddad. Stared him down. Threatened him back. Fucking cheek of the old fart. Old man withered. Started shaking. Mean fucker with the busted nose just stood there, saying nothing. Looking hard as steel.

Dylan sneered through the window at the Raptor. Big. Angry. Fierce. Powerful. Something to be proud of. One of the fleet.

He'd taught the old bastard a lesson he wouldn't forget in a hurry, though. Nobody fucked with Dylan Bentley. Chardonnay and he had driven off from the food hall. Parked around the corner by the petrol station. Watching. Waiting for the old couple and their whiney brats.

Followed them at a distance. Gave their shitty, little car a couple of tiny, little, love taps. Watched them skid off the road in his mirrors. Taught the mouthy fucker not to diss anyone again. Served the bugger right.

Dylan snorted.

"Well?" Dad growled. Anger boiled just below the surface, ready to bubble over.

Cool it, Dad.

"Hit something." Took another slurp. "Dunno what."

Dad turned. Faced him. Leaned closer. Close enough for Dylan to smell the coffee breath and aftershave. Spicy. Expensive. Overpowering. Not the least bit subtle. Dad could be so uncouth.

"Don't give me that bollocks, boy. What d'you hit?"

Dylan sniffed, looked away.

"I told you, Dad. I dunno. A … deer maybe."

Dad ground his teeth. Risked losing his dental veneers. Sucked in a deep breath.

"If you'd hit a deer," he growled, "there'd be blood and fur all over the bars and the bonnet. There ain't. I checked." Dad straightened. Jerked back his shoulders. Looked as scary as he must have done in the army. "I found some flecks of black paint though."

"Black paint?" Dylan asked, defensive. "Like from railings?"

"No, son. Black paint … like from off of a black car!"

Dylan's right hand shook. Would've spilled the coffee if he hadn't drunk most of it already. Lowered his eyes.

"Oh, yeah, that." Scratched the stubble on his chin. Could do with a shave. Always felt better after a shave. Looked better, too. "I remember now. I, er, ... hit a parked car. Toyota, I think. Didn't stop to check, though."

Good save, Dylan.

"Where abouts?"

"Clipped the effing thing's boot. Caved in the rear wing."

Dad shot out his right hand and slapped the back of Dylan's head.

"Ouch. The fuck was that for?" Dylan rubbed his head as though it really hurt. Well, it did, but not from the slap. Too much booze and shit at Baz's gaff. Dad had gone easy with the slap. Thankfully.

"Don't be such a smartarse, son. I meant where was the car you hit parked?"

Dylan shrugged.

"Dunno. Somewhere between the Chinese takeaway and Baz's place. Near the railway bridge." Dylan paused. Time to embellish. "Parked on a double yellow, it was. I reckon it served the owner right. If the Raptor wasn't so powerful, me and Chardonnay could've been hurt."

"Bridge Street?"

Dylan nodded. "Yeah. Prob'ly. Or High Street, maybe. Church Road, p'rhaps. I told you. I don't really remember. Came as a bit of a shock, and I ... I didn't want to stop on account of me having had a couple of pints at the Chinese. While we were waiting. So bloody slow in there, eh?"

Inwardly, Dylan smiled. Didn't let it show. Lying came easy. He was good at it, too.

Dad drained the last of his coffee. Lowered the mug. Thinking, he scratched the bald patch at the top of his head. Scrunched up his face at the same time.

"Who's this Chardonnay bint? You got yourself a new bit of totty?"

"No, Dad. I've been seeing her off and on for a while. You've met her here a few times. She's the skinny bird with blue hair. You know her as Charlotte Smith, but she goes by the name 'Chardonnay' these days. Reckons its classier."

"Classier?" Dad scoffed, onside again. "She reckons Chardonnay's classier than Charlotte?" Shook his head in contempt. "Thick as shit, you ask me. Christ, boy. You don't half pick 'em."

Dylan scrunched up his face.

"Prob'ly, but she's good in the sack. Adventurous, y'know?" He winked. "Really flexible.

"Is she gonna keep schtum 'bout the crash?"

"Yes, Dad. The girl's got the hots for me."

And why wouldn't she?

Dad frowned. Tilted his head to one side. Thinking again.

"She'll keep quiet, then? I don't want the filth sniffin' around. We got things to hide."

"Yeah, Dad. She won't say anything. Like I said, the soppy cow loves me to bits." He shrugged and smiled wide. "Who wouldn't? I mean, she got eyes, right?"

Again, the right arm shot out. This time, the hand mussed Dylan's uncombed hair rather than slapped the back of his head.

"Yeah, son. You're a chip off the old block."

Am I fuck. I take after Mum. Wherever she is.

Dylan kept that part to himself. He'd learned never to mention the bitch. To Dad, she ceased to exist after she'd buggered off.

Dad pulled his arm back. Nodded. "Go upstairs and get dressed."

"Why?"

"We're takin' the Raptor to the garage. Getting' it fixed pronto. Before the filth starts snoopin' round."

"Not a chance, Dad." Dylan shook his head. "Filth don't know nothing about it. Like I told you, we buggered off without being seen."

"Can't take the risk, son. Police got surveillance cameras all over the place these days. Thousands of the bloody things. And there's loads of private ones, too. I want that car like mint, soon as. Today. After we drop it off at the workshop, we'll go pick up some brunch at The Bull. I don't fancy heatin' up none of Doreen's frozen meals."

"It's open on a Sunday? The workshop, I mean."

"Yeah. I called Tony while you was sleepin' it off. He weren't exactly happy, but he works for me and does what he's told. Top it off, he'll be workin' Sunday hours."

"Double time?"

Dad shook his head. "No. Triple. And you're payin'."

Dylan stiffened. "What?"

"What?" Dad's eyes bulged with sarcasm. "You expect me to pay?"

"Oh Dad. It was an accident."

Dad waved a backhand slap at him. Caught him high on the right arm. Bounced off a bunched triceps muscle. Would have hurt Dad more than Dylan.

"Tell someone who cares, son. I ain't payin'. You are. And that's an end to it."

Dylan sighed. "Fair enough. How much is it gonna set me back?"

"New bull bar, a pair of spots, and a full valet's gonna set you back a grand. Plus another monkey for Tony's time."

"Fuck's sake, Dad! That's fifteen hundred quid!"

"I'll take it outta your next month's allowance."

Next month? No way. The old man would probably have forgotten all about it by then, but just in case, Dylan came up with a cunning plan. Delay, delay, delay.

Simples.

"That's gonna leave me a bit light," Dylan said, wincing. "I'm taking Chardonnay and a couple of the lads to Ibiza next month. I'll need plenty of spending money. How's about letting me pay over the next five months?" Dylan smiled, opened his eyes wide. "Three hundred a month from now 'til November."

Dad's eyes narrowed as he thought it over. Could almost hear the cogs grinding away. Eventually, the old man nodded.

"Okay. Deal," he said.

Gotcha!

Dad never could resist one of Dylan's winning smiles. And why would he?

"Three hundred a month. But I ain't forgettin', mind. You've got to learn from your mistakes. Discipline is every-thin'. Without discipline, we're nout but savages. That's what they teach you in the army."

There he was. Off on one of his rants again. Dylan nodded and kept on nodding. Taking it all in. Or appearing to. Had to keep Dad sweet.

"I didn't get where I am today without learnin' from my mistakes," he said. "And I wouldn't have survived Afghanistan without discipline. Without discipline, we're nothin'." Dad tapped a finger to his temple. "Remember that, son."

"Yes, Dad. I'll remember."

Dylan waited for the punchline. Didn't take long.

"Mind you …" Dad said, raising his finger in the air, pausing for dramatic effect.

Here it comes. Get ready to laugh.

"…winning ninety-seven million quid on the Euro Lottery didn't hurt!"

Dad coughed out a deep, belly laugh. Dylan joined in and didn't have to work himself too hard.

"Now," Dad said, "go get dressed. I'm starvin'."

————

TO AVOID the all-seeing traffic cams, Dylan drove the long way around. Took an extra half hour to make it to the industrial estate, but Dad didn't kick up a fuss. He knew the drill. The filth had eyes everywhere, and it paid to know how to avoid them.

They rolled up to the workshop, drove through the gates, through the open shutters, and disappeared inside the old coachworks. Dylan jumped out and pressed the button. The rusty shutters creaked and squealed all the way down.

Tony Epps—narrow-shouldered, grease-stained fingers, mouth a thin-lipped gash—waited for them at the head of the inspection pit. The grease monkey circled the damaged Raptor, doing his usual, headshaking, tutting, sucking-through-his-teeth bit, before grunting and scratching at the stubble furring his pointed chin.

"Bloody hell, Dylan," Epps said, after he'd finished giving the Raptor the once over. "What d'you hit, son? A Challenger tank?"

Typical of Epps to bang on about military hardware, given he'd spent eighteen years in the army, servicing the combat vehicles. Or so he said.

Such a chuffing bore.

"Army's where I learned my trade, son. Great days."

Kept saying it. Never pigging stopped.

For once, Dylan kept schtum about the reference to the tank. Thought it for the best. Let Dad handle the questions. Do the deal.

"Don't be a smartarse, Tony," Dad said, smirking.

"Kidding, Jackie," Epps said, straightening his face. "But it takes some force to bend a chrome-plated bull bar that bad."

"Tell me 'bout it," Dad said, shooting Dylan a dark look. "Replace the bar and the spots, and power wash the whole motor. I want to see my face in them panels when you're done. And you'll keep schtum. 'Kay?"

"'Course I will, Jackie." Epps made a zip-the-lip sign. "You know me, boss. Who would I tell?" He smiled his underslung grin. Made him look even uglier. If that was possible.

Such a hideous bugger. Next to Dylan, someone to be pitied.

"When d'you wanna pick it up?" Epps added.

Dad peeled back the cuff of his calfskin jacket and read the time on his gold Rolex—kosher. Nothing moody about Dad anymore. No cheap knockoffs in sight. Everything he— and Dylan—wore was designer expensive. "Me and Dylan are headin' to The Bull for grub. We'll be back in three hours."

Epps' jaw dropped. "What? You want it done today?"

"Yeah."

"Are you kidding, boss?"

Dad pointed at his face.

"Look at the boat race, Tony," he said. "Does it look like I'm kiddin'?"

Epps slouched his narrow shoulders.

"Where am I gonna find a new, Ford bull bar inside three hours—on a Sunday."

"Fuck's sake, Tony. You were in the army, right? Use your initiative, man. Take a set off of one of the other Raptors and replace that one in the mornin'. As for the spotties, we've got a bunch in the stores, right?"

"But there's only one other Raptor with a chrome bar and it's hired out all day tomorrow. Theo Harrison's picking it up first thing. We wouldn't want to upset Theo. Would we? He's a bloody good customer."

Dad threw out his arms.

"Let me worry 'bout Theo. Give him one with a black bar. I'll knock a ton off his bill to keep him sweet. See you in three hours. 'Kay?"

Epps sucked in a breath. Nodded and added a stiff shrug.

"You're the boss."

"Too right I am. And you're on triple time."

"I am?" He straightened. Smiled. Happy as Chardonnay after a good seeing to.

"Yep."

"Thanks, boss. I'll order three replacement bull bars first thing in the morning."

"Three sets?" Dylan asked. "Why three? That's bloody expensive when we only need the one."

"Camouflage, son," Dad said, tapping the side of his nose. "Camouflage."

"So's the cops don't get sus if they come a-calling," Epps explained.

"Oh, yeah," Dylan said. "Gotcha."

Dad draped a heavy arm over Dylan's shoulders.

"Ready for some grub, son?"

Dylan grinned. "A Full English would hit the spot, and it's on me," he said.

"Too bloody right it is, son."

Dad dropped the Raptor's key fob into Epps' outstretched hand and said, "See you in three hours."

"Better make it four, boss," Epps said. "To be on the safe side."

"Three," Dad insisted. "No longer. I ain't made of money."

Dad winked. Epps snorted a nasal laugh. Dylan sighed.

"Did you change the plates on number two like I said?" Dad asked Epps.

"Sure did, boss. She's good to go."

"Cheers."

The old man tugged Dylan through the small door cut into the roller shutters. They strolled outside and jumped into a Raptor parked around the back of the forecourt—a Raptor with the same plates and colour as the one Dylan bent. This time, Dad took the wheel, and Dylan rode shotgun.

The Bull was only a few hundred metres down the road, but Dad didn't exercise anymore, and Dylan only worked out in the gym—in front of the mirrors.

Chapter Ten

Sunday 27th June - Dylan Bentley

Rigby Road, Stafford, Staffordshire, England

Dylan followed Dad into the pub, keeping two steps behind and allowing the old fool to make his usual, grand entrance. Money talked, and how the old sod loved to natter. Loved to soak in the adulation of arseholes with their hands out looking for a … hand up.

Inside, Dylan laughed at his own joke.

Three deep at the bar, The Bull was jumping on a Sunday lunchtime. As usual. On the huge telly in the saloon bar, white-clothed wallies chased a red ball around a green field. Bloody cricket. Old man's game. Boring waste of time. Pity the footie season had ended. Wouldn't be long before the next one started, though.

Come on you Reds!

Behind Dad's back, Dylan sighed. The Reds had been a joke for years. The glory days of old were long gone, but they'd return. Next season. For definite. Perhaps Dad could buy them a new striker.

Now, wouldn't that be a thing.

Dad barged straight up to the bar, ignoring the queue. Shouted his order. "Full English times two, Gerald. Large. Extra black pudding. And two beers."

"Sure thing, Mr Bentley," Gerald Barnes, The Bull's lard-arsed and red-faced owner said, stopping in the middle of pulling a pint of lager for a frowning, grumbling regular.

Dad stared down the plonker, who looked away first. No one messed with Dad. Built like a brick shithouse with a neck as thick as an oak tree. Took bollocks from nobody.

"Your table's free," Gerald added, nodding towards the only empty table in the whole place.

It looked out over the large beer garden. Had the best view of the big screen TV, too. A white card sticking out of a plastic holder read, "Reserved for J Bentley". Quite right, too. Dad, "Big" Jackie Bentley, didn't stand and wait for anybody. Neither did his son. Not when they were together. Dylan hated playing second fiddle, but Dad had the dosh and with it, the power and the adulation. Fuck him. Wouldn't always be like that, though. Dylan had a plan to get out from under Dad's thumb. Working on it with his man, Baz.

Slowly, slowly.

Dad leading, they mooched over to the table and dropped onto the bench seat against the wall. Nicely padded cushions soft on the arse and back. Specially uphol-stered for Dad, the best-paying regular The Bull would ever have. Dad practically owned the place.

Didn't have to wait long for the beers, neither. Gerald sent the busty Alma with two glasses full to the foamy brim and two sets of cutlery wrapped up in cloth napkins. Proper cloth, not paper. Nothing too good for Big Jackie Bentley. Nothing too good for his son, neither. At least not when he was tagging along as Dad's shadow.

Dad had wielded enough power before the lottery win, but snaffling all those millions only added to his status. Reinforced it. People messed with Big Jackie Bentley at their peril.

Alma served Dad first, Dylan second. Only fair since he was the geezer paying the bill. Despite Dylan's earlier offer, Dad would end up covering the bill. He always did. Smiling, Alma bent low to show off her assets. Nice pair, worth looking at, but Dad didn't seem to notice. Getting old. Old but not weak. Not feeble. No way.

More's the pity.

"Cheers, Alma," Dad said, raising his glass and knocking back a healthy gulp. "I'm starving. How long?"

"Fifteen minutes okay, Mr Bentley?" she said, laying a cute smile on him.

"Sure. I can wait. If I have to." Dad wiped his mouth with the cloth napkin, showing he could do manners if he really wanted to. "And you can call me Jackie. How many times I gotta tell you?"

Maybe he had noticed her baps after all. Didn't miss much, did Dad. Meant Dylan had to be extra careful with his side hustle. Wouldn't do Dylan no good for Dad to catch him in the act. The subsidiary business had to remain on the downlow.

Dylan picked up his beer and sipped. Warm and bitter. He preferred lager, but when drinking with Dad, he wouldn't dare. Didn't want to risk yet another extended earbashing. Dad had his way of doing things, and Dylan had to toe the line. At least when they were together.

"Lager's for louts, Dylan, my boy," he'd say. "We don't call 'em lager louts for no reason."

"Real men drink real ale," he'd say.

"Get some real ale down your neck, son," he'd say. "It'll put hair on your chest."

Yadda, yadda, yadda.

Why the hell would Dylan want hair on his pigging chest when he spent so long in front of the bathroom mirror shaving? And he could never tell Dad he visited a beauty salon every six weeks for a "back, sack, and crack". That would have been worse than drinking lager in front of him. Dad would end up calling him a raging woofter—or worse. Maybe disinherit him. At the very least, Dylan would never hear the end of it. Big Jackie may have been a lot of things, but no one could ever accuse him of being woke.

Not a chance.

Dylan hid a sneer behind his glass, and they settled back to wait. Not talking much. Not in public.

On the TV, the wankers in white, who were standing behind the three sticks, threw their arms in the air. Bloke holding the bat looked pissed, then hung his head. TV showed slow-motion repeats of the red ball passing the edge of the bat, together with a superimposed, squiggly line. After a while, a fat, old guy wearing a white coat raised his arm and the bloke with the bat trudged towards the crowd, his face looking like a slapped arse. The score following him off showed, "97, caught behind", whatever that meant. Either way, Dylan didn't give a toss.

Bloody cricket.

"You reckon Tony's got it covered?" Dylan asked,

keeping his voice low and his mouth hidden behind his raised beer glass.

"Yeah. Tony's good people. Been workin' for me a while now. He ain't never let me down yet," Dad said, draining the rest of his beer in one extended glug. He belched quietly into the napkin and showed his empty to the bar.

Gerald nodded, stopped what he was doing, and started pouring a fresh pint.

"He'll keep his mouth shut?" Dylan added.

"If he knows what's good for him—and he does." Dad turned to face him. Gave him the evil eye. "Why? You worried 'bout summat?"

Dylan flapped his free hand.

"Nah," he said, after taking a second sip. Slipped down better than the first. Always did. "Just wanna make sure the filth doesn't spot anything wrong if they do come calling. Don't need any more points on my licence. Only got three to spare."

"You should drive more carefully, then. I can't keep bailing you out with the beaks every time you bugger things up."

Shut the fuck up, Dad.

"I drive careful enough, Dad. Ain't easy keeping things sweet, with so many aggressive arseholes on the road these days."

Dad cocked an eyebrow. His obvious tell for showing disbelief. He didn't look too happy, neither.

"Like the arsehole who parked on the double yellows last night, you mean?"

Dylan nodded.

"S'right, Dad," he said, keeping his face straight and his voice low.

Dad's eyebrow dropped and turned into a scowl. Something was up. He wasn't buying it. Scalpel-sharp was Big Jackie.

Alma came back with two more full glasses. Dad always left Dylan lagging behind in the beer race. The old sod could hold his booze with the best of them. Way better than Dylan. Not that he'd ever go head-to-head against the old man. Wouldn't be worth the effort. Dad would win hands down, and Dylan would let him. In certain situations, it paid to be tactful.

"Breakfast won't be long now, Mr Bentley." Alma smiled at Dad, and mostly ignored Dylan, before walking away. Woman knew who held the purse strings. Knew whose bread to butter first.

Didn't they all. Moneygrubbing bitches, the lot of 'em.

And thinking about money…

Dylan scratched the top of his head.

"There's something I've been wondering about for ages, Dad."

"What's that?"

"The hire cars."

"What about 'em?"

"Why d'you bother?" he asked.

Dad's frown deepened. Caused his thick, black eyebrows to meet in the middle and his brow to crinkle like a ploughed field.

"What d'you mean?"

"They don't exactly turn over much of a profit, and it isn't as though you need the money nowadays."

Dad's forehead smoothed. Took another swig and dabbed his lips again. Being real prissy about it, he was. Trying to impress Alma, no doubt.

"Son," he said, sniffing, "it's nothin' to do with money, and everythin' to do with self-respect." He grinned. "A man needs to work for a livin'. If he don't work, he's nothin'. 'Sides, I love stretch limos and Raptors. They're my life. Why would I give it up? Can't get enough of it."

"That's it?" Dylan asked, genuinely shocked. "A hobby?"

Dad smacked Dylan's upper arm with the back of his hand. It stung, but Dylan didn't flinch. If he'd flinched, Dad would have smacked him again.

"It's no hobby, son," he scowled. "It's honest graft. Gets me out of bed in the mornin', and I get a real kick from hirin' 'em out. Showin' 'em off. Hen parties. Stag dos. Prom nights. All them happy, smilin' faces. It's great." He tapped his temple. "Like I said, self-respect."

"Yeah, Dad," he said. "I get it. Self-respect."

Did he, bollocks.

Why work if you didn't need to. Dylan certainly wouldn't. A fool's game. The side hustle wasn't exactly work, neither. It was fun. A healthy challenge.

Dylan knocked back the rest of his first pint, lowered the glass to the table, and picked up the replacement. The thumping headache he'd woken with had finally started to ease. Hair of the dog working again.

On the TV, another bloke with a bat trudged off the pitch to loads of cheering and huddled backslapping by the ones on the pitch. The guy's score read, "5, bowled". Didn't sound too good.

Five minutes later, Georgie—a tidy blonde in a pair of skin-tight, black jeans and a sprayed-on, black T-shirt—arrived with a tray full of food piled high on two enormous plates. She bent at the knees, slid the tray onto the table, and handed out the grub. Dad first, then Dylan. Triangles of toast on a silver rack and side plates with little squares of individually wrapped butter followed. Food looked and smelled great. Dylan's mouth watered. Didn't realise how hungry he'd become. Hadn't eaten a thing since last night's Chinese and it was already lunch time.

Georgie smiled at Dad. "Anything else I can get you, Mr Bentley?"

"Tommie sauce for me, love," Dad said, reaching for the salt without tasting his food first. "Brown sauce for the lad."

She nodded, turned away, grabbed a bowl of sachets from a neighbouring table, and placed it in front of Dad.

Dad said, "Thanks."

She said, "Enjoy your meal," and buggered off, swinging her hips like she meant it. Cracking bit of stuff, she was. Cracking. Dylan eyed her up as a potential replacement for Chardonnay, when the time came to move on. Wouldn't be too much longer. Chardonnay was already starting to bore him.

Black pudding went down a treat. As did the bacon and fried eggs. Everything nice and hot, freshly cooked. Delish.

Dad and Dylan raced each other to finish first. Dad won by half an egg and three button mushrooms, but Dylan let him. Didn't pay to beat the old man at anything. Wouldn't hear the end of it.

Dad ordered a second refill, and they settled back to drink and watch the TV, bellies full, satisfied. Happy.

Dylan belched into his fist, trying not to be too noisy about it.

AFTER A WHILE, the wallies in white on the screen trooped off the pitch when it started raining and adverts popped up, trying to sell them toothpaste, sweets, cars, and accident insurance. Non-stop. Accident insurance? How fucking ironic. Dylan snorted into his fourth beer, feeling a little light-headed.

After the adverts came the national news. Dylan scowled.

"Pigging hell," he muttered into his glass.

"What's up?" Dad asked.

Dylan nodded up at the screen.

"Politics," he said. "Who gives a flying fart? They've been banging on about the general election for weeks. So fucking boring."

Dad backhanded his upper arm again. Harder than the last time. Really hurt. Stung.

"Ow," Dylan said. "What was that for?"

"Stop showin' your ignorance, son. Politics is important. Elections form the basis of our democracy. That there"—he pointed at the soot-blackened, old building on the big screen —"is the Mother of All Parliaments. You should be proud to cast your ballot. People died to earn the right to vote. Like I said, the election process is important. Them buggers decide how much tax I pay."

"Bollocks," Dylan said, knowing Dad was taking the piss. "When have you ever been happy to pay your taxes?"

More to the point. When did you ever pay any taxes! The Lotto winnings were tax free.

"Too bloody right, son," Dad said, then laughed. Long, hard, and gravelly.

The news droned on for ten long minutes and the tick-ertape scrolling along the bottom of the screen kept repeating what the newsreaders were mouthing off about. Then they moved on to the local news and the arse dropped out of Dylan's world. The Bull fell silent around him. His stomach lurched. Sweat flowed out of him. The beer in his glass turned sour, and his Full English turned to concrete in his belly.

First story started with film of a black Toyota C-HR, wrapped around a tree halfway down a bushy slope and teetering over the inky-black waters of Rook Pond.

Shit.

Ribbons of crime scene tape fluttered in the breeze, and uniformed filth stood around with their thumbs stuck up their arses, looking clueless. Tickertape headlines running along the bottom of the screen roared in red ink, "Horror on Doom Lane!" Next strip said a woman died, a man had been rushed to hospital, but two children had survived with minor injuries.

Jesus fuck.

Dylan tried not to stare but couldn't drag his eyes from the screen.

A woman dead. Dead!

Fuck's sake. What have I done?

The hand holding his beer started shaking. Dylan lowered it to the table, still unable to tear his shocked eyes away from the pictures on the screen.

"I knew it," Dad growled, quiet. Jaw set firm. "I fuckin' knew it."

He slammed his glass down on the table, slopping beer over his fingers. Shot to his feet.

Dylan looked up.

"Wha—"

"Outside," Dad hissed, wiping beer from his fingers with the napkin. "Right now."

He turned, stomped towards the bar, and dropped two fifties on the counter as he passed. These days, he always carried a thick wad of fifties. He turned and headed for the main doors, waving away Gerald's shouted thanks.

Quaking and nauseous, Dylan climbed slowly to his feet and left the rest of his beer. He followed Dad outside, tail clamped firmly between his legs.

His world was over. His life, too.

The sun shone bright and warm outside, but ice-cold blood ran through Dylan's body. Dad stood around the corner in the beer garden, hidden deep inside the pub's shadow, waiting. Anger showed in his clenched fists and his clenched jaw. Dylan closed on him. Cautious. Shuddering.

"'Double yellow line' be fucked," Dad said, barely holding himself in check. "There ain't no double yellows on Doom Lane. Moron. You killed her." Slowly shook his head. "You fuckin' killed her."

Trembling all over, Dylan shook his head. "It were an accident, Dad. An accident. The bugger came out of nowhere. I didn't see him 'til it were too late."

Dad, red faced, stuck out his square jaw and leaned closer. "Stop lyin' to me, you stupid fuckwit. I know that road. Visibility's good all the way along there. Tell me what happened and stop lyin'."

Dylan looked around, making sure no one was about, no one could hear. He took a breath and started talking. This time he told the truth. There wasn't any point in lying to Dad. Canny, old bastard could always tell truth from porkies. Like he had some sort of built-in lie detector.

"You moron," Dad said when Dylan finished. "What am I gonna do with you?"

"Sorry, Dad," Dylan said, and he meant it. "I didn't expect to bump the old fucker off the road. Wanted to run a scare into him, is all. It was the old man's fault. He got in my face and couldn't drive worth a toss."

Dad ground his teeth. Cracked the knuckles on his fists. Dylan stopped talking. Stopped digging himself a deeper hole. Dad closed his eyes, thinking. Couple of seconds later, he opened them again, stared at Dylan. Again, he nodded.

"This Chardonnay bint," Dad said, "you trust her?"

What? What's she got to do with anything?

"Yeah," Dylan answered. Didn't have to think too hard about it, neither. "'Course I do. She's all over me. Can't get enough."

Dad's eyes narrowed. The monobrow reformed. Made him look mean. Scary as fuck. Dylan struggled to swallow.

"Okay," Dad said, nodding slowly. "We can handle this. Where's she live?"

Dylan thought about it for a second. Trying to remember.

"Timberfield Road," he answered. "Why?"

"Never you mind 'bout that." He reached for his phone and dialled. He waited for a bit, then said, "Tony, you done? … Good man. We'll be right with you. Make sure the tank's full." He disconnected and slid the phone back into his pocket. "C'mon, son."

"Where we going?"

Dad sniffed and stared over Dylan's shoulder. "To pick up the Raptor."

"Then what?"

"Then we're going home. I need time to think. And you need to make a phone call."

"Huh?" Dylan said, stepping alongside Dad, rushing to keep up. "Who am I calling?"

"I'll tell you when we get home." Dad stared hard, looking right through him. He already had something in mind. "Now, shut up and let me think."

Dylan's stomach lurched again. Took all his strength not to puke his ring.

Chapter Eleven

Sunday 27th June - Charlotte Smith

Timberfield Road, Stafford, Staffordshire, England

Oh God. What am I going to do?

Charlotte Smith—she could never think of herself as Chardonnay, the ridiculous name Dylan had given her one booze-filled night—sat on her single bed. She hugged the teddy bear she'd had since her second birthday so tight, her arms ached. Threadbare and stained, she still found comfort in hugging Teddy whenever the world turned to shit. And dear God had it done just that. In spades.

She loosened her grip on Teddy, picked up her phone from her lap, and reread the updating news feed for the hundredth time that day, barely able to make out the text through the tears swimming in her eyes. The hand holding the phone trembled, her stomach churned, and she squeezed Teddy tight again. The comfort he gave was nothing but an illusion.

She'd seen the incident from the passenger seat, and she'd let it happen. Unable to believe what Dylan was preparing to do. Not thinking he'd actually go through with his lunatic plan, she'd said nothing. Why? Shock? Fear?

What was the matter with him? A moment of utter madness.

Charlotte wiped her eyes with a tissue, trying to clear her vision. Once again, she read the lurid headline above the photo of the black car wrapped around a large tree, hanging precariously over the lake's dark waters. An unnamed woman dead, a man seriously injured. Two children in the car had survived unhurt, more or less. A miracle. The police were appealing for information, searching for witnesses.

She'd read the first bulletin while lying, naked, in Dylan's bed after she'd let him screw her again. And she had studied every update since. The day just got worse and worse.

Charlotte had woken earlier that morning in his bed, her head thudding and her mouth dust dry, tasting rank.

Dylan lay on his side, his arm draped over her, hand cupping a naked breast as though laying claim to her. As though he owned her. His drunken, burbled snoring had woken her, and she did what she always did first thing. She'd reached out for her phone to check her messages, and she did it carefully, so as not to wake him. A dozen texts, mostly from Trudy, but nothing important. Trudy simply wanted to check in. Then the local news popped up with a story that made her gasp and chilled her to her core. She almost vomited over the bed.

Dylan grunted, farted, released her breast, and turned over. Oblivious. Lying there, dribbling down the side of his mouth, he disgusted her. What had she ever seen in him? The big car. Big muscles. Decent tats. Full wallet. Empty head. Mean and moody. She had a weakness for bad boys. Found them irresistible. But this? He'd gone too far. Much too far.

After re-reading the article to confirm what it said, she'd slid out of bed and grabbed her clothes and her bag. Charlotte crept from the darkened bedroom and stepped out onto the landing, trying to think.

Standing in the open, stark naked, clothes clasped to her chest, she held her breath and listened. A loud snort from the bedroom along the hall confirmed that Dylan's father still slept, thank God. The brooding, ape of a man scared the stuffing out of her. The few times they'd met, he'd looked at her with unremitting disgust. Charlotte wasn't good enough for his precious boy. Well sod him. Sod them both.

She dressed quickly on the landing and rushed down the stairs barefoot, carrying her high heels. At the bottom of the stairs, she turned left and opened the door into the kitchen —white, granite surfaces, grey units, high-end appliances. Everything spotless. Cleaned to within an inch of its life by the housekeeper. She doubted Dylan even knew how to make himself an instant coffee.

Charlotte hurried inside and closed the door quietly. She raised her phone and dialled. The phone rang seven times before the call connected.

"ACB Cabs," a woman said. "I have your location, where do you want to go?"

"Timberfield Road, please," she said and added the post code. "How long will you be?"

"Fifteen minutes, okay?"

"Thanks. Can you collect me from Brocton Village Hall?"

"Not a problem."

Charlotte had ended the call and taken a few moments to breathe—to try and relax, centre herself. It didn't work.

Her mouth parched, the gold-plated tap over the sink called out to her. She padded across the kitchen, ran the water until it turned cold, and drank straight from the tap. The filtered water tasted great, just like bottled. Much better than the scummy stuff at home. She wiped her mouth with the back of her hand and slipped on her shoes.

The double doors in the hallway looked heavy and secure. Tentatively, she reached for the handle. She cast her mind back to the giddiness of their late-night arrival, high as kites after spending the evening at Baz's flat, drinking and toking on big, fat joints. They'd stumbled through the door, with Dylan's fumbling, grasping hands all over her. Her fake laughing and breathless acceptance of his sloppily aggressive advances. She had to open up to him as per usual. He expected it. They all expected it—all the boys she'd ever known. Had Dylan set a burglar alarm? No. He'd been too keen to take her. Too wrapped up in his own needs. And she'd been keen to let him. She sort of enjoyed the attention.

Stupid, stupid bitch.

Charlotte grabbed the door handle and turned it, preparing to make a dash for the main gates if the alarm sounded. The door opened to silence. No alarm. She breathed again, almost relaxed.

A brisk, five-minute walk to the Village Hall gave her a ten-minute wait. She spent the time pacing the pavement, watching the road one way for the taxi, and the other way in case Dylan woke and came searching for her. Irrational fears, but vivid. While she waited, she created excuses for leaving without telling him, without saying goodbye, without giving him what he wanted—again. She needn't have worried. He didn't come. Too out of it to wake.

Charlotte had only breathed easily when the taxi arrived to whisk her away.

The clock on her phone clicked over to four thirty. Despite the memories, and the news bulletins, her stomach rumbled. She hadn't eaten since the bland takeaway the previous night. Not a morsel all day. Hadn't been able to force any food down. She'd only managed two cups of coffee since waking in Dylan's super-king-sized bed, and she'd spent the day in her bedroom, refusing to eat. She'd said no to each of her mother's shouted offers, and confirmed that she wasn't starving herself, wasn't forcing herself to throw up again. It wasn't like the bad, old days.

"I'm okay, Mum," she'd said more than once. "I had breakfast at Trudy's." The lies came easily. They always did. And Mum fell for them every time.

"If you're sure, love."

"Mum," she'd said. "Don't fuss. I'm not hungry. I'll eat later. Promise."

She'd listened to the vacuum cleaner suck the pile off the downstairs carpets, and then to the *EastEnders* theme tune. Mum recorded each episode to binge on a Sunday afternoon. Her only pleasure in life, she claimed. She worked hard on the tills all week, and cleaned the house all weekend. Bless her. Charlotte helped where she could, but she hated the drudgery of housework, and she had her own life to lead. Working in the salon three days a week and servicing Dylan's needs day after day took its time and its toll. But no longer. She'd had enough.

Since climbing out of the taxi, Charlotte only had one thing on her mind. The poor family in the Toyota. The family Dylan had forced off the road in a fit of childish rage. Leading up to it, Charlotte assumed he'd tailgate the Toyota, flash his headlights, scare the crap out of the feisty, old man and the rest of his family. But no. He'd deliberately rear-ended them, and he'd laughed his head off while doing it. Dylan, the bloody madman.

All the old man had done was ask Dylan to stop swearing in front of the kids. The darling, little things had been terrified. Crying. At the time, Charlotte had felt so sorry for them, but she couldn't say anything. Dylan expected her support and she'd given it. But that was before he'd run the Toyota off the road. Before he'd killed an old lady and injured her husband. And then he'd driven off. Such a cowardly act.

At midday, she'd watched the local news on the TV in her bedroom. They'd covered the story. Of course they had. A death on the roads still carried enough punch to make the lead story in the main, local bulletin. The story ended with an appeal by a dark-haired police inspector. She asked anyone who witnessed the accident to call 1-0-1 or the number running along the bottom of the screen.

Charlotte had reached for her phone and actually dialled the number, but she couldn't make herself hit the green button. Fear had overcome her good intentions. Fear of repercussions. Fear of what would happen to Dylan if she grassed him up. Fear of what Dylan's father would do to her. Big Jackie Bentley had earned himself a fearsome reputation. Former soldier and local hard man.

A hit-and-run, the police called it.

If she phoned them, Dylan would be found guilty of

leaving the scene of a fatal accident. They'd send him to prison for years and years.

Maybe she should keep quiet. Leave well alone. But no. The police would come calling. The damage to the Raptor —the bent bar and missing spotlight—made it obvious that it had rammed into the Toyota. And the police would see the CCTV from the service station. The Raptor wasn't exactly the least conspicuous vehicle on the roads. Bloody thing stood out like a beacon—which was the whole point of having such a garish truck. Nobody drove around in a bright, green Ford Raptor if they wanted to go unnoticed. It would only be a matter of time before the police called to interview Dylan. And they'd call on her, too. They'd see her on the CCTV at the service station. They'd know she'd been in the car. They'd know. Charlotte would be in trouble for not coming forward sooner. What did they call it? Aiding an offender?

Dear God.

What was she going to do?

Her lower lip quivered. Tears formed. She couldn't stop feeling sorry for herself.

Charlotte needed a way out. A way that helped everybody. She needed to talk to Dylan. It would go much better for him if he handed himself in. The police would go easier on him. He could claim it was an accident. He could say he'd lost control of the Raptor on account of the bad weather.

That would work.

It has to work. There's no other way.

Yes, it would be much better for Dylan if he confessed. After all, Dylan wasn't a bad man. Fundamentally, he was a good person. He just got carried away sometimes. She'd call him. Convince him to give himself up. Again, she snatched up the phone.

As she prepared to dial, Steppenwolf's rock anthem, *Born to be Wild*, roared out.

Dylan!

He'd programmed her phone to play it when he called. Her heart lurched. She nearly dropped the phone. Worry coiled its tentacles around her throat, restricting her breathing.

Charlotte shuddered.

She wanted to reject the call, but that would have made things worse. Dylan hated it when she didn't answer. In the ten weeks since they'd first become a hot item, she'd only failed to pick up once—when she'd been in the bathroom—and she'd never heard the end of it.

Fear overtook her caution.

Thumb shaking, she hit the green icon and willed a smile onto her face.

"Hi, Babe," she said, sounding even more tentative than usual.

"Chardonnay," Dylan growled, "what happened to you this morning?"

"S-Sorry, Babe," she said, scrambling for the excuse, the lie, she'd thought of earlier. "I-I ... promised Mum I'd go shopping with her. She can't carry the heavy bags these days."

"You should've woken me up," he said, calming down a little. "Said goodbye. I missed you, Babe."

She hesitated. Time to lay it on thick.

"You looked so peaceful," she said. "I didn't have the heart to disturb you. We had a late night."

"Okay. Sweet." He sniffed. "Er, Babe. We ... we need to talk."

The tentacles around her throat tightened.

"What about?" she asked, scarcely able to drive the words past the restriction.

"About what happened yesterday," he said, sounding tense. "With the … old boy in the Toyota."

"You saw the news?" she said, rushing the words.

"Yeah, and it scared the crap out of me. I fucked up really bad, and I'm sorry. So, so sorry."

His response surprised her. When she expected bluster, he showed remorse. Perhaps there was hope for him—for them both—after all. Charlotte closed her eyes, relief rushed through her.

"What are you going to do?" she asked, sounding less timid, more confident.

"I'm gonna hand myself over," he answered. No hesitation.

"You are?"

"'Course I am," he said. "Did you think I wouldn't? I talked it over with Dad. He's gonna stand by me."

Thank God.

Maybe Jackie Bentley didn't deserve his hard-man reputation after all.

"How?"

"Dad called his solicitor. Best in the area. Most expensive. I'm at home now, waiting for him. We're gonna prepare a statement to take with us to the police station."

"That's a great idea."

"Yeah." His voice caught, tinged with worry. "We're getting out in front of this. I haven't spoken to the solicitor yet, but Dad says it'll be okay."

Relief eased away the fear. Again, she closed her eyes and forced a deep breath into starved lungs. For the first time that day, the heavy clouds lifted. Dylan felt remorse.

Deep down, he was a good man. He *was* a good man. He'd proven himself.

Dylan paused for a moment before carrying on.

"Er, trouble is," he said, being uncharacteristically hesitant, "we need you here, too."

"Really? Why?"

"You were with me in the Raptor. You're a key witness. I didn't mean to hurt that woman, Babe. You know that, don't you?"

"Of course I do," she said, not taking long to convince herself. She'd been wrong about him. Totally, utterly wrong.

"You'll tell them it was an accident. Won't you?"

"Yes, Babe," she gushed. "'Course I will."

"Thank God. Oh thank you so much." He gasped, as though trying to hold back a tear. "Where are you now?"

"At home in my bedroom. Why?"

"Dad's on his way to collect you. I knew you'd help. He left twenty minutes ago. Might even be there already."

Charlotte's heart flipped.

"Hang on, I'll look."

She bounced off the bed, crossed to the window, and drew back the curtains. The only car she didn't recognise was an old, dark blue BMW, parked where the neighbours usually left their rust-bucket Astra. It took up more space and encroached onto the next spot.

"What's he driving?" she asked.

"A BMW Series 5. He … didn't want to use the Raptor … for obvious reasons."

"Yeah, I understand," she said. "I see it."

"Hurry, Babe. Don't keep him waiting."

"I won't. Love you."

"Me too. See you soon."

He ended the call.

Charlotte slid the phone into her handbag and hurried from the bedroom. She smiled. Things were going to be okay. She and Dylan would see this unholy mess through together. Charlotte skipped down the stairs and popped her head around the door to the lounge. Not for the first time, her mother had fallen asleep in front of the TV. Poor thing, she worked so very hard.

Charlotte eased the lounge door closed and crept out of the house.

Chapter Twelve

Sunday 27th June - Jackson Bentley

Timberfield Road, Stafford, Staffordshire, England

Jackson Bentley edged the crusty, old BMW past Charlotte Smith's house and squeezed into the parking spot next door. It didn't leave much room for cars to pass on the outside, but he wouldn't be there long—assuming Dylan did his stuff properly. Surely the dullard could do something right for a change. He gripped the wheel tight, and his leather gloves made the leather cover squeak. The rear-view mirror gave him a good view of the girl's front door. A pale, summer sun broke through the cloud cover, its rays spreading through the scratched and grease-smeared wind-screen. He hadn't driven such a piece of crap in years. Still, the ancient Beemer had its uses. This would probably be its final journey.

His phone chirruped. Jackie grabbed it from the centre console and hit the green button.

"Yeah?" he said.

"Dad? Is that you?" Dylan answered, sounding nervous.

Who the fuck else would it be?

"Yeah, it's me," Jackie said, patient as possible. "You called her?"

"Yeah. Told her about the solicitor. She's in."

"Good." Jackie smiled. He loved it when a plan came together. A real plan that didn't include any fucking solicitors. Not that Dylan had a clue about what was really going down. Still, what he didn't know couldn't hurt him.

"She knows you're waiting for her," Dylan said. "She's on her way now."

"Good. I've just heard from the solicitor."

Yeah, 'course I have.

"He's runnin' a little late. Had to pick up some papers from his office. He'll be with you in about an hour. Hang tough, son. Grab yourself a coffee. Sober up."

"Okay, Dad."

"Good lad."

"Oh, Dad?"

"Yeah?"

"Thanks for everything. I mean … you know. Thanks for standing by me."

"You're my boy," Jackie said, smiling. "What else am I gonna do?"

He ended the call and waited. In the rear-view mirror, the front door opened, and the spiky-haired, slip of a girl stepped through the opening. She smiled and waved at him.

Jackie poked his arm through the open driver's window and gave the thumbs up.

She trotted down her weed-strewn path, reached the BMW's front passenger door, and tugged it open.

"Hello, Mr Bentley," she said, climbing in and buckling up for safety.

Safety is important.

"Whatcha, Charlotte," he replied, all nice and friendly. "Thanks for comin'. Dylan and I appreciate what you're doin' for us."

She nodded and winced. "It's a bad business."

"Yeah." He nodded. "It is, but one little mistake shouldn't ruin my boy's life, and you can help."

"I'll do everything I can, Mr Bentley."

"Jackie," he corrected, adding his friendliest smile. "Please, call me Jackie."

She glanced around the inside of the car and her gaze landed on his gloved hands, which looked out of place on such a warm, summer's day.

"Eczema," he said, holding up his hands. "Flares up summat rotten from time to time. Especially when I'm stressed. This is one of them days."

She pouted in sympathy. "My gran used to suffer from that. Terrible, it was. She's gone now, though. Passed away two years ago."

"I'm sorry to hear that, love. Ready to go?"

The daft bitch nodded.

Jackie fired up the Beemer, indicated, and pulled out. A couple of hundred metres later, he turned left into Mahogany Drive, drove around the loop, and ended up back on Timberfield, below Chardonnay's house. He made a left on Doxy Road and put his foot down, heading straight for the roundabout. With the light, Sunday afternoon traffic, he pushed the Beemer up to forty, then slowed to take the first exit onto Pans Road. For once, the lights held on green. He turned right and slowed to a crawl behind a plonker on a pushbike.

"Nice car," she said, making conversation. "Didn't expect to see you in a BMW. I thought you preferred Fords."

Jackie indicated right and overtook the cyclist, giving the fluorescent warrior a nice, wide berth. Playing the good, careful driver. For camouflage.

"Ordinarily, I wouldn't be seen dead in a Beemer," Jackie said, smiling. "Not good for business or my street cred. But the family Raptor's out of commission and this was the only car available at short notice."

"I like it," she said. "It's easier to climb into for someone my size."

She shot him an apologetic smile, and he returned it.

"Good things, little packages," he said, adding a wink.

He had to play the nice guy. At least for the moment.

The lights at the end of Foregate stayed green—yet another miracle—and he filtered around to the right, then swung left onto the A34.

A dark green Renault Kangoo cut him off without indicating. Ordinarily, Jackie would have leaned on the horn and yelled something fruity out the window, but to keep a low profile and to keep the girl sweet, he gave ground to the tosser. For the same reason, he maintained a modest thirty-eight mph in a forty zone. He didn't want to alert any passing patrol cars or to put the girl on her guard.

Their luck turned and they were forced to stop at a red. The twenty-something driver of a Kia Picanto in the inside lane took an interest in Jackie's passenger, her blue, spiky hair drawing attention. Jackie rubbed his temple to hide his face and waited for the lights to change. It took an age, but the second they turned green, the Kia driver burned rubber and left them for dead. Jackie pulled away slowly and allowed the Kia to disappear into the distance.

"Everyone's in such a hurry these days," he said, smiling.

She nodded but said nothing.

They joined Lichfield Road and headed out of town.

The girl opened her handbag, dug out her mobile, and started tapping.

"You're not callin' anyone?"

She looked up from her screen and shook her head.

"Nah," she said, "just reading some messages. Why?"

"It's probably best to keep things quiet for a while," he said. "At least until after we've talked to the solicitor. You know what legal eagles are like. Don't want nobody sayin' nothin' to no one unless they've okayed it first."

Her brows creased, apparently in concentration.

"We've got to make things right for Dylan," he added. "'Kay?"

The hard lines on her forehead softened and she nodded.

"Okay, yeah. Makes sense. But I'm not saying anything. Just reading my messages. There's a sale on in Next, and I was looking for a new top."

Jackie relaxed. With so much shit going down, all she could think about was shopping. What an airhead. She'd be no loss to the world.

He left her to her online browsing and concentrated on his driving.

Trees crowded up around them on both sides of the road, and the area started looking less populated. They'd soon reach the country. Another set of lights showed green and let them through without him needing to slow. Brick-built, terraced houses rolled by on the left, and a heavily wooded park passed by on the right in a blanket of dark greens and browns. The flashing blue lights and wailing sirens of an ambulance bore down on them from straight ahead. Jackie pulled tight into the kerb, giving the bus plenty of space to pass. He hadn't driven so carefully in years. So carefully, it made his palms itch inside the gloves.

They passed a small shopping centre on their right and carried on out of town.

Not long now.

Although the nerves should have been building, Jackie felt nothing. Nothing but calmness and determination. Nerves were for people with no balls. Gutless bastards who got nothing done in their lives.

"Darn it," the girl said and looked up at him. "Sorry."

"What's wrong?"

"They don't have my size."

"Oh," he said. "That's a shame."

Airhead.

She swiped her screen a couple of times, dropped the mobile back in her bag, and leaned back against the head restraint. She spent the time looking through the window at the houses scrolling past.

Straight over at the next roundabout, past the Aldi on the right, and out into the country. Finally.

Soon be there.

"Mind tellin' me what happened?" he asked, finally broaching the subject—the elephant in the car. On his honour, he had to at least give her one chance to save herself.

Her dark blue eyes turned towards him. "Sorry?"

"Yesterday evenin'. Tell me what happened with the Toyota."

Once again, creases formed on her otherwise-smooth brow, and she shook her head.

"We stopped at the services to fill the tank."

Jackie nodded, indicated right, and overtook a granny in an old, but spotless, VW Golf.

"The Raptor's a thirsty beast," he said, moving back to the inside lane and slowing to the speed limit. "But they're fantastic motors. Built like tanks. You can go anywhere in a Raptor."

She smiled, took a tissue from her handbag, and blew her nose.

"Go on," he encouraged, keeping her engaged, putting her at her ease.

"We were supposed to be meeting my friend, Trudy, but we were early. So, we popped into the food hall for a coffee." She winced, wiped her nose again. "Dylan was being a bit … lairy. You know, loud? Swearing down the phone. You know what he's like."

Jackie stopped behind three cars waiting at another set of lights.

"Yeah," he said, through gritted teeth. "I know what he's like."

A loud-mouthed, opinionated git. But he's my *loud-mouthed, opinionated git.*

He didn't need a brain-dead tart like Charlotte-bloody-Smith telling him about Dylan's strengths and weaknesses.

Not that there are many strengths, mind.

"What happened next?"

The lights turned green, and after the usual, stupid delay waiting for the dozy wankers to find the right gear, they started moving again.

She told him about the rumble in the café, and how Dylan backed down to an old man and a bruiser. That was another thing about Dylan. Kid had no balls. All mouth and nothing to back it up. Heavy muscles, but a coward's heart. A bully. Soft bugger wouldn't last five minutes in the army. Or in prison, come to that. The lad was Jackie's responsibility. He had to save him. Nothing else for it. No other option.

Town turned to outskirts and then to countryside, and all the while, the girl droned on, ending each statement on the rise as though it was a question. By the time she reached the part where Dylan had parked by the petrol station, lying in wait for the Toyota, they passed The Wheatsheaf on the left. Ten seconds later, they were alongside the car showroom on the right—a moron selling jap crap—and were on their way towards the double roundabout. The second exit on the first roundabout led to Brocton and home, Cannock Road.

Her description of the crash matched Dylan's detail for detail. No doubt about it. The boy had dropped a major bollock. Jackie would have played it different. He'd have followed the Toyota home and gone back later. Torched the car, or the house, but he would've done it alone. Wouldn't have taken along a bloody witness to tell tales. Especially not an airheaded girl barely old enough to drive.

"I-It was terrible," she said, reaching into her handbag for another tissue and wiping her eyes. "I t-tried to stop him, talk him out of it, but Dylan sort of went crazy, y'know? He laughed when the Toyota crashed through the fence. He actually laughed. He needs help, y'know? Psychiatric help."

Jackie nodded the whole way through her story, encouraging her to continue, making out as though he agreed with her.

Stupid, naïve bitch.

Her chin dimpled. She sniffled and blew her nose on the tissue. Slim built, she didn't really fill out her thin top too well, but he could see why Dylan fancied her. Although no tits to speak of, she had a pretty face, big, cow eyes, and a nice smile when she chose to use it. Didn't look so hot with the eyes all blotchy and red, though. Not so hot at all.

Jackie listened and nodded but focused on his driving.

Here we go.

He ploughed straight past Brocton Village and turned right into Teddesley Lane. It ran downhill. Nothing but countryside all around. He slowed to make the sharp right-hander before pulling away as the road straightened.

"You've gone the wrong way," she said, worry in her voice. "Your house is back there." She pointed over her shoulder.

"There's roadworks on Shipton Lane. We've got to go around the back. This way's much quicker."

"Oh," she said. "Okay. So, where was I?"

"My son ran the Toyota off the road."

"Oh yes," she said, sniffling. "I tried to get him to stop, and go back to help, but he just carried on. We ended up at Baz's flat. You know Baz?"

The sycophantic, no-nuts clown.

"Yes," he said. "I know Baz. Nice bloke. Reliable. A good friend to Dylan."

"Hmm," she said, guarded.

She'd twigged to Baz. Not all that naïve, then.

Four miles on winding, country roads later, Jackie turned right into the always-deserted Hope Way. Single track, unruly hedgerows each side, farmer's fields beyond. Two hundred metres in, he checked the rear-view. Road empty. No one about. No tractors in the fields that he could see. He eased his foot onto the brake. Gravel crunched under rubber, and the old car shuddered to a stop. He turned to face her.

"What's wrong?" she asked, curiosity on her face, not fear.

"Fifty grand," he said.

"Sorry?"

"I'll give you fifty grand to tell the police it were an accident, and you were drivin'."

She frowned, shook her head as though she didn't understand him.

"What? No. I-I can't do—"

"Think about it, Charlotte. Think what you and your mother could do with fifty grand. Think about it."

"No. I-I can't lie to the police. I'll go to prison."

Better than Dylan going down.

"You've never been in trouble with the police before, have you?"

She hesitated, then said, "No. Never. But—"

"Good. They'll go easier on you than him. Tell them it was an accident. Tell them you were drivin' the Raptor for the first time, and you lost control. You ran into the Toyota by accident."

"No! I can't lie to—"

"A hundred!" he said, almost shouting. "One hundred thousand pounds. I'll pay all your legal fees, and I'll look after your mother, whatever happens. Please!" Even to himself, he sounded desperate. Maybe he should take up acting.

At least he was giving her a chance. If he had a conscience, he would be easing it by making her such a generous offer. But he didn't have a conscience. His time in the army had seared it out of him along with his soul.

"No!" she said. "I can't lie. And no matter how much money to offer, it wouldn't work."

"Why not?"

"I don't have a driving licence. I-I never learned to drive."

Shit.

"That don't matter," Jackie said, reaching the end game. "Make out that Dylan were givin' you a lesson. After all, you were on a quiet road."

"But … I wouldn't have been insured. It would make it even worse for me. I-I can't do it. I won't lie to the police."

That did it. The bitch had all the answers. Nothing else for it.

Jackie struck.

"Get out!" he raged.

She lurched backwards in her seat, raised her hands as though worried he'd hit her. Not a chance of that happening. He didn't want to leave any giveaway marks on her face.

"What?" she asked, chin dimpling again.

"Get outta my fuckin' car!"

She looked around her, through the windows, and saw nothing but hedges and fields.

"But we're in the middle of nowhere," she said, a tremble in her voice. Pleading.

Jackie sneered.

"I don't give a rat's arse. Get out before I throw you out!"

The bint grabbed her handbag—a cheap, knockoff Louis Vuitton—held it up to her chest, using it as a shield. He leaned closer. She squealed and backed further away. He reached for the door handle, pushed. The door screeched open. Crying openly, she unfastened her seatbelt, slid out of the car, and slammed the door shut.

"Bitch!" he shouted and shifted into reverse.

"Bastard!" she shot back, finding strength from somewhere.

He selected reverse and stamped on the throttle. The rear wheels spun, spat gravel into the floor pan, gained traction, started reversing up the hill. The stupid bitch stepped into the middle of the lane. She raised her fist and hurled obscenities. Begging for it.

Happy to oblige, Jackie stamped on the brake and threw the Beemer into drive. He mashed his foot on the throttle and buried the pedal into the worn carpet. The engine roared. The crappy, old car lurched forwards.

The stupid bitch screamed.

Front grill and bumper slammed into soft tissue and bone.

Terror and pain twisted her features. Eyes wide, mouth open, her scream partially masked by the engine's roar, she folded over the bonnet. Her face slammed into the metal. Jackie ploughed on, dragged her under the wheels. Hands grasping for a hold, she disappeared.

Tyres thumped and bounced.

Bones snapped and crunched.

The screaming cut off. Jackie kept going. The rear wheels bumped over something soft and sludgy. He rolled the car ahead ten metres, fifteen, until the pulpy, red mess revealed itself in the rear-view.

He slammed on the brakes, and the big, heavy Beemer shuddered to a stop.

The blue, spiky head crushed almost flat said enough. The blood and brains splattering the road, the distorted arms and legs said even more. Charlotte Smith no longer posed a danger to his boy. She no longer represented the weak link in the chain.

Family bonds were stronger than any others.

Dylan could rest easy.

Jackie cast his searching gaze around the car. Nothing showed that she'd ever been in it.

He scanned the rest of the scene. Lodged on a branch in the hedgerow hung the handbag. Thrown there by the impact. He scrambled out of the car, grabbed the knockoff bag, and dived back behind the wheel. He dropped the bag onto the passenger seat and glanced in the rear-view mirror. An opportunistic crow flopped down for an unexpected, early supper. It joined the growing bloom of flies.

Jackie released the handbrake, eased a little pressure onto the throttle, and rolled the Beemer forwards. He drove slowly away from the gloopy mess.

Jackie drove three miles, pulled into a passing place, and jumped out. The front of the Beemer showed little evidence of having connected with a human body. A set of dirt-encrusted headlights, a bent and buckled grille, but no obvious blood spatter. The underneath would be covered in gore and human tissue, but no passing motorist would spot that. He was free and clear to head for the farm. With any luck, they wouldn't find the corpse for a while. A couple of days maybe. Precious few vehicles travelled Hope Way. Few dog walkers would ever venture that far from the village.

He reached the T-junction where Hope Way met Acton Hill, turned right, and followed the road leading away from Brocton Village. Ten minutes after the crest of a hill and a left turn onto Sawdust Lane, he made a sharp right into the farm he'd bought for a few hundred grand after Old Man Harrow died. Jackie acquired the place through a holding company. Few people in the world knew who actually owned the farm now.

Chapter Thirteen

Sunday 27th June - Dylan Bentley

Bentley House, Brocton Village, Staffordshire, England

Dylan paced the kitchen floor, carrying his third mug of strong coffee. His heart raced. Caffeine wasn't helping. Burning a hole in his throat and guts. No news from Dad. He'd been gone for ages, working on a way to fix things.

Come on, Dad. Where are you?

Dylan paced alone. Festering. Wondering what Dad was up to. How long he'd be. Any moment, the filth could burst in, and he'd have to face them solo. He swallowed thick, sticky phlegm. Made him gag.

Cool it, man. Cool it.

The filth wouldn't find anything. As usual, Tony Epps had done a bang-up job on the Raptor. The big beast looked mint. Showroom perfect. Only fly in the ointment was Chardonnay, but if anyone could handle her, it was Dad. He'd wave a bunch of cash under her nose as a convincer. Do anything for money, would Chardonnay. Greedy, little cow. Why else would she be hanging around, begging for a piece of Dylan's action? On the other hand ...

"Easy, Dylan," he said to his reflection in the microwave. "Things are cool. Dad's got this covered. Dad's always got things covered."

Outside, something creaked.

Dylan turned to watch through the window as the front gates swung open and Dad arrived in his black Raptor with the gold eagle's wings on the bonnet. Looked so damned cool. Dylan wanted one just like it, but Dad refused to have a copy made. Said there could only be one Midnight Eagle in the world.

Dylan set his mug down in the sink and hurried into the hall. Opened the front door and waited for Dad to park. The old man climbed down from Midnight Eagle, stomped towards the house, and barged past. No sign of Chardonnay. Where'd she gotten to?

A gaping hole opened in Dylan's stomach. He swallowed acid.

What the fuck? He didn't. Did he?

Dad headed straight to the bar in the front room. Hands shaking, he poured himself a whisky. Large. Neat. Knocked it back in one. Slammed the glass down on the bar and turned to face Dylan.

"Where's Chardonnay?" Dylan asked.

Dad sniffed, shook his head.

"She's gone."

"Gone?"

He blinked a couple of times and nodded.

"How much did it cost?"

"A knackered, old BMW 5 Series," Dad mumbled, showing him a sad smile. Hands no longer trembling, he reached for the bottle. Filled the glass to the top.

"What d'you mean?"

"She wouldn't go for it. In the end, I offered her a hundred grand. She turned me down flat."

"Fuck." Dylan swallowed hard. "Where is she?"

"Like I told you. She's … gone." He lifted his glass. Took a big gulp.

"What happened?"

Hesitation. Not like Dad to hesitate. Normally he had all the answers down pat.

"She jumped out the car," he said, taking another gulp.

"Where?"

"Hope Way."

Dylan frowned.

"Bloody hell, Dad. That's in the middle of nowhere."

"Yeah, that's what she said," he said. Another mumble wrapped up in another tight smile.

"And you just left her there?"

He shook his head. "She started runnin'. I chased after her in the car. Just wanted to talk to her, is all. Shit."

Dad downed the rest of the second whisky. Held the empty glass like he wanted to crush it in his fist.

"Dad," Dylan said, hating the haunted look on the old man's face. Wasn't like him to be worried. "What happened?"

"I shouted out the window for her to stop, but she … she … fuck."

"Dad, you're scaring me," Dylan lied. "What the fuck happened?"

Head down, shoulders slumped, Dad stared at his feet. Shook his head.

"Dad. Tell me."

He looked up, eyes glazed. Dad never cried. Not even when Mum buggered off and left them. An act. Dylan knew it but he didn't let on.

"She stumbled," Dad said, words apparently catching in his throat. "Fell under the wheels. I … I ran her over, son. Killed her."

"Fuck."

Brilliant. Pure, dead brilliant.

Dylan could see the upside—of course he could—but made sure he didn't whoop with joy.

"Yeah," Dad said. "Fuck."

"You sure she's dead?"

Dad nodded. Breathed in a sigh.

"Yeah. I'm sure. Crushed head. But at least it were quick."

Who cared how quick it was, so long as the daft bitch was dead and no longer a liability? No longer a witness against him.

Thank fuck for that.

"What we gonna do?" Dylan asked, trying to sound grief-stricken and managing quite well. He tried to force tears into his eyes but failed.

"Nothin'," Dad said.

"Did you call an ambulance?"

Dad shook his head. "No point. She were dead. I've seen dead bodies before. There weren't no savin' her."

Of course there wasn't. Dad wouldn't fuck up like that. He was nothing but thorough.

"So, what'd you do?"

"I scarpered. Rapid quick."

Dylan blinked. Three times. Added one more for luck.

"You just left her there? In the middle of the road?" he asked, as though he cared.

Dad tilted his head. "She were dead, son. Nothin' I could do for her." Wiped away his false tears with his fists.

Dylan dropped into the nearest chair. Dad's hand-built, leather recliner. Figured he could get away with it just the once. He sat and thought about how he felt. Relieved? Certainly. Turned on? Absolutely. Either way, Dylan had to hide his excitement. Had no idea how the old man would react if he knew the truth.

"You just left her there?" Dylan repeated, play-acting being stunned.

"Well, I couldn't exactly hang around, could I?" Dad said. "I mean, I ran the poor lass over. It were an accident, like, but who'd believe me? You know the rep I've got. Filth woulda stitched me up for murder in a heartbeat. Like they're gonna try to do with you for the woman in the Toyota."

"Christ Almighty."

He buried his face in his hands like he was in shock, crying.

Play the part, Dylan. You're good at this.

"Yeah, right," Dad said into his hands. "Christ Almighty."

"What we gonna do?"

Dad squatted at the side of the recliner, grabbed Dylan's forearm.

"Look at me, son."

Dylan turned his head, faced Dad. Stared into his eyes and saw nothing but calm certainty. No more fake tears.

"It's you and me against the world, son," he said, jaw tense. "You and me. No one else has got our backs."

"But the solicitor … he's on his way."

Dad shook his head. "No, he ain't. I … cancelled him. Said it was all a big mistake."

"But he knows the truth."

"That don't matter, son. He can't say nothin'. It's called privileged information."

"But I thought we were going to the cops. I was planning to confess."

The fuck I was.

They were planning to pay Chardonnay to take the blame.

Dad sighed. Gave another shake of the head. "That would never have worked, son."

"Why not?"

"When we fixed the Raptor, we was tamperin' with evidence. We'd have all been in the shit. Including Tony. And he were only helpin'." He paused. Took a deep breath. Continued. "You understand, don't you?"

"Yeah. I suppose."

'Course I understand. What's difficult about that?

"So," Dad said, "you'll stand by me? You'll keep schtum about what happened with Chardonnay?"

"Yeah," Dylan said. "I will. 'Course I will."

"And you'll keep schtum about the Toyota?"

Dylan nodded. Forced himself not to smile when he wanted to howl in delight. Yell at the ceiling.

He'd dodged the bullet, big time.

"Yeah," Dylan said. "It'll be our secret. One thing though. I got a question."

Dad stood. Knees creaked on the way up. When had he turned into such a doddering, old man?

"Go on. Ask away."

"What happened to the Beemer? There'll be evidence all over it. Blood and stuff."

Dad sniffed, raked his fingers through what remained of his hair. The bald patch shone in the sunlight flooding through the French doors.

"Oh," he said, "didn't I tell you?"

"No, Dad. You didn't."

"Fancy a snifter?" he asked, pointing at the whisky bottle with the fancy label. Something with loads of vowels and an unpronounceable, Scottish name.

"Don't mind if I do," Dylan said, nodding and rolling his finger forwards. "But what about the Beemer?"

Dad turned, reached over the bar, and grabbed another glass. Filled it close to the brim and handed it across. Refilled his glass and raised it high.

"You and me against the world!" he said.

Dylan repeated the toast and knocked back a mouthful. The whisky scorched his throat on the way down. He'd normally sink a few lagers before turning to the fiery stuff. Didn't complain, though. Dad paid a fortune for the jollop and would've hated for Dylan to diss it.

"So, you wanna know about the Beemer?"

Dylan nodded.

"I dropped it off at the farm when I collected Midnight Eagle," he said, pointing to the black Raptor with his glass. "And you'll never guess what happened to it the moment my back was turned."

He had an idea, but said, "No, Dad. Do tell."

Dad took another sip of the amber liquid.

"Some nasty bastard torched it."

Dylan grinned. Matched Dad slurp for slurp.

"You're kidding."

"Nope. Went up like a firework on bonfire night."

"Oh dear, oh dear. Kids, you reckon?"

"Prob'ly. It's the parents I blame. No control. Wouldn't surprise me if the fuckin' thing's still burnin'."

Another sip made Dylan a little dizzy. The Full English wasn't soaking it up too well. Good job he was sitting down, or he might have taken a tumble. Strong stuff, the whisky.

"Want me to call the fire brigade?" he asked.

Dad sucked a breath between his teeth. Shook his head.

"Nah. Don't bother, son. It's well away from the barns. Best to let it burn itself out."

"Good idea."

Dad laughed. Relieved, Dylan joined in.

He hadn't felt so good since the last time he'd watched the dashcam footage.

They finished the first bottle. Broke open another. Dad drank most of it, but Dylan knocked back his fair share. Eventually, Dad drowsed in his chair. Somewhere along the line, Dylan had moved from Dad's recliner into his own. Later, with darkness fallen, he woke to Dad mumbling to himself.

"What was that, Dad?" he asked, slurring his words.

"I done it for you, son," he said, speaking quiet, almost a whisper. "Couldn't let you go down for killin' the old woman in the Toyota. You can see that, right? You're too pretty to end up inside. You'd make some hairy-arsed fairy a lovely cell wife. And I wouldn't be around to protect you. My money only stretches so far. You'd end up toppin' yourself, and I can't have that, son. I love you."

"What you saying, Dad?"

Dad told him what really happened. Stark and simple. Tantalising. Secretly, it gave Dylan a hard-on.

"Jesus, Dad!"

"Done it for you, son."

"Bloody hell."

"It were the only way."

Dylan shut his mouth and started thinking. Whisky had loosened Dad's tongue. Never seen him drink so much in so short a time.

"You and me, son," he said, tapping the side of his nose. "We're the only ones we can trust. We stick together and nobody can touch us. Right?"

Dad stopped talking. Waited. Looked like he was holding his breath. Actually seemed worried. Dad never worried.

Dylan tried to answer. Couldn't form the words. Wanted to laugh but couldn't. It would give the game away.

Dad leaned over. Grabbed Dylan's shoulder. Squeezed.

"Right?" he repeated, louder. More forcefully.

Dylan coughed. Swallowed. For effect.

"Yeah, Dad. I … I got it."

Dad squeezed harder, then let go of his shoulder.

"Good lad. You know it makes sense."

Oh Jesus. What a total gas.

It all boiled down to one simple truth. Accept Dad's intervention or suffer twenty-odd years banged up in a cell, being arse-fucked day after day for a simple mistake. An accident. Dylan or Chardonnay. Her guaranteed silence, or a life behind bars.

Made perfect sense.

Her or me.

No contest.

Dad made the right choice. Only one thing wrong with it. One problem that couldn't be fixed. Dylan would have loved to see the stupid bitch die with his own eyes. Such a shame the old Beemer didn't have dashcam. Still, the

Raptor did, and he'd keep watching the footage of the Toyota crashing through the wooden fence and rolling down the bank. Every time Dylan watched it, he tingled all over.

Such a blast.

Chapter Fourteen

Sunday 27th June - Tobias Fabien

Location Unknown

Toby floated into dull awareness through a haze of pain.

Where am I?

Everything hurt. Head, neck, right arm, ribs. But … he felt nothing below the waist. The bleeping alarms and the harsh tang of disinfectant shouted hospital. He was safe.

Thank God.

Melissa. The twins.

Tears formed behind his closed lids. He tried to open his eyes but couldn't find the strength.

Where were they?

Where?

Where was his family?

Darkness and silence closed around him.

———

SOUNDS. A voice.

Toby's subdued senses swam into consciousness. He pulled up through the haze of darkness into vague awareness. Muddiness fogged his mind. Sharpened by the unremitting pain.

Something touched his right eyelid. Gently tugged it open. Blinding light flooded his eye.

A groan roared inside his head. Thudding. Pounding. A firework display popped and crackled through his brain.

Something moved. A shape. Out of focus. The light snapped off.

Another groan, this one quieter, less painful. Sounding from within.

He tried to lift his head. The throbbing increased. He dropped it back into the firm embrace of a pillow.

"Try to relax, Mr Fabien."

A woman's voice. Calm. Confident. Soothing.

Toby opened his mouth. Lips cracked. Chapped. He ran the tip of his tongue over them. Tried to speak. Couldn't. His voice didn't work. The words wouldn't form. They came out as a croak. He took a shallow breath. His lungs rattled. Filled with fluid. He wanted to cough but didn't have the strength.

Cool dampness dabbed at his mouth. A cloth. Something hard passed between his closed lips.

"Take a sip of water, Mr Fabien. That's a straw."

Toby groaned, sipped. The cool liquid bathed his mouth. He swallowed. It tasted wonderful. Another sip. The straw disappeared.

"That's enough for now," the woman whispered.

Torturer.

Toby tried again. The words formed.

"My ... f-family," he croaked.

No answer. No response.

"Where ... Where are they?"

Darkness returned.

———

CLICKS. Bleeps. Muffled voices. Footsteps.

Toby, lying on his back, opened his eye. Only the right worked. The left eye remained swollen shut. His vision focused on a white ceiling in a white room.

Two figures floated over him, dressed in medical scrubs. A tall, stooped man and a slight woman. The man wore lavender, the woman green. Their faces were dark behind clear, plastic visors.

"Mr Fabien," the man said. "Can you hear me?"

Toby swallowed. Nodded. Pain seared through his brain.

"Y-Yes," he managed, keeping his head still to lessen the throbbing. "Where ..."

"You're in the intensive care unit of Cavell Hospital, Stafford."

"My family ... Where?"

The man stiffened. Frowned. Looked away. The woman shook her head.

Ignoring the thumping agony, Toby tried to raise his head from the pillow. Couldn't. Too heavy.

"The twins?"

He tried to sit up.

The small woman pushed his shoulders back down, the pressure firm and strong. Too powerful for him to fight.

"The twins are safe," she said, her voice quiet, soothing. "A few bumps and scratches. Nothing serious. They're being looked after."

Thank God.

Toby relaxed. But something was missing.

"Melissa? ... Wh-Where?"

The man looked at the woman before fixing his pale blue eyes on Toby.

"Mr Fabien," he said, "I'm really sorry, but ..."

The words flowed and swirled. Made no sense.

Darkness fell again.

———

TOBY HAD A DREAM. A horrible nightmare.

Words flowed from a man wearing a lavender gown.

"...paramedics tried everything ... heroic measures ... CPR ... forty-five minutes ... they were unable to save her ... so very sorry for your loss."

In his delirium, the words slammed through Toby in a series of sledgehammer blows, fading in and out of focus.

In his dream, Toby screamed. He railed against the loss. Melissa wasn't dead. His beautiful wife, the love of his life couldn't be dead.

No! No! No!

It wasn't true. The dream was a lie.

Tears of rage, fury, self-pity tore through him.

Melissa wasn't dead. She wasn't. She couldn't be.

My darling. My love.

What was he going to do without her?

Chapter Fifteen

Monday 28th June - Jackson Bentley

Bentley House, Brocton Village, Staffordshire, England

Wearing silk pyjamas, dressing gown, and slippers, Jackie shuffled into the kitchen, yawning. Doreen, the frumpy, old biddy who'd been in his life for more years than he cared to remember, turned to greet him.

"Oh dear," she said, bushy right eyebrow cocked. "You look rough."

Jackie ignored her comment, schlepped to the breakfast bar, and climbed onto his favourite barstool. He reached for the radio but decided against. He doubted he could put up with the added noise. Behind Doreen, a harsh sunshine glared through the window, slicing into Jackie's eyes and adding fuel to his pounding headache. Twisting the stool, he turned away from the blinding light.

"Coffee," he croaked.

"Cream?"

"Black."

Chuntering to herself, Doreen filled a mug from the carafe and pushed it towards him. The mug scraped along the marble surface, the screech slicing through Jackie's brain. Much more and his head would split.

"Doreen!"

"Oops," she said, straight-faced. "Sorry."

"Keep that up and you bloody will be."

The cocked eyebrow lifted again.

"Oh dear, we are in a bad mood this morning, aren't we?"

Jackie sniffed, ignored the snarky comment, and slurped a mouthful of the coffee. It tasted of burned mud and gurgled all the way to his stomach. He took another slug. No better.

He didn't often suffer from hangovers, but the crashing, blinding headache and the delicate stomach ranked way up there along with some of his worst.

Must be getting old.

How much had they put away? Couple of bottles of the good stuff. Maybe more. He'd tell himself, "Never again," but if he did that, he'd be lying.

"Me and Dylan spent the night in for once," he said, priming the pump. If he ever needed an alibi for the Charlotte bitch, Doreen and Reg would provide it as they lived in the granny annex at the end of the drive, but he had to play it smart. Couldn't make it obvious.

"I know," she said, scowling. "Took me over an hour to tidy the front room this morning. What a mess you made. I counted three empty bottles of *Laphroaig*. Don't know how you manage."

"Bentley men can hold their whisky," Jackie announced, proudly. He sat up straighter and tried not to wince as his brain slammed against the inside of his skull, his stomach roiled, and the stool tilted beneath him.

"Over an hour to clean up in here, too." She ran a damp cloth over the spotless surface of the island. "How can anyone create such a mess making cheese and tomato sandwiches?"

"Pack it in, Dor," he said. "I had enough naggin' in the old days, with Babs."

"I mean," the grumpy mare continued, "I left a shepherd's pie in the fridge for you. All you had to do was heat it up."

"You did?"

"Don't know why I bother sometimes."

'Cause it's your job, woman.

"Sorry, Dor. We'll have it for dinner tonight."

"No chance. It was out all night. I threw it in the bin."

Took it home for your supper, more like.

"I'll make something fresh."

"Thanks, Dor," Jackie said, humouring the old sow. "You're a peach. And thanks for holdin' off on the vacuumin'."

"Yeah," she said, "I thought you'd need a bit of quiet this morning. I'll do it later."

She stopped polishing the marble surface, hung the cloth on the handle of the cooker, and turned to face him again. Built like an overstuffed sofa, her tight-fitting overall —flowery grey with white trim—bulged in all the wrong places. How Reg found her attractive enough to take to bed, Jackie would never know. Took all sorts.

"Breakfast?" she asked, an evil glint in her eye. "How 'bout a nice fry-up? Bacon and eggs? Mushrooms? Fried bread?"

Jesus.

The idea of tucking into one of Doreen's breakfast specials made Jackie's stomach churn. He raised the mug to his lips and knocked back another mouthful. It tasted less like mud and more like coffee.

Thank fuck for that.

"Toast," he answered and took a bigger mouthful.

"Toast?"

"Yeah," Jackie said. "Toast. Two slices."

"That won't line your stomach. I picked up some nice, streaky bacon yesterday. I could fry you a couple of rashers. Go on. It'll do you the world of good."

Jackie shook his head. Instantly regretted it.

"Toast and butter," he insisted. "No marmalade."

Doreen sighed, grabbed a granary loaf from the bread-bin, and set it on the breadboard. She cut two thick slices and dropped them into the toaster. He could have done it himself, but she liked to feel useful, and what else did he pay her for?

He sniffled. Wiped his nose with the back of his hand. Doreen scowled, ripped a tissue out of the box, and slapped it down on the counter in front of him.

Jackie took the hint and blew his nose. He scrunched the tissue into a tight ball and dropped it into the pocket of his dressing gown. Then he emptied the mug and looked at her.

"Another?" Doreen asked, glowering at the mug.

Jackie nodded. Again, he wished he hadn't as another wave of pain blasted through his throbbing head.

"Yeah," he croaked, swallowed.

Doreen poured him a refill and returned the carafe to the hotplate.

He took a tentative sip.

Eventually, the toast popped. She smeared an unhealthy dollop of butter on each slice, cut them in half diagonally, plated them, and slid it across. That time, she did it quietly.

"Thanks, Dor," he said.

He bit into the first triangle and chewed gently. Hit the spot. His mouth watered.

"Celebrating?" she asked.

"Huh?"

"Were you celebrating last night?"

"Nah," he said after swallowing the second mouthful. "Not really. Me and Dylan just had a quiet night in for once. Don't happen often. Made a nice change."

She sighed and shook her head.

"So much whisky. Will you never learn?"

He snorted. "Doubt it."

Outside, the ride-on lawnmower fired up. The chattering roar of its powerful engine rattled through the kitchen, pounding through Jackie's head.

"For feck's sake," he moaned, clapping his hands over his ears. "What the hell?"

"Reg is making a start on the lawns."

"Yeah," Jackie snarked. "I gathered that. Can't it bloody wait?"

Doreen shook her head. "It's forecast to rain later. He needs to get on."

"Too bloody early."

"It's gone nine."

Jackie read the time off the microwave's display. 09:07.

"Only just. Shut the window, will you?"

She turned and pulled the casement behind the sink closed. The sound eased, along with Jackie's headache.

"Thanks."

"Seems a shame to block out the fresh air."

"Open it again when he's done."

Jackie picked up the half-eaten triangle of toast and took another bite. The melted butter dribbled down his chin. Doreen opened a drawer on her side of the island and handed him a cloth serviette. He wiped his mouth and chin, and said, "Ta."

Without asking, she poured herself a coffee and stood to one side, nursing the mug, but not drinking. Jackie never liked eating alone. Didn't like being watched while doing it, neither. Doreen and Reg had been working for Jackie since well before Babs buggered off—Jackie's term for it. Doreen knew what he liked. She knew the ropes.

"Did you watch the local news this morning?" she asked.

Jackie's heart raced. He stopped chewing and pushed the wad of toast into the side of his mouth before answering.

"Nah," he said. "I've only just surfaced. Anything interestin'?"

Doreen leaned closer, excited to share the juicy gossip.

"There was a hit-and-run on Hope Way."

Jesus. They'd found her already.

"Yeah?" he said, trying not to appear too fussed.

He grabbed his mug, held it up to his face, and sipped. Steam from the coffee made his eyes water. He blinked them clear.

"A woman was run down. She died."

"Oh dear. That's awful."

Jackie sipped again, for want of something better to do.

"Shocking." She nodded. "Police say the driver ran her over and left her for dead. The poor thing."

"Do they know who she is?"

"No," Doreen answered, after finally tasting her coffee. "Police don't have a clue. There was no identification on the body. Nothing in her pockets. No phone. No handbag."

Such a shame!

"They're asking for witnesses," Doreen added, "but they'll be lucky. No one uses Hope Way but farmers."

"Someone must do," Jackie said. "How else would she have been run down."

Doreen gave an absent nod. "Yeah. Good point."

She frowned, apparently deep in thought.

"What?" he asked.

She lowered her cup to a coaster and leaned further forwards.

"I've been thinking."

That'll be a first.

"Go on."

"It seems suspicious to me."

"In what way?"

Doreen wagged a finger in the air between them.

"Well," she said, "how many youngsters these days don't carry a mobile phone around with them? And her handbag's missing. What if it was a hit? A deliberate attack?"

Shut up, you moron.

"Don't be ridiculous, Dor," Jackie scoffed. "You read too many crime thrillers. And anyway, how'd you know she were a youngster?"

"The police put her age between fifteen and twenty-five. Going by her clothes."

"Have they released a photo?"

Doreen shook her head. "No, the body was too badly damaged."

Yeah. I know.

"That's a shame."

"It means her face would have been mangled."

Jackie winced and held up a hand. "That's enough, Dor. I'm eating."

"Oh sorry," she said, not looking at all apologetic. "Didn't realise you were so squeamish."

"I ain't. Saw plenty of blood and gore in the army. I just don't need it over me breakfast. Stick the box on, will you? Let's see what's going on in the world. But not too loud, eh?"

Doreen grabbed the remote from her side of the island, hit the power button, and lowered the volume. On the screen, a bedraggled, grey-suited reporter stood under a brolly in the driving rain. In the background, the Houses of Parliament peeked through a heavy mist.

"...less than three weeks to go before polling day, the campaign is in full flow. With the acting Prime Minister attending a NATO summit in Brussels, it leaves the field clear for the other party leaders to—"

"Bloody general election," Jackie growled over the reporter's excited words. "Turn it off."

Doreen hit the red button again and the TV powered down.

"Thanks. We'll turn it back on for the local news at half past."

Behind them, the kitchen door opened, and a sorry-looking Dylan staggered in. Bleary eyed, unshaved. Such a mess. It made Jackie feel so much better.

"Mornin', son."

"Morning, Dylan," Doreen said, eyes narrowed. "You look worse than your father."

Dylan grunted an incoherent response. He made his way to the island and fell into the stool beside Jackie like a sack of spuds dropped from the back of a tall lorry. He pointed to the coffee. Said nothing.

She smiled and poured. She'd known Dylan forever and loved him like a mother. To Doreen, the kid could do no wrong, which would come in handy, when the filth came calling.

"Here you are, son," she said, love glowing in her eyes.

She passed Dylan the full mug and offered Jackie a freshener, which he accepted.

"You're awake early," she said.

Dylan closed his eyes and sniffed the coffee. He blew over the top and slurped.

"Bloody mower woke me," he said and slurped again.

"Sorry, love," she said, and obviously meaning it. "Forecast says it'll rain all afternoon. Reg needs to—"

"Yeah, yeah, okay," Dylan interrupted. "Any chance of some grub? I could murder someone for a bacon buttie."

Doreen beamed at him.

"Excellent," she said and turned to Jackie. "What about you, Jackie? Changed your mind?"

"Go on then," he said, pushing his plate of cold toast towards her. "You've convinced me. I'll have one. But only one."

"Two for me, Dor," Dylan added. "I'm starving."

"You're always starving," she said, still smiling. "Three bacon butties coming right up."

She opened the fridge door, retrieved a vacuum pack of bacon, and got to work. It didn't take long for the rashers to start sizzling. Jackie's mouth watered as the aroma of smoky bacon filled the kitchen.

Jackie took the opportunity. He dropped a hand on Dylan's shoulder.

"How you feelin' son?"

"Okay."

"We had a good session," he said. "Last night, I mean."

Dylan frowned. Not understanding where Jackie was heading.

"Yeah." He nodded. "Good."

"Stayin' in all night. We ought to do it more often."

"Yeah," he said. "Maybe."

"We don't often spend the weekend together, do we?"

Jackie shot a look at Doreen's wide back and then locked eyes with Dylan. The lad's frown deepened, still not taking the hint. Jackie jerked his head towards her and glared at Dylan.

"Aren't I right, son."

The light dawned. The dullard finally twigged.

"Yeah, right," Dylan said, nodding and tapping his nose with an index finger. "I really enjoyed it. A quiet, Sunday night in. We'll have to make a regular thing of it. Just the two of us. Chilling."

Jackie nodded his encouragement.

"Yeah. Let's do that," Jackie said. "Have you seen the news?"

"Nah. Bugger that," Dylan scoffed. "It's wall-to-wall election. Bores me rotten."

"Local news is interestin', though," Jackie said. "Isn't that right, Dor?"

"Too true," Doreen said, using a pair of tongs to flip the sizzling bacon. "There was a hit-and-run on Hope Way. A girl died."

"You're kidding," Dylan said, looking at Jackie.

The frown returned, but Jackie shook his head and patted his hand in the air between them.

Cool, son. Play it cool.

Doreen turned to face them, excitement playing on her pudgy and wrinkled face. She picked up the breadknife and split her concentration between slicing the bread and feeding Dylan the information. It was a wonder she didn't hack off her fingers.

"Crushed, she was," Doreen said, her voice hushed in wonder. "Beyond recognition. The monster just drove off … drove off and left the poor little darling to …"

Chapter Sixteen

Tuesday 29th June - Tobias Fabien

Cavell Hospital, Stafford, Staffordshire, England

"Mr Fabien?"

The deep voice floated through a muffled gauze of physical and emotional agony.

Toby opened his eyes.

"Mr Fabien? Can you hear me?"

The man in the lavender scrubs spoke from behind his face visor. The visor made his voice sound hollow—as though talking from inside a tunnel.

Toby squinted out from the bed. His head still throbbed, but not as badly as it had done. An aching sadness swirled around him. The sadness of loss.

Melissa was gone. Gone forever. He would never recover.

"Y-Yes," he answered, his voice strained and scratchy. "I hear you."

His jaw ached along with everything else, but it didn't affect his speech.

Toby had developed an irrational hatred of the man in the lavender scrubs. The bringer of dreadful news. The worst imaginable. A doctor. Not one of the nurses who poked and prodded and kept waking him in the middle of the night. The same nurses who were looking through the glass panel that separated him and the other patients from the rest of the hospital—the rest of the world. Toby struggled to think straight with the constant thumping in his head, with his desolation, and with the incessant bleeping of the machines attached to his bed.

Why do they have to be so loud?

How long had he been in the room? The room with six beds, two of them empty. The ICU, which reeked of disinfectant, soap, and desperation.

Another wave of loss overwhelmed him.

Deep sadness. Gloom. Desperation.

How could he survive without Melissa by his side? Why would he bother?

The answer arrived in an instant.

Olivia and Rupert.

The twins.

They needed him, but what good would he be to them? What use?

Toby stared hard at the doctor. Tall, as far as Toby could tell from his position, lying on the hospital bed. Slim and wearing the absurd, lavender scrubs. Short-cropped, fair hair, clean shaven. Clear, pale blue eyes. Slightly stooped at the shoulders. He held a tablet computer in his left hand and typed quickly with his right.

"How are we feeling today, Mr Fabien?"

"Desolate," Toby said.

What else could he say?

The doctor's expression darkened.

"I understand."

"Do you?" Toby snapped and instantly regretted it.

No need to be unkind. Not the doctor's fault. Not his fault at all.

Shame on you, Toby.

Melissa would have been mortified.

Dear God. Melissa. Why?

"Sorry," Toby said, opening his left hand in apology. "That was uncalled for."

"That's okay." The doctor showed him an understanding smile as though he'd seen and heard it all. "I understand."

Toby licked his parched lips and coughed.

A blinding shaft of pain shot through his head and his ribs. He groaned.

"Water?" the doctor asked.

"Y-Yes ... please."

The man reached across to the plastic cup with the straw sticking through the lid and held it to Toby's lips. He drank. The cool liquid soothed his dry throat. He remembered the taste from earlier. Delicious.

"Th-Thank ... you."

The fair-haired doctor took away the cup and set it down on the bedside cabinet, slightly out of Toby's reach. Once again, an overwhelming sadness draped itself around him—a cloak of dread.

"Who are you?" Toby asked.

"You don't remember me?"

Toby would have nodded, but he didn't want to risk the pain.

"I-I do, but … did you tell me your name?"

The doctor's smile fell.

"I did, but given the circumstances, it's hardly surprising you don't remember." He spoke gently. "You've been through quite the ordeal. My name is Klaus Ferber. I'm the surgeon who operated on you."

"Surgeon?" Toby frowned.

The damn burst and the information flooded back. He'd seen the man, Ferber, before and after the surgery. Toby recalled the piercing, deep blue eyes, the sloped shoulders, and the dreadful news he'd delivered.

"Yes … I remember," Toby said and added, "Vaguely."

"I must say, you presented me and my surgical team with quite the challenge. But we"—Ferber paused, dropped the smile, and replaced it with a serious expression, one more in keeping with the sombre nature of the discussion—"we succeeded in the end. I imagine you have a few quest—"

"The twins?" Toby asked.

"Sorry?"

"The twins. Where … are they?"

"They're safe."

"Can I see them?"

"I'm sorry, but visitors aren't allowed in the ICU."

"Please?"

Ferber hesitated before nodding.

"I'll see what I can do."

"Thank you."

"Before that, I need to run a few tests," Ferber continued. "May I?"

Toby blinked rapidly, trying to clear an unexpected river of tears.

"Okay," he said.

"Look straight ahead."

Ferber shone a fancy light in Toby's right eye, flicked it away and back, away and back, and asked him to look up, down, left, and right. He repeated the test with the partially closed left eye. After each movement, Ferber signalled his approval with a nod and a, "Good. Yes. Very good."

He put the pen away and asked, "Can you move your fingers?"

"I don't know."

"Try, please. First your right."

Toby made a fist with his right hand. The fingernails dug into his palm. He pressed them harder, enjoying the sensation, and the relative relief it brought.

"Excellent," Ferber said, nodding. "And now the left."

Toby did the same to his left hand and earned the same reward.

"Very good," Ferber said. "Now hold your arms off the bed, above your body."

Toby complied, working through the pain in his chest.

Ferber placed his hands over Toby's.

"Now try to stop me pushing your arms down."

Ferber added a little weight to Toby's hands and Toby worked against the surgeon's strength. He lost the fight easily.

"Good," the surgeon said. "Very good."

"It didn't seem … good to me. It hurt my chest, and I couldn't stop you."

"I'm looking for bilateral balance. You were able to exert a similar amount of strength on both sides. That's very good. Very good indeed."

Toby accepted the surgeon's explanation and asked, "You want me to move my legs ... my toes now?"

"That won't be necessary, Mr Fabien."

Toby tried to move the toes on his right foot. Felt nothing. Tried his left. Same thing. No movement. No sensation. Nothing.

He raised his head to look down. The blankets stood proud. Held away from his legs by a cage.

Sweat exploded out of every pore. Toby's heart pounded, and his throat constricted.

"I can't feel my legs!" Toby cried.

Ferber raised a hand.

"Please, Mr Fabien," the surgeon soothed. "Try not to worry." He pointed to one of the machines at the side of the bed—a machine with numbers Toby couldn't read without his glasses. "We've put a nerve block in place. It's keeping you immobile. You've suffered a serious compression to your spinal column."

"What?" Toby gasped.

The surgeon frowned and tilted his head to one side, as though deep in thought.

"During the accident, you were whipped around inside the car quite violently."

You think?

"Yes ... I-I know."

"You suffered a number of serious injuries, including a double fracture to your left femur, five cracked ribs, and a partially ruptured spleen. However, the most significant injury was the damage to your spinal column. Specifically the fourth and fifth lumbar vertebrae. During the surgery, we had to fuse them together. The nerve block is to stop you moving and to numb the pain."

Gorge rose to Toby's throat. It scorched the lining.

"Y-You mean I'm paralysed?"

"Not necessarily, Mr Fabien," Ferber said, remaining so calm and cool, he might have been discussing his investment portfolio. "The MRI scan showed no obvious damage to the nerve cluster around the spinal injury. In fact, there is every reason to be optimistic. Given time, I am hopeful for a full recovery of function.

"Are you sure?"

Ferber hesitated before answering.

"With injuries such as these we can never be certain, but as I said, there is every reason for optimism. We'll know more when the swelling subsides."

"Why the cage?" Toby asked.

"Ah, yes," Ferber said. "That."

He nodded and smiled, seemingly on firmer ground.

"After we fused the vertebrae, we called in an orthopaedic surgeon to operate on the fractured femur. She performed a procedure called 'intramedullary nailing'. During this process, a metal rod is inserted into the femoral canal to fix the bone in position. This cage"—he rested his hand on top of the raised bedding—"is keeping the bedclothes away from your leg. Nothing more."

Toby tried to take in the enormity of what the surgeon had just told him. "Thank you," he said, unable to think of anything better.

"It was a team effort, Mr Fabien."

Toby pulled in as deep a breath as he could manage without causing a flareup of pain.

"What about the twins. Do they know … how bad things are? Do they know about … their granny?"

Ferber shifted his bodyweight. He looked uncomfortable. No longer on such solid ground.

"Not yet. We thought it best not to give your grandchil-

dren any details. They're very young. Too young to understand the possible long-term implications of your injuries …
or of your wife's … loss."

"Don't be so sure about that," Toby said, chafing at the
way the surgeon was talking the twins down. "Olivia and
Rupert are very bright children. Olivia's talking about
becoming a doctor. And Rupert might be quiet, but he's cut
from the same cloth as Olivia. They are my son's children. I
know you said they aren't allowed in the ICU, but can I see
them, please?" Tears threatened to fall again. He hated
showing weakness. "I-I need to see my family."

What's left of it.

Ferber winced.

"Please? Toby begged.

He hated begging, but for this, he'd demean himself.

"Okay," Ferber said, adding a half-hearted nod. "I'll see
what I can do."

"Thank you, Doctor." Toby sniffled and blinked away
the stinging tears.

Ferber took the box of tissues from the bedside cabinet
and placed it on the side of the bed within easy reach. Toby
tugged one from the box, wiped his injured nose delicately,
and crushed the paper into a tight ball.

"How bad is the pain?"

"Pretty bad," Toby said, "But I can cope."

"Do you need more sedative?" Ferber asked. "I can talk
to the nurse."

"No, thank you. I just need to see the twins." Toby
dropped the wadded tissue into the bin and gently shook his
head.

"If I can organise the twins to visit, would you like me
to tell them about your wife?"

"No!" Toby snapped. "That's my job."

God help me.

Ferber pursed his lips, and again, he nodded.

"I understand, Mr Fabien."

The surgeon patted his hand on the cage and turned away, leaving Toby to his own private world of pain. The bleeping machines helping to keep him relatively pain free could do nothing for his mental anguish.

Melissa was dead and he was alone.

Alone.

Alone with the twins. What on earth was he going to do?

For the second time in a year, Toby Fabien wept hot, desperate tears. Almost a year earlier, he'd lost his beloved son and daughter-in-law. Now, he'd lost his wife, his life-partner, the only woman he'd ever truly loved. All he had left were Olivia and Rupert. He desperately needed to see them.

Chapter Seventeen

Tuesday 29th June - Tobias Fabien

Cavell Hospital, Stafford, Staffordshire, England

Two fraught, pained hours later, the door to the ICU opened, and two little mites dressed the same way as the nurses—including oversized, for them, visors—entered the ICU. They arrived with a similarly dressed nurse. The two children approached the bed warily. As usual, Olivia walked slightly ahead of Rupert.

"Granddad," she said, lower lip wobbly, "you look awful."

Toby forced a smile onto his damaged face, trying to hold back the tears. "Thank you, my darling. It's lovely to see you, too. You and Rupert look like astronauts."

"Where's Granny?" Rupert asked, stepping out from

behind his sister. He rested a tentative hand on the edge of the bed but made sure not to touch or jog Toby. They'd clearly been told to keep their distance.

Toby lost the fight to remain calm. Hot tears ran down his cheeks. He swiped them away with a tissue.

"Where have you been staying?" Toby asked, sidestepping Rupert's question to earn himself a reprieve. Doing so made him feel like a dreadful coward.

"We stayed with Emily's family," Olivia said.

"Emily?" Toby recognised the name but couldn't place it.

"You know Emily, Granddad," Olivia said, eyes wide. "My best friend from school."

"Of course I do." Toby smiled. "Emily Kendall."

"Yes, Granddad. Emily's my BFF."

"The Kendalls have been looking after you?"

"The police took us to them." Olivia rushed the words. "Annie's very nice."

"Annie?" Toby frowned, and pain sliced into his left eye. "Who's Annie?"

He definitely didn't know anyone called Annie.

"She's the police Family Liaison Officer," the nurse explained. "PC Annette Riggs. She's waiting outside. Mr Ferber would only allow the twins in here for a few minutes. You need your rest and ... visitors aren't really allowed in the ICU."

Toby dipped his chin and turned his watery gaze on the twins.

"Olivia," he said, "you must be a brave girl and look after Rupert. He needs you to be strong."

Rupert dropped his hand from the bed and stood taller.

"I'm strong, Granddad. And I'm brave."

"I know, Rupert," Toby said, "and you need to look

after Olivia, too. I won't be able to take care of you for a while. Not until I get better."

"What's wrong with you, Granddad?" Olivia asked, her eyes resting on the cage keeping the bedclothes away from his legs.

How could he answer without scaring them? He opted for partial truth.

"I have a broken leg and some other injuries. But I'll be up and about again before you know it. I promise." He'd have crossed his fingers but the twins would have seen it and known he was fibbing. "In the meantime, you can stay with Emily's family. Would you like that?"

Olivia nodded but, being so big and loose, her visor didn't move.

Rupert frowned.

"Do we have to stay at Emily's for long?"

"What's wrong? Don't you like it there?"

"No … it's nice. Emily's okay, but …" He breathed in and released it in a deep and heavy sigh.

Toby lifted his head to stare at the lad. The strain caused one of the machines at the top of the bed to bleep faster. The nurse glanced at the monitors, frowned, and shook her head. For fear of an early end to the visit, Toby relaxed back against the pillow and tried to slow his racing heart.

"But?" he prompted the lad.

"But," Rupert said, "Arthur's really annoying."

"He is?" Toby asked.

"Yes," Rupert said. "He keeps pestering me to play football in the back garden." Rupert did the thing with his mouth—a cross between an apologetic smile and a wince—that Toby knew so well. At a similar age, Robert used the exact same expression.

"I hate football," Rupert added, unnecessarily.

Toby grimaced as a shaft of pain shot up through his leg and drove into his lower back. Again, the bleeps increased in frequency.

"Is anything wrong?" the nurse asked, her gaze locked on the monitor above his head.

"My leg," Toby gasped. "It … hurts."

The nurse pressed a button on one of the machines.

"Analgesia," she said. "It will help in a few minutes. Try to relax."

Easy for you to say.

Toby breathed as deeply has his cracked ribs would allow. The twins waited, showing great patience. Seconds extended into minutes.

"Olivia, Rupert," Toby said, forcing himself to speak without gritting his teeth against the shock of the pain. They deserved the truth. He couldn't hold off any longer.

"Yes, Granddad?" they said together.

"I have some very bad news. You need to be brave."

"Is it about Granny?" Olivia asked. She blinked but her blue eyes remained dry. Rupert's rimmed with tears.

"Yes, darling."

"Sh-She … passed away, didn't she." Olivia said, a statement, not a question. "She's gone to be with Mummy and Daddy, hasn't she." Another statement.

Oh God. Out of the mouths of babes.

"Y-Yes, darling. She's with …"

Toby broke down. He couldn't finish. Tears fell. Olivia and Rupert rushed forwards and fell against the bed— against Toby. He hugged them as best he could, ignoring the agony as their heads pressed against his ribs.

They cried together. The nurse stood back and let them.

Although the pain from his leg and ribs had eased, the

ache in his heart remained, and it would do forever. Toby stroked the twins' hair and held them gently. Slowly, their crying subsided.

The nurse raised her arm and tapped the wrist. Toby closed his eyes for a moment and nodded.

"Olivia, Rupert," Toby said quietly. They lifted their heads and looked up at him. "You have to go now, but before you do, you need to promise me something."

"Yes, Granddad?" they asked.

"You need to be strong and brave. And you need to be well behaved for Mr and Mrs Kendall. Will you do that for me?"

"Yes, Granddad," Olivia said. "Of course I will."

"Good girl. I knew I could rely on you."

Rupert's right hand shot into the air.

"I'll be good, too, Granddad," he said, almost breathlessly.

"I know, Rupert," Toby said, forcing out an encouraging smile. "I know."

Rupert dropped his arm and stood closer to Olivia. Close enough for their arms to touch.

"Now," Toby said, blinking away the latest set of tears. "I'd love to give you both another big hug, but I'm afraid I'd squeeze you so tight you'd break."

Or I might.

"Instead, can you hold my hand please?"

The twins eased forwards and placed their hands on top of Toby's. They squeezed and Toby absorbed their warmth and what little strength they could offer.

Olivia, the most reserved and self-contained, nine-year-old girl Toby had ever known—a reserve born of suffering and loss—broke down. Again, tears washed her cheeks.

"We love you, Granddad," she cried. "Please get better soon. We need you."

Not only reserved, but perceptive way beyond her years. The poor, poor darling.

Teary-eyed and equally as perceptive, Rupert reached for his sister's hand and pulled her closer.

"We love you, Granddad Toby," he said.

The nurse, who was only a little taller than the twins, gathered them up and hurried them from the room.

As he watched them leave, Toby tried to swallow past the solid lump that had formed in his throat. He failed, as he'd failed to keep his family safe.

How was he going to cope without Melissa? How could he look after the twins on his own?

Dear Lord. Please help me.

Chapter Eighteen

Wednesday 30th June - Tobias Fabien

Cavell Hospital, Stafford, Staffordshire, England

To Toby's astonishment and relief, the crushing, thumping pain in his leg turned out to be a really good thing. According to Mr Ferber, it showed he hadn't suffered any serious spinal cord damage. It didn't stop the bloody thing hurting when they removed the morphine drip at Toby's request, though. All his life, he'd hated taking medication. On the rare occasions when he became ill, he resisted popping even the mildest of over-the-counter pain meds. Fortunately, he'd been blessed with robust, good health all his life and rarely suffered illnesses.

Before the car crash, he'd only been admitted to hospital when his appendix burst. He'd been a kid, fifteen, and nearly died of peritonitis. The family GP had misdiagnosed his chronic, abdominal pain as indigestion and prescribed him antacids. As a result, Toby had been left with a decidedly jaundiced view of the medical profession.

Not that he hadn't been in hospital on other occasions.

Most happily, he'd been in the delivery room with Melissa when she gave birth to Robert, who turned out to be their only child, despite their heroic and thoroughly enjoyable attempts to give him brothers or sisters. Robert's birth was a wonderful event filled with joy and hope. That happy time was offset when Toby spent an endless day and night in the children's ward of County Hospital after Robert had broken his leg playing football.

To counteract the bad, another joyous hospital visit came when Helen delivered the twins. On that occasion, Toby had spent the hours pacing the corridor outside the maternity suite, with Melissa trying to keep him calm. Robert took the delivery in his stride, but the delight on his face when the twins finally arrived couldn't have been bettered. Toby had immortalised the event in a series of photos taken with his Canon SLR. He'd been a keen photographer at the time and had no truck with mobile phone camera apps.

Nobody could ever accuse Tobias Fabien of abusing the NHS system. Nor could they accuse him of being the world's most demanding patient, but on this one instance … he kicked up a fuss and the medics relented. After all, if he was prepared to suffer the pain, who were they to force him into drug-induced analgesia? Besides, no amount of pain killers could relieve his real suffering. He would be living with the agony of Melissa's loss for the rest of his life.

Earlier that day, the fourth of his incarceration, they finally moved him out of the ICU and into a well-appointed, private room—covered by Toby's expensive health insurance policy, which in turn, had been funded by the supportive 83 Trust. The twins were allowed to visit as often and for as long as they liked, limited only by the requirement to attend school and their need for sleep.

Lucinda and Kenneth Kendall, Emily's parents, proved to be absolute Godsends. Angels. They took in the twins without hesitation and apparently smothered them with love and support. A mildly reluctant Rupert bunked in with Arthur and slept on a blowup mattress. On the other hand, the enthusiastic Olivia and Emily happily shared the same room, and no doubt lost a great deal of sleep as a result.

Lucy and Ken promised to ferry them to and from hospital and refused to take a penny piece for the petrol. Lucy even drove the twins to the family home and helped them pack clothes for their extended stay, after Toby told her where they kept the spare housekeys.

Overwhelmed with gratitude, Toby couldn't thank them enough for opening their home to a pair of traumatised twins, but he knew it could only be a temporary measure. He would have to find a more permanent arrangement. But how could he manage that from a hospital bed?

The junior doctor, Brinsley, interrupted Toby's musings by saying, "Good afternoon, Mr Fabien. How are we today?"

What was it with medical staff and their use of plural personal pronouns? Toby considered responding with a sarcastic, "I don't know about you, Dr Brinsley, but I'm not too bad, considering I've been involved in a fatal car crash and lost my wife," but decided on, "Much better, thanks." He didn't want to upset the overworked doctor.

In truth, Toby's ribs ached with each breath, his left leg throbbed with each heartbeat, every joint in his body cried out in pain whenever he moved, and his lower back was a cauldron of fiery agony from which he could not find a moment's relief no matter which way he lay. Apart from that—and the crushing, hollow emptiness of Melissa's death—everything happened to be hunky-bloody-dory.

One bright spot gave Toby tentative hope for a tolerable future. The twins. Toby lived for them. Only for them.

Without lifting his eyes from the chart he'd taken from the end of the bed, Brinsley nodded. His fringe of shaggy, dark hair kept flopping into his eyes, and he regularly flicked it away with a jerk of his head. An intensely annoying habit, he'd have been better off taking a pair of shears to the damned mop. Either that or the man could try wearing a headband.

Stop it, Toby.

He was letting the pain get to him, fray his nerves. If things got much worse, he'd end up accepting the painkillers all the hospital staff kept trying to force down his throat.

"Very good," Brinsley said, absently. "Any pain in your abdomen?"

Toby paused to consider the answer and finally found something positive to say.

"Funnily enough, my abdomen's just about the only area that's pain free, Doctor."

"Very good," Brinsley repeated, nodding in encouragement. "The lack of pain and the results of your latest blood tests suggest that your spleen is repairing itself. That's excellent news."

About time. It had been a while since he'd had any good news.

"When can I get out of bed?"

Brinsley finally raised his brown eyes from the chart and

turned his tired gaze towards Toby for almost the first time since entering the room.

"That's a question only Mr Ferber can answer. We wouldn't want to rush things, now would we."

"No, *we* wouldn't."

I might, though.

"When can I see him?"

"He'll be doing his rounds this evening. You should ask him then."

"I will," Toby said, keeping his tone dry. "Thank you, Doctor."

Brinsley returned the chart to the foot of the bed and rested his hand on the metal rail. After a moment, he fixed his eyes on Toby again.

"I've asked you this before, but I need to ask—"

"No painkillers," Toby said, shaking his head slowly. Since rejecting the meds, he'd learned to do everything slowly as a matter of self-preservation.

"Mr Fabien," Brinsley said, dropping his shoulders, and all but rolling his eyes, "judicial use of analgesia has been demonstrated to enhance the recovery process. These days, there really is no need for a patient to suffer discomfort."

"No painkillers," Toby repeated, trying to add a finality to his voice.

"Very well," the young doctor conceded.

"Please don't ask again."

"I can't promise that, Mr Fabien."

"I tell you what," Toby said, raising his left hand and pointing the index finger to the ceiling. "The moment I need painkillers, I promise to ask for some. Deal?"

The medic smiled and the shoulders drooped again.

"Deal," he said. "And on that note, I'll be on my way."

"More patients to browbeat?"

The smile widened and took even more years from the young man's exhausted face.

"Exactly. But most of them tend to accept my advice. In fact, the majority of patients can't get enough pain medication. You're bucking the trend, Mr Fabien."

As always.

Whenever he had a cold or an ache, he used to drive Melissa wild with frustration.

Tears stung his eyes, and he fought the urge to cry. To rage at the walls. Melissa. His poor, beautiful darling. What was he going to do?

Stop it, Toby. The twins need you.

"That's not always a bad thing," he croaked, still fighting the urge to bawl.

He couldn't let himself go. Brinsley might end up misinterpreting the tears as the result of physical, rather than a buildup of emotional, distress. Toby couldn't go through the same argument again. He'd had more than enough.

"Perhaps not." Brinsley turned to leave. Halfway to the door, he stopped and retraced his steps. "I almost forgot. There are two police officers outside who'd like to speak to you. It's the second time they've visited. I have no idea why they don't call ahead. Such a waste of their time. Normally, I tend to put the police off to shield my patients, but as you aren't taking medication, and they're investigating a fatal … well, you know"—he grimaced—"I promised to ask. Are you prepared … willing to answer their questions?"

Toby hesitated. From the first moment he'd woken in the ICU, he'd been desperate to talk to the police, but the medical staff had been highly protective of him.

"Yes, please," Toby said at length. "Send them in."

Brinsley frowned and tilted his head towards Toby.

"Are you sure?"

"Of course. Why wouldn't I talk to the police?"

The young doctor shook his head. "No reason. It's just that police interviews can sometimes be a little … fraught. In light of the serious nature of your injuries, I'll instruct them to go easy on you. If things become too … intense, you should press the emergency call button."

"Thank you, Doctor, but I'll be okay."

He had nothing to hide from the police, but, by God, he did have plenty to say.

Chapter Nineteen

Wednesday 30th June - Tobias Fabien

Cavell Hospital, Stafford, Staffordshire, England

Toby prepared for the police arrival by slowing his breathing and trying to compartmentalise each separate pain and tamp it into quiet submission. He didn't have long.

A few minutes after the door closed behind Dr Brinsley, it opened again to allow entry to two men who couldn't have looked more like plain-clothes police officers if they tried. Unsmiling and serious, they had an air of quiet confidence and authority that bordered on superiority.

The one in the lead sported a dark grey suit, a white shirt, and a plain, dark tie. He wore highly polished, black shoes, stood tall and straight, and carried barely an ounce of spare flesh. Heavily tanned as though he'd recently returned from a beach holiday in the Med, his light brown hair was cropped short, and he had a clean-shaven chin with a deep, vertical cleft. From the lack of crow's feet circling his light brown eyes, Toby put him in his late twenties or early thirties.

The one trailing in his shadow was short and squat. He wore a pair of black jeans and a tan jacket over a dark blue polo shirt. Green eyes sat behind black-framed glasses which glinted as the lenses caught the sunlight. A five o'clock shadow darkened his soft chin. Toby put him in his mid-forties. A leather satchel hung from a strap across his shoulder. From the way it crinkled the jacket, the satchel appeared heavy.

They marched straight into the room as though they owned the place and stopped at the foot of the bed.

"Mr Fabien?" the taller man asked.

Who else?

"Yes," Toby answered. "Excuse me for not getting up."

A joke? Really. Where had that come from? Nerves. He tried a welcoming smile, but his mouth didn't want to obey the mental command.

"That's okay, sir," the younger man in the grey suit said, missing the joke, his tone stiff. "We understand."

He reached into his jacket, removed a small, black wallet, and flipped it open to reveal a police ID card complete with an impressive, serrated-metal badge. Toby had never seen a warrant card up close. He couldn't avoid being impressed and, if he were honest with himself, slightly intimidated. He swallowed past a dry mouth.

Don't worry, Toby. There's nothing to be scared of.

"Good afternoon, sir," the man said. "I'm Detective Inspector Fellows, and this is Detective Sergeant Skarrats. From the Staffordshire Police. Are you able to answer a few questions about your accident?" He slid the warrant card back into his jacket pocket.

Toby frowned. Shook his head and received a shaft of pain in his neck for his troubles. From the outset, the police had it all wrong.

"It wasn't an accident," Toby said, fists clenched. "We were deliberately run off the road."

Fellows shot his junior partner a glance that Toby struggled to interpret. If pushed, he might have called it "knowing".

"Before we go any further," Fellows said, "there are a few formalities we have to address."

"Formalities?"

Toby pressed a button on the control panel hanging from the side rail and raised the top third of the bed by a few degrees. He grimaced against the discomfort to his back and leg caused by the movement.

"Yes, sir," Fellows said, after Toby finished adjusting the angle of the bedstead. "Are you comfortable?"

"As comfortable as I'm ever likely to be with a broken leg, a damaged back, and cracked ribs. What were you saying about formalities?"

Fellows hesitated and the tension ratcheted up a notch.

Heat spread through Toby's body, warmed his face. Heat caused by worry as much as pain.

Fellows shuffled to the left side of the bed and edged closer. Skarrats stepped around to the other side. He removed a computer tablet from the satchel, and tapped the screen awake. Their separation made it difficult for Toby to see both officers at the same time and moving his head too much made him uncomfortable. He focused on the man in charge, Fellows.

"First," Fellows said, "I must tell you that we would like this to be a voluntary interview, taken under caution."

Alarm bells rang in Toby's head—alarm bells that had nothing to do with the hospital's PA system.

"Under caution?" he asked through a dry mouth. He struggled to swallow.

"Yes, sir," Fellows said. "It's a formality, but we are investigating a serious RTC—a road traffic collision. One that led to a fatality. The results of our investigation could lead to serious charges."

"Charges?" Toby gasped. "What sort of charges?"

"Charges that could include death by careless driving or death by dangerous driving. The sentence for the latter is life in prison."

Dear God!

Toby struggled to understand what he'd heard. Were they being serious?

"Wait a minute," he said. "You think it was *my* fault?"

Fellows frowned and pulled in his chin.

"You *were* driving the vehicle, sir. And you *did* leave the road, which resulted in the death of your wife."

"But we were run off the bloody—"

Fellows held up his hand to stop Toby mid-sentence.

"Please, sir. Don't say anything more until I've cautioned you."

Toby scowled and ground his teeth until the pain in his jaw overrode the anger.

"Go on then," he said, teeth barely unclenched. "Do it."

"Thank you, sir." Fellows flipped open the wallet again, removed a card from one of the slots, and turned to his partner. "Are we recording?"

"One moment, guv."

Using the tablet's built-in stand, Skarrats propped the

tablet on the bedside cabinet and adjusted it until satisfied the camera pointed where he wanted it to. From where he lay, Toby couldn't see the screen.

After another minor tweak, Skarrats nodded.

"Ready, guv."

For the recording, Fellows reintroduced himself and Skarrats, and continued with, "Mr Fabien, I am required by law to tell you that you do not have to say anything, but it may harm your defence …"

The words flowed from Fellows' lips without pause, clearly memorised verbatim despite him holding up the card. Toby recognised the script from a thousand TV police dramas and documentaries, but never in a million years expected to hear them directed at him. He seemed to be sinking through the bed, to be drowning in the crisp, white sheets. What was happening? He couldn't think, couldn't breathe, couldn't speak.

"…may be given in evidence. Do you understand this caution?" Fellows finished and gave Toby time to gather his thoughts.

"A-Am I … under arrest?" Toby asked after what seemed like an age of silence.

"No, sir. As I said, we're simply interviewing you under caution. This is a formality designed to protect your rights. Do you understand these rights as I have explained them to you?"

Toby tried to clear his throat.

"Yes," he croaked.

"Would you like a solicitor?" Fellows asked.

Toby finally managed to swallow. "Do I need one?"

"You are entitled to legal representation if you deem it necessary," Fellows said, "but that will only delay the process. Our only intention here is to discover exactly what happened last Saturday evening."

Toby didn't take long to consider his response.

"I don't need a solicitor to help me tell the truth. Let's get on with this."

"So, you're happy to continue?" Fellows asked.

"Yes."

"Are you certain?"

"Yes," Toby snapped. "I have nothing to hide. Ask me anything you like."

"I must remind you that we are recording this interview," Fellows said, pointing to the tablet and adding what, to some, might have been a pleasant smile. To Toby, it seemed predatory.

"I understand," Toby said. "Please get on with this. I'm developing a headache."

"I'm sorry to hear that, but thank you, sir." Fellows drew a visitor's chair close to the bed and sat. Skarrats remained standing.

Quietly, Fellows cleared his throat.

"First," he said, "I'd like to discuss the RTC … the collision."

"Of course."

"How much do you remember, Mr Fabien?"

Toby ran the sequence of events through his mind in a horrible, rapid montage of fractured images, screams, excruciating pain, and fear. And loss. Terrible, heart-wrenching loss.

Toby closed his eyes. Tears formed behind the lids. He let them flow.

"I remember every moment," he said, his voice breaking. "Until we smashed into the tree. After that … things are a little hazy."

Fellows nodded but didn't respond. He seemed happy to wait for Toby to continue.

"We were run off the road," Toby added. "Deliberately run off the road."

Fellows arched an eyebrow.

"Really, sir," he said, his tone flat, if not bored, then sceptical.

"By a lime-green pickup truck," Toby insisted. "A Ford."

"Really, sir?" Fellows repeated, this time as a question.

He shared another look with Skarrats. The sergeant shook his head slowly. Another sceptic.

Toby frowned at the lack of any follow-up questions. What was wrong with these people?

"You don't believe me?"

"We found no evidence of another car being involved in the crash."

"What!" Toby gasped.

Once again, the bed seemed to tilt and open up beneath Toby. He felt himself slipping into the depths. Falling. Drowning. Panting, he closed his eyes and clenched his hands into fists. The pain in his ribs flared. It formed an anchor. It stopped him sliding deeper. Toby forced his breathing to slow. Surfaced. Swam clear of the encircling water.

Fellows stared at Toby, keeping his expression unreadable.

"We found no evidence of—"

"That's not possible," Toby said. "Have you looked properly?"

"Yes, sir. We've conducted a thorough investigation of every aspect of the incident. That includes taking witness statements from your grandchildren."

Toby jerked upright. A shaft of fire shot up his leg, into

his lower back, and radiated throughout his body. Sweat prickled his scalp, bathed his face, and sprouted under his arms. The price he paid for moving so sharply.

"You did what?" he gasped.

Fellows raised a conciliatory hand. "We were very gentle with them, sir. I promise. Followed all the correct, safeguarding protocols. And a responsible adult was present the whole time."

"What responsible adult?"

"A woman from the Appropriate Adult Services," Fellows said, lowering his hand and speaking quietly. "We can give you their contact details if you need them."

"The twins didn't tell me anything about it. When and where did this happen?"

"Yesterday afternoon. In the front room of Mr and Mrs Kendall's house. As I said, sir, we were very gentle with them. However, we did need to progress the investigation, and since we weren't given access to you until this morning ..." Fellows allowed the sentence to fade, but he did add an apologetic tilt of the head and a lift of his right shoulder.

"You should have asked me first," Toby said.

"Under the law, we aren't required to, sir. But I can assure you, all the safety protocols were followed."

I should hope so!

"What did they tell you?"

"About the accident?"

"No! About the attack! I keep telling you, it wasn't an accident."

Fellows and Skarrats shared another glance.

They were starting to annoy Toby with their sly looks. Perhaps that was their intention.

Keep calm, Toby.

He was telling the truth and needed to convince them of it. He wouldn't do that by shouting.

"We were intentionally run off the road," he said, moderating his tone. "The man driving the pickup deliberately rammed us."

"Did he now?" Skarrats said, speaking directly to Toby for the first time.

"Yes, Sergeant. He did!"

Skarrats sniffed. Unconvinced.

"Did you get the Ford's licence number," Fellows asked, patience itself.

Toby's frown deepened. It added pressure to his injured nose and made his eyes water again.

"No, of course I didn't. His lights were dazzling, and I was trying to avoid being hit. But he rammed us twice!" he repeated, raising his voice a little, unable to prevent himself.

"So you say, sir," Skarrats said, his cold, green eyes staring directly into Toby's. For a moment, the sunlight reflected in his lenses, making them opaque. It hid his emotions and his humanity, and was truly disconcerting.

Toby turned from the overbearing Skarrats and focused on Fellows.

"What did the twins tell you?"

"The little girl ..." Fellows hesitated and glanced at Skarrats, seemingly for a hint.

"Olivia, sir," Skarrats said.

"That's right, Olivia," Fellows said. He turned back to Toby. "She didn't see another car. All she remembers is hearing you shout before the car crashed through the fence and ploughed through bushes. She"—he averted his eyes for a moment—"also remembers your wife screaming."

Oh God. Melissa.

Tears rolled down Toby's cheeks. He tugged a tissue

from the box—one of the many he'd used since regaining consciousness—and gently wiped his eyes.

"What about Rupert?" Toby asked. "Didn't he see anything?"

Fellows shook his head. "No, sir. The lad said much the same thing as his sister."

Toby's world shuddered.

This can't be happening.

He wiped his runny nose. It hurt like the devil.

"They didn't see the Ford?"

Again, Fellows shook his head. "No, sir."

"Maybe you left the interview too long," Toby suggested. "Maybe they're too traumatised to remember properly."

"On the contrary, sir," Fellows announced, confidence flowing through his words. "Research has shown that witness statements are best taken a few days after a traumatic event. We've found it optimal to leave a gap of twenty-four to forty-eight hours to avoid what's called perceptual distortion. As I said, we followed—"

"All the safeguarding protocols," Toby blurted out. "I know, I know. But I'm telling you the truth. We were rammed—"

"By a big, green, Ford pickup," Skarrats said, speaking through a sarcastic sneer. "Is that correct, sir?"

"Yes. That's right. It had a bull bar."

Fellows seemed to perk up and take notice. Skarrats retained his sneer.

"You saw it that clearly?" Fellows asked.

"Of course. And the driver rammed us. Deliberately."

"As you say, sir," Skarrats said. Once again, disbelief ran through his words.

Toby nodded slowly, ignoring the pain pulsing through his head and neck.

"Yes. I do say, Sergeant. The driver rammed us twice. The first time he hit us, I managed to control the skid and tried to speed away. The second time, I lost the rear end ... we smashed through the fence ... and then"—Toby swallowed hard, unable to prevent his lower lip quivering—"we slammed sideways into a tree."

Toby found it more difficult to describe the crash than he'd imagined. Voicing his thoughts solidified them, made them more powerful. More painful. More final.

Melissa's gone. She's gone!

What was he going to do without her?

Oh God.

"In one way," Fellows said, breaking into Toby's dark thoughts, "it was a good thing, sir. Crashing into the tree, I mean."

"A good thing?" Toby hissed, anger overtaking caution and sadness. "A good thing! Hitting that tree killed ... killed Melissa." He could hardly bring himself to say the words.

"I really am sorry for your loss, sir." Fellows words barely carried across the short gap between them, and they sounded hollow. "It was a terrible thing, but the tree stopped you plunging into Rook Pond. And that would have been even worse. Rook Pond is much deeper than it looks. Your car was suspended over the bank. It may not appear that way, but you were very lucky."

"Lucky? But Melissa ..."

Toby couldn't continue and allowed his words to die, unspoken. Again, tears welled. He ripped another tissue from the box, dabbed his eyes, and wiped his nose. After rolling the used tissue into a ball, he dropped it into the nearby bin and clasped his hands in his lap.

Fellows allowed the silence to sit for a few moments before speaking again.

"Are you okay, sir."

No, I'm bloody not!

Toby focused on his hands. They trembled. Things were slipping out of control. What could he do?

Desperation sparked an idea.

"The dashcam!" Toby said, latching onto the hope. "I can give you access to our dashcam recording!"

Chapter Twenty

Wednesday 30th June - Tobias Fabien

Cavell Hospital, Stafford, Staffordshire, England

Toby waited for a response, but Fellows seemed unmoved.

"We already have access to your dashcam, sir," Skarrats said, and the aggressive grin made a return appearance.

"You have?"

"Yes, sir." Fellows said. "We have. The traffic police—members of the Serious Collision Unit—collected the camera immediately after you were freed from the vehicle."

Toby frowned.

"Are you allowed to do that?"

"Yes, sir." Fellows nodded. "We are permitted access under the provisions of both the Road Traffic Act, 1988 and the Police and Criminal Evidence Act, 1984."

Toby gasped, struggling to pull in enough air.

"And?" he urged. "What did you see?"

"The recording showed you skidding, increasing speed, then leaving the road. It then showed you smashing through the fence and hitting the tree."

"That's all?"

"Yes, sir," Fellows answered. "That's all. The recording doesn't show any other vehicle on the road at the time of the ... incident."

Toby didn't like the way Fellows hesitated before saying "incident".

"Oh God. But ... but, that's impossible. The pickup rammed us. Twice!" Again, Toby had to force out the words.

"It's a shame you didn't install a rear-facing camera, sir," Skarrats said, his voice calm but his expression smug, accusatory.

"So, it's my fault?"

"I'm sorry, sir." Skarrats didn't look sorry. "But, as we said, there's no evidence of another vehicle being involved in the crash."

Again, the bed tried to swallow Toby whole. The blood drained from his face. He felt lightheaded, ready to retch.

Fellows leaned closer.

"Mr Fabien, are you okay, sir? Shall I call a doctor?"

Toby breathed easier. In and out. In and out. Shallow and slow.

"No ... No, thank you. I'm okay. Headache. Backache. It's nothing."

"Good. Are you okay to continue?"

Toby lifted his head and stared into the senior officer's dark eyes.

"Will you answer a question?"

"If I can, sir."

Toby swallowed. It wasn't getting any easier.

"If we weren't rammed, what do you think caused me to leave the road?"

Fellows returned Toby's stare, his expression flat and emotionless. He shrugged.

"The weather that day was appalling. Heavy rain. Poor visibility. Flooded roads. And … your car's black-box recorder—the one you had installed to reduce your car insurance—showed you were travelling at fifty-three miles an hour at the time you left the road."

"The posted speed limit on that road is fifty, sir," Skarrats butted-in, speaking up to drive home the point, a poorly concealed accusation.

Careful, Toby.

Toby blinked. The only movement he could make without causing discomfort. "But I was scared. I was trying to get away from the pickup truck."

"So you say, sir," Fellows said, his voice a monotone.

"But as we've already said, there's no evidence to support that claim," Skarrats said.

"Did you drink any alcohol that day, sir?" Fellows asked.

Toby's heart lurched.

Dear God.

"You think I caused the crash, don't you! You think I was drunk."

"I'm simply putting the question to you, sir," Fellows said. "You *were* heading home after an evening meal."

"At a service station, not a restaurant. And I never drink and drive. Never."

Fellows nodded slowly.

Skarrats quirked his thin lips. It made him look cruel. He seemed to be enjoying himself.

"There is a way you can prove that, sir," Fellows suggested.

"How?" Toby asked, reaching out and grasping the potential lifeline.

"We have a blood sample taken when you arrived at hospital."

"You took it when I was unconscious?"

"Yes, sir, but we did have the permission of an independent medical practitioner as required under Sections 7 and 9 of the Road Traffic Act, 1988."

"What did the results tell you?"

Fellows paused before answering. "Although we were empowered to take a pre-transfusion sample, we do need your consent to run the analysis. Do you give that consent, Mr Fabien?"

Toby took a breath, but before he could speak, Fellows held up his right hand, index finger extended.

"Before you answer that question, I am required to tell you that if you do *not* give consent for the analysis, you will be committing an offence, and you may therefore be liable to be prosecuted. Do you understand these conditions as I have explained them?"

Fellows' confusing words swam through Toby's head. Consent. Offence. Prosecuted. What the hell was happening? He'd never been in trouble with the police before. Never received so much as a speeding fine. Never had any points added to his driving licence. For pity's sake, he'd never received anything more serious than a parking ticket, but there he lay, in his hospital bed, being treated like a criminal.

When driving home from the service station, he had Melissa and the twins in the car. He'd been responsible for their safety. They were his precious cargo. Nothing could have made him lose sight of that responsibility. Nothing. He'd been stone-cold sober, and the police had the evidence to prove it. Why shouldn't he give his permission?

"Test it," Toby announced.

"You give your consent for the analysis?" Fellows asked.

"Yes. I do. Like I told you before, I have nothing to hide."

Fellows shoulders relaxed. This time, his smile seemed genuine.

"Thank you, Mr Fabien. Can you sign a release to that effect?"

"Yes. Of course I'll sign it."

Still smiling, Fellows nodded to Skarrats, who dug inside his satchel and pulled out a single sheet of paper. The sergeant handed it to Toby.

Official-looking. it had a crest in the top centre of the page. Toby narrowed his eyes but struggled to read the closely printed script.

"I'll need my reading glasses." He pointed to the bedside cabinet to the right of the bed. "They're in the drawer. The cleaners keep putting them away."

Skarrats leaned forwards and pulled the drawer open, jogging the tablet as he did so. The sergeant found the glasses case, removed the specs, and handed them across, scowling the whole time. Then he turned and resettled the tablet.

Taking care not to cause any more discomfort to his bruised and battered face than necessary, Toby balanced the reading glasses on the plaster stuck to his broken nose. The words on the page swam into focus and said exactly what Fellows suggested they would.

"I'll need something to rest the paper on."

Skarrats slipped the satchel's strap from his shoulder, flipped the bag onto its back, and held it out for Toby.

"The blood sample will be clear," Toby said, as confident as he could be of anything.

"I'm sure it will be, sir," Skarrats said, smugness itself.

Hand trembling, Toby signed along the dotted line, shocked at the semi-legible scrawl he'd made of his signature. Fellows smiled and nodded at Skarrats, clearly satisfied with the way their day had developed. Skarrats took the form from Toby and returned it to the satchel.

"How long before the results of the blood test come through?" Toby asked Fellows, ignoring Skarrats.

"Don't worry, sir. We will be putting a rush on it."

"That doesn't answer my question. How long?"

Fellows stuck his tongue into his top lip and scratched his chin.

"We can expect the results in around twelve weeks, sir."

"Three months! Is that what you call a rush job!" Toby gasped. "Are you serious?"

Fellows tilted his head to the side. "The lab we use, Racer-Colby, is inundated. To be frank, when I say, 'around twelve weeks', I'm being optimistic."

"And in the meantime, I'll be under a cloud?"

"Try not to worry, sir. I'm sure it'll be okay."

Easy for you to say, mate.

Toby pressed his left hand to his chest and tried to breathe normally. He glowered at Fellows.

"I want my name cleared faster than that. Can't you use another lab?"

Fellows shook his head.

"I'm afraid not, sir. Racer-Colby is the only police-accredited, testing centre in the region."

Toby tried to sit up straighter, but pain forced him back

against the pillows. "Can't you go outside the region?" he gasped. "If it's a matter of cost. I can pay to speed things up."

"No, sir. That's not a viable option. Every police-accredited lab in the country is likely to be equally stretched. You'll just have to be patient."

"Patient?" Toby growled. "Patient, you say. And in the meantime, what will you be doing? Sitting on your hands, I suppose?"

Fellows thinned his lips and came close to matching one of Skarrats' scowls. Toby had hit a nerve. He'd overstepped the boundary.

Well, sod him.

"Thank you, Mr Fabien," Fellows said, his chin set firm. "That will be all for now. Interview terminated at"—he read from the screen of the tablet—"sixteen fifty-three." Then he stood.

Skarrats retrieved his satchel and slid the strap over his head and onto his shoulder. Then he picked up the tablet, tapped the screen to end the recording, and slid the device into the bag. He tugged the satchel's zip. It snagged half way around.

"That's it?" Toby said, incredulous. "That's all?"

"Yes, sir," Fellows answered, looking down at Toby. "We'll leave you in peace to recover from your injuries. We will be in touch when we have some news ... or if we need anything more from you. And we'll email you a copy of the recording for your records."

Toby frowned. Another shaft of pain rifled across his forehead and his nose throbbed. He snatched off the reading glasses and folded the arms together.

"You have my contact details?" Toby asked.

"Yes, sir," Fellows answered. "They're on your phone,

which we recovered from your car along with your wallet. Didn't I tell you?"

"No, Inspector," Toby said, trying not to grind his teeth again—he was already in enough discomfort. "You didn't. And I suppose you're allowed to do that?"

"Yes, sir," Skarrats said, still fiddling with the zip. He nodded and let another smug grin play on his lips. "We have the authority granted to us by the—"

"Road Traffic Act, 1988?" Toby interrupted, anger bubbling close to the surface.

"Yes, sir. Quite right. They will be returned to you in due course." Fellows smiled. "Thank you for your time, Mr Fabien. I'd like to wish you a speedy recovery."

Fellows nodded to Toby and turned away. Toby stared at the inspector's back and smouldered.

The hell with your good wishes.

Skarrats, his satchel finally in possession of the tablet and hanging from his shoulder again, spoke for his boss.

"Mr Fabien," he said with enforced patience, "we will continue to investigate this case to the utmost of our abilities. However, until the blood results are back, there is little more we can do."

"So you're going to sit on your hands until the blood results come up clear? And, in the meantime," Toby said, quietly, under tight control, "the man responsible for Melissa's death gets away with murder?"

"There's not an awful lot more we can do, Mr Fabien," Fellows snapped. His patience stretched to breaking.

"What have you done so far?"

Fellows returned to his position near the visitor's chair. "We've made a public appeal for witnesses in the local press and on the local TV news. We've had a roadside appeal board in place on Doom Lane since the morning after the … accident."

Again, the mocking delay. What was the matter with him?

"It wasn't an accident," Toby insisted. "We were attacked!"

"And," Fellows continued, ignoring Toby's outburst, "up to this point, no witnesses have come forward."

"None?"

"Not one, sir," Skarrats said, apparently keen to heap on the bad news.

"There must be something more you can do!"

Fellows shook his head in exasperation.

"Try to see it from our perspective, sir." He held up his right hand and counted off the points on his fingers. "We have no independent witnesses to support your claims. There's no evidence of your car having been rammed. No obvious damage and no paint transfer. There are no dashcam clips of the collision, and there are no surveillance cameras near where your car left the road. To be honest, sir, if you'd *intended* to crash your car—and I did say 'if'—you couldn't have chosen a much more isolated spot than Doom Lane."

Oh my God.

Toby swallowed.

The police really *did* think him responsible for the crash. Again, the world opened up beneath Toby, threatening to swallow him whole. Nausea rolled over him in hot, sweaty waves. His head throbbed, adding to his banks of pain.

"So, Dylan gets away with murder?" Toby barked.

Fellows froze, then turned.

"Dylan?" he said, edging closer to the bed. "Who's Dylan?"

"He's the man driving the Ford that rammed us."

Fellows braced his shoulders.

"He gave you his name?" Fellows demanded.

"No," Toby answered. "I overheard Chardonnay calling him Dylan. Why, do you know him?"

Fellows broke eye contact and shook his head, but he wasn't at all convincing.

Skarrats stared at his boss, a confused frown creasing his forehead. He stopped playing with the zip.

"And who's Chardonnay?" Fellows asked, a strange glint in his eyes. A glint of interest.

"Dylan's girlfriend."

Fellows looked at Skarrats and pointed to the satchel.

"Matt," he said, "I think we'd better restart the recording."

Skarrats shot his boss a questioning frown, a look that Fellows blanked.

Toby sagged back into the pillows. He'd finally gained their attention.

Chapter Twenty-One

Wednesday 30th June - Tobias Fabien

Cavell Hospital, Stafford, Staffordshire, England

Toby waited for his heart rate to settle. It took a while.

Fellows stepped forwards and dropped back into the visitor's chair. He waited for Skarrats to retrieve the tablet from the overstuffed satchel and set up the recording again.

After a few moments, Skarrats nodded.

"Ready, guv," he said, tapping the screen.

Although Skarrats followed Fellows' instructions, his confusion couldn't have been more obvious. Dylan's name had sparked a reaction in Fellows, but not in Skarrats. Toby didn't care, he'd drawn Fellows' interest, and he planned to keep it.

"Mr Fabien," Fellows said, "I must remind you that we

are being recorded, and you are still under caution. Now, for the record, can you repeat what you just told us."

Toby took a breath and swallowed.

"A man called Dylan was driving the pickup truck that ran us off the road and killed my wife."

"How do you know the driver's name?" Fellows asked, his eyes alive.

Toby swallowed. This was it. His chance to make his point. He had to make the most of it.

"I overheard his girlfriend, Chardonnay, talking to him in the food hall of the Hilton Services."

Fellows nodded his encouragement. "Where you ate immediately before the crash?"

Toby nodded, relieved and a little surprised that Fellows hadn't called it an accident again.

"Yes, that's right," he said.

"Would you like to tell us what happened?"

"It was … tense," he said, understating the fear he'd felt at the time, "but I thought it was over." Toby took as deep a breath as his sore ribs would allow. "Turns out I was wrong."

Hideously wrong.

"Go on, sir," Fellows said. "Tell us in your own words. Take your time."

Relief mixed with anxiety. Relief that Fellows was finally prepared to listen, but anxious that the police still wouldn't believe him. Toby ploughed on. He needed to tell his story. Put the police in the picture. On the right track.

"While we were eating, a big, green pickup truck—a Ford—roared into the car park, making enough noise to attract everyone's attention. A man and a woman in their early twenties climbed out of the Ford and entered the food hall. They bought drinks and sat at a table close to us. The man, Dylan, was on the phone, talking very loud. Almost shouting. Foul mouthed. Every fourth word a curse. It was shocking. I wanted to tell him not to swear in front of the twins, but … Melissa was worried and held me back. Then Dylan slapped Chardonnay. It was terrible. I couldn't let it pass. Not with the twins looking on in horror." Toby paused for breath again.

"What did you do?" Fellows prompted.

"I-I stood and asked Dylan to stop swearing."

"What happened next?"

Toby shook his head. "We exchanged a few words. Dylan started shouting. He marched towards me, threateningly. I was scared. So were the twins and Melissa. The twins were crying."

"Did it come to blows?" Skarrats asked, probably hoping to add assault to the charges he planned to level against Toby.

Toby recoiled into his pillows. "Don't be ridiculous. I'm an old man, and he's a gym jockey. You know the sort. Thick arms and neck. Sleeves of ugly, black tattoos. To be honest, I was terrified."

He saw nothing but disbelief in Skarrats' green eyes. He moved his head, and again, his glasses flashed blank. Toby frowned and another thought popped into his head as he clutched at any straw he could find.

"CCTV," he snapped, desperation lifting his voice. "There were surveillance cameras in the food hall. You can confirm everything I've told you."

Fellows fingered the cleft on his chin.

"We'll look into it, Mr Fabien."

He nodded to Skarrats, who pointed at the tablet, and mimed taking notes. A slight smirk played across his fat lips.

Toby wouldn't, couldn't let it drop.

"If you can't access the recording, the other man will confirm what I've told you."

"What other man?" Fellows asked, clearly more prepared to listen than his dismissive colleague. His response gave Toby hope. Not much, but hope just the same.

"The man who came to help. … Damn it, what was his name?" Toby closed his eyes, desperate to remember. "Barrowman? No … no … Barraclough." Toby sighed with relief as the name resurfaced. At least his memory still worked. "That's it. … Jerry Barraclough. He gave me his business card. It'll be in my wallet. Call him. He'll tell you what happened."

"Thank you, sir," Fellows said. "Rest assured. We'll follow it up."

"You will?" Toby asked, doubtful.

"Yes, sir. You have my word."

Toby had to believe him. He had no other choice.

Again, Fellows nodded to Skarrats, who sat still and silent. Brooding rather than thoughtful.

"How did the confrontation end?" Fellows asked.

"Dylan backed down."

"Just like that?" Skarrats asked through a sneer.

"Yes," Toby agreed. "He took one look at Barraclough and backed down. Barraclough's a big man. He looked like he could handle himself."

"Dylan ran away," Fellows said, nodding as though it was something he'd expected. As though he knew Dylan.

What's going on here?

"Yes," Toby said. "After threatening me."

"He threatened you?" Fellows asked, left eyebrow raised. "What did he say?"

"I can't remember exactly. Something about not being finished with me yet. And then he and Chardonnay left."

"And they drove away?"

"That's right," Toby said, nodding. "In the green pickup."

"Can you describe the vehicle? Make? Model? Registration number?"

Toby frowned and shook his head.

"Other than it being lime green and a Ford, not really. I don't take much of an interest in cars ... or trucks."

"One moment, sir," Fellows said. He dug into his pocket and pulled out his phone. Frowning in concentration, his thumbs dabbed the screen until he found what he wanted.

"The pickup," he said, "does it look anything like this?" Fellows turned the phone towards Toby.

Two images filled the phone's screen. Images from Ford UK's latest, online catalogue. The first showed a side view of a gleaming, black pickup, and the second showed the same vehicle head-on, revealing a black bull bar festooned with spotlights. The text below the photos read, "The Victorious Ford Ranger Raptor! Power in Spades!"

Toby's heart rate jumped.

"That's it," he said, his voice raised. "The colour's wrong, but that's definitely the pickup Dylan was driving."

Fellows leaned back in his chair, nodding.

"How did you know?" Toby asked.

"Educated guess," Fellows answered, shooting a sideways glance at his sergeant.

Skarrats shook his head and looked blankly at Fellows' phone as though he didn't have a clue.

"You can check Dylan's Raptor for damage!" Toby announced, excitement speeding his words.

Fellows pursed his lips in consideration before he nodded and slid the phone back into his pocket.

"Yes, sir."

"You will?"

"Yes, sir," Fellows repeated. "We will."

"Thank you," Toby said, tears of relief welling. "Dylan killed Melissa. Murdered her. Promise me you'll catch him. Promise me."

"Mr Fabien," Fellows said, his voice calm and considered, authoritative, "you must try to keep calm. I can assure you, we will act on this new information, but you really can't go around accusing people of murder without proof. You can find yourself in all sorts of trouble that way."

"But you accused me of being drunk, causing the crash. You think I'm responsible."

"No, sir. We did nothing of the sort. All we're doing is trying to find out what happened."

"But I told you what happened. Dylan rammed us off the road. My car will show it, as will Dylan's Raptor."

Fellows slowly shook his head, showing exaggerated patience.

"As I've already mentioned, Mr Fabien. We found no evidence of your car having been forced off the road."

"But there must be," Toby said, his voice cracking. "Did you look properly?"

Fellows stretched his neck.

"Our best technicians have been all over the crash scene and all over your vehicle. Of course, there's plenty of damage to the Toyota, but we found no signs of a rear-end collision."

Toby couldn't—wouldn't—believe it.

"That's not possible. Dylan rammed me twice."

"As you say, sir."

"There must be some paint transfer. There must be ... Wait, the Raptor's bull bar! It was shiny. Chrome. It would have made contact with us."

Fellows and Skarrats shared another telling glance. Doubt showed on Skarrats' face for the first time. The absolute certainty had gone. Were they finally starting to believe him? Had he convinced them?

Fellows scratched his strong jaw.

"I suppose the chrome may explain the lack of paint transfer," he said, almost to himself.

Fledgeling hope swelled in Toby's chest.

"So, you believe me?" Toby heard desperation in his question.

"You've certainly opened up a new line of enquiry, sir," he said, noncommittal.

"You'll search for Dylan and the Raptor?"

Fellows sat up straighter. A knowing expression appeared on his tanned face. He knew something, but wasn't prepared to share it with a suspect.

"Do you have anything else to add, sir?" Fellows asked after a brief pause.

"No, I don't," Toby said. "All I will say is you need to find Dylan's Raptor before he has a chance to repair it."

Fellows nodded.

"Very good, sir," he said, adding a thin smile. "In that case, we'll leave it there. Thank you for your time. You've been most helpful." He nodded at Skarrats and then turned back to Toby. "Interview terminated at"—for a second time, he read from the tablet's screen—"seventeen fourteen. Again, I'd like to wish you a speedy recovery."

At the signalled end to the interview, no, the interrogation, exhaustion overwhelmed Toby, and he sank heavily into the pillows. He'd done his best to convince them and could do no more. Nothing else to do but let them do their work. Assuming they were going to do anything other than try to prove Toby guilty of causing the crash.

Toby shuddered at the thought.

Don't go there, Toby. Don't.

Fellows pushed his hands into his thighs to help boost him to his feet, acting as tired as Toby felt. He stood and watched Skarrats end the recording and slide the tablet into his satchel.

They were on their way, and good riddance.

Fellows' mobile buzzed. He dropped a hand into his trouser pocket, dragged out his phone again, and read the caller ID.

"Excuse me, sir," he said to Toby, "I need to take this."

With shoulders hunched, Fellows turned his back and edged towards the door. He accepted the call and spoke quietly.

With Fellows' back turned, an evil smile formed on Skarrats' pudgy face. He worked the satchel's zip. This time, it ran smoothly the whole way around the rim. Skarrats hung the satchel over his shoulder. With his boss occupied, he edged closer to the head of the bed and leaned in close.

"Don't think all that 'Dylan' bollocks is gonna save you, Fabien. I've never heard so much crap in my life."

His breath stank of cigarettes, and tobacco fumes oozed from his clothes in a dreadful wave. The man was a real throwback to darker times.

Toby shook his head. "But—"

"Do you know what 'familicide' means?" he asked, lips peeled back in a sneer, his voice barely loud enough to carry the short distance between them.

Toby's jaw dropped.

"You think I *wanted* my family dead?" he gasped. "That's madness."

"You said it," Skarrats growled. He stretched out another sneer, straightened, and stepped back.

"How could you think that?" Toby demanded, voice raised. "How?"

Skarrats glanced at Fellows, who continued his call. He still had his back turned, which seemed to embolden Skarrats.

"Look at it from our point of view, *sir*," he said, speaking up a little. He emphasised the "sir" and loaded it with menace. "For no apparent reason, you ran your car through a fence on a straight road. And this happened within a few months of you losing your son and being lumbered with your grand—"

"Lumbered?" Toby snapped, shouting through the pain. "How dare you! I love my—"

"Some might suggest the pressure got to you," Skarrats continued. "Financial and emotional worries can have a strange effect on the recently bereaved. It happens all the time in cases of murder-suicide."

No. This can't be happening.

"But Dylan ran us off the road," Toby said, shocked at how pitiful he sounded.

"So you keep on saying, *sir*," Skarrats said, pressing the satchel hard against his side.

Fellows ended his call. He turned to Skarrats and jerked his head in the direction of the door. Skarrats nodded and moved away, but not before staring pointedly at Toby, his meaning clear. The accusation blatant.

"Rest assured, sir," Fellows said, smiling as though he hadn't heard Skarrats' lunatic allegation, "if any fresh evidence comes into our possession, we will give it due consideration."

Toby, stunned, could think of nothing to say.

The detectives turned away. They didn't seem able to leave quickly enough. As the door swung closed behind them a deep sense of unease and hopelessness settled over Toby. Despite Fellows' bland assurances and his apparent interest in Dylan, Skarrats actually thought Toby capable of intentionally harming his own family.

As if he could ever deliberately hurt the twins or Melissa when he loved them all more than life itself.

Unbelievable. Complete madness.

Toby had been naïve. He'd been too open with the police.

Melissa would have told him to be careful. She would have insisted he consulted a solicitor before saying a word. It would have been the sensible thing to do. Melissa. Always the rational one. He would have listened, but …

The sudden realisation struck like a physical blow. Shook him to his core. Nausea roiled up and around and through him.

Melissa was gone. Gone forever.

Melissa. What am I going to do without you?

Tears fell.

Chapter Twenty-Two

Wednesday 30th June - Riley Fellows

Cavell Hospital, Stafford, Staffordshire, England

Angry as all hell, Fellows marched from the private room, stomped along the corridor, and stopped at the lift. He waited for Skarrats to catch up.

"Did you hear that bollocks, guv?" Skarrats asked, not picking up on Fellows' mood.

Hell of a detective you are.

Fellows ignored the question and jabbed the lift's call button.

"I mean," Skarrats continued, "'Dylan ran us off the road in his big, green, pickup truck.'" He waggled his head while mocking Tobias Fabien's cultured accent. "Total crap. You did well to humour him, guv."

Give me strength.

"I wasn't humouring him," Fellows snapped.

Skarrats stared up at him. Disbelief worked its way onto his sagging face.

"You weren't?"

"You're new to Stafford, Sergeant," he said. "You haven't heard of Jackie Bentley and his delinquent son … *Dylan*." He stared pointedly at Skarrats and left the name hanging.

"Dylan exists?"

Fellows nodded. "Fabien's description matches Dylan Bentley to the letter. Right down to his sleeve tats."

"Bloody hell," Skarrats said.

A porter and a nurse walked past, chatting. The porter pushed a trolley loaded with laundry. The nurse carried an armful of folders. Neither spared them a second glance.

Fellows raised a finger to his lips.

"Let's pick this up in the car."

While they waited for the lift, a brooding silence permeated the space between them. Fellows ground his teeth, willing the lift to hurry the hell up. It would have been faster taking the stairs.

Finally, the doors slid apart to reveal an empty, brushed-steel box large enough to hold fifteen passengers or a hospital bed and two porters. He stepped inside. Skarrats joined him and pressed the button for the ground floor. The twin doors slid closed. As he'd feared, a waft of stale, tobacco smoke assaulted Fellows' senses.

Skarrats leaned against the corner of the lift, shifting the satchel around to the front.

Fellows turned to face his new partner, unable to hold himself in check any longer.

"What the bloody hell was that all about?" He spoke quietly, but his anger bubbled through clearly enough.

Skarrats stood up straighter. He pushed away from the corner and moved too close for comfort. Fellows started breathing through his mouth.

"Sorry, boss?" Skarrats said. "I've no idea what you—"

Fellows clenched his fists. "Familicide? God above!"

Skarrats blanched.

"You heard that?"

"Of course I bloody heard it. I'm not deaf!"

"But you were on the pho—"

"It's a bloody good job you'd stopped recording the interview before you accused him of deliberately killing his family." Fellows paused long enough to take another open-mouthed breath and added, "What the hell were you thinking?"

"It was a legitimate interview technique, boss."

"We'd already terminated the interview. You were out of order."

Skarrats' nostrils flared. "It's a valid theory, guv."

"Is it?"

"It's as valid as thinking he got pissed and lost control of the car."

"Is it?" Fellows repeated with greater intensity.

"Or that he was driving too fast for the conditions."

Fellows caught Skarrats' eye and held it.

"If anyone else had witnessed that outburst but me, you'd be out on your bloody ear."

"You're kidding, right?" Skarrats said, still trying to defend the indefensible. "It was a legitimate tactic."

"No. It wasn't!" Fellows snapped. "It was cruel." He pointed in the approximate direction of Fabien's sickroom. "That man's just lost his wife. He's lying in a hospital bed, not knowing whether he's going to walk again, and you've just accused him of killing her and trying to murder his grandchildren!"

Skarrats' neck and cheeks flushed, and a vein in his forehead ballooned.

"Hang on a minute, guv," he said, voice raised. "Look at what's happened to Fabien over the past year. His son and daughter-in-law die aboard Flight BE1555. He hasn't even had a chance to start grieving when he's forced to take on twin grandchildren. All of a sudden, there are young kids in the house. School runs. Parent-teacher visits. Medical appointments. You know what kids are like. Nothing but trouble. The pressure mounts. Then some young thug threatens him in front of his newly expanded family. He's impotent. Embarrassed. He loses it. Blows a fuse. Decides to end his suffering and take the family with him. Murder-suicide. Classic." His emerald eyes glinted with anger and excitement.

The lift alarm dinged. Fellows raised a finger to his lips.

Skarrats shut his mouth.

The carriage clattered to a stop and the doors slid apart. Fellows marched through the foyer, stepped out into early-evening sunshine, and retraced the circuitous route to their car.

With ten metres to go, he pressed the button on the key fob, and the central-locking system deactivated. He opened the driver's door, slid behind the wheel, and waited. Skarrats, breathing heavily in the attempt to keep up, yanked open the passenger door and climbed aboard. The Insignia's suspension dipped under the added load before correcting itself. He removed the strap from his shoulder, placed the satchel between his legs, and buckled himself in.

God, the man stank of smoke. He'd have to mention it at some stage, but first things first.

Fellows pressed the ignition button and rolled his window all the way down. To ensure a through-flow of air, he did the same to the passenger's window—the hell with Skarrats if he didn't like fresh air—then he launched into it as though they'd not broken off.

"Listen to me, Sergeant, and listen carefully. If you can't let the familicide thing go, I'll have you transferred off the team."

"You wouldn't."

Their eyes locked, Skarrats' expression imploring.

Fellows gripped the steering wheel but left the car in park. He didn't plan to move until he'd finished. Delivering a severe reprimand to a junior officer didn't exactly lend itself to safe driving.

"I know where this is coming from, Matt," he said, speaking with enforced control. "Tobias Fabien is *not* Grant Stokes."

Skarrats jerked upright as though he'd been tagged with a stun gun. He set his jaw.

"I know that, sir." His lips barely moved.

"Do you?"

"Yes, sir. This has nothing to do with Grant Stokes."

"I read your personnel file before you transferred in from the Met."

"Of course you did," Skarrats muttered, treading really close to insubordination.

"I've seen the mugshots," Fellows said, "Tobias Fabien looks like Grant Stokes."

"Does he?" Skarrats asked, guarded. "I hadn't noticed."
Liar.

"Similar age. Same colouring. Grey hair, brown eyes. If

you can't see the resemblance, you're not much of a detective." Fellows loosened his grip on the wheel. "Admit it, Matt. You're biased against Fabien because he reminds you of Stokes."

Fellows held his breath and waited.

"Okay," Skarrats said, finally spitting it out. "You're right. I agree. There's a *slight* physical similarity, but that didn't affect my reasoning."

"Bullshit."

"Excuse me, sir?"

"You heard me, Matt. I called 'bullshit'."

Fellows stopped talking. Skarrats sat still, fuming. The silence stretched out, growing in its intensity.

"Think about it, Matt."

Skarrats blinked, shook himself, and seemed to snap out of a daze. He twisted in his seat and finally met Fellows' angry glare.

"Stokes killed his wife and kids, and then the sick fuck topped himself," Skarrats said, quietly, "and I should have stopped him."

"You couldn't have known what he—"

Skarrats turned his imploring, green eyes on Fellows. "That's just it, guv. I *did* know. The bugger threatened to do it, and I thought it was the booze talking. Did nothing about it."

"You applied for a restraining order."

"Which the CPS refused to run with. Another case of 'there's insufficient evidence' and it 'not being in the public interest'! Sometimes I don't know why the fuck we bother … sir."

"I understand, Matt," Fellows agreed. "I really do, but we can only work with the tools we're given."

Skarrats shot him an angry scowl.

"With respect, guv," he said, "that's a platitude, and you know where you can stick your platitudes." He shook his head and ran a hand through his thinning hair. "Sorry about that, guv. I really am. Sometimes ... I get ... worked up ... fixated. You're right, though. Fabien does remind me of Stokes." He dropped his hand into his lap. "It screwed with my head." He sucked in a deep breath and blew it out, long and slow. Thankfully, he turned his head and spared Fellows a hot blast of his smoker's breath.

"What happens now?" Skarrats asked, worry tinging his tentative question.

Fellows rubbed his face with both hands, trying to drive some life into it.

"By rights," he said, surprised at how defeated he sounded, "I should talk to HR, get you some counselling." Skarrats opened his mouth to speak, but Fellows drove on. "But that can wait. Do I have your word that you'll drop the familicide bollocks?"

Skarrats hesitated, then sat up straighter.

"Yes, guv," he said. "I promise."

"Good," Fellows said, shifting the selector into drive. "Now let's get back to the shop. We have work to do."

"I'm with you, sir," Skarrats said. "What's the next step?"

"You're going to send a uniform to the Hilton Services food hall to seize that surveillance footage. Then you're going to read the file we have on the Bentleys. I think you'll agree that father and son both stink to high heaven."

Not unlike you, Sergeant.

"And you, sir?"

"I'm going to delegate one of the team to apply for a warrant to impound Dylan's lime-green Ford Ranger Raptor."

"Dylan owns a Raptor?"

"No, Sergeant," Fellows said, trying to ease up on the smugness. "Jackie owns the Raptor. In fact, he owns a whole fleet of the bloody things. Dylan will have borrowed one from Daddy."

"A fleet of Raptors?" Skarrats said. "Who the hell is this Jackie Bentley?"

Fellows shot Skarrats a grim smile.

"Read the file, Sergeant. It's all in there."

"Right you are, guv. I can do that on the move."

Skarrats pulled the satchel from between his legs, and placed it on his lap. He removed the tablet, and accessed the blue-and-white home page on the secure server.

"Jackie Bentley," Skarrats said. "Spelled with an E like the car?"

"Yes, but the first name's Jackson. Jackson Bentley, aka Jackie."

Fellows indicated left, consulted his wing mirror, and filtered onto the hospital ring road. They nurdled along in slow-moving traffic until the second set of traffic lights they reached turned red. Fellows stopped in a seven-car queue.

"Bloody hell," Skarrats said, holding up the screen to show Fellows. "The lucky bastard."

"You found the case file then," Fellows said, throwing him another smile, this one ironic.

Skarrats nodded and continued reading.

"Sometimes," he said, two minutes later, "life just ain't fair."

"Tell me about it," Fellows shot back. "Better still, tell Tobias Fabien about it."

Skarrats' shoulders slumped. "I think I might owe Fabien an apology."

"You only *think*?"

"I know, I know," Skarrats said. "I'm a first-class arse-hole. Want to drop me off here so I can go say sorry to him? I can take a cab back to the station."

The lights turned green, and Fellows waited for the cars to do something useful. Move even.

"No. You'll only make things worse. Best way we can make amends is to work the case and maybe confirm Fabien's accusation."

"Yes, guv. I'm with you on that."

The first five cars made it through the lights before they turned red again. He rolled the Insignia a few metres forwards and pulled to another stop. Beside him, Skarrats kept shaking his head and muttering to himself as he read the Bentleys' case file.

Chapter Twenty-Three

Saturday 3rd July - Evening

Mike's Farm, Long Buckby, Northants, England

The air-conditioning unit hummed in the background, keeping the comms room at a comfortable eighteen degrees. During the attic's refurb, they'd packed state-of-the-art insulation between the roof trusses and added sheets of high-density boarding. They'd also fitted bullet-resistant glazing to all the windows. The temperature inside the wooden barn's roof space could rocket to uncomfortable levels when the sun hammered down from a clear sky. Aircon was a necessity, not a luxury.

Kaine and Lara sat in front of the bank of monitors in their nicely upholstered office chairs, watching Corky and listening to his detailed briefing.

"Staffordshire Police have convinced themselves that Toby's guilty of causing death by careless driving. They haven't charged him yet on account of him still being in 'ospital, but from what Corky's read in the police file, it's only a matter of time. Trouble is … careless driving's the least they're going for."

Lara leaned forwards and typed "death by careless driving" into a search engine. The results on her screen showed the penalty for such an offence as up to five years imprisonment.

Kaine blew out his cheeks. Five years was serious time for a man of Toby Fabien's age. Could he survive it?

"What other charges are they considering?" Kaine asked.

Corky shot back the answer.

"They is waiting on blood test results," he said, for once being deadly serious. "If the lab finds anything dodgy—like high levels of alcohol or illegal drugs—they'll likely increase the charge to death by dangerous driving. And that's a whole different level of mire."

Lara added a new search string to the engine. Her fingers flew over the keys at a rate Kaine couldn't hope to match.

"The maximum punishment is life imprisonment," she said, frowning and speaking quietly.

"Bloody hell," Kaine sighed.

"If he drove under the influence and caused his wife's death, the bugger deserves to go down for it," Corky announced in a manner so implacable that it didn't sound like the jovial, IT wiz they had grown to depend on.

"No," Lara said, shaking her head. "I can't see it. The Toby Fabien I met during the Trust assessment didn't seem the type to drink and drive. He was too responsible, and he loved the twins to bits. Toby would never willingly put them at risk. That much was obvious."

Cheering and laughter outside indicated that the spontaneous party had spilled out into the courtyard. The guys were really tying one on. So much for Cough's ability to rein in the rabble. Not that Kaine minded. They all deserved to let off steam. In fact, Mike would have insisted on it.

Mike's gone. He's really gone.

Kaine's heart flipped at the loss, and he made himself concentrate. A member of The 83 needed his attention, his support. Mike would understand.

"How long did your meeting with the Fabiens last, Doc?" Corky asked, frowning, and as deathly serious as Kaine had ever seen him.

"I spent an afternoon with them."

Corky scoffed. "So, after a couple of hours, you'd learned enough to tell that this geezer weren't a drunk?" Corky shook his head. "You got any idea what alkies are like, Doc? What they go through to conceal their drinking? The buggers become experts at hiding bottles and—"

"Are you speaking from experience, Corky?" Kaine asked, already guessing the answer.

"Too right, Mr K. As it happens, Corky's doin' just that." He raised a hand, index finger extended. "And, don't ask."

Kaine nodded. "I won't."

"I met Melissa, too, don't forget," Lara said. "She didn't strike me as the sort of woman to allow her husband to drink and drive. She'd have driven them home herself."

Blinking rapidly, Corky pulled in his chin.

"Yeah, right," he said. "But we can't ask her what happened on account of her being dead, now can we?"

"No," Kaine said, teeth gritted. "We can't. How long will it take for the blood test results to come in?"

"At least three months. Prob'ly longer."

"For God's sake. How long?"

"You heard, Mr K. Three to four months."

Kaine shared a glance with Lara.

"Bloody hell. Where did they send the sample? The moon?"

Corky scrunched up his face and shook his head.

"Nope," he said. "The Racer-Colby Crime lab in Brum. And before you ask, Corky talked to Mr J about it and the old boy weren't having none of it. He spouted a load of guff about procedures and hierarchy and not wanting to 'exert any more pressure on an already overloaded system'." Corky pushed his face closer to the camera and looked sideways at them. "You ask Corky, the old boy don't want to risk upsetting his new lady friend by asking her to break the rules. It's sweet, really. The poor bloke's totally smitten. And Corky can't blame him. Robyn Spence is a real babe." Corky blushed. "But don't tell him Corky said nothing when you go speak to him, Mr K."

Kaine arched an eyebrow.

"What makes you think I'm planning a face-to-face?"

Again, Corky scoffed.

"You telling Corky you ain't?"

Kaine threw him a tight smile. "I'm telling you nothing of the sort."

"Yeah. Corky thought not." He chuckled and the world tilted back onto its correct axis.

Outside, someone with a really decent baritone, who sounded a little like Stefan, started singing a sad song that Kaine didn't recognise. A few verses later, a couple of off-key tenors joined in the chorus—they could barely hold a note. Thankfully, within a few bars, a peel of ragged laughter silenced the rest of the song. Seconds later, a chorus of cheers greeted the arrival of a car. Kaine stood and peered through the window in the barn's gable end which gave a decent view of the courtyard. The sun's final rays highlighted superfine particles of dust floating in the cooled air. Nathan Montero and Jeff Baines had made the journey from Yorkshire a couple of hours behind their overly optimistic schedule. They must have kept within the speed limits for once.

Shouts welcomed the new arrivals to the revelry. Knowing them as well as he did, Kaine had no doubt they'd taken time out of their journey to find an off-licence and load up for the party, which seemed set to last long into the night.

"Work hard, play harder," the unofficial, second motto of the UK's Special Forces would be honoured at Mike's farm that night.

Kaine returned to his seat.

"The lads are celebrating Mike," he explained to a smiling Corky.

"Yeah," he said. "The surveillance cameras are picking it up. Want Corky to put the feed on one of the monitors for you?" He raised his hands in preparation for attacking one of the many keyboards on his desk.

"No, thanks." Kaine didn't need to witness the spectacle of half a dozen men rolling around under the influence. He'd seen it often enough in the past. Before too long, the cheers and laughter would degenerate into maudlin toasts and sad reminiscences. He didn't need to join them. He was already sad enough and, unfortunately, he had other things to focus on.

The 83 come first.

"Let them see it through in peace," Kaine said.

Corky nodded and lowered the hands of a maestro.

"So," he said. "What else can Corky do for you today, Mr K, Doc?"

"If you have access to the police case file"—and Kaine would bet big money that he did—"I'd love to see a copy."

Corky let out another high-pitched chuckle. "It's already on the main server, Mr K. Latest file. Title is 'The Fabien Family'. It's all there. Murder book. Autopsy. Crime scene video. Witness statements. There's also a digital recording of the police's interview with Toby Fabien, with the bloke lying in his 'ospital bed."

"Now that I have to see."

"Geezer looked in a bad way. Like he'd gone ten rounds with a two-hundred kilo gorilla. There's detailed pics of the Raptor, too."

"Raptor?" Kaine asked.

Corky frowned.

"Yeah. The Raptor. Didn't Corky tell you?"

"Tell us what?"

"Fabien's claiming he were deliberately run off the road by a bloke driving a lime-green Ford Ranger Raptor, of all things."

"No, Corky," Kaine said. "You didn't tell us."

Kaine could have done with the information at the start of the discussion. It potentially put a whole new spin on things.

"Yeah. It turned out to be a load of bollo—nonsense." He pinched his face and raised an apologetic hand at Lara. "The cops didn't find no evidence on the Toyota of a collision with another vehicle." Corky's expression showed derision—he didn't believe Toby Fabien's story for one moment. He continued. "They did identify the lime-green Raptor—

one of only four in the whole of Staffordshire—and towed it to the police garage. That's where them pics were taken. The Raptor's in the queue for testing, but there ain't no obvious signs of damage. The cops reckon the bloke's telling porkies. Trying to shift the blame away from his own dangerous driving. And there's the blood test results still to come in, don't forget."

Kaine hadn't forgotten the blood test, and he'd already worked out a way to minimise the delay with the results.

"Okay, Corky," Kaine said, ready to wrap up the mini conference. "Thanks for everything. You've done your usual, excellent job."

Corky raised a hand and scratched at the top of his head, almost looking embarrassed at the compliment. A rarity for their self-styled "information acquisition specialist".

"You is welcome, Mr K." Corky pulled his lips into a thin line. "And Corky's sorry about the rant earlier. Didn't mean to slag off Fabien like that, but Corky's got a thing 'bout drink drivers." He shrugged. "Bad history."

"I understand," Kaine said, "but Fabien's innocent until proven guilty."

"And if the blood test comes back positive for booze or drugs?" Corky asked.

"If that happens, I'm going to do my best to make sure Fabien never gets near the twins again."

"Yeah," Corky said. "In that case, the poor, little mites will be better off without him. Tra for now, Mr K, Doc."

He threw them a backhanded wave and melted from the screen, leaving Lara and Kaine alone in the comms room.

Lara spun her seat to face him.

"I suppose you'll be heading to Stafford?"

"After reading the police file," he said, nodding, "and after a brief stopover in Shropshire."

"You really think you can convince David Jones to break the rules?"

Kaine smiled. "Why not? He's done it before. And he is one of the good guys."

"But you heard what Corky said. David's already refused to help."

"Maybe Corky didn't ask properly. You saw the way he reacted to the idea that Fabien might have been drunk at the wheel."

"Yes, I did. And it didn't seem like him."

"Agreed. Can you access the files, please?" He pointed to her keyboard.

"You really should learn to do this yourself." She spun to face the monitors and attacked the keyboard with mild ferocity.

"I can, but you're much quicker than me. See?"

The Fabien Family folder appeared in the centre of the main screen. Lara double-clicked the icon and a dozen or so subfolders appeared.

"Thanks."

"You're welcome." She stood and slid the wireless keyboard closer to him. "I'll leave you to it."

"You're not staying?"

"No. I have other things on my plate. I'll go through it" —she nodded at the screen—"in my own time. Don't break anything." Lara smiled, bent to kiss his cheek, and turned towards the door.

"I won't, love."

Kaine waited for her to go, watching her the whole way, before he turned to face the keyboard and started pecking.

After trawling through the files, he found the one he

wanted—the two-part interview with Fabien in his hospital bed. He selected the first file, hit run, and winced at the image of a man who had been involved in a serious road collision. A bandage covered Fabien's head, heavy bruises darkened his bloodshot eyes, a nasal splint protected his nose, and cuts scored his lower lip. And they were only the visible injuries. More would be hidden beneath the blanket.

Kaine watched and listened carefully, pausing and repeating the recording for clarity where necessary. The detectives remained largely out of shot, making good use of the classic "good cop, bad cop" routine, with DS Skarrats clearly enjoying his role as the aggressor. For his part, DI Fellows dialled in his role as the good guy. He played it strictly by the numbers until the second video, when he became more animated, especially when Fabien mentioned the aggressive Dylan. Fellows clearly recognised the man from Fabien's description.

For Fabien's part, he was clearly out of his depth and showed intense naïvety by refusing the offer of a solicitor. Whether the naïvety of an innocent or a calculating man, only time would tell.

After two full viewings, Kaine had seen enough. He opened the murder book and started reading. By the time he'd finished the first readthrough, the sun had set, darkness had fallen, and the guys had taken their drunken carousing inside. Mike deserved the best sendoff in the world.

But Kaine couldn't join them. He'd only kill the mood, and besides, he had work to do. Important work.

He reopened the video of the hospital interview, fast-forwarded to the best headshot he could find, and paused the recording. He zoomed in until Toby Fabien's face filled the large screen and studied the still image at length. Was he looking at the face of a guilty man? His gut said no. But his gut hadn't exactly shown itself to be infallible.

In Fabien's favour, the police had found nothing in his history to suggest he was anything other than an honest, law-abiding citizen. In addition, Fabien had passed the "Lara test", which was good enough for Kaine. For the present, Fabien deserved the benefit of any doubt on offer. On top of which, as a member of The 83, he had a special pass.

Kaine rubbed the grit from his dry eyes, leaned back in his chair, and stared through the darkened windows into a gloomy night. He allowed his mind to wander.

Toby Fabien was in trouble. He needed help, and Kaine would provide it. The twins were in trouble, too. Kaine had turned them into orphans. He'd ruined their lives and would do everything in his power to ease their suffering. He would do it in honour of the eighty-three people he'd shot down over the North Sea, and he would do it in memory of Mike and Danny.

Mike and Danny.

He pulled in a deep, shuttered breath and released it slowly.

Five minutes later, Kaine closed the video file, collapsed the folders, and put the system to sleep. He left the comms room, locked the door securely behind him, and descended the wooden stairs. With a two-hour drive to David Jones' isolated cottage in the depths of Shropshire to come, he required a big hit of caffeine to help him on his way.

Chapter Twenty-Four

Monday 5th July - Morning

Cavell Hospital, Stafford, Staffordshire, England

Kaine strode towards the reception desk as though he'd spent half his professional life entering private wards in NHS hospitals. He wore an expensive, dark grey suit, light blue shirt, maroon tie, and highly polished but well-worn leather loafers. He'd oiled and combed his unruly hair flat, wearing it neatly parted on the left, and had perched a pair of horn-rimmed glasses with tinted but uncorrected lenses on his nose. In his left hand, he carried a battered, leather briefcase. Hopefully, he looked every bit the solicitor visiting his latest, unfortunate and needy, client.

With no queue at the desk—unlike at the reception area in the main entrance—he didn't have to wait.

"Good morning, sir," the smartly dressed receptionist, with too much makeup, said. "How can I help?" She showed him a welcoming smile that actually appeared genuine.

"Arnold Jeffries to see Mr Ferber."

She consulted her computer screen and frowned. "I don't see your name on the list, Mr Jeffries. Is he expecting you, sir?"

Kaine shook his head. "Not exactly, but I can assure you, he will want to see me. I represent The 83 Trust."

"I'm sorry, sir. Mr Ferber is a busy man and there's no appointment in the—"

"Would you mind telling him I'm here, Ms Gilbert," he said, reading the name badge pinned to her lapel. "He really will want to see me, and I promise not to take up much of his valuable time."

She shook her head, the barrier descended, and the frown locked in place. The gatekeeper would protect her star player with all the power at her disposal.

"I'm sorry, sir," she repeated, "but Mr Ferber can't—"

"Ms Gilbert," Kaine interrupted, his tone officious, "I can assure you that Mr Ferber will be extremely upset if you don't at least tell him I'm here."

The gatekeeper hesitated, trying to decide whether she could dare to risk upsetting her boss.

"Very well, Mr Jeffries," she said, her features stiffening. "I will tell him, but Mr Ferber is in the middle of rounds. I'm afraid you'll have to wait."

She stole a quick glance to her left, along a corridor dotted with closed doors.

Kaine smiled in condescension. "Very well, Ms Gilbert. If I must. While I'm waiting, I'll visit my client, Mr Toby Fabien. What's his room number?"

Again, she looked down the corridor and smiled as a door opened.

"Room Six, sir. It's at the far end of the corridor. On the right."

She signalled to her left. Kaine turned in time to see a slim, stoop-shouldered man with short-cropped, blond hair step out of the room she'd indicated, and march briskly towards them. The man wore a dark suit, wire-rimmed specs, and carried a voice recorder into which he spoke while on the move. Multi-tasking at its finest. Kaine recognised the senior surgeon from the hospital's website and his social media profile.

"I take it that's Mr Ferber?" Kaine asked the star-struck receptionist.

"Yes, sir." She beamed with pride. "But—"

"Excellent."

He stepped out in front of the fast-approaching surgeon, who had to stop or risk an unfortunate collision.

"Mr Ferber?" Kaine said, pushing out his right hand. "I'm Arnold Jeffries, from The 83 Trust. It's a pleasure to meet you at last."

With clear reluctance, Ferber dragged his attention away from his recorder and focused on Kaine. He ignored the offered hand, and Kaine lowered it. No offence taken. A surgeon would value his hands above all else and would think twice about who he offered them to.

"Mr Jeffries?" he asked. "Do I know—"

"Might I have a word with you about Mr Fabien, sir? As I said, I represent The 83 Trust," he said in his most ingratiating voice. "You had a telephone consultation with our chief medical officer this morning. Dr Grace Sloane? She would have mentioned me."

As usual, Lara had done a great job completing the groundwork for Kaine's unannounced visit.

"Ah, yes, Mr Jeffries," Faber said, nodding in recognition. "Dr Sloane did suggest you might wish to pay a visit at some stage, but I didn't expect it to be so soon. You really should have made an appointment with my secretary."

Ferber shot Ms Gilbert an annoyed glare. She'd failed in her prime directive of protecting one of the hospital's star players.

"But now I'm here," Kaine said, pushing his glasses up to the bridge of his nose, "would it be possible to have a quick word in private? I can assure you that I won't take much of your valuable time."

Ferber frowned.

"You know, I really can't discuss the health of a patient with a non-family member."

"I'm sure you'll be able to make an exception for the patient's legal representative," Kaine countered, shooting Ferber an obsequious smile. "As I said, this is rather important. We need to discuss Mr Fabien's medical care *vis-à-vis* the ongoing … costs."

That's it, Kaine. Dangle the carrot.

Kaine offered Ferber his business card, which the man took and handed to Ms Gilbert. The surgeon hesitated, read the time from the clock hanging on the wall above the distressed receptionist, before releasing a heavy sigh. "Very well, Mr Jeffries. Follow me."

Ferber skirted around Kaine, headed past the desk, and entered an empty waiting room lined with well-upholstered and comfortable-looking chairs. Serene landscapes—original oils—graced two of the four walls, and the window opposite the door looked down on a nicely tended flower garden, eight storeys below, and the rolling fields beyond.

The room virtually guaranteed the occupants comfort and tranquillity while they awaited news of their loved ones.

"Thank you, Mr Ferber."

"I imagine you'd like a prognosis for Mr Fabien?" the surgeon opened.

"Yes, please."

Ferber hugged the voice recorder to his narrow chest, as if using it as a shield.

"I have good news, Mr Jeffries." He gave Kaine the benefit of a weak smile. "Mr Fabien is showing remarkable recuperative powers for a man of his age. If he continues to improve at the same rate, we will be able to send him to our postoperative convalescent facility within the next few days."

"Your 'postoperative convalescent facility'?"

"It's a private care home staffed by specialists dedicated to the patient's recovery."

"And where is this?"

"Outside Coton Clanford. Five miles from here."

"No, no," Kaine said, shaking his head. "That won't do at all, Mr Ferber."

"It won't?"

"Mr Fabien has guardianship of his grandchildren."

"Ah yes, the twins," Ferber said, nodding.

"He needs to return home to look after them or they will be taken into care. Would that be possible?"

Ferber hesitated. He raised a hand to his chin.

"Well," he said, "if a suitable care package can be arranged, we may be able to discharge him, but ..." He shook his head.

Kaine beamed. "That *is* excellent news."

"Let me reiterate, Mr Jeffries. A *full* care package must be in place before he can be allowed to return home. The package must include around-the-clock nursing care, attendance at outpatient clinics, and ongoing physiotherapy. The cost of such a package would be … prohibitive."

Kaine nodded sagely, taking in the meaning.

"The 83 Trust is prepared to cover all the ongoing, medical costs, Mr Ferber," he said and repeated, "*All* the ongoing costs," for emphasis. "There are no financial limitations," he added.

The surgeon's eyes widened in surprise, and he tilted his head to one side. "Suitably qualified nurses are not always easy to locate, Mr Jeffries."

"As it happens," Kaine said, revealing another smile, "The 83 Trust keeps a number of highly qualified nurses and doctors on retainer. Staffing levels won't present us with any problems."

Ferber hiked his eyebrows. As Kaine expected, the surgeon seemed impressed with the scope of The 83 Trust's operation—and the depth of its pockets.

"Now," Kaine said, going in for what he hoped would be the clincher, "these outpatient clinics …"

"Yes, Mr Jeffries? What about them?"

"Two simple questions. What do they entail, and would it be possible for them to take place at home?"

After an in-depth "consultation" with Lara, Kaine already knew the answers to both these simple questions.

Ferber spoke without hesitation.

"Apart from regular X-rays and soft-tissue scans, outpatient clinics are a chance for the consultants to see the patient in person. These clinics give us the opportunity to monitor the ongoing health of the people under our care."

"In Mr Fabien's case, are the consultants always available? I mean, Mr Fabien would never have to drag himself away from home only to end up seeing a junior doctor, for example?"

Ferber winced and delayed his response. Kaine allowed the silence to hang until the surgeon relented.

"Given the nature of the situation," he said, "that can happen from time to time. But I must assure you that the junior doctors in question are all highly qualified, and they would report directly to the consultant in charge of the case. The patient will always receive the best possible—"

"Would out-of-hours home visits be possible?"

An interested glint flickered in Ferber's blue eyes. He could see where Kaine was headed.

"Consultant visits, you mean?" Ferber asked.

Kaine nodded. "I do, indeed."

Kaine's earlier words, "There are no financial limitations," hung heavy in the conversation.

"Only in highly exceptional circumstances," Ferber said. "And such visits would be prohibitively expensive."

"But they would be possible?"

"Well, yes," the consultant said. "They would be."

"And they would be in the best interests of the patient."

Ferber stiffened.

"Of course," he snapped. "Everything we do is in our patients' best interests."

"Excellent," Kaine said, still smiling. "In which case, I have a proposal that might be of interest …"

Chapter Twenty-Five

Monday 5th July - Morning

Cavell Hospital, Stafford, Staffordshire, England

Kaine knocked on the door to Room Six and awaited the summons, before opening it and stepping into another well-appointed room. Spotless, light, and airy, it couldn't have been any more conducive to a patient's swift recovery if it tried. He kept hold of the handle and remained in the open doorway, not wanting to appear too pushy.

Tobias Fabien sat up in bed, leaning against a stack of plump pillows. He showed a significant improvement on the swollen-eyed, bruised, and damaged individual on the police's video footage. The head bandage was gone, the black eyes had faded to green and yellow, and the once-pale skin of the face and neck had turned to a much healthier pink. The nasal splint had been removed, and the patient no longer needed to be hooked up to the various machines.

"Mr Fabien?" Kaine asked.

"Yes," Fabien said, nodding.

"I'm Arnold Jeffries, from The 83 Trust. May I come in?"

"The Trust?"

"Yes, sir. May I come in?"

"Of course," Fabien said, beckoning him inside. "Is anything wrong?"

Kaine stepped further into the room and closed the door behind him. He removed the uncomfortable glasses and slid them into the breast pocket of his jacket.

"Not at all, Mr Fabien. This is a standard welfare visit. We want to make sure that you're receiving the best care possible."

Fabien relaxed.

"That's very good of you. I was worried you were going to remove your support."

Kaine tilted his head in question.

"Why would we do that?"

"I don't know," Fabien said after a brief pause. "We … that's Melissa and I,"—a flicker of emotion crossed his expressive but still-swollen face—"always thought it was too good to be true. We were waiting for the other shoe to drop, but … I'm sorry. We were clearly doing you a disservice."

Kaine nodded slowly.

"That's understandable, Mr Fabien. Many of our clients feel the same way … to begin with." He edged forwards and pointed to one of the visitor's chairs. "Would you mind if I take a seat?"

"Please do."

"Thank you."

Kaine dragged a chair alongside the bed and groaned as he lowered himself into it, as though heartily relieved to take the weight off his aching legs. It made him sound like a much older man, which happened to be the intention. He lowered the battered briefcase to the floor, sat up straight, and placed his hands on his knees.

"Mr Fabien, rather than removing our support, we intend to increase it in response to your current ... situation."

Fabien's forehead creased into a deep frown.

"Really? How?"

"I've just spoken with your consultant, Mr Ferber. When you are discharged—which will be sooner than you might imagine—he has agreed to visit you at home until you've made a full recovery. We are also arranging around-the-clock nursing cover to help with your day-to-day care. We will also provide housekeeping services."

"You're joking," Fabien said, in hushed disbelief.

Kaine sat up straighter. "The 83 Trust doesn't joke about such serious matters."

Fabien closed his eyes, and set his jaw. Deep emotion played havoc with his innate, British reserve.

"How long can you afford to do that?"

Kaine showed Fabien what he considered his most reassuring smile.

"As long as is necessary, Mr Fabien. Which won't be as long as you fear right now. According to Mr Ferber, with the proper, ongoing care, you should make a full and relatively swift recovery. Apparently, you have the recuperative powers of a man half your age."

Fabien grunted.

"Melissa"—he gulped—"Melissa and I always looked after ourselves. Never smoked. Drank only in moderation and took regular exercise. We had hoped for a long and healthy retirement together." Tears rimmed his eyes. "The best laid plans …" Fabien covered his eyes with a hand and allowed the adage to remain unfinished.

"I really am very sorry for your loss, Mr Fabien."

"Please," he said, a catch in his voice, "call me Toby."

Kaine nodded and leaned back in his chair.

"Why did you come in person?" Toby asked, locking eyes with Kaine. "Don't get me wrong, I appreciate all you've done for my family … for the twins. You've been so supportive with the finances, but you could have dealt with this meeting over the phone."

Kaine wondered where to begin and decided that the direct approach would be best.

"The 83 Trust offers more than financial support to its clients, Toby. And when we learned about your accident—"

"It wasn't an accident," Toby snapped. He struggled to sit up, grimacing from the effort. "We were deliberately run off the road by a madman. Like I told the police."

"And how did they respond to that?" Kaine asked, feigning ignorance.

Toby gasped and flopped back against the pillows. "They didn't believe me. They think I'm responsible for the crash. In fact, they're waiting on the results of my blood test. Hoping I'll show up as being over the alcohol limit. It'll make their jobs easier." Again, he swallowed. "But I won't be over the limit. I *do not* drink and drive. Never. I'll swear to whatever God you believe in. I'm not responsible for the crash … for Melissa's death. I was *not* drunk."

"We know," Kaine said, keeping his voice low but firm.

Toby gasped.

"What?" He gritted his teeth, raised himself from the

pillows again, and leaned on his right elbow. "What did you say?"

"I said, 'We know', Toby," Kaine repeated, straight-faced. "We know you hadn't been drinking that evening. As do the police."

Toby blinked rapidly.

"How?" he asked, shaking his head. His face had reddened with the exertion and from the heightened emotion. "How do you know?"

"The blood analysis came back clear for alcohol and recreational drugs."

Again, Toby collapsed back against the pillows. "But the police said they wouldn't have the results back for months. I've been worried sick."

Kaine smiled, delighted to be delivering more good news. God knew how much Toby needed it.

"We … The 83 Trust … has a certain influence with senior members of the police service and with officials at the local crime lab. Enough influence to have the process fast-tracked. One of the laboratory's senior scientists gave up her Sunday evening to run the analysis for us."

Silently, Kaine thanked David Jones and his new friend, Robyn Spence, for their efforts on Toby's behalf. It had taken some time to convince Jones to make the approach, but after a full rundown of the case, he and Robyn were delighted to help.

"And the results were clear?"

"Exactly. Did you have any doubt?"

"No." Toby paused for a moment, before adding, "Well, yes. Actually, I was scared that someone would make a mistake somewhere." He swallowed and exhaled deeply. "Have you ever heard of the statistical phenomenon called a 'false positive'?"

Kaine smiled knowingly and nodded.

"Yes, I have. But that hasn't happened in this case. You're in the clear as far as the blood tests are concerned."

"Thank God." Toby closed his eyes only to open them a few moments later and drill his gaze into Kaine. "What did the police say?"

"Nothing yet. They're still … digesting the information. The lab only delivered its results this morning."

"They can still charge me with death by careless driving. They have me down as speeding."

"And were you?" Kaine asked, tilting his head. "Speeding, I mean."

"No … yes. A little. But only because we were being chased by a man driving a Ford Raptor. A man by the name of Dylan."

Kaine pursed his lips and nodded. "How do you know the driver's name?"

"It's a long story."

Kaine held open his hands. "I've got time if you have."

Toby started speaking, and Kaine allowed him to tell his tale without interruption. It matched the story he'd told the police during their bedside interrogation. He left nothing out and added nothing in. It had the ring of truth to it and, given what Kaine had read in the police's case file, Kaine believed every word.

"Thanks, Toby," Kaine said after he'd finished, and the silence had stretched out for a few moments. "Going through that again can't have been easy."

"It wasn't, but I … I had to. That man, Dylan, is responsible for Melissa's death, and he could have killed the twins. It's true. I swear it. You have to believe me!"

"We do, Toby." Kaine nodded. "We believe you. Unreservedly."

Tears burst from the man's bruised and bloodshot eyes. "Thank God."

Now all we have to do is prove it.

Toby grunted as he reached for a box of tissues on his bedside cabinet. Kaine jumped up and handed it to him.

"Thanks." Toby plucked a tissue from the box and dabbed his eyes. "You don't know how much it means for someone to believe me. I've been terrified."

I can imagine.

"Toby," Kaine said, keeping his tone serious, "just because *I* believe you, doesn't mean the police will. There's a long way to go before we're clear of this."

"I know, but it's a start." Still drying his eyes, Toby drew in a long, slow breath. "And thank you for saying 'we'. It means a lot to know I'm not going through this alone. The 83 Trust has been wonderful. I don't know how Melissa and I would have coped without your support when Robert and Helen ... passed. And now ..." He broke off and shook his head. "Oh God, what am I going to do?"

"What's wrong?"

"I've just thought. How am I going to cope with the twins. Look at me." He waved a hand over the cage protecting his legs from the weight of the bedding. "And my back ... I don't know how soon I'm going to be able to walk again. If ever."

Kaine held up a hand.

"Toby, as I just told you, Mr Ferber's prognosis is highly encouraging. You can expect a full recovery, but it will take work, and you'll have to give it time."

"It's going to take ages. Months. I can't expect the Kendalls to look after the twins for that long. They have two children of their own. And ... and I can't stand the thought of the twins going into care. I've heard so many horror stories."

"What about Emma?"

Toby gasped, and his eyes narrowed. "You know about Emma?"

Kaine nodded and released another gentle smile. "We try our best to learn as much as we can about our clients. Do you have an issue with your sister-in-law?"

"No," Toby said, without wavering. "Not at all. Emma's wonderful. It's just that"—he frowned and scratched his chin—"she lives in Harare and hasn't been back to the UK for nine years. Her last visit was just after the twins were born. She came for the christening."

"If The Trust funded her visit, might she be prepared to come and help look after them during your recuperation?"

Toby hesitated, then his eyes widened.

"I really have no idea. She might be. Since her husband passed away, she hasn't had much to keep her in Zimbabwe. In fact, she's been talking about coming for an extended visit. Although she hasn't met the twins in person since the christening, they video chat regularly. She won't be a total stranger to them."

"Would you like us to contact her for you?"

"And say what exactly?" Toby asked after a momentary hesitation. "'You don't know us, but your big sister's dead and we'd like you to come and look after her grandchildren?'" He scoffed. "What sort of a coward would that make me?"

"We'd be much more tactful than that, Toby. During your video calls, did you or Melissa tell Emma about The Trust?"

"I don't—" Toby placed his fingers to his temple, deep in thought. "Actually we did. At least, Melissa did. I've just remembered. Melissa referred to you as 'our wonderful benefactors'. She couldn't speak any more highly of you." Tears formed once again and threatened to spill over. "Emma really appreciated the way you supported us."

"So, that's settled. We'll call her for you."

"No you won't," Toby said, his delivery firm, absolute. "No, thank you. I'll call her. I've been meaning to do it for days, but I don't have access to a phone, and I don't have access to my contacts list. The police seized my mobile. Hoping to find evidence against me, I suppose. I was going to ask them for Emma's number, but the way they treated me, I wouldn't dream of it. They'd probably eavesdrop on the conversation. Not that I have anything to hide, but … you know? It's wrong."

"Yes, it is," Kaine agreed, as though he would never do such a thing—as though butter wouldn't melt. "They can occasionally resort to highly questionable practises."

Kaine tugged his briefcase from the floor and rested it on his lap. He opened it and pulled out a new and fully charged smartphone and its charging cable.

"Here," he said, leaning forwards and setting them on the bedside cabinet, within Toby's reach. "Courtesy of The Trust. I asked a colleague to set it up for you. I'm useless at that kind of thing. Apparently, he's installed all the usual apps, and I've added my details to the contacts list. Call me any time you need me. Night or day. I'll be staying in the area for a while."

"Thank you," Toby said, admiring the state-of-the-art device. "It's the same as the one I have."

"It is?" Kaine asked, keeping a straight face. "You'll know how to use it then?"

"Yes, thanks. I'll be able to download my contacts list

from the cloud. Assuming I can still remember my password." Again, he tapped his temple with an index finger.

"Good luck with that, Toby. I'm afraid I won't be able to help you with accessing the cloud thing," Kaine said, speaking the whole truth, although he did know a man who could do that very thing, should he be asked to do so.

Someone rapped twice on the door. It opened and a large, black woman wearing a cheery smile popped her head through the opening.

"Mornin', Mr Fabien," she called, laughter shining in her dark brown eyes. "Would you and your guest like anythin'? Tea? Coffee? Biscuits?"

"Decaf?" Toby asked, eyes wide.

"O' course." She laughed. "No caffeine allowed in here."

"Low-fat bikkies?" he added.

"Likewise," she answered through another chuckle.

Toby glanced at Kaine. "Mr Jeffries?"

"No, thanks. It's not long since I had breakfast."

The idea of drinking decaffeinated tea or coffee left Kaine cold, and it made him fear the approaching end of civilisation as he knew it. Decaffeinated coffee mystified him. He'd rather do without and resort to water.

"Nothing for my guest, Gladys, but I'll have my usual, please."

"Comin' right up," Gladys said, ducking back out through the door and returning with a tray which she placed on the bedside cabinet.

"Thank you, Gladys."

She smiled at Toby and then at Kaine, said, "Enjoy," and bustled from the room.

"I won't," Toby muttered to her back as the door swung quietly closed.

Alone again, Toby reached for his cup, leaving the saucer on the tray. He left the packet of Rich Tea biscuits on the side plate.

"Decaffeinated coffee," he said, quirking his upper lip as he peered at the dark brown liquid. "I ask you, what's the point?"

Kaine shrugged. "I have no idea." At least they'd found something in common.

Toby took a tentative sip, shook his head, and sipped again.

"Horrible stuff."

"Why suffer it, then?" Kaine asked.

"It's marginally better than the tea, and a definite improvement over the fruit juice." He sipped again, still grimacing, but not as much. "Besides, I don't have the heart to say no to Gladys. She's so resolutely cheerful, I'd hate to upset her." He finished his drink in three more sips. His hand shook as he returned the cup to the saucer.

"Would you do me a small favour?" Toby asked after pressing his hand to his ribs and settling back against the pillows once again.

"If I can."

"It's nothing onerous, I promise."

Kaine grinned. "I'll be the judge of that."

"Please take those things away with you," Toby said, eyeing the untouched Rich Teas. "If you leave them, Gladys might shame me into eating the blessed things. I really can't face them today."

"Okay, I can manage that," Kaine said. "Just as long as I don't have to eat any."

"Low fat, low sugar." Toby sneered. "No taste."

"Exactly. I think I'd rather go hungry."

Kaine dropped the biscuits into his briefcase, shut the lid, and snapped the catches closed.

"Now," he said, "is there anything I can get you before I go?"

"You're leaving?"

"Afraid so," he said, climbing to his feet. "I have other clients to see, but I will only be a phone call away. I promise."

"Would you mind passing me my reading glasses? They're in the cabinet drawer. The cleaners keep putting them away for some reason."

Kaine opened the drawer, found the glasses in their case, and handed them across.

"Anything else?"

"No, thanks. And thanks so much for all your help. You've been truly wonderful."

"Remember, I can make myself available anytime you need me."

Kaine pushed out a hand and they shook.

He left what he imagined was a much-relieved Toby and hurried from the hospital. Not a fan of health foods and drinks, Kaine didn't care much for hospitals either. He'd spent more than enough of his life in a surgical recovery ward.

Chapter Twenty-Six

Monday 5th July – Midday

Calliss Close, Stafford, Staffordshire, England

Kaine discovered The Green Man pub within a mile of the hospital. A weather-bleached banner on the side of the building promised, "Good Quality Food & Drink". He ordered a large, full-strength coffee and a goat's cheese salad from the bar and found a table in a quiet corner of the sun-drenched beer garden. He wore a plain, black, baseball cap, and the lenses of his non-prescription glasses had darkened in the sunshine, making it difficult for any nearby surveillance cameras armed with facial recognition to work their dark magic. At least, that was the hope.

He pulled a mobile from his pocket—a duplicate of the

one he'd given Toby—connected the earphones, and opened Corky's latest spyware app. The screen mirrored Toby's phone, and Kaine watched his client scroll through his recently recovered contact list. He found the entry for his sister-in-law, Emma Trulove, and the image paused. Kaine could imagine Toby working out how to break the terrible news. It wouldn't be easy.

Toby's handset picked up a knock on the hospital room's door, and Kaine listened through the earphones to a relentlessly cheerful Gladys collect Toby's crockery and wish him a pleasant day.

In the beer garden, a fresh-faced waitress in a blue-and-white-striped apron brought out his meal on a tray, smiled, and left him to it. At midday on a Monday, he was alone in the garden, which suited him. He placed the mobile on the table beside his plate and worked his way slowly through the meal which, surprisingly, lived up to its billing. The dressing on the salad was first class.

Five minutes after Gladys left, Toby picked up his phone again and finally gathered enough courage to dial Emma. Kaine closed the app to give them the privacy they deserved. He scrolled through his own contacts list and hit the requisite number. The call connected instantly.

"Whatcha, Mr K. How you diddling?" Corky's cheerful tones matched those of Gladys and seemed very much in keeping with the summery weather.

"Afternoon, Control. Any news from the Boys in Blue?" He spoke quietly, scanning the area for anyone taking undue interest, but the garden remained empty.

"Sure thing, Mr K. They've updated the file with the blood test results, and DI Fellows has called a briefing for the full investigative team at five o'clock this afternoon."

"Pity we can't be a fly on the wall for that," Kaine said, hiding his mouth behind his raised coffee mug as a middle-aged couple strolled into the garden and sat three tables away. The man—silver hair, neatly-trimmed, grey beard, casually dressed—nodded to Kaine while his partner reached for a menu. Kaine nodded back and added a polite smile.

"What makes you think Corky can't arrange that?" the IT guru asked.

"Okay, Control. I'll bite. What can you do?"

Corky chuckled. "Assuming DC Skarrats attends the briefing with his tablet activated—and since he never goes anywhere without it, that's a given—Corky's gonna be able to put you in the room right alongside 'em all."

Kaine smiled.

"Control," he said, "you never cease to amaze me."

"Yep. Corky's good, ain't he," Corky said through another chuckle.

"Yes, Control. You really are."

"Need anything more from ol' Corky?"

"Not at the moment, Control. Thanks again for everything."

"Not a problem. One of these days, Corky might need something from you in return, Mr K. Corky's just markin' your card, is all."

Kaine's ears pricked up. Corky had never asked for anything from him before. He'd never even hinted at the need for a favour. Whatever it entailed, Kaine wouldn't hesitate. He owed the IT wizard more than he could ever repay. One thing alone—removing all record of Lara from the internet—had earned Kaine's eternal gratitude.

"Not a problem, Control. You only have to ask."

"Thanks, Mr K. Corky knew he could rely on you. It ain't urgent, though. Not yet. He'll let you know if and when."

The call clicked into silence, leaving Kaine to wonder what Corky had in mind for him. Rather than waste time on idle speculation, Kaine reactivated the spyware, listened for a moment to a desolate and teary Emma Trulove, and powered it down again, leaving them alone to their shared grief.

Kaine finished his very decent meal, ordered a second coffee, and drank it while searching the web for the nearest comfortable hotel.

THE ABBEY PARK HOTEL, ideally located between Cavell Hospital and the Staffordshire Police HQ, offered expensive suites, a good-quality restaurant, and free Wi-Fi. Kaine chose a single room on the top floor with its own private fire escape. To the south, the room provided an excellent view of the Beaconside Sports Fields and the adjacent Stafford Crematorium. To the east, on Weston Road, stretched out the low-level buildings of Staffordshire Police HQ. If he knew the location of DI Fellows' briefing room and it had a window facing the hotel, Kaine might have been able to watch the meeting through a scope while listening to it through Skarrats' tablet.

Kaine lay on the soft bed, set his phone alarm for 16:30, and closed his eyes. He'd only caught a few hours' sleep since leaving the farm, and a siesta would set him up for the rest of the day. As a highly experienced, special forces operative, Kaine knew that rest could be as important a part of his prep as cleaning his weapon—which he'd done—and stocking his ration pack.

———

THE ALARM WOKE him from a refreshing, two-hour nap. Kaine showered, dressed, and powered up the recharged mobile. He connected the earphones, pressed the buds into his ears, and waited for the show to start.

Chapter Twenty-Seven

Monday 5th July - Riley Fellows

Staffordshire Police Station, Stafford, Staffordshire, England

Fellows, with Skarrats in tow, entered a stark but sunlit briefing room and stood in front of the smartboard. He waited. Three rows of hardbacked chairs, arranged in semi-circles, pointed towards the smartboard, their backs to the large window. Silence rippled from the front of the room to the back in a slow wave. Seventeen faces of varied ages stared up at him. Some expectant and keen, others world-weary and bored.

"Afternoon, all," he opened. "Sorry for the late call, but we've had some fresh intel on the case, and I wanted to bring everyone up to speed."

"Fabien's in the clear, guv?" Sergeant Edgar Clayton, a grey-haired and saggy-eyed veteran in charge of the CCTV unit piped up. He'd taken up his usual spot in the middle of the back row.

"As far as the blood work goes," Fellows said, "yes." He scanned the room and added, "For those who haven't heard yet, Tobias Fabien's blood results have come in. They're clean."

A loud murmur flowed around the room. Fellows waited for his troops to settle.

"Okay, more on that later, but you're up first, Annie."

For form's sake, Fellows started with the FLO. Showing concern for the innocent victims of the crash would look good in the duty log.

PC Annette Riggs—dark haired, dark eyed, and pleasantly rounded—sat up straighter. As the twins' FLO she knew the drill.

"The Protection Order is still in place," she said, "and the social worker, Leigh Bronze, has been paying regular visits to the host family, the Kendalls. Leigh has submitted an interim report"—Annie swiped to a new page on her tablet—"which states that as far as she is concerned, the twins are healthy and are being well cared for." She lowered the tablet to her lap and fixed Fellows with a bright smile.

"Excellent," he said. "Anything else?"

Annie shook her head. "No, guv. That's it."

"Thanks, Annie," Fellows said. "Right, now the blood results are in, what do we have?" He scanned the room, staring at all the blank faces. "Come on, people. Speak to me."

A hand at the back of the room rose slowly into the air. The hand and attached arm belonged to Sergeant Clayton.

"Yes, Sergeant?" Fellows asked, bracing for impact.

"How the hell did they come back so fast, sir?" Clayton asked. "The blood results, I mean. We weren't expecting them for months."

"No idea," Fellows answered.

"The tests were run by someone called Dr Robyn Spence," Skarrats piped up, reading the name from his ever-present tablet. His crutch.

"Not that it matters," Fellows added.

"Oh it matters alright, sir," Clayton said, adding the slightest of frowns.

"Really?" Fellows said.

"Well, if Racer-Colby are prepared to bump the Fabien test up to the top of the queue, maybe they can be persuaded to do the same thing for a few others." He sniffed. "I've got a dozen scrotes waiting on blood test results. Right now, those same scrotes are driving around free as birds. Probably high as kites, too. Accidents waiting to happen. It's bloody criminal having to wait so long."

A few of the officers close to Clayton nodded or grumbled their agreement. The nearest slapped him on the back and said, "You got that right, Edgar."

"Maybe the team at Racer-Colby are open to persuasion," Fellows said, staring hard at the senior sergeant. "Why not give them a call?"

"Yeah," Clayton snorted, "and risk them taking offence and relegating all my samples to the bottom of the queue? Not likely. Just making a point, guv."

"Okay, Edgar," Fellows said, "now you've broken the ice, why not take the floor."

"Sir?"

Fellows stared hard at the man who was old enough to be his father. "Any results from the accident boards or the media appeal?"

Clayton leaned forwards in his chair and rested his fists on his thighs. He looked uncomfortable. Trouble with his back again, no doubt. The old codger would complain about his raging lumbago to anyone who stood still long enough to receive the earbashing.

"No one's come to us with any dashcam footage of the incident, and there are no surveillance cameras within two miles of the crash site."

Now tell me something I don't know.

"Any film of the Raptor in the area?" Skarrats asked.

"Yes," Clayton said, sitting up a little straighter, easing his back. "We have it leaving the motorway services' car park seven minutes before the Fabiens' Toyota fills up at the petrol station. After that, it doesn't show up anywhere until later that night in the town centre."

"Any signs of damage to the front end?"

Clayton grimaced and inclined his head.

"'Fraid not sir. The only clear pics we have are from the rear. The front-facing images are too fuzzy or distant to show any detail. It's as though Dylan Bentley knew exactly where he needed to go to avoid all the head-on shots."

"Either that or he got lucky," a nearby constable suggested.

"Nobody can get that lucky," Clayton grunted. He clenched his fists and dug them into his thighs. "The kid's as bent as his old man. Are you sure the Raptor's clean, sir?"

"Spotless," Fellows said. "The SCIU has cleared it. Isn't that right, Doc?" He nodded to PC Jake "Doc" Kildare, who represented the Serious Collision Investigation Unit at the briefing.

"We went over it twice, sir. Eight thousand and seventy-five miles on the clock," Kildare said. "The truck's near-enough spanking new. Barely a mark on it and definitely no indication of any front-end impact."

"And it wasn't fitted with a dashcam?" Clayton asked, relaxing his fists, but keeping his hands in his lap as though using his arms to hold himself upright.

"Not when we examined it," Kildare said. "No dashcam, no cabling, no holder. Although it could have been removed before we impounded it."

"What about the crash scene?" Skarrats asked.

"We found nothing to confirm the involvement of a second vehicle. No skid marks. But given the amount of rainwater on the road surface, I wouldn't have expected to find any."

"Trace evidence?" Fellows asked. "Detritus?"

"None. No pieces of broken Raptor. No paint transfer on the rear of the Toyota, either. In fact, as our interim report stated, there was nothing to indicate a rear-end collision. However," he paused, seemingly for emphasis, "that's not surprising, considering how badly damaged the Toyota was. Crushed almost beyond recognition. Bent around the oak tree like a horseshoe. How the twins walked away without any serious injuries beggars belief. If I were a religious man, I might be inclined to call it a miracle."

"So," Clayton said, "what's your *diagnosis*, Doc?" Once again, he smiled, as did his three-person team and a number of the others around them. "Definitely no second car involvement?"

Kildare scrunched up his face and took a moment to think.

"We can't say anything that categoric," he said, hedging his bets as would be expected, "but there's no evidence at the scene to show it was anything other than a single-vehicle incident." He paused again before raising his index finger. "In fact, if not for the black-box unit showing the Toyota's speed at the time it left the road, I might have gone so far as to call it a tragic accident."

"Thanks, Doc," Fellows said.

"However," Kildare said, his finger still raised, "I can't be one hundred percent definitive about the 'single-vehicle incident' diagnosis, either." As he finished, he smiled, falling in with the joke at his expense. "It's a real shame the Toyota didn't have a rear-facing dashcam."

"Isn't it just," Fellows said.

"And," Kildare added, "it's even more of a shame that Jackie Bentley didn't install a dashcam in his Raptor."

"Yes," DC Jenny Stockton, the team's lead Digital Forensic Technician, agreed. "And it's not at all suspicious, that. Is it?"

"Not at all," Skarrats said.

Fellows nodded his thanks to Doc Kildare and said, "Over to you, Jenny."

All eyes turned to the woman sitting in the front row. A new-age Goth, she had dark eyes and darker hair, shaved tight at the back and sides but left tall and spiky on top. Pencil thin to the point of emaciation, with high cheekbones sharp enough to slice paper, she nodded.

"Yes, sir?"

"Come up with anything useful?"

"Nothing, sir," she said, scrunching up her nose so much, the silver nose ring she wore glinted in the sunlight shining through the side window. "There's no footage of the acci—er, the incident."

"I understand Jackie Bentley gave you access to his dashcam cloud account?" Fellows asked.

"Yes, sir. He did."

"Very public-spirited of him," Clayton groused.

Fellows frowned at the disgruntled sergeant but otherwise let the interruption pass.

"Okay, Jenny," Fellows said, rolling his hand forward. "Keep going."

She nodded.

"As everyone here knows, Mr Bentley"—Clayton snorted at "Mister" and earned one of Fellows' silent rebukes—"owns a fleet of vehicles including Raptors and stretch limos. He hires them out for special events. You know the sort of thing. Hen and stag nights, bar mitzvahs, weddings, school proms, birthdays."

"And none have dashcams?" Skarrats asked.

"No, Sarge," Jenny said, a note of triumph in her voice. "They *all* have dashcams, and all are linked to the company's cloud. That is, all except …" She paused and hiked one of her pierced eyebrows.

"The lime-green Raptor we impounded," Fellows announced, filling in for her.

Jenny tapped her nose and again the silver ring glinted. "Spot on, sir. How did you guess?"

"Call me psychic. So, Dylan or Jackie may have deleted the accident footage. Can you restore it?"

"No, sir. You don't get it," Jenny said, patience itself. "If the Raptor in question ever did have a dashcam fitted, it was never linked to the cloud. No link means no footage to delete … or recover."

"And what did Jackie have to say when you asked him about it?"

"He said … just a sec and I'll give you the direct quote." She lowered her gaze to the tablet on her lap and read from the screen. "He said, 'Oops, sorry 'bout that, love. We mainly use that particular Raptor as a family runabout. We did plan to fit a dashcam but never got around to it. Didn't I tell you?'. Laughed when he said it, too. Smarmy beggar."

"The arsehole was yanking your chain," Clayton grumbled.

For once, Fellows let the interruption pass. He could understand where the veteran sergeant was coming from.

"So," Fellows said, "there's no dashcam footage?"

"None in the cloud," Jenny agreed, "but that doesn't mean there's no primary recording saved on a stand-alone dashcam somewhere."

A fresh-faced PC Wigton, sitting in the middle row, raised his hand.

"Yes, Wiggy?" Skarrats called. "Speak up, lad."

"I was wondering," Wigton said, his delivery timid. "I don't suppose there's any chance of us getting a warrant to search the Bentley's workshop and home, is there?"

"With what we have now?" Fellows answered, his energy levels fading. "I doubt it."

"I could pull an application together if you like, sir," Wigton suggested, keen as a knife. He'd made an early application to join CID, and the bright spark would do anything to support his case.

Another murmur of comments undulated around the room. Some approving, most not. A male voice close to Wigton muttered, "Brown-noser."

Fellows held up his hand and patted the air for silence.

"Thanks for the offer, PC Wigton, but let's park that for now," he said, stepping back and perching the cheeks of his arse on a sturdy table, after testing it first. Some were less solid than others, and he'd have looked a right plum if he ended up on his rump.

"Okay, let's take a step back and look at what we have. Matt, throw up the presentation, please."

Skarrats dipped his head, tapped the screen of his tablet a few times, and the smartboard attached to the wall behind them burst into life.

Fellows had seen the presentation ahead of the briefing, and he already knew what to expect.

Chapter Twenty-Eight

Monday 5th July - Riley Fellows

Staffordshire Police Station, Stafford, Staffordshire, England

A row of five rectangular images popped onto the top of the smartboard.

The first image showed a downhill shot of the scene of the RTI—the Toyota C-HR wrapped around the base of a large, oak tree, hanging over the inky waters of Rook Pond. Below the picture ran a few lines of text, detailing the date and time of the crash, the road conditions in place at the time, names of occupants, name of decedent.

Image two showed the same car as it appeared at the police garage, with details of its date and time of arrival and a brief rundown of its crumpled condition.

Image three represented a headshot of Tobias Fabien, a screenshot taken from the bedside interview. To Fellows, it indicated a bruised and battered man struggling to come to terms with his loss and his injuries. The first row of text read, "Victim/Suspect #1". The subsequent rows gave Fabien's details, including date of birth, home address, and occupation—high school English teacher, retired. A paragraph at the bottom of the column outlined Fabien's claim that he'd been deliberately forced off the road.

Image four displayed the lime-green Ford Raptor at the police garage. Five lines of text below the photo gave the truck's registration number, the date and location of manufacture, the VIN, the time and date it had been collected from the Bentleys' workshop, and the single word, "Undamaged".

Image five had been taken from an online news story with the headline, "Local Businessman Wins Euro Lotto!" In the shot, Dylan and Jackie Bentley stood holding up either end of a supersized cheque representing Jackie's massive Euro Lottery win. Skarrats had allocated a mere three lines of text for Dylan, including the date and time he'd been interviewed, and his assertion that he had no knowledge of, nor involvement in, the fatal crash. Skarrats had allocated a load more space for Jackie, leading with his rep as a former soldier, a well-known, local hard man, and a suspected drug baron. How he'd managed to avoid more than one prison sentence in his miserable life who knew. For such a man to have won millions in the lottery demonstrated the innate unfairness of life.

"Matt has already loaded the presentation onto the PNC," Fellows said. "Access it in your own time, but let's go through the obvious. Point one"—he raised his right, index finger—"Tobias Fabien claims to have been run off the road by that Raptor." He pointed to the fourth picture.

"But as PC Kildare confirmed," Skarrats said, speaking up clearly, "there's nothing to show that the Raptor ever came into contact with the Toyota."

"Why would Fabien lie?" Fellows asked, waving his hand to encourage a response from the team.

"That's obvious, isn't it?" Clayton called out.

"Go on, Edgar," Fellows said.

"To deflect attention away from himself," Clayton answered.

"Keep going."

"Because he's a crap driver who caused his wife's death and he's scared witless about shouldering the blame."

"But he's been driving for over forty years," PC Wigton said, speaking up above the growing chorus of agreement. "He's never had so much as a speeding ticket, and we now know he definitely wasn't driving under the influence."

"It only takes one time to screw up, Wiggy," an older PC sitting next to him said. "The weather at the time was appalling, and he was speeding."

Wigton shook his head, showing enough spirit to advance his case for a move into CID.

"At the time of the crash, he was three miles an hour over the limit," Wigton said. "And that's well within the margin of error for measurement. Ordinarily, at that speed, no traffic cop would even have pulled him over."

"But the bugger killed his wife," Clayton announced.

"According to Mr Fabien, he was trying to get away from Dylan Bentley in the Raptor," Wigton responded, standing up well under the onslaught.

"So why did Fabien pick on the Raptor?" Fellows asked the room.

"If I may," DC Stockton said, holding up a hand.

"The floor's all yours, Jenny," Fellows said, giving her another go.

"Well," she said, her lips thinning, "according to Mr Fabien, twenty minutes before the crash, he had that stand-up confrontation with Dylan Bentley. A confrontation that nearly came to blows, which would have terrified him."

"Does the surveillance footage confirm any of that?" Fellows asked Clayton.

"Unfortunately not," the irascible sergeant piped up. "The cameras didn't pick up the altercation. The angle didn't allow it. We have images of all the participants entering and leaving the food hall seating area, but there's no footage of the argument."

"Anything we could use to support a case against Dylan Bentley?" Fellows asked. "Should we need to."

"Nothing, guv. Nothing useable and there's no sound on the recording."

"Thanks, Sergeant."

"You're welcome, guv," Clayton said.

"Who contacted the Good Samaritan?" Fellows asked, although he'd already received DC Stockton's full report.

"I did, guv," she answered, playing up to the crowd. "I finally got hold of Mr"—she read from her tablet—"Barraclough on Friday. He confirmed Fabien's story. Dylan Bentley was the aggressor, but he backed away when Barraclough stepped up. Barraclough also confirmed that Dylan threatened Fabien before he ran away … tail between his legs."

Fellows nodded. Typical behaviour for Dylan Bentley—a first-class bully and a coward.

One of the guys sitting close by sniggered at Stockton's parting comment.

"Thanks for your input, Jenny."

"You and the sarge interviewed Dylan, guv," the annoyingly youthful PC Ashcroft in the back row asked. "What did he have to say for himself?"

"Not a lot. He gave a prepared statement through his solicitor, and followed it with the standard 'no comment' interview."

"Surprise, surprise," Clayton said, and followed with a muttered, "The smug, little toerag."

This time, Fellows couldn't find a reason to contradict the grey-haired sergeant. He'd heard enough, and he stood.

"Okay," he said to the whole room, "the way I see it, we've got at least two viable scenarios here. First, Fabien drove too fast for the conditions and caused his wife's death through carelessness. Second, Fabien's telling the truth and Dylan Bentley deliberately ran him off the road." He took a moment to scan the room before continuing. "Question regarding scenario one. Can we put a case together that will convince the CPS to press charges against Fabien?"

He waited. For once, the room fell silent.

"Anyone?"

PC Janet Boscombe, sitting four chairs to Clayton' left, raised her hand.

"Yes, Janet?"

"There's a simpler alternative," she said.

"Which is?" Fellows asked.

"Fabien aquaplaned through a puddle and lost control. Simple accident." She shrugged. "Tragic, but an accident just the same."

"But he was speeding," Skarrats said, his voice losing some emphasis. "We can do him for that."

"He wasn't speeding by much. There's a margin of error," Wigton said, reinforcing his earlier comment.

Fellows drew in a breath and released it slowly.

"Once more, I ask you, can we make that case to the CPS?" he asked. "Answer? Not with what we have here. Sorry, Matt, but they'll throw speeding and careless driving charges back at us as 'not being in the public interest'."

"And the second scenario," Jenny Stockton said, "the Raptor attack?"

"Right," Fellows answered. "Let's assume Fabien's telling the truth and Dylan Bentley *did* run him off the road —which is starting to look more and more likely—how can we prove it? Anybody? Doc?" He nodded to PC Kildare.

"Yes, sir?"

"Remind me. When did you impound the Raptor?" he asked, even though the date was on the smartboard.

"Last Thursday, sir. July the first. Late afternoon."

"Five days after the crash."

"Yes, sir," Kildare answered, nodding.

"Five days," Fellows repeated. He turned, stepped closer to the smartboard, and stabbed his index finger into the fourth picture. "Jackie Bentley owns a garage with a work-shop, and five days is more than enough time to repair any damage to the Raptor. That's one hell of a window of opportunity."

"I'm afraid not, sir," Clayton said, an apologetic look on his crumpled face. For once, he appeared deadly serious.

"Why not?"

"We have CCTV images on the afternoon of Sunday the 27th, around three forty-five. It shows the Raptor driving towards the Bentley's home in Brocton Village. And the front end's undamaged."

"Could he have repaired it earlier in the morning?" Fellows asked, looking at the doc.

"It's possible," Kildare said, nodding, "but it'd be tight."

"But possible?"

"I suppose so."

PC Julian "Tuck" Friar, one of the officers in Clayton'
CCTV unit—who'd been uncharacteristically quiet up to
that point—cleared his throat loudly.

"Sir," he said.

"Yes, Tuck?"

"Jackie and Dylan were in The Bull on Rigby Road for
most of Sunday afternoon."

"What time?"

"We have them on CCTV entering the pub at"—he
glanced at his notepad—"eleven forty-seven. They stayed
until five minutes to three."

"How did they get there?" Skarrats asked. "On foot?"

"No, Sarge. They drove. Parked in the car park," Friar
answered, drawing it out.

"What in?" Fellows asked.

Friar grimaced. "Would you believe a lime-green
Raptor?"

"The same lime-green Raptor as that?" Fellows asked,
jerking a thumb at the fourth image on the smartboard.

"Looks like it," Friar answered. "Same colour. ... Same
number plates."

"And it's condition?" Skarrats asked.

Friar stared at the smartboard and said, "Undamaged."

"Bugger," Fellows said and raised a hand in apology. "I
don't suppose it could be a different car?"

"Possible, but unlikely," Friar answered, shrugging. "Like
I said, it was showing the same licence plates as the one on
the CCTV at the service station."

"A clone?" someone in the front row offered.

Again, Friar shrugged. "It's not impossible, I suppose.
Difficult to prove after the event, though."

"How many lime-green Raptors do we have in the county?" Skarrats asked.

"At this point," Fellows said, sighing, shoulders sagging, "more than one would be enough to leave enough room for doubt. Anyone check with the DVLA yet?"

"I did, sir," Friar answered. "On Friday. They finally got back to me this morning. Apparently, they've had a massive system failure."

Now tell me something new.

"And?" Skarrats snapped. "Christ, this is painful. Like pulling teeth."

"In Staffordshire, there are four Raptors in lime green, three in ivory white, and one in gunmetal black," Friar said. "They're all registered to ... wait for it ..." He paused to build up the tension.

"Bentley Hire Fleet?" Clayton butted in, left eyebrow hitched.

Friar nodded.

"S'right," he said. "Got it in one. You must be psychic, Edgar."

"*Psycho*, more like," someone in the back row snarked.

Fellows let the jibe pass.

"You couldn't have told us this earlier, Tuck?" Fellows asked, slowly fuming.

Friar sat up straighter. "No one asked me earlier, guv."

"So," Fellows said, biting back an angry retort, "we have at least four of these bloody green pickups running around the county?"

"Yes, sir." Friar nodded.

"All with the same licence plate?"

"No, sir," Friar answered, deadpan. "That would be illegal. They are similar, but sequential. BHF 101 to BHF 108. That's eight Raptors in total."

"Bloody hell," a PC sitting in the middle row said. Fellows never could pronounce his Polish surname properly —too many consecutive consonants. "That must have cost a mint."

"Around five grand a piece," Friar announced.

A chorus of groans ran around the room along with a few muffled expletives. One joker complained that his car cost less than that.

"Bentley's a multimillionaire," Friar said. "Forty grand means nothing to him."

"And he isn't going to dirty his hands as a grease monkey," Fellows said, stepping further away from the table. "He has a mechanic, right?" He shot Skarrats an enquiring look.

"He has, sir," Skarrats said, reading from his tablet. "Bloke called Tony Epps."

Fellows nodded his thanks.

"Okay," he said, "who interviewed Epps?"

Kildare's hand shot up. "I did, guv."

"What did he have to say for himself?"

"Said that no work had been done on any of the Raptors in the past fortnight apart from the usual servicing and valeting."

"And where was he on Sunday the 27th?"

"Claims he was at home all day, fighting a hangover and watching Sky Sports on the telly."

"Can he prove it?" Skarrats asked.

Kildare shook his head. "Not really. Epps lives alone. I paid a visit to his next-door neighbours. They heard his TV that day. Apparently, Epps is a little mutton. Always has the box turned up loud and the walls are paper thin. They didn't see him leave the house or return to it."

"Could he have slipped out," Fellows said, "and slipped back in unnoticed?"

"It's possible, guv," Kildare admitted.

"All things are possible, Doc," Clayton said, unhelpfully.

Kildare continued. "There are no traffic cameras in the area, and no one in the street has a doorbell cam."

"Where did you interview Epps, Doc?" Fellows asked.

"At the workshop."

"With Jackie Bentley looking on?"

"Well," Kildare said, scratching his chin, "he wasn't exactly in the office with us, but he was hanging around, looking moody."

"Making sure Epps kept schtum, you reckon?" Skarrats asked.

"Possibly," Kildare answered, "but I couldn't exactly do the 'perp walk' and drag Epps down to the station, could I? I mean, he wasn't actually a suspect."

"This whole thing stinks," Fellows snapped. "Bentley's bent, and so's his bloody son."

"We don't have anything solid on either of them, sir," Annette Riggs said, adding a note of restraint. "Not enough to arrest them or interview them under caution."

"Nonetheless, I want them taken in and taken down. Any suggestions?"

"If Epps worked on the Raptor, or swapped the plates with that clean one on the Sunday, he's the weak link. We should talk to him again," Skarrats suggested. "Put some pressure on."

Fellows nodded. "Agreed. But we'll do it away from the workshop."

"Bring him in, you mean?"

"No, Matt," Fellows said. "You and I are going to call

on him at home this evening, where he feels safe. And tomorrow, we'll visit the hospital."

"What for, guv?" Skarrats asked.

"You're going to tell Fabien about the blood test result," Fellows said, his face a blank mask. "And I'll tell him we're not going to press charges for careless driving or for speeding. I imagine the poor man could use a bit of good news about now."

"Yeah," Skarrats said, unable to look Fellows in the eye. "I guess he could."

And you're going to apologise for the "familicide" bollocks.

Fellows turned to face the rest of the team. "Briefing over. I'll expect every team leader's report on my desk by close of play tomorrow. And please"—he paused to add emphasis—"someone come up with something. If we can't take this case to the CPS soon, we'll have to drop it. And that goes against the grain. A woman is dead. Don't forget that. Dismissed."

Before anyone could move, Fellows headed out of the briefing room, beckoning Skarrats with a crooked forefinger.

"You're with me, Matt."

Chapter Twenty-Nine

Tuesday 6th July - Pre-Dawn

Eccleshall Way, Stafford, Staffordshire, England

Kaine checked the time on his diver's watch. 02:42.

Situated in a discreet quadrant of a rundown, industrial estate, the premises of Bentley Hire Fleet stood alone and deserted, surrounded on three sides by deep woods and thick scrubland.

He'd been on site since before midnight and had yet to see a single vehicle, let alone a security patrol. The building —a fifteen-metre-tall warehouse with brick and corrugated-metal walls and a steep, A-framed roof—held enough room to house half a dozen double-decker buses and all the equipment required to service them.

Kaine, dressed for clandestine, night manoeuvres—all in

black with camo paint breaking up the exposed skin on his face—had scouted the perimeter fence, looking for a weakness. Made of rusted steel-mesh and topped with spirals of razor wire, he'd found no obvious point of entry apart from the double gates at the front of the commercial unit, that used to be a workshop for a defunct bus and coach company. A tarnished, stainless-steel chain and a heavy-duty padlock held the gates together. With no razor-proof matting available and no desire to slice himself to ribbons, it left picking the lock as his only option for entry. But that had its own problems—he'd have to stand in the open for as long as it took to pick an unknown padlock. Not a happy thought, but one he'd have to overcome if he wanted to force his way inside. At least he'd brought along his proper, metal pick set this time. His small, ceramic pick—the one he always secreted in his palm for missions such as this—wouldn't be up to the job.

Kaine melted into the shadow formed by a row of dumpsters and the corner of a brick building across the road from the gates and dropped to one knee. He pressed the earpiece and held it down for a two count.

"*Whatcha, Mr K. How you diddling?*"

"I'm fine, thanks, Control. Have you done your thing? Over."

"*Sure have, Mr K. The industrial estate's surveillance system has fallen over. … Wonder how that happened? Shame though, eh?*"

"It is," Kaine answered, smiling. "Such a shame. And the workshop? Over."

"*Their internal surveillance cameras deffo ain't hooked up to the net. It means Corky can't gain access remotely. Which is why you need to do your stuff with the dongle.*"

"So, I'm going in blind? Over."

"Not necessarily." Corky chuckled.

"What do you mean? Over." Kaine looked over his shoulder, half-expecting a repeat of the Walthamstow incident, where Corky unexpectedly foisted Sean Freeman on him.

"Corky's arranged a drone flyby. It's overhead right now. Frodo's piloting it."

Bloody hell.

"He is? Over."

"Yeah, the bloke's at it like a kid with a new toy. Lovin' it."

Kaine listened. Apart from the gentle wind sighing through the mesh fencing, and the constant, low rumble of middle-of-the-night traffic on the nearby M6, there was silence.

"Are you sure?" he asked. "I can't hear a drone. Over."

"It's high up and running on stealth mode."

"Spectacular. It's as silent as the grave here, Control. Over."

"That's good," Corky shot back, happily.

"Where did you launch from? Over."

"Wouldn't you like to know."

"That's why I asked. Over."

"Corky and Frodo are in a van on the industrial estate half a kilometre south of you, Mr K. Makes a nice change for us to get out and about. Stretch our legs, like. Say hello to the captain, Frodo."

"Hello to the captain, Captain," Frodo said in his singsong voice.

Kaine hadn't heard him speak since delivering him into Corky's care. The youngster sounded chipper and not at all distracted. Again, Kaine smiled.

"So you're nearby? Over."

"That's what Corky said, isn't it? Fancy a meet and greet after you're done there?"

"That would be great, Control," Kaine said, trying not

to sound too shocked at the idea. "I'd like to shake the hand of the man who does so much for us. Over."

"*Corky don't do handshakes, Mr K. A person can catch too many nasty, little germs that way.*"

"Fair enough, Control. Let's table that for the moment. How's the drone looking? Over."

"*The IR camera's coming up clear. There ain't nobody in the immediate vicinity or inside the workshop. No one warm-bodied at least. We can see you, though. Shining bright in the corner by them rubbish bins. Looks like you is good to go.*"

"Thanks, Control. I'm going silent, but keeping the comms open. Over."

The wind shifted direction and Kaine caught the merest hum of an electric motor overhead. The drone. He waited for the noise to fade before preparing to move out. Kaine stood, but movement in the periphery caught his attention. He reversed back into the shadow and crouched.

Slowly and with caution, a skinny fox wandered into the middle of the road. Head raised, sniffing the air, its heavy brush trailed on the tarmac. The animal stopped and looked directly at Kaine long enough to confirm the absence of a threat. He turned, trotted across the road, and came up short of the fence. He sniffed again, then turned left, heading away from the double gates. The fox followed the wire along the front, around the corner, and disappeared into a tangle of undergrowth.

Seconds later, the same fox reappeared inside the fence. He scampered across the parking bays in front of the workshop and vanished into the shadows of the enormous building.

"Hello, Mr Fox," Kaine muttered. "How d'you get in there?"

With eyes peeled and ears open, Kaine darted across the

road and followed the route the fox had taken. He reached the corner where the fence ducked back into the darkness. Five paces in, he saw it—a flattened patch of long grass in the verge at the foot of the chain-link. A patch so small and seemingly insignificant in the overgrown verge, he'd missed it during his initial recce. He ducked down, patted the area where the grass hadn't been strimmed for months, and found a rusted break in the mesh at the base where the aged fence had been anchored into the concrete footing. A small gap—no more than sixty centimetres wide and eight at its highest. Too small.

Kaine kneeled and grabbed the exposed links. Sharp points dug into his thin, leather gloves. He took a breath. Heaved. Nothing happened. He gritted his teeth, tensed his shoulders, heaved again. The muscles in his arms and back strained. Despite the cool air, sweat broke out on his face, dripped into his eyes, and stung. He blinked them clear. Two more links popped out of the cement. A third. The gap lengthened to a metre wide, twenty centimetres high, maybe twenty-one. He strained again, but the fencing held tight. He gasped, released his hold, breathed again. His hands ached, and he flexed his fingers to restore the blood flow.

Despite Corky's overwatch, Kaine stole a quick look around the perimeter to confirm that tearing the fence hadn't raised any alarms. All clear. He shrugged the thin and lightweight backpack from his shoulders. If the backpack wouldn't fit through the gap, neither would he.

He grabbed the loosest link, tugged on the fence, and stuffed the backpack through the opening. It passed easily enough.

Now it's your turn, old man.

Kaine dropped prone, flipped onto his back, and wriggled through the hole. His head—turned sideways to protect his face—made it through easily enough, but a protruding wire snagged on his jacket, caught, and pinned him in position.

Bugger it.

Over his head, the fox barked three times in rapid succession. It sounded like derisive laughter.

"No need for that, mate," Kaine grumbled. "If I'm stuck in here, so are you."

An owl hooted in the nearby woods, calling to its mate. The mate didn't answer. Traffic still thrummed on the motorway. Life continued around him, and he lay stuck to the fence like an insect pinned to a display board.

C'mon, Kaine. Can't lie here all night.

Kaine forced the air from his lungs to collapse his ribcage and heaved the bottom of the fence away from the concrete. Straining, forcing, he wriggled his shoulders, shuffled his hips, and dug his heels into the turf. The wire link tore away from his jacket and released his chest. He slipped free and continued to writhe, keeping up the momentum. The fence tugged on his waist and hips but didn't catch. Seconds later, he squirmed free.

Kaine rolled onto his front, scrambled to his feet, and snatched up the backpack. He raced across the concrete car park to the deep shadow cast by the side of the building and slammed his back against the brickwork. Breathing deep and fast, he listened carefully, but heard nothing he didn't expect to hear. He shot a quick glance back to where he'd scrambled under the fence. Thankfully, in the shadows thrown by the undergrowth, the break remained pretty much invisible. Quickly, his breathing returned to normal.

He tapped the earpiece once.

"Alpha One to Control. Are you still reading me? Over."

"*Corky's still here, Mr K,*" he said, his response instant.

"Anything? Over?"

"*No alarms. You're in the clear so far.*"

"Excellent," Kaine said. "I'm going in. Over."

"*Good luck. Corky's gonna keep listening.*"

"Thanks, Control. I'll keep the comms open. Over."

Hugging tight to the brickwork, Kaine hurried along the side of the building, turned right at the end of the wall, and ducked further into darkness. The fence stood three metres back from the rear wall, separated by a gravel path dotted with thistles, dandelions, and buttercups.

Ten metres along the back wall, the rusted metalwork of an external fire escape pushed up into the night sky. Kaine climbed the metal staircase. Each tread creaked as he added his weight. Unavoidable. He reached the top platform unchallenged and studied the solid-looking fire door. Its flat, metal panel and riveted, horizontal bars seemed strong and impressive. It appeared like a solid barrier to forced entry, but exposure to the elements, the passage of time, and the lack of maintenance had played its part. Without its protective layers of paint, the wooden frame surrounding the fire door had rotted and warped. The gap between the edge of the door and the jamb had widened. Not much of a gap, but wide enough for his purposes.

"Alpha One to Control. I've reached the fire door. Over."

"*Corky's still here, Mr K. All's quiet on the northern front.*" As usual, he chuckled at his own naff joke.

Kaine removed two lengths of titanium-aluminium-alloy microwire from the backpack. The first had a right-angled arm formed on one end. The second had a hook instead of the straight arm. Both had padded, D-shaped handles on the non-operative ends. He'd ordered the tools from Sean Freeman after an online discussion about different methods of breaking and entering, and Freeman knew how to fabricate such equipment. After months of redundancy, Kaine had finally found a use for them.

Kaine fed the first wire into the gap two-thirds of the way up the non-hinged edge of the door. He turned the handle anticlockwise through ninety degrees and locked it against the inner face of the fire door.

Here goes nothing.

Kaine tugged on the handle, slowly adding more tension. The microwire was so thin, he found it impossible to believe the handle wouldn't snap off in his fingers, but it held firm. The door eased further away from the frame, not much, but enough to allow the hooked wire to pass between the edge of the door and the shoulder of the jamb.

"Hook in place. I'm searching for the push bar. Over."

Kaine slid the hook downwards, away from the lever. After travelling fifteen centimetres, it found an obstruction. The push bar. He rotated the handle clockwise and engaged the hook.

"Push bar found. Ready? Over."

"*Corky's ready, Mr K. Go for it.*"

Kaine held his breath and tugged on the handle. The fire door clunked open.

A siren blared.

Kaine's heart lurched.

Chapter Thirty

Tuesday 6th July - Pre-Dawn

Eccleshall Way, Stafford, Staffordshire, England

An ambulance siren wailed in the middle distance, the Doppler effect showing it moving away at high speed.

Kaine's heart rate slowed. He breathed again.

"Control? Anything? Over."

"All clear, Mr K. You is good to go."

Kaine tugged on the door. It creaked outwards against the slight resistance of a soft closer. He hung the backpack from his shoulder and crept inside, allowing the door to close quietly behind him.

High-level windows and double rows of translucent rooflights allowed a pale, amber glow to filter in from the streetlights outside. The resultant, ambient light rendered the NVGs in Kaine's backpack redundant. One less thing to worry about.

The fire escape's platform—its textured tread plates worn nearly smooth from years of heavy use—emerged into a rear corner of the building. It formed a gap between rows of cubicles that created a high-level, wrap-around, mezzanine floor on three sides. The fourth wall, the far side, remained clear, leaving room for a set of full-width, roller shutters.

Ahead of him, a wide, open-treaded, metal staircase descended to the ground floor.

To his left, the row of units—the nearest of which smelled rank enough to be a toilet—stretched the full, one-hundred-metre length of the rear wall. To his right, a shorter row of office pods clung to the short-side wall. Opposite, another row of storage cubicles ran along the front wall.

A one-metre-wide balcony stepped out in front of the units, and metal railings bolted to its outer edge offered a degree of protection against a five-and-a-half-metre plummet to the unforgiving, concrete floor below.

The pods hung suspended from the eaves and supported by vertical I-beams formed from structural steel. During its time as a bus depot, the units would have housed dozens of maintenance crew and office staff.

A deep chill ran through the workshop which smelled of damp, engine oil, and car polish. In winter, it would have been impossible to heat properly, and the balcony's worn treadplates represented a significant health and safety issue. Any moisture on the plates would have created a dangerous slip hazard.

Kaine dropped into a crouch, crept towards the edge of the balcony, and stopped before breaking the line of pods, trying to keep hidden. He kneeled on the cold, textured tread plate and took in the vast cavern that spread out below him.

He whispered, "I'm inside, Control. Over."

"*Corky needs pictures, Mr K.*"

"One moment. Over."

Kaine pulled the burner phone from his trouser pocket and dialled. The video call connected and revealed a smiling Corky dressed in a green polo shirt. Kaine flipped the camera and pointed it out over the void.

"Are you getting this? Over."

"*Yep. Picture's perfect. Can you scan the place, please?*"

For Corky's benefit, Kaine stood and poked the burner out past the edge of the office unit and panned the camera slowly from right to left.

The workshop opened out below, its concrete floor cluttered with maintenance equipment. Five white, stretch limos lined the rear wall, parked in an angled row, side by side, their rear ends backed into the wall. Opposite the limos, hugging the front wall, stood a row of Ford Raptors. Four green and three white. A gap showed the black one as missing. Jackie Bentley's preferred ride.

Between the rows of flashy vehicles, an inspection pit had been cut deep into the floor. It ran half the length of the building, the only nod to health and safety being the reinforced, one-metre-tall, guard rails running parallel to each long side of the pit and set wide enough to allow room for busses and coaches to drive over the top. The narrow ends, near and far, stood open and unprotected.

At the far end of the garage, a set of roller shutters with a built-in, wicket door provided normal, day-to-day access to the building.

"*Point it up, Mr K.*"

Kaine angled the camera lens towards the roof.

Structural-steel, A-frame trusses extended across the width of the roof. Spaced four metres apart, they ran overhead and away into the distance. A cluster of four surveillance cameras hung from the middle of trusses two and fourteen. Together, the cameras would provide a comprehensive, bird's-eye view of the floorspace below and the suspended balcony. The layout gave Kaine a bad feeling. A really bad feeling.

"There you go, Mr K. Just like Corky said."

Yep.

He bloody knew it.

"Tell me what you need again, Control. Over."

"Corky wants you to plug one of the dongles into the back of a camera. Any camera will do, so long as the dongle's not in plain sight. The choice is yours." He released one of his annoying, high-pitched chuckles.

"You're kidding, right? Why can't I plug it into the system's drive unit? The drive's bound to be in the office, right? Over."

"Nah, that ain't gonna work, Mr K. Can't risk some bozo security guard seeing it and pulling it out. Besides, them units often have the ports in the front."

"That's ridiculous. Why the hell can't we just try it? We won't need access for all that long. I don't plan on leaving the client swinging in the wind forever. Over."

"Because, Mr K, what would you do if you found some tech what don't belong plugged into your camera set up?" Corky paused for a moment, then continued with more intensity than usual. *"You would shut up shop and lock the place down tighter than a duck's nether regions. And that would leave Mr F hanging out to dry."*

Kaine sighed and rubbed his face with his gloved hands.

"You're sure there's no other work-around? Over," Kaine asked, reaching for any straw he could find.

"*Sorry, Mr K. The dongles don't have an internal battery, so they need to be fitted permanently and out of sight. It's essential if you want Corky to have full access to the system.*"

"You couldn't have told me this earlier? Like, *before* I broke into the workshop. Over."

"*Corky did say you should be prepared for a bit of climbing. And Corky also said we was both going in bat-like. Remember?*"

"Yes, Control. I remember. Over."

Although forewarned, Kaine had imagined the climbing to entail ladders and staircases rather than stepping out on a narrow, metal bar over a yawning chasm. As a result, he'd failed to bring along rope or a safety harness.

Bloody idiot.

Kaine removed the dongles from a side pocket of the backpack and turned them over in his hand, studying one closely. It didn't look much. He couldn't find a maker's badge or serial number. Nothing but a plain, white cube the size of a box of matches with a USB socket built into one end. Each looked identical, save a different connector protruding from the other end on a short length of cable that looked like a tail. No doubt the device was packed with little pieces of high-tech magic designed and built by Corky and Frodo, which they'd couriered to Kaine the previous evening. Kaine hoped to God one of the bloody things worked. He slipped the lightweight units into the map pocket of his trousers and lifted his gaze to study the building's internal skeleton, focussing on the A-frame trusses.

The feet of each triangular truss were bolted onto vertical, steel posts which formed the framework—the ribs—for attaching the corrugated-steel walls. Reaching the trusses wouldn't present much of a challenge. A steel ladder attached to the end wall of a pod, running alongside the fire exit, gave access to roof storage. The real challenge came with the trusses themselves. Towards the centre of the span, the diagonal cross-bracing welded to the trusses stretched more than an arm's length apart. Way more. He'd have to tightrope-walk three or four metres between the braces, untethered, and he'd be some twelve metres above the concrete floor.

He shuddered at the thought.

Another fine mess.

"C'mon, Kaine," he muttered. "Get on with it."

"*What was that, Mr K?*"

"Nothing, Control. Just thinking out loud. I'll need radio silence for the next part. Alpha One, out."

Kaine tapped the earpiece inactive and threw the back-pack's strap over his shoulder. He backed away from the edge and climbed the metal ladder.

Nine rungs later, he scrambled onto the top of the first unit and had to duck to avoid cracking his head on the sloping roof panels. He lowered the backpack to the dirt-and-rubbish-strewn surface—the added weight and awkward shape would do nothing to improve his balance.

Moving silently, Kaine picked his way over the unit roofs, keeping to the reinforced walkway. When he reached the second truss, he stopped, turned, and looked out over the span for the first time at that angle. The camera cluster seemed miles away when, in reality, it was little more than twenty metres from the outside edge of the unit. Twenty metres that included two gaps where he'd have to ghost-walk or crawl across the beam.

He took time to study every detail of the truss, working out his moves in advance.

Three diagonal, bracing struts and a vertical tie-bar

running down from the apex to the centre of the horizontal member stood between Kaine and the camera cluster. Each steel member was no more than fifty centimetres wide and covered in decades of accumulated filth.

What the hell are you doing?

The longer he stared at the truss—the awkward angles of the supporting struts and the impossibly wide gaps—the more dangerous the crossing seemed to become.

Why take the risk?

He was doing it for Toby Fabien and the twins. They needed—they deserved—his help.

Crack on, Kaine. You can do this.

He grabbed the first diagonal strut with both gloved hands and shuffled towards the front edge of the office unit.

The grey, concrete floor spread out far below him. From such a height, the limos and Raptors looked like children's toys. He made himself focus on the camera cluster.

Agitated by thermals and the roof's ventilation fans, chill, dank air wafted around his head, cooling the sweat on his face. White splodges on the red-alkyd paint showed that birds had gained access to the roof space over the years and had made their deposits.

Pigeon shit. That's all I need.

Praying that it was dried, not runny and slippery, he took a deep and steadying breath and waited for the breeze to still. He swallowed hard.

"C'mon," he muttered. "Let's get this over with."

Leaning against the reinforcing strut, Kaine removed his canvas belt, draped it around his neck, and stepped up onto the horizontal I-beam. Standing sideways, he edged out as far as he could while still holding onto the first strut and stretched out his right arm. His reach fell short by half a metre.

"Damn it."

Kaine shuffled back to the first diagonal support and slid the belt from his neck. He looped it around the metal-work, tucked the end through the buckle, and tugged it tight. Using the belt as a tether, he slid his right foot ahead of his left, edged away from the inner strut, wobbled, stead-ied, and stretched out again. This time, his right hand reached the second strut easily. He grasped the metal bar and released the belt. No longer under tension, the belt's end flopped, the buckle loosened, and it slid down the diag-onal strut to clank against the horizontal I-bar. The belt had served its secondary purpose in a one-time-only deal.

Kaine worked his way around the second strut, paused, and breathed deep and slow. Four metres separated him from the vertical tie-bar in the middle of the span. A four-metre gap he had no option but to cross.

He pulled in a final deep, steadying breath, and stood tall. He leaned out from the brace and slid his right foot forwards.

Headlights raked the front of the warehouse.

Shit.

Kaine stopped, pulled back into the brace, hugged it tight, and waited.

An engine approached. One vehicle. Large, heavy. A van? Tyres crunched on gravel, stopped. A man shouted something Kaine couldn't quite make out. A vehicle door opened and slammed shut. Footsteps jogged over tarmac. Seconds later, a chain rattled.

Visitors at this time of night?

"Come on, Baz. Pull your finger out!" a man shouted in the distance.

"Bloody padlock's stiff," Baz called back. "Why don't you oil the bloody thing?"

"You can stick your oil up your—"

"Ah, got it."

The chain rattled again. Hinges creaked as a gate swung open, the lower edge scraping on rough concrete.

"About fucking time," the driver shouted.

The diesel engine revved and the vehicle rumbled closer.

Trapped halfway across the roof truss, Kaine had no choice other than to stay put. Heart thumping, he squatted, hugged the cross brace, and squeezed into a tight ball. A couple of metres away, the end of his belt dangled below the crossbar.

What the hell's going on?

The vehicle rumbled to a stop near the roller shutters. Two doors creaked open, and one set of footsteps approached.

Below and to Kaine's right, a lock clicked, the wicket gate in the roller shutters opened, and a man stepped over the high threshold. Strongly built, wearing a padded, black hoodie, blue jeans, and black trainers with white soles, he stepped to the side and reached out to the wall. A heavy, industrial, light switch clunked. One of the two rows of fluorescent tubes, the row directly beneath Kaine, flickered and held steady, their brightness blinding, searing. Kaine flinched, slammed closed his lids, hugged the brace tighter.

Bugger.

He had one thing in his favour. Being above the hanging lights would throw him into deeper darkness and hide him from the visitors. Probably.

"C'mon, Baz," Driver shouted. "We don't got all fucking night."

The orange-and-white afterimages behind Kaine's lids

faded. He opened his eyes a crack. Beneath him, in the open wicket door, stood Dylan Bentley.

What the hell was he doing in his dad's workshop in the middle of the night? More to the point, how long would he and Baz be, and ... would the buggers look up?

Kaine held on tight to the cross brace, hardly daring to breathe. His heart rate spiked, and he wondered why Dylan couldn't hear the pounding from where he stood, a few metres below and sixty metres away from Kaine's exposed position.

"Are you gonna give me a hand?" Baz shouted. "I can't carry 'em all, man."

"Okay," Dylan called. "Keep your bloody wig on. I'm coming."

He ducked back out through the wicket door. Muffled grunts and grizzles preceded Dylan's return, carrying a large, blue, cardboard box. A picture on the front of the box showed a plastic bottle, and the label above it read, "Concentrated Screen Wash, 0.5 litre x 12".

Baz—long, dark hair, scraggy beard—followed him through the door. Dressed the same as Dylan, but wearing walking boots rather than trainers, he carried an identical box.

"Why are we luggin' these bloody things?" Baz asked.

"They ain't gonna walk themselves to the storeroom, are they?" Dylan answered, leading the way past the row of stretch limos, and passing directly below Kaine. "Careful of the inspection pit, mate. Wouldn't want you falling in and damaging the gear." He sniggered.

"Ha ha. Very funny, man," Baz snorted, his deep voice rumbling through the workshop. "Nah, what I meant was why don't you open the shutters so we can drive the van inside. That way, we wouldn't have to carry the boxes so far."

Dylan reached the metal staircase leading up to the fire escape and the run of office and storage units. He started climbing and Baz tramped behind him.

"There's a counter on the shutters," Dylan said. "We open them, and the counter cranks up another notch. Dad's paranoid. Logs the numbers every night. Checks the fuckers every morning. I don't want him finding out we've been in here."

"Oh, right," Baz said, breathing hard. "The old boy wouldn't like what we're storing, huh?"

Dylan reached the balcony, turned the corner, and strolled along the front of the units. He passed the toilet and kept going to the end. He lowered the box to the tread plate, then unlocked and opened the door marked "Storeroom #5".

"No, man," Dylan said, shaking his head. "The old boy wouldn't mind too much, but he'd charge us for storage, and his cut would eat into our profits."

"Why don't you offer him a share? It'd save us havin' to come here in the middle o' the bloody night."

Dylan picked up his box and entered the storeroom.

"Fuck that, man," he said, emerging from the darkness. "The old fucker's mega rich already. He don't need any more wedge. This is our deal, Baz. Yours and mine. A fifty-fifty split, right down the middle—after I've taken out my expenses, of course."

Dylan took the second box from Baz, carried it inside, and reappeared five seconds later, brushing dust from his hands.

"Go on then," Dylan said, waving the back of his hand at Baz. "Off you pop."

Baz frowned. "Where to?"

"Go fetch the other box."

"What? Me?"

Dylan placed his hands on his hips and bent forwards at the waist.

"Fuck's sake, man," he growled. "You expect me to go?"

Baz reeled in his neck.

"Why do I have to do all the runnin' around?"

"I paid for the gear," Dylan snapped. "So far, all you've done is sit on your arse, griping."

"Fuck off. Booger's *my* contact," Baz said, digging his thumb into his chest. "I negotiated the deal, I bought the ferry tickets, and I organised the collection."

"So what? I paid for the gear, and I'm the brains behind the operation. Get on with it," Dylan said, checking his ostentatious Rolex. "Times a-wasting."

Grumbling under his breath, Baz turned away, and stomped along the balcony. By the time he'd reached the staircase and started his descent, Dylan had lit a cigarette and begun sucking on its butt. He leaned against the creaking railings, tilted his head, and blew smoke towards the ventilation duct. He seemed to look straight at Kaine while doing so.

Round-shouldered, Baz plodded along the floor, placing a grubby hand on the bonnet of each limo as he passed.

"Pack that in, dickwad!" Dylan shouted. "Dad's gonna make me polish those fuckers in the morning."

Baz looked up, shot Dylan the finger, and shouted, "Up yours, dickwad."

Dylan leaned out over the railing, snorted, and spat. The gobbet of thick, brown phlegm splattered the concrete one meter behind Baz. It had the desired effect of making him scurry along.

"Dickwad," Baz repeated and walked through the open wicket door.

Dylan laughed and continued toking away on his cigarette.

Seconds later, Baz, carrying a third box identical to the first two, ducked back through the door, pausing halfway.

"What you waiting for?" Dylan called down, taunting.

"You stopped gobbin'?"

Dylan sneered and held up a hand.

"Yeah, yeah. You're safe, man."

Dylan dropped the stub of his tab to the balcony and ground it out under the toe of his trainer.

Clearly not one to accept Dylan's word, Baz stepped out into the open, balanced the box on his head, and jogged towards the staircase. Panting and laughing, he climbed the steps and delivered the third box to his vulgar mate.

Dylan snorted, said, "Took your sweet time," and carried the box into the storeroom.

Three minutes later, he came out empty handed, locked the door, and brushed his hands clean again.

"That's it, we're done."

"Good job, too," Baz grumbled. "I'm knackered. Been up since before the sparrows started fartin'."

Dylan slapped his mate on the shoulder.

"Missing your beauty sleep?"

"Too bloody right, man," Baz said, laughing. "Let's go."

Kaine watched them retrace their way along the balcony. Five metres from the staircase, Baz turned his head and glanced up. A quizzical frown formed.

"Fuck's sake!" he said, pointing straight at Kaine.

Chapter Thirty-One

Tuesday 6th July - Pre-Dawn

Eccleshall Way, Stafford, Staffordshire, England

Kaine snap-calculated the odds of retracing his steps to the safety of the cubicle roofs before Dylan and the deep-voiced lunkhead could intercept him. Not good. In fact, non-existent.

"What's up," Dylan asked.

"The bloody cameras," Baz barked.

Kaine blinked. Swallowed in relief. The idiot hadn't seen him. He'd been blinded by the bright, strip lights.

"What about them?" Dylan asked.

"Do they work?"

"'Course they bloody work. Why wouldn't they work?"

Baz frowned and gave himself a moment to think before answering. "Won't your dad know we've been here?"

Dylan snorted and started walking again, leading Baz towards the staircase.

"Don't be daft," he said, laughing. "Stupid fucker never looks at the surveillance footage. To be honest, I'd be buggered if he knew how to work the system. Nah, mate. I'll delete the files tomorrow morning. Dad'll never know we were here."

"If he don't know how to use the system, what's the point in havin' the cameras, then?" Baz asked, following close behind.

Dylan stopped and turned. Baz nearly bumped into him.

"If the place ever got burgled, he'd—"

"Hand the disk to the cops?" Baz suggested.

"Would he fuck," Dylan scoffed, shaking his head and taking off again. "Dad and the filth don't get along. Nah, he'd get Marco to access the tapes and find out who did it. Not that any local scrote would be stupid enough to rob this place. Dad would find the buggers and run them through a meat grinder."

Baz snorted.

"Don't laugh, mate. I'm serious. Fucker told me about this one time in the army when he had a bit of bother with an officer. He tore …" Dylan scrunched up his face. "Nah. I'd better not say anything more. Dad told me in secret."

"So, who's Marco? You talkin' 'bout the minder?"

"That's right, man. Marco's more than a minder, though."

"Yeah?"

Dylan skipped down the staircase and stepped out into the garage with Baz in his wake.

"Yeah," Dylan answered. "Marco's a dab hand at the techie stuff. Almost as good as me, he is."

"That good, huh?" Baz asked, his words loaded with sarcasm and his eyebrow arched. Perhaps he wasn't as slow-witted as he appeared.

They passed to the far side of the inspection pit and strolled alongside the row of Raptors, passing directly below Kaine. Dylan grabbed the safety rail, spun around, and stepped directly into Baz's path. Baz jerked to a stop and raised his hands.

"Whoa, man. Easy."

"Are you taking the piss?" Dylan growled.

From his angle, looking down on the tops of their heads, Kaine could make out a bald patch on Baz's shaggy crown.

"What, me?" Baz said, shaking his head. "Nah, mate. No way."

Dylan jabbed an index finger into Baz's chest.

"Sounded to me like you were taking the piss!"

Baz shook his head.

"Why would I do that?" he said, his voice rising in pitch.

"Dunno, mate," Dylan said, frowning. "Maybe you were being a smartarse!"

"Not me, Dylan," he said, still shaking his head. "I ain't no smartarse. You know that."

They faced each other in a silent and angry standoff. Seconds passed. Dylan blinked first. He laughed, clapped Baz on the shoulder, and a forced smile broke out on his square-jawed face.

"Gotcha!" he said, laughing. "Just messing with you, buddy."

Baz relaxed his shoulders and nodded.

"Yeah, man," he said, matching Dylan's forced smile,

but clearly having to work harder at it. "You got me alright. Nice one."

Dylan spun around and carried on walking. The moment Dylan turned his back, Baz's smile dropped. If fiery looks contained any real heat, Dylan would have ended up a heap of charred ash on the floor before he'd reached the far end of the inspection pit.

Baz rushed forwards, keen to catch up.

"Fancy a spliff at my gaff?" Baz asked, his delivery light and friendly as though all was forgiven.

"I thought you were heading for your pit?"

"Yeah, I am, but I'll always make time for a bifter, man. What you reckon?"

"I'd say you're on."

At the wicket door, Dylan stepped aside and allowed his buddy through first. Baz lifted his foot over the raised sill and ducked under the low, head jamb while Dylan mimed side-footing him in the rear to help him through. They laughed—the earlier anger having dissipated in the time it took them to walk halfway through the building. It demonstrated the volatile nature of the relationship. Reaction, overreaction, and reconciliation in little more than a few heartbeats. It made them seem like an old, married couple.

Dylan paused long enough to snap off the lights, plunge the workshop into instant darkness, and slam the door shut. The lock clicked and Kaine found himself alone again.

Seconds later, van doors opened and slammed shut. A starter motor whirred, a deep-throated engine caught, and tyres screeched. They stopped long enough to close and padlock the gates before powering away in a tyre-squealing race start.

Kaine waited for his night vision to return before pulling on the cross brace and climbing to his feet. Gently, he eased the cramp out of his legs. Pins and needles had set in. He released his left hand and tapped the earpiece.

"Alpha One to Control. Over."

"*Whatcha, Mr K.*"

"You couldn't give me any warning? Over."

"*Sorry 'bout that, Mr K. By the time Corky knew what was happening, they were already through the gates and in the car park. Corky knew you'd hear them, and he didn't want to disturb you in case ... well, you know.*"

"Okay, Control. Understood. Over."

"*Corky takes it you haven't done the business yet, right? Can't find the signal.*"

"No, Control," Kaine answered, managing not to snap. "I was interrupted. Over."

"*Okay. Corky gets it.*"

"I'd better get on, then. Alpha One, out."

Kaine tapped the earpiece again and turned to face the tie-bar. Somehow, it looked further away. Five metres, not four. He stood up straight and shook out his legs, one at a time. The pins and needles had faded to a minor tingle as the blood flow to his legs returned to normal.

Now or never.

Grasping the brace firmly with his left hand, he twisted to face forwards. He locked eyes on the vertical strut and slid his right foot ahead of the left, searching for his point of balance. At the limit of his reach, he stopped.

Although only three metres were left, it still seemed like five.

He tried not to look down, but his eyes were drawn to the concrete floor and the elongated gash of the inspection pit. During training and in the field, he'd crossed many such gaps before but never without a safety harness.

Kaine fixed his gaze on the target—the vertical, jet-black tie-bar—took a deep breath, and held it.

He released his grip on the cross brace, threw his arms wide, and edged out into the airy gloom. Four shuffled, sliding steps and one serious, heart-stopping, half-wobble later, he reached the tie-bar and wrapped his arms around it. He hugged tight and blew out the pent-up breath.

Piece of cake.

His racing heart rate recovered quickly.

Kaine peeled one hand free of the cold, metal bar and tapped the earpiece again.

"Alpha One to Control. I made it to the middle. Over."

"*'Course you did, Mr K. Why wouldn't you?*"

Easy for you to say!

"Okay, now what? Over."

"*Plug the dongle what has a squashed-oval-shaped cord into the technician's troubleshooting port of any camera, and Bob's your aunt's hubby.*"

"You're certain it'll fit? Over."

Why hadn't he asked that earlier? Perhaps *before* he'd risked the crossing.

"*They got standard USB-C sockets, Mr K. It'll fit.*"

They'd better.

"*And besides,*" Corky said through a quiet chuckle, "*Corky knows the spec of that there system.*"

"How the hell …? No, don't tell me. I don't need to know. Starting the insertion now. Over."

Still hugging the tie-bar, Kaine bent at the knees and slid down to sit on the horizontal, truss bar. He gripped with his knees and crossed his ankles under the bar. As secure as he would ever feel in such a position, Kaine tugged the right glove from his hand with his teeth and stuffed it into his jacket pocket. Next, he removed one of the dongles from his map pocket—miraculously the right one—and, after clamping it between his teeth, leaned down, and reached for the back of the nearest available camera.

Despite the chilly air, sweat ran from his forehead and down his nose, dripping from the tip. It plummeted into the inspection pit and disappeared. A second and a third drip followed it. He straightened, wiped his face dry with his sleeve, and licked salt from his lips.

Again, he leaned out and stretched down, holding the tie-bar with his left hand, arm strained and extended to its limit. The blood rushed to his head. He blinked twice and struggled for grip. He swiped his hand on his trouser leg, reached out again, and tightened his grip. The camera twisted, nudged downwards, changing the angle of shot. Kaine lurched sideways, nearly toppled, righted himself.

Bloody hell.

A breath of cool air chilled his sweaty face. He removed the dongle from his mouth and checked the tail for signs of crimping. Nothing. It appeared undamaged. He couldn't believe he hadn't bitten clean through the cable.

"You're getting too old for this nonsense," Kaine mumbled.

"What was that, Mr K?"

"Nothing, Corky. Just thinking aloud. Over."

Kaine scrunched down, studied the back of the camera, confirmed the USB-C port's alignment, and made sure he had a firm hold of the dongle's male connector. For the final time, Kaine leaned out and down again. Carefully, he lined up the male and female connections, and pushed. They slotted together perfectly. With one hand, he pulled himself upright and waited.

"Excellent work, Mr K. Corky's into the system."

Thank God for that.

"Piece of cake," Kaine said, lying through his teeth. "Over."

"There is a slight problem, though."

Damn. He'd spoken too soon.

"I'm listening, Control. Over."

"The camera you messed with is out of alignment with the others. It needs to point up a little more."

Kaine sighed.

"Okay, Control. Give me a second. Over."

He resumed the inverted, hanging position, and nudged the rear of the camera downwards.

"A smidge more."

Kaine nudged it again.

"That's it. Perfect."

"It better be. I'm done here. Over."

Kaine returned to the vertical and climbed to his feet, sliding his hands up the tie-bar.

"Corky's a happy bunny, Mr K. You keep safe, now. Going silent again."

"Thanks, Control. Alpha One, out."

As he prepared to retrace his steps along the truss, a pigeon fluttered past his face, its wing feathers missing his nose by a whisker. Kaine jerked his head back and away, still grasping the tie-bar. A few seconds later and it would have been disastrous. As he waited for his heart rate to settle, Kaine pulled the glove from his pocket and worked it onto a sweating, right hand, before striking out again. He made the return trip without further interruption. It took less than three minutes, including the brief pause to retrieve and refit his belt. Before stepping off the truss and onto the roof of the pod, he stopped and tapped the earpiece.

"Alpha One to Control. Over."

"Yes, Mr K?"

"I'm about to climb onto the office roof. Will you be able to see me? Over."

"*No. Up there, you'll still be out of shot. Corky's working through the earlier footage now. The cameras picked you up when you opened the fire door and crawled along the balcony, but that's an easy fix. Corky's gonna doctor the tapes when you've gone.*"

"Thanks, Control. Make sure you leave the part where Dylan and his mate break in. Over."

"*Is you trying to teach Corky to suck eggs, Mr K?*" he asked, adding another of his trademark chuckles. "*And what makes you reckon they broke in?*"

"Listen to the recording, Control. The soundtrack says it all. Over."

"*Righto. Will do.*"

Keen to leave, Kaine climbed off the truss and hurried over the storage unit roofs. On the way, he collected his backpack and slid down the ladder. Back on the balcony, he turned right towards Storeroom #5. Although he had his suspicions, he wanted to know what the screen-wash boxes contained and the reason for Dylan's furtive break-in.

The storeroom lock, a three-lever mortice, didn't present much of a barrier. He picked it inside ten seconds.

The door opened into a stockroom, the floor covered in rat droppings and lined floor-to-ceiling with metal shelving made from the same, textured, tread plates as the balcony. It revealed itself as a dust-filled, treasure house of rubbish and old stock. The long, back wall contained rodent-chewed, cardboard boxes part-filled with plastic containers of antifreeze, cans of brake fluid and engine oil, bottles of distilled water, and aerosol cans of de-icer. The left-hand wall housed old, plastic, wheel trims, used numberplates, boxes of headlight bulbs, old, rubber, floor mats, sachets of unused wiper blades, and dead car batteries. The right-hand wall held cartons of hand gel, rolls of blue paper, rubber gloves, dust masks, and part-used cans of spray paint. Everything was covered in a thick layer of dust, draped with cobwebs, and looked as though it hadn't been touched since the building had been a fully operational, bus garage.

On the floor, taking pride of place, and the only boxes not covered in grime, stood Dylan's three cardboard boxes, stacked in a tower. The flaps of the top box had been opened and interlocked back into place. Kaine peeled the flaps apart, peered inside, and found the bottles of concentrated screen wash as advertised. Twelve bottles in two layers of six, separated by a sheet of stiff, corrugated cardboard.

Kaine frowned. It looked innocent enough, but he didn't buy it. Not for one moment.

He removed one of the bottles and pressed his finger into the cardboard sheet. It deflected a little and turned out a great deal thicker than he expected—six centimetres deep.

"Hello, hello," he muttered. "What do we have here, Dylan?"

Kaine removed the remaining five bottles, exposed the cardboard sheet, and smiled.

"Very clever."

Someone had cut three slices into the cardboard sheet, five centimetres from each edge. They'd left the fourth side intact to form a hinge. Kaine tugged open the flap and revealed a neat layer of white, medical packets held in place by thin wafers of cardboard. Forty-six packets in all, with two missing.

He took out one of the packets and found the front branded with the logo of a well-known, Swiss, pharmaceutical company. It had embossed, braille lettering and bore the product name, "Mestodidolone AAS". It looked impressive, but the logo and barcode were slightly blurred and clearly forged. A knockoff. A good one, but a knockoff, just the same. He broke the seal and found a blister pack inside containing seven small vials of a yellow liquid. One week's supply of something probably illegal.

Interesting.

Kaine replaced the blister pack inside the packet, grabbed the burner from his pocket, and took a quick snapshot.

"Alpha One to Control. Over."

"*Corky's still here, Mr K. What d'you need?*"

"Can you run a quick search for the drug, "Mestodidolone AAS", please." Kaine spelled out the name. "I've a good idea what they are, but I'd like you to confirm it for me. Over."

"*Corky's right on it, Mr K.*"

While he waited, Kaine replaced the bottles of screen wash and interlocked the flaps again.

The earpiece clicked.

"*You still there, Mr K?*"

"Yes, Control. Over."

"*There ain't no such thing on the market, Mr K. Nearest Corky can find is an anabolic-androgenic steroid with a similar name. That do you?*"

"Perfect, thank you. It's exactly what I suspected. I'll be leaving the workshop now. Anything you need before I go? Over."

"*Not a thing, Mr K. Be safe.*"

"Thanks for your help, Control. Alpha One—"

"*A quick question before you go, Mr K.*"

"Shoot. Over," Kaine said.

"*Do you still fancy a meet?*"

So much had happened since Corky had made the suggestion, Kaine had forgotten all about it.

"If you're up for it. Over."

"*Corky can't wait for a face-to-face. Even Frodo's keen to see you again.*"

"He is? Over."

"*Yes indeedie. Corky's sending a location to your burner.*"

"Thanks, Control. Alpha One, out."

Kaine tapped the earpiece inactive.

Before leaving, he scanned the storeroom one last time. The stacked boxes of disposable gloves on the middle shelf gave him an idea. He grinned, snatched a glove from an open box, and stepped out onto the balcony.

Kaine ran his eyes over the tread plates and soon found what he was searching for. He squatted, used the disposable glove to pick up Dylan's flattened cigarette butt, and carried it back into the storeroom.

A few moments later, he returned to the balcony and locked the storeroom door. He retraced his steps to the fire exit, pushed on the slam bar, and strode out into the fresh, night air. His mobile vibrated with an incoming message—Corky and Frodo's GPS location.

A quiver of tension rippled through Kaine's body. He had no idea why.

Chapter Thirty-Two

Tuesday 6th July – Jackson Bentley

Eccleshall Way, Stafford, Staffordshire, England

Jackie Bentley stood at the window, surveying a significant part of his business empire from the suspended, metal-and-glass box that was his office. A row of milk-white, stretch limos lined up on one side of the hangar-sized workshop, and the assorted mix of Raptors on the other. All the cars gleaming, all perfect, all with gold, eagle wings on their bonnets—the eagle wings that Jackie had chosen as the company's logo after he struck it lucky. Pure class, they were. Every one of them. Drop dead gorgeous.

Jackie's chest swelled with pride.

Something was missing from the scene, though. No mechanic. No Tony Epps. Strange. Geezer never turned up late. Not once in the three years he'd been on the books. People could set their clocks by his timekeeping.

The Chrysler 300 wouldn't service itself. Bloody car was needed for a stag do that evening.

C'mon, Epps. Where the fuckin' hell are you?

Jackie turned from the window to face the office interior. Clean, spacious, comfortable, it matched the professional vibe he was aiming for. The vibe of a successful entrepreneur. Who cared if Bentley Hire Fleet never made a penny in profit? Jackie didn't need a profitable business when he had millions in the bank. Legit millions, too. And tax free.

No. Bentley Hire Fleet was nothing but what the press might call a "vanity project". Jackie loved stretch limos and adored the Raptors even more. Limos for their class and luxury, and Raptors for their gut-wrenching power and ferocity. Useful when he wanted to look down on the pygmies driving past in their tiny, little motors, which he did every time he hit the road in one.

"Marco?" he growled.

The thick-necked, broad-shouldered, and heavily tattooed minder, tech guy, and occasional chauffer-for-hire dragged his eyes away from his tabloid. Feet crossed and stretched out on the glass-topped coffee table, he jerked up his head.

"Yes, boss?"

"What's up with Tony?"

Marco hiked the powerful shoulders.

"Dunno, boss."

"He said anythin' to you?"

"'Bout what, boss?"

"'Bout not turnin' up for work today?"

Marco stretched his thick neck and arched an eyebrow.

"Tony's never late, boss," he said, his slow and low, West-Midlands accent stretching out into forever. "Loves those motors like they were his own."

"Well," Jackie said, "where is he then?"

"Isn't he in?"

"Would I be askin' why the bugger weren't here if he *were* here, you dozy pillock?"

Grunting, Marco dropped the paper to the coffee table, swung his legs onto the floor, and sat up.

"Want me to phone him for you, boss?" Marco stretched out one leg and dug inside his trouser pocket.

Something screeched down below. Jackie spun.

The small door cut into the shutters at the far end of the workshop clattered open and the man himself stepped inside. Instead of the usual, spotless, boiler suit, Epps wore a faded-denim jacket over a white T-shirt, skinny jeans, and a pair of white trainers.

"No need," Jackie said to Marco. "Bugger's just walked in. Don't look like he's turned up for work, though. Not in that clobber."

Marco climbed to his feet and stood next to Jackie by the window.

Epps cast a glance up to the office, spotted Jackie and Marco standing together behind the glass, and fixed his eyes on Jackie. He hitched his eyebrows and nodded towards his workstation on the far side of the inspection pit.

Jackie nodded.

Epps nodded back and headed for his locker.

"Looks like he wants a quiet word," Jackie said.

"Want me to give you some space, boss?" Marco asked. "I can go stretch my legs if you like."

Meaning the dozy mutt wanted to bugger off for a

smoke around the back of the workshop, well away from all the flammable liquids.

"No, you stay here," Jackie said, scowling at the tabloid on the coffee table. "And keep your eyes 'n' ears open. Don't like surprises, me."

Jackie edged away from the window.

"Okay, boss," Marco said. "I've got your back." He glanced at his chair, the paper, and the packet of ciggies next to it, sighed, and took up a lookout post near the window with the best view of the garage floor. Simple soul he might be, but he came in handy during a rumble. Marco had power to spare. The bugger was surprisingly good with the tech, too. Didn't come cheap, but was a useful mutt to have around.

Jackie turned his back on the hired muscle and pushed through the office door. He clomped down the metal staircase and landed on the concrete floor at the same time as Epps opened his locker and started throwing his stuff into a canvas holdall.

What the fuck's he doin'?

Jackie stopped well back from the edge of the inspection pit and stood still, waiting.

Finally, Epps turned. He zipped up the holdall and dropped it onto his pristine workbench. Say whatever anyone liked about the scrawny mechanic, the bloke did keep his workstation clean and tidy. The sign of a real pro.

"What's up?" Jackie demanded, eyeing the stuffed holdall. "Why didn't you come up to the office?"

Epps shot a furtive glance over Jackie's shoulder and shuddered.

"Big bugger gives me the creeps," he said, lowering his voice.

Jackie snorted.

"Marco's okay. Once you get to know him."

Epps looked down, met Jackie's eye. "I'll take your word for it, Mr Bentley." He spoke so quietly Jackie had to strain to make out what he said.

Jackie stood tall and crossed his arms.

"So," he said, "you gonna tell me what's wrong?"

Epps twisted his upper lip, and his dark eyebrows met in the middle.

"The cops showed up at my place last night," Epps bleated, his words muted. "At my home!"

"They did?"

"Yeah," he hissed. "They fucking did."

Whoa.

Jackie stiffened, dropped his arms to his sides. He couldn't remember ever having heard Tony Epps swear before. The bloke was so squeaky, the drivers had taken to calling him "Reverend".

"Why are we whispering?"

Epps glanced up at the roof trusses, where the surveillance cameras hung from a ceiling brace.

"You fucking know why," Epps shot back.

That was twice. The grease monkey was losing it.

"Okay, Tony. I get your point. What did the filth want?" Jackie matched Epps for volume.

"What do you think they bloody wanted?" Epps huffed.

"Tell me, Tony." Jackie fought to keep calm. Epps knew things and needed careful handling.

"Same as before. They asked about the Raptor and the bull bar."

"What d'you tell 'em?"

Epps blinked, took a breath and started talking, faster than normal.

"What do you think I told 'em? Nothing, that's what I told 'em. Bugger all."

Jackie relaxed a little. He nodded.

"That's good, Tony. Very good."

"No," Epps whispered. "It's not good. They know, Mr Bentley. They bloody know."

Jackie frowned, turned his head to give Epps a sideways glare.

"What do they know, Tony?"

Epps moved away from his workbench and shuffled closer.

Again, the mechanic glanced up at the office window where Marco stood, looking down. Jackie didn't need to turn and see for himself. He just knew. Marco followed orders. Reliable that way, he was.

"They know what Dylan did," Epps said, edging even closer, staring Jackie down. "They know he ran that Toyota off the road."

Jackie stared at Epps, unblinking.

Shit. Bugger's worked it out.

"I have no idea what you're talkin' 'bout, Tony." He tried to sound relaxed, but it came across as stiff and aggressive.

"Don't give me that bollocks, Mr Bentley. I didn't just come down with the last shower."

Epps stepped around the end of the inspection pit, keeping well clear, closed on Jackie, and stopped out of arm's reach. He swallowed. Then carried on talking.

"You're moron of a son ran that Toyota off the road and killed the old lady. I knew it the moment you called me in to replace the bull bar on the Raptor." He nodded to the row of beauties parked opposite the string of pearl-white limos. The third in line, the one with the brand-new bull bar, the perfectly aligned spot lamps, and the pristine paint-work that blended in with all the others. The only difference between it and its brothers was the slightly higher mileage. As the family's second runabout, it had clocked up an extra five thousand miles.

"How?"

"How what?" Epps frowned. Confused. Bugger wasn't as smart as he made out.

"How did you know?"

Epps pulled in his pointed chin.

"I heard the story on the local radio before you called me in that Sunday. When I saw the damage to the Raptor, I put two and two together—"

"And come up with five," Jackie growled.

"No, Mr Bentley," Epps sneered. The smarmy bugger actually sneered. "I came up with four." He tapped his temple. "Your dickhead of a son killed that woman. Stupid twat. What the fuck was he playing at?"

"Don't talk like that about Dylan," Jackie growled without moving his lips although he had his back to the overhead cameras.

"And now the cops are onto it. They're onto me!"

Jackie shook his head and peeled back his upper lip.

"The filth don't know squat. Can't prove nothin'."

Epps took a step closer, but stayed just out of range of a straight jab to the throat.

"When you got me to work on the Raptor," Epps continued, spitting out the words and getting carried away in his anger, "you made me an accessory after the fact. And all for a measly five hundred quid!"

Money. The bugger wanted more money.

Greedy fuckwit.

"So," Jackie said, trying to keep calm, "you keep quiet,

and they won't be able to prove nothin'. Keep schtum and we're all in the clear. All three of us."

Epps shook his head.

"It won't work that way."

"Yes," Jackie said. "It will."

"I know what the police are like when they have a theory. They worry away at it like a dog with a bone. They'll keep coming back and asking their questions until they have the answers they want. They'll keep digging. Well that ain't happening here. Not with me!" He punched his chest with the side of his fist. "I ain't having the cops digging into my past. No bloody way. I'm off. I'm leaving. Tonight."

"You're what?" Jackie snapped, leaning closer.

Epps backed away, his eyes locked on Jackie.

"I've got a buddy in Spain who'll put me up for a while," Epps said, hitching one of his scrawny shoulders. "Flying out tonight. Just stopped by to collect my gear and have this little … chat."

Money. It was all about money.

Always is.

Jackie nodded.

"Okay," he said, "that's a good idea. Go to Spain. Stay there 'til the heat's off."

Eyes sparkling, Epps stretched out a crooked smile.

"I intend to, Jackie."

Jackie scowled.

Cheeky sod.

Since when did a snot-nosed grease monkey think he could call Jackie by his first name?

Epps raised a hand to scratch his chin, hiding his mouth from the cameras.

Here it comes.

"But," Epps said, "I'll need a little spending money."

Everything came down to money.

"How much?" Jackie asked, jaw clenched.

"One hundred grand," Epps spouted without hesitation. "To help cover my travel and living expenses." He locked eyes with Jackie again.

Jackie thought about it.

One hundred wasn't too bad. It wasn't as though Jackie couldn't afford it. Wouldn't make much of a dent to his bank account. Sod it, he earned more than that on his investments most days. But giving up that much without a whimper went against the grain. Not only did it set a dangerous precedent to the world, it wound Jackie right up.

"You greedy fu—"

"And another one-fifty for my continued silence," Epps added behind his hand.

Jackie shook his head as though his hadn't heard right.

"You what?"

"That's right, Jackie. I want a quarter of a million and for that, you get way more than my guaranteed silence."

Jackie scowled.

"What the fuck you talkin' 'bout?"

Behind the hand, Epps' smile widened.

"I'm talking about a bent bull bar with Dylan's finger-prints and DNA all over it." He sniffed, stood up even straighter, and glanced up at the office again. "And I'm talking about chips of black paint belonging to the Toyota your moron of a son barged off the road. The paint chips I taped to the bull bar and have safely stored away in a place you'll never find them. That's what I'm talking about, Jackie."

The bottom fell out of Jackie's world. He swallowed.

"You kept them?"

Epps nodded. Victory shone in his piggy, brown eyes.

"'Course I bloody kept them," he said. "They're my ticket out of this shithole. I was going to hold onto them for a while. String you along until you reckoned that you and Dylan were in the clear before I asked for my fair share. But last night, when the cops came calling ..." He shook his head. "It made me move my schedule up. I can't have the cops on my back. I value my safety and my anonymity. Always have. They'll try to pin accessory charges on me, and I can't have that. I need the cash today. Right now. And don't go telling me you don't have the money handy. I know you keep that much in the safe upstairs. You've bragged about it often enough."

"In cash," Jackie said, nodding. "Right. And what happens when I hand over the two hundred and fifty grand?"

"I bugger off into my mate's place in Malaga. And into my early retirement."

"And the bull bar?"

"The evidence, you mean?" The snide smile returned.

Jackie so much wanted to bludgeon the smile off the scrawny arsehole's face.

"Yeah, that's right. The evidence." Jackie scowled. "What happens to that?"

"Oh that," Epps said, releasing a near-silent cackle, "I keep that locked away where you can't find it. I figure it's my ace in the hole. So long as I have it, not only will I be safe from you, but Dylan will be safe from the cops."

Jackie's heart pounded against his ribcage.

"What's to stop you demandin' more money?"

"Nothing," Epps said, hiking his eyebrows. "Absolutely nothing."

He lowered his hand and burst out laughing.

"When I reach Spain," he added through the laughter, "I'll text you my bank details. Every month you'll send me ten grand in euros. You can reference it as my pension. That way, you can claim it back on your tax returns."

Jackie curled his hands into fists.

"You fuckin' bastard!" he growled and prowled forwards. "You piece of shit."

Epps raised his hands, cowered away.

"Easy, Jackie," he bleated. "You wouldn't want—"

"Boss!" Marco yelled through the open office door. "You okay?"

Epps jerked his head up and around. He lurched back and trod in a patch of old, engine oil. The training shoe shot out from beneath him. He screamed. Terror-filled eyes flashed wide. Arms splayed, flailing, struggling for balance.

In reflex, Jackie darted forwards and shot out his hand, reaching for a flap of denim jacket. Missed.

Screaming, eyes wide, terrified, Epps fell backwards, arms still thrashing, still whirling. On the way down, an arm and the side of his head smashed into the sharp, unforgiving edge of the pit.

The hollow crack of bone slamming against concrete echoed through the workshop. Blood spewed from the head wound. Epps' scream cut off dead. His body slid into the grease-blackened hole and sank to the sludge-filled bottom.

Chapter Thirty-Three

Tuesday 6th July - Morning

Abbey Park Hotel, Stafford, Staffordshire, England

After delivering a blow-by-blow account of the overnight break-in—leaving out the part where he narrowly avoided plummeting twelve metres to a painful death—Kaine dropped the bombshell and watched the screen carefully as Lara tried to take it in. Her shocked expression made him smile.

"Say that again," Lara said, finally finding her voice. "You actually met Corky?"

"Yep. In person," he said, smiling. "Face-to-face."

"How did that happen?"

Kaine explained the circumstances.

"What was he like?"

Kaine paused, giving himself time to consider his answer carefully.

"As you'd expect, but ... different."

"Different? In what way?"

The harsh lighting on the videocall washed out her healthy, outdoor tan, but she still looked damn fine.

"Well ... for a start, he's much taller than I imagined. I've always thought of him as being short and round, but he's way taller than me. Six one, six two. A tad overweight, but that's not surprising considering his lifestyle."

She nodded.

"It must have been good to shake his hand after all this time."

"That didn't happened, love. Corky doesn't shake hands."

"Ah, I see." She nodded. "Our Corky's a germophobe."

Kaine smiled and nodded. "Yep."

"That's interesting."

"Frodo was there, too," Kaine said. "In the back of the van."

"What van?"

"Sorry, I didn't say?"

"No, you didn't," Lara said.

"Corky turned up at the meet in a four-berth camper-van. Nothing to extreme or eye-catching. On the outside, it looked like something a retired couple might use for weekend camping trips. On the inside, though ... highly impressive."

"In what way?"

"The back was tricked out like the comms room in the barn, only more compact. It even had a retractable section in the roof so they could launch a drone without having to leave the van. Like I said, highly impressive."

"And Frodo was in the back?"

"Yep." Kaine nodded. "He was sitting at the controls in something that looked like a pilot's chair. Looked happy enough but didn't say much. Didn't make eye contact either, but I imagine that's normal for him."

"So," she said after a moment's pause and after a slight frown had formed on her brow, "why did Corky arrange the meeting?"

"He wanted to sound me out about something."

Kaine winced in anticipation of the next question.

"About what?"

"Sorry, love. I've been sworn to secrecy for the moment. I'll tell you as soon as I can."

Lara's frown deepened.

"If you can't tell me the reason for the meeting," she snapped, clearly upset, "why bother telling me you met up at all?"

"You've been worried about Frodo, and I wanted you to know that he was fit and well. As happy as he can be."

"Hmmm," she growled, only partly appeased. "What's Corky getting you into?"

"It's nothing to worry about, love," he said. "Might not even happen, but I will tell you as soon as I can. Promise."

Kaine yawned and rubbed the dryness from his eyes. It had been a long and stressful night, and he'd only managed a couple of hours shuteye. To cap it all, the overly soft mattress on his hotel bed didn't help.

"By the way," Lara said, the frown gone and the soft voice back, "have I told you how tired you look?"

"Have I told you how wonderful you look?" he countered.

"Nice comeback, but don't deflect. You need your rest."

Kaine nodded and held up the same hand he'd used to rub his eyes.

"Yes, I know. I'm angling for a siesta this afternoon. I couldn't lie in this morning because I had to make this report." Again, he smiled, glad to be returning to normal. "I didn't want you worrying about me."

"Cut the bull, Arnold!" she snapped, not buying it for a moment. "What's the real reason?"

"Like I said, I wanted to present this report," he repeated, "and ... I needed to be awake. DI Fellows and DS Skarratts are due to visit Toby Fabien in"—he read the time from his diver's watch—"about three minutes."

"You're running late if you want to make that meeting."

"No," he said, smiling, "I'm going nowhere near that hospital room for the moment. I don't know whether you're aware of this"—he grinned—"but the police and I don't get on all that well. And besides, I don't need to be there in person. I didn't tell you, but Corky installed a mirror app on the new phone I gave Toby. If you have time to listen, I'm sure Corky'll drop an app onto the main system."

Lara shook her head.

"I'm busy today. The lads and I have a memorial service to organise. And somewhere along the line I have to interview for a couple of stable hands. I won't be able to look after all the horses alone—not when we're a sanctuary. And I can't take on more horses without staff. It's a chicken and egg thing."

"Have you had many responses from the Royal Naval Association announcement?"

"Seventy-three so far," she announced, a note of pride warming her voice.

Kaine absorbed the warmth.

"Mike was well liked. He deserves a good send-off."

"Pity you can't attend."

"I'll be there," he said.

"In spirit?"

More or less.

He nodded and cleared his throat.

"And on that note," he said, smiling, "I have to sign off now. See you soon."

She glanced to her left, and a black horse appeared in the shot, nodding his dark head and snickering.

"That's sweet," she said.

"What is?"

"Dynamite's saying goodbye."

Kaine snorted. "Begging for food, more likely. Cheers, love."

"Bye." She blew Kaine a kiss and cut the connection.

Kaine checked his watch again. He switched apps and opened the mirror app on Toby Fabien's phone. Fellows and Skarrats had already arrived, but they were still in the middle of their greetings.

Kaine settled back on the yielding mattress and listened intently.

Chapter Thirty-Four

Tuesday 6th July - Jackson Bentley

Eccleshall Way, Stafford, Staffordshire, England

Shit! Fuck. What the hell?

Jackie stood at the edge of the pit, looking down at the bloody mess.

Epps lay crumpled at the bottom, the side of his head split and cracked open like someone had butchered the top of a soft-boiled egg. A flap of hair-covered scalp attached to a piece of bone hung from the skull. Dark red blood, purple muscle, and white clumps of porridge tumbled out of the wound. Epps eyes were open, glazed, seeing nothing. His chest didn't move. The blackmailing bugger wasn't breathing.

Dead.

No doubt about it.

Good fuckin' riddance.

"Marco!" Jackie screamed. "Marco!"

The minder stood in the office doorway, mouth hanging open.

"Fuck!" he shouted, heading for the stairs.

Jackie held up his hand.

"Marco," he yelled again, loud and clear, "Tony's had a terrible, terrible accident."

"Yes, boss," the minder shouted back, stopping on the landing at the top of the staircase. "I saw it happen."

I know, dingbat.

"I tried … couldn't catch him," Jackie called, making sure he spoke clearly—for posterity.

"Yeah, I saw that, too."

"Dial 9-9-9. Ask for an ambulance."

"Sure thing, boss." He dug a hand into his trouser pocket and tapped on the screen. "Ambulance, please," he said and wandered back inside the office to complete the call. When he wanted, Marco could be really quick on the uptake.

Leaving the minder to do the business and keeping in full sight of the all-seeing cameras, Jackie moved cautiously to the end of the pit and hurried down the concrete steps into the sludgy bottom. He stepped over the corpse and kneeled at its side. Hiding his actions from the cameras, he searched Epps, found a set of house keys, and slipped them into his pocket. As part of his job, Marco had been keeping an eye on all the employees—including Epps—and he'd learned that Epps had recently hired a lockup. He wouldn't have hidden the bull bar too far from home. Fuck him. The mug didn't have the smarts to outwit Jackie Bentley.

Taking excessive care, Jackie lowered Epps onto the bottom of the pit and stretched him out flat. Ignoring the blood and the other glop, he started chest compressions.

"Breathe, Tony," he shouted for the benefit of the cameras. "Come on, mate. Breathe. You can do it."

He counted in time with the compressions but didn't bother with the rescue breaths. No way could he bring himself to give the dead bugger the kiss of life. Too much blood and gore smeared all over the arsehole's boat race. He wouldn't even do it for the cameras. He could only take the play-acting so far.

"Boss!" Marco yelled. "Where are you?"

"Down here … in the … pit," Jackie shouted, gasping for breath, making it look good for the cameras hanging directly over the pit. "Doin' compressions."

"Didn't think you knew how," Marco called.

"Learned it in the army, years back. … Dunno if I'm … doin' it right, though. I think I bust … one of his ribs."

"Doing something's better than doing nothing, boss."

Gee, thanks for the support, Marco.

"How long's the … ambulance gonna be?" Jackie gasped, sweat already dripping off his face and cramp stiffening his arms.

When had he become so unfit?

"Twenty minutes … thirty, tops," Marco answered.

"Fuck's sake. How long?" The compressions faltered. Jackie forced himself to keep going. "Get down here. Give me a hand."

Marco could do the rescue breaths. Earn his wedge for once.

"I'm on it, boss."

Rubber-soled shoes squeaked and clanked as Marco descended the metal staircase.

"Breathe for me, Tony," Jackie gasped. "Help's on the way."

Another compression, another rib cracked.

Oops.

Chapter Thirty-Five

Tuesday 6th July - Morning

Abbey Park Hotel, Stafford, Staffordshire, England

"…upshot is, Mr Fabien, unless more evidence arises, we won't be taking this matter any further," DS Skarrats said, his tone flat, as though reading from a script.

Kaine listened in silent disgust. DI Fellows and DS Skarrats had spent twenty-five minutes in Toby Fabien's hospital room reviewing their investigation in detail. They'd been polite, precise and, in the end, completely inadequate.

Fellows took over from his sergeant.

"There will be a coroner's inquest," he said. "There has to be in the case of an unexpected death, but the police will not be offering any evidence against you. The coroner's verdict will most likely be one of accidental death. As my colleague said, we won't be proceeding with charges against you."

"I should bloody well think not!" Toby said, his voice raised.

"Really, sir," Fellows said. "There's no need to upset yourself."

"What about the Raptor?" Toby demanded, nearly shouting. "We were run off the bloody—"

"As I said, Mr Fabien," Fellows interrupted, "we found nothing to substantiate your claim. The only Ford Raptor in the area at the time of the ... incident was undamaged, and the driver has been interviewed and cleared. To be honest, it would be better for you not to pursue the matter any further."

"But—"

"Really, Mr Fabien," Fellows interrupted, "take my advice on this, sir. Grieve for your loss, take time to recover from your injuries, and move on with your life. You have two wonderful grandchildren who need you to be there for them. Concentrate on your recovery. It'll really be for the best."

Kaine ground his teeth.

For pity's sake.

How many more platitudes was the man going to spout?

"Who is he?" Toby demanded. "What's the driver's full name?"

One of the cops cleared his throat. Kaine couldn't tell which, but Fellows dead-batted Toby's questions with yet another cliché, "We are not at liberty to divulge that information, sir."

"So," Toby snarled. "The bugger gets away with murder?"

"Really, Mr Fabien. That's not at all helpful."

"Not helpful? Not helpful! This is bloody ridiculous," Toby ranted, losing control. "First you accuse me of being drunk—"

"We did nothing of the—"

"Then you accuse me of dangerous driving, and now your letting the man who actually killed Melissa get away with it. I wonder what the papers are going to say about this ... this bloody shambles."

"I wouldn't do that, sir."

"Do what?" Toby asked, breathing hard from his exertions. "Go to the papers? Why not?"

"It wouldn't be helpful."

"Why not?" Toby repeated.

"It can lead to ... complications."

"What complications?"

A mobile phone rang.

"Excuse me, Mr Fabien," Fellows said. "I need to take this."

"Please do," Toby announced, sounding bitter. "I imagine you're about done here, *Officers*."

Shuffling in the background suggested movement.

"Fellows here," the DI said, his voice growing quieter. He'd either turned his back to Toby or walked away. Or both. "I'm still at the hospital ..." A door swung open and then closed on the rest of Fellows' phone conversation.

"Is that it?" Toby asked. "Are you done now?"

Chair legs screeched on floor tiles.

"Yes, Mr Fabien," Skarrats said, grunting as he stood. "And before I go, I'd like to offer my sincere apology for what I said during our first interview. I was out of order."

Toby grunted.

"You accused me of deliberately crashing my car and killing Melissa. You can stuff your apology up your—"

"I understand how you must feel, sir," Skarrats said. "I really do. Nevertheless, I still apologise." After a slight pause, he added, "Let me offer you a word of advice, sir. For your own good, don't even think about going to the press about this. The person you are accusing has powerful friends. Powerful and dangerous friends." He allowed another pause to stretch out for a moment. "These people won't take kindly to their ... friend being accused of murder, and they don't play nice, sir. Please be careful."

"Thanks for nothing, *Sergeant*. Goodbye."

"Get well soon, Mr Fabien."

"Up yours," Toby muttered loud enough for Skarrats to hear.

The door squeaked open.

"Detective Sergeant Skarrats," Fellows called, his voice distant, "we have a potential NAI at the workshop."

"Bloody hell," Skarrats said, his voice muffled. "Who?"

"Tony Epps."

"You're kidding?"

"A what?" Toby asked.

"It's a police matter, Mr Fabien," Skarrats answered. "Good day, sir."

Footsteps hurried away, the door closed, and Toby muttered a sheaf of curses under his breath.

The mirrored smartphone showed Toby typing into his internet search browser. He typed slowly. The search string asked to identify the police code, NAI, which saved Kaine the trouble of running the search for himself. The browser's answer, "Non-accidental Injury", was illuminating, and Kaine knew exactly what Fellows' reference to the "workshop" meant.

Interesting.

Kaine wondered what had happened to the mechanic

but dismissed the question. If anything relevant had happened, Corky would let him know. As he continued watching Toby work his phone, Kaine's discomfort grew.

The second search found a list of local companies who sold or hired out Ford Ranger Raptors. Apart from the two main Ford dealerships in the region, there was only one in Stafford—Bentley Hire Fleet. Toby visited the firm's website and hit paydirt. The homepage contained a photo of their fleet of hire cars, which consisted entirely of stretch limos and Raptors.

A second photo immediately below the first showed father and son, Dylan and Jackson Bentley, holding up an oversized cheque. The same photo DS Skarrats had used in his briefing presentation. Toby scrolled down the page, reading the text which detailed the share of the money that Jackson Bentley had invested in his private hire business.

After a short while, Toby's phone became inactive. Presumably, the grieving and injured man was trying to decide his next move. Kaine's phone bleeped with an incoming SMS. The message from Corky simply read, "Earpiece".

Kaine sat up, unplugged the warm earpiece from its charger on the bedside table, and gently pressed it into his ear. He tapped it once.

"*Whatcha, Mr K. How you—*"

"Morning, Control. Have you been watching the work-shop footage? Over."

"*Frodo has. It's upset the poor guy. He's sitting in the corner of the room, rocking.*"

"What did he see? Fellows and Skarrats just blew out of the hospital as though their shirttails were on fire. Something about Tony Epps and an accident at the workshop. Over."

"Yeah. That's right. Corky's only just watched the footage. Want him to send it to you?"

"You can do, but I won't be able to view it for a while. I'm watching Toby's smartphone. I'm worried he's going to do something stupid. Over."

"Corky knows that, Mr K. Which is the reason for the earpiece. Corky didn't want you to miss nothin'."

"Can you talk me through what happened at the workshop?"

"No probs. The mechanic and Jackie B were chatting. Animated, it were. Some might call it a 'full and frank exchange of views'. After a bit, Epps slipped and fell into the inspection pit you was danglin' over last night." Corky stopped talking.

In the background, Frodo quietly repeated the same phrase over and over. "Not Frodo's fault. Not Frodo's fault."

"It's alright, mate," Corky soothed. *"No one's blaming you. Grab yourself a sherbet lemon and have another stab at solving the Hodge Conjecture."*

After another three phrase repetitions, Frodo fell silent, but a keyboard started clicking.

"Loves his sherbet lemons, Frodo does," Corky said, sounding like a proud father. *"Even more than chocolate limes. And he goes absolutely potty over his maths conundrums."* He chuckled.

"Is he okay now? Over."

"Happy as Fat Larry in an all-you-can-eat buffet, Mr K. So, where was we?"

"You were telling me how Tony Epps fell into the inspection pit … or was he pushed?"

"Nah, Mr K. Epps definitely fell. Jackie B were close, but not close enough to push the geezer. Ironically, it looks like he slipped after stepping in a puddle of engine oil he didn't clean up after himself. Go figure."

"Any idea of the topic of this 'full and frank exchange of views'?"

"*Sorry Mr K. Although it were animated, they was whispering. It were just like they didn't want the CCTV to earwig.*"

"No chance of lipreading what they said?"

"*Sorry again. The angle of shot's all wrong. The camera's looking down on them from above. Interestingly, Jackie B performed CPR while a big guy named Marco called for an ambulance and then helped with rescue breaths. Corky's searching for data on Marco as we speak. By the way, the ambulance just left with the body, but it don't look good for the mechanic. The bloke's toast. Uniformed cops are staying around.*"

The screen on Toby's phone changed to the workshop's "Contact Us" page and the active link on the phone number changed colour.

"Damn," Kaine said.

"*Corky's watching what you are, Mr K. Don't look good, does it.*"

"No, it doesn't, Control. I think Toby's about to make a big mistake. I need to concentrate on this. Alpha One, out."

Kaine leaped off the bed, grabbed his small backpack, and raced from the room, keeping one eye on the mirrored phone.

Chapter Thirty-Six

Tuesday 6th July - Jackson Bentley

Eccleshall Way, Stafford, Staffordshire, England

Exhausted, filthy, and knees aching from kneeling in the base of the inspection pit, Jackie watched the ambulance drive slowly away—no blue lights or sirens needed for a corpse. He sagged against the track of the open shutters, staring at the bloodstains on his hands. The sweat from his exertions had long since dried, but his filthy, crinkled clothes might have belonged to a rough sleeper. Still, he looked the part of an employer traumatised by the accidental death of a valued worker. He pulled in a deep breath and released it in a heavy sigh.

Easy, Jackie. No need to overdo it. There ain't no Oscars up for grabs.

A shadow fell across his feet.

"Are you okay, Mr Bentley?"

Jackie dropped his hands to his sides and stared at the uniformed constable. She had dark hair, blue eyes, and the kind of face and body no hot-blooded male would mind waking up to in the morning. Pity she was the filth. After all, Jackie had his standards. He didn't fraternise with bacon. He ate it.

"Okay?" he snapped. "No I'm not 'okay', Constable. One of my employees just fell. Cracked his head open, and I spent thirty-five minutes sweatin' my ... nuts off doin' CPR. 'Course I'm not 'okay'."

"I'm sorry, sir." A frown crinkled her pleasant face.

The woman glanced towards her two colleagues who stood guard over the inspection pit. Probably wished she hadn't approached him.

Cool it, Jackie. She's only doing her job.

Jackie held up his hand, pleased it still trembled.

"Nah," he said. "I'm the one who's sorry. Didn't mean to snap, but I were right there next to him. Saw him fall. Tried to catch him, but ..." He gasped, slowly shook his head, and left the rest unspoken.

"That's okay, Mr Bentley," she said, her expression full of concern, the sweet thing. "I understand you've had a genuine shock."

"It was a shock alright," Jackie said. "Tony Epps is— was the best mechanic I've ever employed. Don't know what I'm gonna do without him."

Easy, Jackie. Don't push it. Less is more.

At times such as these, it were best to keep quiet. He didn't want them to keep digging.

"Boss!" Marco shouted down from the office balcony.

"What?"

"Coffee's ready. Get it while it's hot."

'Bout bloody time.

"Comin'," he called.

Jackie pushed away from the wall, walked through the workshop, past all the cars, and skirted the "inspection pit of doom".

He made sure to look sad.

Slowly, using the handrail to help him up as though it were hard work, Jackie climbed the metal staircase and wandered into the office, feeling the inquisitive eyes of all three cops—the plonkers—watching his back. He closed the door behind him and hurried over to his desk.

"You set it up yet?" he asked Marco, pointing to his laptop.

"Sure have, boss," he said. "Just like you told me. I downloaded the relevant file to the laptop. Sweet as a nut."

"What's it show?"

"Exactly what happened. No more, no less."

"Can you hear what me and Tony was arguin' about?"

"No, boss. Nothing 'til I called you and Tony screamed. Tap the spacebar if you wanna check the pics for yourself."

"Good," Jackie said. "Now, where's that coffee? Instant will do for now."

"Coming right up, boss."

While Marco sloped over to the kitchenette and got to work with the kettle, Jackie jabbed the spacebar, and the video started rolling.

He watched the first few minutes of screentime and loved what he saw. True enough, he couldn't hear any of his and Epps' whispered conversation. Better still, the overhead angle of the shot obscured Epps' mouth and Jackie had his back to the cameras. The filth wouldn't be able to use lipreaders. When Epps took his tumble, Jackie was standing well away from him. Out of reach. The pictures made it looked exactly like it was, a highly fortunate—or should that be *un*fortunate—accident. No way the filth could claim it as anything different. On top of everything else, it looked like he and Marco were trying everything they could to save the poor bugger. The film showed Jackie as a hero, moving heaven and earth to help.

Marco arrived with the instant coffee and one for himself.

"Here you go, boss."

"Cheers."

Jackie grabbed the mug and took a slurp. Hot, overly sweet, but acceptable.

"Okay?" Marco asked, nodding to the laptop.

Jackie smiled. "Good enough."

"Makes us look like heroes, dunnit?" Marco said, nodding at the image on the laptop.

"Too right it does."

Marco puffed out his massive chest.

"No doubt about it, boss." He smirked. "You tried to catch him, then did all of those compressions—"

"And you did all them rescue breaths."

Marco grimaced and wiped his mouth with the back of his hand, the one not holding the coffee mug.

"No need to remind me, boss. I can still taste his blood."

Jackie took another slurp.

"Video makes it look like you were suckin' faces. Very romantic."

Jackie smiled but made sure not to laugh out loud. Not with three members of the filth crawling all over the garage.

Nah, that wouldn't do at all.

Chapter Thirty-Seven

Tuesday 6th July - Tobias Fabien

Cavell Hospital, Stafford, Staffordshire, England

Seething from the injustice of it all, Toby dialled the number on the website's "Contact Us" page and waited for the system to make the connection. It seemed to take forever. His heart raced behind the cracked ribs, and his broken thigh pounded with every thudding heartbeat. He tried to calm down, slow his breathing, but it didn't work. Normally slow to anger, losing Melissa and suffering the constant, sharp pain resulted in the explosion. Dylan Bentley—he recognised the younger man in the photo instantly—had run them off the road and killed the woman Toby had loved for every moment of his adult life.

Murdered her with a ridiculous, monster truck. Toby couldn't let him get away with it.

He simply couldn't.

"Bentley Hire Fleet and Car Sales," a woman's recorded voice said, "your call is important to us … Hello?" A man interrupted the recording, his voice deep, gruff. His accent heavily West Midlands.

Toby's heart lurched. He shuddered. Nearly cancelled the call.

"H-Hello?" Toby said. "I'd like to speak to Jackie Bentley, please."

God. He sounded so weak. So polite. So pathetic.

"This ain't a good time. Call back tomorrow."

"Is that Jackie Ben—"

"I told you, mate," the man interrupted. "Now's not a good—"

"Don't hang up, Mr Bentley. I need to talk to you about your son. It's important. He's in trouble. Big trouble."

"Hang on. I'm not Mr Bentley. I'll fetch him. … Boss," the man called out. "You'd better take this."

The sound muffled as he covered the microphone. A few seconds passed before muted scratching indicated the phone passing from one hand to another.

"You still there?" A second man, his voice as deep and rough as the first, the accent different. A Londoner.

"Are you Mr Bentley?" Toby asked. "Jackson Bentley?"

"Yeah. That's me. What's this about my boy? Has he been hurt or summat?"

"You son's a coward and a murderer!" Toby blurted out the accusation before he could stop himself, anger over-riding caution.

"What's that?" Bentley snarled.

"You heard me," Toby grunted. "Your son's a coward and a murderer."

"Hang on a minute! You can't go round accusin' Dylan of murder. It ain't right. I'll call the cops."

"Your son ran my car off the road. He killed my wife!" Toby raised his voice.

"Oh fuck. You're him, ain't ya?" Bentley said, his voice calmer, slightly softer. "You're the mutt what's spreadin' lies about my boy. Settin' the cops on us."

"My grandchildren were in the car. They could have been killed, too. Your son's out of control. A danger to everyone. As a father, you can see it, can't you? He needs help before he does it again."

"Fabien, ain't it?" Bentley said, "Toby Fabien. Listen, pal. I dunno what your game is, but Dylan didn't do nothin'. There ain't no evidence against him."

Toby caught the hint of a smirk in the man's words.

"He ran me off the road and killed my wife, and I'm not going to rest until I've proved it. I'll shout it from the rooftops if I have to!"

Bentley paused for a moment. Toby's heart pounded. A chasm opened up in his belly. What was he doing? What good would come of it?

"Listen, Mr Fabien. Let's calm this down, shall we? I can hear how upset you are. You was hurt in the accident, and you lost your missus. I can understand you want someone to blame, but it ain't fair to accuse my boy. Okay, he can be a bit lairy at times, but, deep down, he's a good kid. ... Heart of gold just like his dad."

Bentley scoffed. The man actually scoffed.

"A good kid?" Toby spluttered. "Do you actually know your son?"

"'Course I know my son, dickwad," Bentley answered,

anger deepening his voice and making it louder. He paused, coughed. "Are you after money? Is that it? You want money?"

"You can keep your blood money, Bentley. I don't want it."

"How does one hundred grand sound?"

"What?"

"You heard me," Bentley said. "One hundred thousand pounds. Call it a donation to help your recovery. I've heard you're in the hospital. Must be difficult for you. Scary even."

"I told you to keep your money."

"Two hundred grand. Final offer. Take it or leave it. There ain't gonna be no more."

Toby's shoulders sagged as his energy depleted.

"All I want is for you to convince your son to hand himself over to the police and confess."

This time, Bentley cackled.

"Why the fuck would I wanna go and do a thing like that?"

"Because it's the right thing to do."

Bentley snorted.

"Bollocks!"

In the background of the call, another man coughed out a derisive laugh. Bentley must have put his phone on speaker.

"We both know he's guilty," Toby continued, nearly shouting. "What happens if he loses control again and someone else dies? Could you live with yourself?"

"Shut your stupid mouth! Okay? My boy didn't do nothin' wrong!"

"If you don't do something to stop him ... if you keep protecting him, you'll be complicit. Just as guilty as he is."

A car horn blared. It sounded hollow down the phone line, echoey.

"Hang on. … Who's that?" Bentley whispered, his head turned away from the phone's mic, talking to the other man.

"Fellows and the fat one," the man answered.

The detectives had reached the garage.

"Tell them I'm in the crapper. I'll be right down."

"Okay, boss."

Heavy footsteps clumped away. Boots squeaked on metal.

"You still there, Fabien?" Bentley asked, his voice slow and low. Ominous.

"Yes. I'm here."

"Right," he growled, "I've had enough of this bullshit. Listen to me, pal. You got no idea who you're talkin' to."

"Yes, I—"

"Don't interrupt me, you fuckwit. Listen to me and listen good. If you don't keep your stupid mouth shut, there'll be consequences."

Toby swallowed. Things were getting out of hand. It had all gone horribly wrong.

"Wh-What do you mean?"

"Consequences," Bentley repeated. "And that ain't a warnin', it's a promise. I don't give warnin's."

"What sort of consequences? Prosecute me if you like. I don't—"

"You've got grandchildren, haven't you," he said, his voice quiet, relaxed, and, as a result, even more threatening. "Nine-year-old twins. Olivia and Rupert. Sweet, little kids."

Oh God.

Toby closed his eyes.

"H-How do you know—"

"I know everythin' about you, Fabien. Everythin'. I know where you live. Nothin' gets past Jackie Bentley."

Toby's stomach churned. His world imploded.

"Does Burton Hall Primary ring a bell?" Bentley asked.

Toby gasped.

Bentley knew where the twins went to school. How? How was that possible? How had he found out so quickly?

"Great school. Ranks right up there on the league tables. Must be nice. I got nephews. Maybe I'll send 'em there."

"What—"

"Changin' the subject," Bentley continued, his manner conversational, almost pleasant. "I drove past Hilton Park Arena & Stables the other day. Like to drive, me." He laughed. "Nice-lookin' place, the stables. Secluded. Real quiet."

Oh God.

Acid bile rose up from Toby's stomach. He dry heaved. Sucked in a deep, shuddering breath. Bentley knew where Olivia went riding on Saturday mornings. Her visits to the stables.

"I've often thought about takin' up horseridin'," Bentley continued, his tone becoming more and more casual, "but it can be dangerous. I mean, horses are so easily spooked, ain't they. One blarin' car horn and ..." He paused for a moment before adding, "You still there, Fabien?"

Tears filled Toby's eyes, blurring his vision. He dry retched again. Bentley might as well have booted him in the stomach.

"Fabien ... Toby?"

"Yes?" he answered, a catch in his voice.

"Are you okay, mate? You've gone all quiet."

"Please don't hurt them," Toby begged.

"Sorry, what was that, mate?" Bentley jeered. "I got no idea what you're talkin' about."

"Please don't—"

"You got anythin' else to say to me, Toby? Only I've got visitors. Wouldn't want to keep the filth waitin'. Now, would I?"

Bentley laughed and the call clicked into silence.

Dear God. What have I done?

Toby dropped the mobile into his lap and burst into tears.

———

TOBY LAY in bed for what seemed like hours, tears flowing, terrified.

What have I done? Dear God, what have I done?

A soft knock on the door made Toby jump. He blew his nose on a tissue, wiped his eyes with another, and called, "Yes?"

The door opened and Arnold Jeffries, the man from The 83 Trust, popped his head through the opening.

What's he doing here?

Toby reached for a clean tissue and wiped his eyes again.

"May I come in?" Jeffries asked.

"Yes," Toby answered, sniffling into the tissue, "of course. Please do."

What else could he say to the man who offered so much support? Even though Toby could think of nothing he wanted less than a visitor.

Jeffries stepped into the room, pushed the door closed. He stood at the foot of the bed, hands clasped in front, his expression serious. He'd changed clothes. Rather than the smart, business suit of his previous visit, he wore walking boots, black jeans, and a plain, dark sweatshirt. He'd lost the glasses and looked much more a man of action than a bookish solicitor.

"Sorry," Toby said, "I-I wasn't expecting you. Did we have a meeting planned?"

Jeffries shook his head. He looked deadly serious.

Chapter Thirty-Eight

Tuesday 6th July - Midday

Cavell Hospital, Stafford, Staffordshire, England

Toby Fabien sat up in bed, looking a little stronger than he had the first time they'd met. The bruising to his face had faded and the head bandage was gone, but the puffiness and redness around his eyes suggested a brush with tears. Hardly surprising considering his recent telephone conversation with Jackie Bentley.

"Toby," Kaine said, speaking quietly, calmly, "we have a … situation."

He'd been wondering how to approach the subject of Jackie Bentley's threat without telling Toby about the tap on his phone. He had no idea how that information would have gone down.

"How do you know?"

Kaine frowned, tilted his head to one side.

"How do I know what?"

"About …" Toby sighed, shook his head. "Sorry, I'm a little confused. What 'situation'?"

"Do you mind if I sit?"

"Please." Toby pointed him into the same chair as before.

Kaine shuffled around the bed, reached for a coloured pencil that had fallen between the seat and the arm, and held it up to Toby.

"It's Olivia's," he said. "The lamb spends all her free time drawing. She's very artistic. Takes after Melissa." He gulped. "Her … grandmother."

Kaine placed the pencil on the bedside cabinet and lowered himself into the chair. He leaned forwards, rested his elbows on his thighs, and considered how to proceed.

"What's this about a 'situation'?" Toby asked.

"Before I start," Kaine said, "is everything okay with you?"

Toby stiffened. "Why do you ask?"

"If you don't mind my saying, it looks as though you've been crying."

"Well, that's a shock, isn't it?" Toby snapped. "I've lost my wife, and I'm in a great deal of pain. You don't think I'm allowed to cry?"

"I'm sorry," Kaine said, holding up his hands, "I didn't mean to sound insensitive."

Tears flowing, Toby shook his head.

"No," he said, "no, please. I-I'm overreacting. Please … forgive me. I know you're only trying to help." He reached for a tissue and dabbed his streaming eyes. "What were you saying about a 'situation'? It sounds ominous."

"Nobody's called you recently?" Kaine asked, glancing at the phone he'd given Toby, which sat on the bedside cabinet alongside Olivia's colouring pencil. "You've not received any threats?"

"No," Toby lied. "Why."

Kaine settled back and lowered his hands to his knees.

"As your legal representative," Kaine opened, "I've been looking into Dylan Bentley's background. This includes his immediate family." He paused, still unsure of the best way to continue.

Toby frowned.

"You've discovered Dylan's full name?" he asked.

"We have."

"How?"

Kaine shot him a grim smile.

"There aren't too many lime-green Ford Ranger Raptors in the Staffordshire area, Toby. And working from your description, he wasn't difficult to identify."

Toby swallowed but said nothing.

"My research team unearthed some rather disturbing intel related to Dylan's father, Jackson," Kaine continued.

Toby's face paled.

"Wh-What do you mean, 'disturbing'?" he asked. His eyes watered and his blink rate increased.

Kaine dived straight in, not sugar-coating it.

"Jackie Bentley has a reputation for violence. In his late twenties, after a dishonourable discharge from the army, he served three years in prison for assault. There's been nothing since, but that doesn't mean he's turned over a new leaf. It simply means the police haven't been able to prosecute him successfully, although they have tried on a number of occasions."

Kaine paused again, giving Toby time to absorb the

implications and make him more amenable to Kaine's rapidly evolving plans.

"What exactly are you saying?" Toby asked.

"I don't want to worry you unduly, but Jackie Bentley isn't the type of man to upset. He's ruthless, and he's rich. A dangerous combination."

"Oh God," Toby said, breaking down. "What have I done?"

He lowered his head and covered his mouth with his left hand.

"Toby?" Kaine said. "What's wrong?"

Toby raised his head and looked deep into Kaine's eyes.

"This morning," he said, a catch in his voice, "I called Bentley."

"You did what?" Kaine gasped, feigning surprise.

"I-I called him. Tried to convince him to make Dylan confess."

Kaine lifted an eyebrow. "How did he respond?"

Toby's lip quivered. He blinked and more tears fell.

"He threatened the twins."

Kaine stiffened.

"Good grief. That's terrible."

"Not in so many words," Toby gasped, "but I-I knew what he meant. Basically, he told me to shut up or he'd hurt them."

Kaine gritted his teeth and gave a short nod.

"Did you record the phone call?"

"No," Toby answered. "You can do that?"

"On some phones it's possible. But it doesn't matter. I doubt Bentley would have made the threats obvious or legally actionable."

"No, they were implied, but I knew exactly what he

meant. He knows all about the twins. Their names, where they go to school, Olivia's riding lessons … everything."

He dried his eyes with a fresh tissue after disposing of the used one in the plastic bag next to the phone and the pencil.

"Toby, listen to me," Kaine said, locking eyes with his client. "The Trust won't let anything happen to you or the twins. *I* won't let anything happen."

Toby lowered his eyes to take in the whole of Kaine. He didn't seem overly impressed with what they told him.

"What can *you* do?"

Plenty. Believe me.

Kaine didn't answer.

"Should we contact the police?" Toby asked.

"What would the police do?"

"They could talk to Bentley. Warn him off."

Kaine nodded.

"Yes," he said, "we could do that. If you think it would do some good."

"Would it?"

"In my experience," Kaine said, "people like Jackson Bentley don't take much notice of the police. If anything, it might antagonise him further."

Again, Toby's lower lip quaked. The man was close to breaking down.

"Do you have an alternative suggestion?" he asked.

"There are a number of options open to us, Toby."

"Such as?"

"Well, we could ignore Bentley and hope his threats were nothing more than bluster. However …" Kaine paused to drive the message home.

"What?"

"The Trust takes threats to its clients very seriously. We don't like it at all. I have a second option."

"Tell me," Toby said, staring hard at Kaine. Imploring. Grasping for any hope that he could cling to.

Kaine leaned closer.

"I could go and have a quiet word with Bentley myself. Point out the error of his ways and explain the consequences of his proposed actions."

"Wouldn't that be the same as the police talking to him? Wouldn't it antagonise him just as much?"

Kaine delivered a grim smile.

"I don't have to follow the same rules as the police, Toby. I don't have the same restrictions."

"You might make the situation worse."

"You'll be surprised what the right quiet word will be able to achieve. However, I promise not to do anything hasty. I need to put certain things in place first."

"What sort of things?"

"The Trust has a security department that specialises in personal protection. Our operatives are very discreet and highly professional. With your permission, I'll arrange for them to protect the twins."

Toby reached out a hand.

"You really think that's necessary?"

"I hope not, but in my opinion, there's no such thing as being too careful. Not when the twins' safety is at stake."

"God, you're starting to scare me."

Good.

Being scared would help keep him and the twins safe.

"I'm not trying to scare you, Toby. It seems to me that Jackson Bentley has already done that. My job—The Trust's job—is to keep you safe. So, can I talk to my security people? Start the ball rolling?"

Toby fell silent, and Kaine allowed him time to think.

"How would it work, exactly?" he asked after a short time staring at the crushed tissue in his hand.

"In what respect?"

"I mean, how would it work, logistically? How would Ken and Lucy Kendall react if a pack of uniformed, security guards suddenly knocked on their front door and invaded their lives? They'd be terrified. They've got kids, too, don't forget. It wouldn't be fair on them to even ask. They've already done so much for us … for the twins."

Kaine smiled at the idea of Cough and Stephan or Nate and Jeff—dressed as security guards—rocking up at a suburban home, demanding admittance.

"It wouldn't work that way. For a start, my team would be undercover."

"How?" Toby scoffed. "I suppose you'd have them park outside the house and try to look inconspicuous. Have you seen where the Kendalls live?" He took a breath. "Around the corner from us. The place is so quiet that strangers in a parked car would stand out a mile. You might as well shine a searchlight on them. And how would they explain themselves to the twins? It would terrify them. And how long would we have to live with security guards watching our every move?"

Not long, Toby. Not long.

"And how would we explain it to the twins' school?" Toby continued. "No, it wouldn't work."

"You're quite right," Kaine said. "It wouldn't work. Not like that, but …" He scratched his beard.

"But?"

"If you were at home, my people could act as your live-in carers."

"But I'm not at home. I'm here!" Toby said, raising his voice slightly. "In this hospital bed."

Kaine held up a finger.

"That's right," he said, smiling, "I haven't told you, have I?"

"You haven't told me what?"

"You're being discharged tomorrow."

"I'm *what?*" Again, Toby shook his head.

"I spoke with Mr Ferber on my way in," Kaine said, adding an air of optimism. "He's happy to discharge you into the care team we have organised."

"A care team?" Toby asked. "What care team?"

"You'll meet them tomorrow. It'll be led by Nigel Cathcart." Kaine smiled sadly. "Nigel's a first-class nurse. As I said, two of The Trust's security officers will help with day-to-day tasks like cooking and ferrying the twins to and from school. A third will take the night shift."

"You've organised all this very quickly."

"The team is in place and ready to go at a moment's notice. All we need now is your permission. Do you give it?"

"Yes," Toby said, without hesitation. "Yes, I do. I can't wait to get home."

"Good," Kaine said, offering up a relieved smile. "I'll confirm the arrangements this afternoon."

"The twins will be safe?"

"Yes," Kaine said. "They'll be as safe as I can make them. You have my word."

He stood, leaned forwards, and offered Toby his hand. They shook slightly awkwardly.

"Try not to worry, Toby," he said. "I know that's easy for me to say, but we know what we're doing. We've done this sort of thing before, and we're good at it."

He left the room, hoping he hadn't just tempted fate.

Outside in the hospital car park, Kaine slid behind the wheel of his Ford. He hit the ignition button, waited for the phone system to connect, and dialled Lara's number. She answered within seconds.

"Hi, love," he said brightly.

"Did he agree?" she asked, breathing heavily.

Whickering in the background and wind whispering through the trees gave away her location as one of the paddocks near the stables.

"Yes. It's a go for tomorrow. Is Nigel on board?"

"He is," she answered. "I've given him a full, medical handover. He's happy to take on an open-ended contract."

Whinnies suggested Lara had left one horse and moved onto another.

"Why wouldn't he be?" Kaine said. "We're paying him the same as the average, NHS consultant."

"He's not only doing it for the money, Arnold," she said, her tone gently scolding. "I gave him a brief overview of the situation and he's really keen to help."

"How much have you told him?" Kaine asked, although he really should have known better. Lara knew what she was doing.

"Only that the client has been in a car crash and needs full-time, nursing care during his rehabilitation. I also told him there were children involved. Cough, Stefan, and Connor have agreed to provide logistical support for the first few days, and I have the others on standby if protection is needed over the long term."

It won't be.

"That's brilliant, love. Thanks for doing that. How are things on the other matter?"

"It's progressing. We're fielding calls from all over the

country. The memorial service will be packed. Plenty of prep needed."

She paused but Kaine didn't have anything to say. At least, not over the phone.

"Oh," she said, "before I forget. We heard from Emma."

Kaine had to think for a moment before the name jogged a memory. Emma Trulove, Toby's sister-in-law.

"Her flight's due in early on Friday. Hunter offered to collect her from the airport and drive her to the client's home."

"That's good news. Thank him for me, will you?"

"Already have," she said, a smile edging into her voice. "And what are your immediate plans? Are you coming home?"

Kaine smiled. He liked the idea of having a permanent home with Lara. Maybe one day. At one stage, he thought it might be the villa in Aquitaine, but the farm would do equally as well. The villa would make a great holiday retreat.

"'Fraid not," he said softly. "There's a few things I need to do here first."

"Can you give me any examples?"

"Darling, if we're going to move here, one of us needs to scope out the local primary schools," he said, being deliberately vague over the phone, as usual, "and as I'm here on business ..."

"Good idea," Lara said, quick on the uptake. She understood his intention.

"Little Stefan will be old enough to attend school soon," he added, making her laugh.

"You can be so cruel."

"He's a big boy, love. He can take it."

"Being serious for a moment, what do you have planned for the … car hire firm?"

"What makes you think—"

"I know you, Arnold. C'mon, fess up."

"No firm plans, but I might arrange to test drive one of their pickup trucks. They look so darned cool."

"Don't you even think about buying one of those monstrosities," she warned. "I'll disown you."

This time, Kaine laughed.

"But they're spectacular, love. Powerful beasts. I love them. It would be great to take them off-road."

"Hmm. You're definitely planning to see the owner?"

"Yep."

"Why take the risk?"

"You know why, love," Kaine answered. "I need to look him in the eye, to see if he's a serious menace. His aggression might just be bluster."

"And if it is bluster?"

"I'll leave well alone."

"If not?"

"You know the answer to that already, love."

"I think I do," she said, after a momentary hesitation. "Take care, and keep in touch."

"Will do, love. Give Dynamite and the brown one my regards."

"Her name's Lexie," Lara snapped. "As you very well know."

He ended the connection on another gentle laugh.

346

Chapter Thirty-Nine

Tuesday 6th July - Early Afternoon

Uplands Road, Stafford, Staffordshire, England

Kaine turned the page of his newspaper and absorbed his favourite news article for the third time. It made pretty good reading. The previous night's, televised, election debate had shown the new leader of the incumbent party falling flat on his face. He'd been caught in a bare-faced, statistical lie and his opponent—the long-serving and well-respected leader of the opposition—had pounced, scoring hit after unchallenged hit. The post-debate snap polls showed the opposition with a twelve-point lead. Although not a political animal, Kaine had a vested interest in the outcome of the imminent general election. If the opposition won with a strong majority, Kaine would have a shot at clearing his name without any legal wrangling. The same would not be the case if the governing party somehow clung to power. Kaine sighed. The final poll couldn't arrive soon enough.

He checked his watch. 14:48. Half an hour to wait.

To claim a prime parking spot, one with a decent view of the entrance to Burton Hall Primary, he'd arrived an hour before the end of the school day and had spent the time engrossed in his tabloid. The news was interesting enough, and the paper gave him cover. He didn't often have the time to read something that wasn't a mission briefing and considered it a rare luxury. One to appreciate.

Slowly, the road started filling with parents on the school run. Some doubled parked, others climbed grass verges, no doubt to the frustration and annoyance of the householders. Pedestrians—the vast majority women—arrived in dribs and drabs, and clung to the school's dark green, metal railings, waiting. Dressed in lightweight, summer gear, some showing more flesh than seemed appropriate, they smiled and chatted and soaked up the sun's warmth. Some hid in the shade of the overarching conifers, while the scantily clad sun-worshipers stood in its full glow—dicing with the onset of melanoma.

The Kendalls' bright, blue Peugeot 308 drove past the front of the school and carried on. Kaine felt sorry for having taken up a prized parking space, but it would only be the one time. Hopefully.

Five minutes later, with school kicking-out time nearly upon them, Kaine spotted Lucinda Kendall in his rear-view mirror, walking. She'd clearly completed a full circuit of the block, parked around the corner, and was rushing to avoid being late. Kaine opened the door of his dull, grey Ford Focus and climbed out. As she approached the school gates, she slowed, and he matched her pace.

"Mrs Kendall?" he said, strolling alongside her. "I'm Arnold Jeffries. We met briefly at the hospital the other day."

Lucinda's concerned frown transformed into a bright smile.

"Of course I remember you," she said. "You're Mr Fabien's solicitor."

"That's right."

Kaine didn't mind lying for a good cause.

They stopped close to the gates but far enough away from the groups of parents to avoid being overheard. Lucinda turned to face him.

"What are you doing here?" she asked, her educated, Home Counties accent slow and soft. "Is anything the matter?"

"Not at all, Mrs Kendall," Kaine answered in his poshest voice. "I just wanted to make sure everything was okay with you and the twins."

"Things are fine. The twins seem to be coping well given the ... circumstances. They miss their grandmother, of course."

And their parents, no doubt.

Her smile dropped and Kaine nodded slowly, showing his appreciation of the situation.

A serious-looking, young woman in loose-fitting, sports gear rounded the side of the school's main building. She marched towards the gates, spinning a small bunch of keys on a cord around her index finger. She bent to open the padlock on the gates, but kept the gates closed.

Three minutes to go.

"Mr Fabien asked me to give you the good news," Kaine said.

"Oh?"

"He's being discharged tomorrow and returning home."

She smiled. "That *is* good news."

"Yes. And Mr Fabien's sister-in-law, Emma, will be arriving on Friday. Which means we'll be in a position to take the twins off your hands much earlier than we first anticipated." He softened his voice to counteract the silence of the nearest group of parents who'd started to take an interest in their conversation.

"It really isn't a problem, Mr Jeffries. We're more than happy to help. The twins are so well behaved, they really are no trouble. Olivia and Emily are thick as thieves, and Rupert's such a quiet lad. He's having a calming effect on little Arthur. There's really no rush. In fact, it might be a good idea to let Melissa's sister recover from her journey before she has to look after what will be two relative strangers. Don't you think?"

Kaine took a few moments to explain the care package they'd put in place. Despite her assurance to the contrary, Lucinda seemed pleased with the preparations and relieved that the twins would soon be off her hands. Perhaps she was being polite earlier. Giving up the twins would take the pressure off her young family.

Who can blame her?

The main doors of the school building opened, and a pinch-nosed, grey-haired woman in a dark skirt suit stepped out. She stood to one side, straight-backed, hands clasped at her ample chest. A solemn expression hung on her authoritarian face. Kaine expected to see an immediate eruption of screaming, yelling kids keen to escape the confines of the classroom. Instead, a line of tiny tots filed out, led by an adult Kaine could only assume to be their form teacher. The pupils' impeccable behaviour would have been a credit to any military drill instructor. The grey-

haired woman nodded benignly and spoke to the occasional child.

Movement in the corner of Kaine's eye drew his attention. He half-turned towards it but kept the conversation
going, nodding and smiling.

"That's Year 1," Lucinda said. "Arthur's in Year 3.
They'll be out soon."

A black, Mercedes-Benz G-Class wagon approached,
driving slowly up the one-way street. It pulled to a stop
alongside the school gates. The driver seemed unaware that
he was blocking the road. Unaware or indifferent.

"They're very well behaved," Kaine noted, nodding to
the line of kids. "Wouldn't have happened like that in my
day. We couldn't wait to escape school."

"Mrs Franklyn's rather fearsome, but she does get good
results. The school's Ofsted rating is 'Outstanding'."

Kaine nodded sagely, as though he knew what that
represented.

The woman in sports gear finally opened the gates and
released the little ones into the arms of their eager
guardians.

"Ah, there's Arthur. Excuse me."

Kaine stepped away, his attention split between the
Mercedes and the kids exiting the school. The next class
appeared, led by a fair-haired man in light grey trousers and
a polo shirt, Year 4. Olivia and Rupert led the troop, two
abreast, hand-in-hand. So obviously twins.

The Merc driver raised a mobile phone to his eye for a
few seconds, then dropped it into the passenger's seat and
drove away. Kaine's senses tingled, and anger flared. The
bugger had taken a photo of the twins. Kaine could see no
reason for it but the obvious. Intimidation.

You bastard.

With teeth gritted, Kaine spun. He hurried back to his Ford, jumped in, and fired the engine into life. He reversed out of his parking spot and backed into Burton Hall Road, incurring the horn-blaring wrath of a driver in a white Kia Sorento. He smiled, waved his abject apology, and rolled his car towards the T-junction where Uplands Road joined Burton Hall Road.

The Merc sat third placed in a queue, the driver illegally thumbing a message into his mobile, oblivious to the rules of the road. Kaine advanced slowly, allowing a gap to form between his car and the ones in front. At the T-junction, he flashed his lights and allowed the cars on Uplands Road to go in front of him. The first two drivers nodded their thanks. The driver of the Merc—a heavy-shouldered, white guy in a black, muscle shirt with a sleeve of tats scrolling down his right arm—ignored Kaine's kind gesture, and jumped out into the road as though he owned it. Kaine didn't mind. It suited his purposes, and he followed at a safe distance.

Five minutes later, the Ford's infotainment system announced an incoming call. Caller ID, Toby Fabien.

"Accept call," Kaine said.

"Mr Jeffries?" Toby asked. "Is that you?" He rushed his words in agitation.

"Yes, it's me," Kaine answered, already suspecting the reason for Toby's distress. "What's—"

"I've just been sent a picture of the twins. They're leaving school. It's Jackie Bentley. He's threatening me." Toby gasped, his fear obvious.

"Toby," Kaine said, "try to keep calm. I'm on it."

"What? How?"

"I'm following the man who sent you the—"

"Jackie Bentley?"

The Merc driver indicated left and made the turn. Kaine followed him into a drive-through restaurant that sold chicken by the bucketload.

"No," Kaine answered, "but he'll be working for Bentley."

"What are you going to do?"

"Not sure yet. I'll keep following. See where he goes. If he stops somewhere quiet, I might just have a little word. Warn him off."

"Dear God. Is that wise? Won't it make matters worse?"

How can it be any worse?

"Please try not to worry, Toby. I can be quite persuasive when I put my mind to it."

"Don't worry?" Toby barked. "Don't worry! I'm terrified. The twins are my whole world. I can't help but wor—"

"Toby," Kaine interrupted. "You and the twins are under my protection, and Jackson Bentley's cronies need to be made aware of that fact. Starting with the man who sent you the photo. I know this is a difficult situation for you, and it's hard to trust someone you don't know, but this is what I do. Trust me."

The Merc edged forwards in the short queue. The driver stopped at the kiosk, leaned through the open window, placed his order, and tapped his bank card on the pad. Then he pulled the SUV ahead.

"I-I … can't … I-I don't know what to say," Toby said. "Please, be careful."

"I will. I promise."

Kaine ended the call and rolled up to the kiosk.

"Hello, sir," the bored-looking, spotty-face teen behind the glass shield said. "How can I help you today?" His smile couldn't have been much more plastic.

Kaine shook his head.

No, thank you, son.

For Kaine to order chicken in a bucket, he'd have to be a damn sight hungrier than he was. In fact, he'd have to be starving. Tapping on death's door.

"Sorry, mate," he said. "I turned left by mistake back there. I'll just filter through."

"You're not the first to do that, sir," the kid said, more animated. "Happens all the time." His smile broadened—this one genuine.

At least Kaine had made someone's day.

True to its "fast-food" credentials, the Merc reached the service counter and collected a bucket of some kind of chicken and a giant, takeout mug of drink. He drove away and Kaine followed him back onto the open road.

The Merc drove under the M6, passing a grammar school on the right. They powered along, ignoring the speed limit and heading out into the countryside. Half a mile later, after running through an avenue of trees that threw down a dimpled light, the Merc's left indicator flashed again. They turned into a secluded layby and the Merc skidded to a sudden stop. Kaine pulled up close behind, stopping the Ford's bonnet centimetres from the Merc's tailgate.

The driver threw open his door and jumped out. He stood, feet shoulder-width apart, hands on narrow hips. Arms bare, heavy biceps and triceps bulging, he jumped his pecs and tightened his abs in a threatening, muscular display of pure, animal power. Gym-built muscles, useless for anything but inept posturing.

Kaine all but burst out laughing.

"Are you following me, pal?"

Driver roared the challenge, his voice deep and booming. The man's acne-covered cheeks and neck gave away that he was one suspected recipient of Dylan Bentley's illegal product.

Kaine scanned the area. The layby stood empty, shielded from the road by copper beech trees and an overgrown, hawthorn hedge.

Perfect.

He opened his door and climbed into the glowing sunshine.

"Are you a paedo?" he asked, speaking with calm consideration. Keeping things casual.

Driver dropped his hands from his hips, formed fists, jutted out his chin. His eyes bugged.

"Say what, arsehole?"

Kaine repeated his question, loud and slow enough for the hard of understanding.

"Fuck you!" Driver said, tracking closer.

Kaine held up an open hand. Driver stopped. Jaw still clenched.

"Show me your phone."

"What? Fuck off," Driver barked. A man of few words and a limited vocabulary like so many of the mouth breathers Kaine often had to deal with.

"I saw you outside the school," Kaine said, "taking photos of the kiddies. We don't like paedos hanging around our school."

Driver pulled his angry eyes away from Kaine and glowered at the Ford. Finding it empty, he sneered.

"Who's the 'we', little man?" he snarled. "The way I see it, you are all on your lonesome." Again, he stuck out his chin, delivering the last remark as a taunt.

Kaine puffed out his chest. "I'm speaking as co-leader of the Uplands Road Neighbourhood Watch Association."

He held out his hand and beckoned with his fingers. "C'mon. Hand over your phone, *Paedo*."

Driver's face reddened.

"Call me that again, and I'll break your fucking neck, you scrawny arsehole."

"What's wrong, *Paedo*?" Kaine sneered. "Don't you like being a called a paedo, *Paedo*?"

Driver roared and lurched forwards, arms swinging, throwing wild but clubbing blows. Kaine ducked under a haymaker right which whipped harmlessly over his head. He slid to his left and stuck out his rear leg. Driver tripped, staggered, righted himself. He spun to face Kaine, who'd slipped behind him, moving away from the Ford and closer to the Merc.

Kaine laughed. "Is that all you've got, *Paedo*?"

Driver's eyes bulged and his thin lips peeled back to reveal a row of off-white choppers so small they could have been milk teeth.

"I'm gonna break your fucking neck!"

"You've already said that, *Paedo*." Kaine smiled, held up both hands, and motioned him closer again. "C'mon then. Here I am. Come get me."

Furious, Driver growled. He stomped towards Kaine, fists raised, chin tucked into his lead shoulder. Kaine moved to his right, threw a short left and straight right. Driver jerked his head back and leaned away. With his balance compromised, Driver stopped advancing and dropped his left arm, exposing the left side of his face.

Kaine lunged and slammed his open right hand against the unprotected left ear in a ringing, deafening blow. Driver screamed, jerked his head away. Kaine followed the slap with a vicious, two-fingered jab into Driver's eyes. His fingernails dug into soft tissue. Eyeballs squelched.

Driver squealed, drew his head away, threw his hands up to his face, and crumpled to his knees in the dirt.

"My eyes!" he shrieked. "Oh God. My eyes!"

Kaine hadn't pulled the jab. Didn't give a damn if he'd blinded the arsehole. The bugger deserved everything he got. He'd been happy to threaten the twins, and Kaine had been delighted to maim him in return.

"That's what happens to paedos around here, *Paedo*."

"I'm not," Driver cried, waving his right hand in front of him in an ineffective attempt to fend Kaine off. "I'm not a paedo. I'd never hurt kids. Honest."

Kaine approached from the side, silently. He leaned close to Driver's right ear and whispered, "You lying piece of shit."

Driver squealed, jerked back, and shrank away.

"I'm not," he screamed. "Please believe me."

Kaine stood tall, stepped back a pace, merciless. He needed to put the pitiful creature out of the game for a while.

"Why should I?"

"I-It's true," he cried, eyes weeping. "Oh God. I-I can't see nothing. Help me. Please, help me!"

"What's your name?"

"Logan," he wailed instantly. "L-Logan C-Cambridge."

"Well then, Logan Cambridge, give me your right hand," Kaine said, soothing, "I'll help you to your car. You can phone for an ambulance."

Still covering his eyes with his left hand, Cambridge hesitated for a moment before pushing out his right, blindly searching the empty space in front of him. Kaine stepped closer, reached out, and grabbed a pair of the outstretched fingers in each fist. He ripped the fingers apart and bent them backwards, dislocating knuckles and breaking all four fingers.

Bones snapped, joints popped, and again, Cambridge screamed.

Kaine released the shattered fingers and stepped away.

A crumpled Logan Cambridge hugged his broken right hand tight to his chest and curled into a foetal ball. He rocked and wept.

Kaine stared down at the sorry mess, unmoved. He deserved nothing less for threatening the twins.

"Serves you right for being a paedo, *Paedo*!"

Too busy blubbing, Cambridge no longer had the spare capacity to contradict the accusation. He simply rocked in place, weeping.

Keeping a close watch on the incapacitated thug, Kaine approached the Merc. He yanked open the driver's door, snatched the mobile from the passenger's seat, and touch-activated the screen. It required a password.

Kaine slammed the door shut.

Cambridge whimpered, lowered his left hand from his face, and raised his head. He opened a pair of bloodshot and inflamed eyes, blinked rapidly, and squinted through swollen lids. On Kaine's slow approach, he dug in his heels and scrambled away, scraping his backside in the dirt.

"N-No," he pleaded. "Please don't."

"You can see me?"

Cambridge nodded. Snot ran from his nose and mixed with the tears.

"J-Just about."

"Lucky boy." Kaine held up the mobile. "What's your PIN?"

"9-8-7-6," Cambridge blurted out, no hesitation. Desperate to appease.

Kaine dialled in the numbers.

The phone opened to the photo app. The most recent pics showed three shots of the twins framed in the school entranceway.

"What are these?" he demanded, showing the screen to Cambridge.

The thug didn't answer.

"Like I said," Kaine mocked. "Paedo. The police are going to love these."

Cambridge hung his head. Still, he didn't speak.

"Hand me your car keys," Kaine demanded, holding out his hand.

Cambridge looked up through weeping, reddened eyes.

"But—"

"Keys!" Kaine snarled, taking a threatening pace closer. "Now!"

Awkwardly, grunting, Cambridge stretched out his right leg, dug his left hand into his right jeans pocket, and tugged out a set of keys on a fob. He held them up.

Kaine snatched them from Cambridge's outstretched hand, locked the Merc, and lobbed the keys high into the nearby hedge.

"Goodbye, Logan Cambridge," Kaine said, cheerily.

He turned to leave.

"Wait," Cambridge cried out. "You can't leave me here. I-I need a hospital."

Kaine stopped and closed on the thug.

"Listen to me, *Paedo*. If I ever see you hanging around the school again, I'm going to tell the mothers what you are." Kaine sneered and shook his head. "Believe me, you won't like their reaction. It'll make what I've just given you seem like a series of gentle, love taps."

He turned and left a pitiful, snivelling lackey scrambling in the dirt where he belonged.

Chapter Forty

Wednesday 7th July - Jackson Bentley

Eccleshall Way, Stafford, Staffordshire, England

"Get on with it," Jackie said, leaning over the balcony railing and cranking out an evil smile.

Time to pay your dues, son.

Dylan looked down at the workshop and frowned.

"What?"

Jackie pointed at the inspection pit and the splash of dark red gore painting the far edge.

"Clean it up."

"What, me?"

"Of course, you," Jackie snapped. "Fuck's sake, boy. You expect me to do it?"

Dylan's faced turned white.

"Can't you get someone in?"

"What? And pay good money for some overpriced, clean-up firm to throw a bucket of soapy water over it and wipe it with a mop?" He scoffed. "Get on with it." Jackie leaned forwards and lowered his voice. "You owe me, remember."

Colour flushed Dylan's face, and he added a dark scowl. It made him look like a spoiled schoolboy.

"Did the filth give permission to clean up the mess already?" Dylan asked, clutching at straws.

Jackie glanced around the workshop to make sure they were alone.

"Don't call them that in public, you dick. They're 'the police' or 'the cops', understand?"

"We ain't in public, Dad," Dylan said, drawing out the words and shaking his head. "We're in the workshop. So, did they?"

"Yeah," Jackie answered. "They're happy it were an accident. Couldn't do nothin' else. The CCTV proves it. Now you can clean the place up. And don't forget to use bleach. I want that area spotless. And make sure you mop up that oil spill, too. Don't want another accident, do we?"

Dylan's broad shoulders dropped, and he lowered his head.

"'Kay, Dad. How do I clean the oil?"

"You'll need builder's sand to soak it up first. There's some in Storeroom Five. I'll show you."

Jackie turned and headed for the door at the end of the row beyond the loo.

"No, Dad!" Dylan snapped. "Don't bother. I'll find it."

He brushed past Jackie and stomped along the balcony,

his boots squeaking on the metal plates. Daft bugger still thought Jackie didn't have a clue.

"Wait!" Jackie barked.

Dylan stopped, turned.

"Yeah?" he asked. Another deep frown wrinkling his forehead.

"You'll need the key, idiot."

He up-nodded. "Oh, yeah. Right."

Dylan reversed course, ducked into the main office, and plucked the store key from the unlocked hook board. He held it up to show Jackie and slid passed him again.

It weren't like Dylan to be so Goddamn helpful. Inwardly, Jackie smiled. He knew exactly what was going on. What the fool was trying to hide.

For the hell of it, Jackie followed the lad towards the storeroom, but only took three paces before Marco yelled at him from inside the office.

"Boss?" he called. "Call for you."

"Who?" Jackie asked, retracing his steps, nudging into the warm, and shutting the glass door.

"Customer," Marco announced, pointing to the handset lying on the desk. "Wants to hire a car or two."

"Can't you handle it?"

Marco pulled in his neck and shook his head.

"Bloke asked for you by name. Said he needed to talk to the man in charge—and that's you, boss."

It sure is.

Marco held up his hand and rubbed the tips of his fingers together. There was money in it. Big money.

"Okay," Jackie said, crossing to his desk and dropping into the comfy chair behind it. "I'll take it."

"It's on mute, boss."

Jackie nodded.

"When's Tracy due back from Marbella?"

"Monday."

"Good. She's better at the customer-facing stuff than you. More professional."

Marco snorted.

"You don't pay me to answer the phones or suck up to the punters, boss."

Jackie snorted. "That's true enough."

Dylan walked past the office door, lugging an open sack of builder's sand. As he passed, he smiled and nodded to Jackie.

I know what you're up to, son. Can't pull the wool over my eyes!

"Hey, Dylan."

The lad stopped and retraced his steps to the door, hugging the sand as though it weighed a ton. And him with all them bulging muscles. Daft bugger.

"Yeah?" he said, resting the bag on his hip, and leaning against the doorjamb.

"Spread the sand over the spillage and let it soak in for at least fifteen minutes. Then sweep it up and mop the stain with detergent. Do it proper, okay?"

Dylan rolled his eyes to the ceiling.

"Yes, Dad."

"Go on, then. Get on with it."

Dylan bunted himself away from the doorjamb and sloped off, muttering to himself.

Marco smirked.

"Don't say nothing, Marco."

"Who, me, boss?" he said, smiling wide. "No way, boss."

"Smartarse," Jackie said, smiling.

"Sorry, boss."

Jackie reached for the phone and released the mute.

"Hello," he said, using his best telephone voice. "Jackson Bentley here."

"Ah, Mr Bentley. My name's Jeffries, Arnold Jeffries." The man sounded cultured, posh. Made of money.

Jackie noted the man's name on his pad. He was crap with names. Couldn't hardly remember his own some days.

"Good morning, Mr Jeffries, how can I help you today?"

Jeffries cleared his throat gently and excused himself. Very posh. Most people didn't bother.

"My fiancée and I are getting married next June."

Another lamb to the slaughter.

Jackie tried to stifle a yawn.

"Congratulations, Mr Jeffries."

He tried hard to play nice.

"Thank you. We're looking at Westbury Hall for our wedding venue."

Jackie sat up a little straighter. Westbury Hall charged an arm and half a leg for hosting a wedding bash. Jeffries clearly had real money to spend.

Might be worth schmoozing the mug.

"Westbury Hall is lovely, Mr Jeffries," Jackie said. "You couldn't wish for a better venue. The future Mrs Jeffries will be delighted."

Yes, Jackie. Lay it on with a trowel.

"I certainly hope so, Mr Bentley. And that's where you come in. We'll been looking to hire chauffeured transportation for the whole weekend."

"How many vehicles will you be needing?"

"Half a dozen, I imagine. Maybe more. Most of our guests will be travelling up from London by train. We'll be reserving first-class train tickets for most of them. We'll need transportation to and from the station and between the Hall and the church on the Saturday."

Guy's loaded.

Jackie smiled at the thought of stiffing the wanker for a huge fee.

"Will you be looking to hire our stretch limos?"

"Of course, old man," Jeffries said through a laugh. "Nothing but the best for our guests. But we'll be needing some Raptors, too. On self-drive."

"Self-drive?"

"Yah. Like I said, most of our friends will be coming up from London, they'll be wanting to tackle the green lanes. That's one of the prime reasons we've chosen Westbury Hall. They have good access to the green lanes."

"Ah, I see."

Tosser.

"Yes, we want to make the most of the long weekend. My mates are all petrol heads. And most of Martha's friends—Martha is my fiancée, by the way—are keen to give off-roading a go. I've visited your website and love the look of your Raptors. They're so … beefy. If you don't mind my asking, how easy are they to drive?"

"Just like a normal, big car, Mr Jeffries. Only better. You're up high and with nearly three hundred horses under the bonnet and three hundred and sixty foot-pounds of torque at your disposal. That power will slam the Raptor from nought to sixty in less than eight seconds, which is hot hatch territory. You'll find it a real blast."

Jackie reeled off the numbers he'd "borrowed" directly from the manufacturers blurb. Reckoned it made him sound like he knew his shit—which he did. He knew all there was to know about Raptors. And the stretches, come to that. It always paid to know what you were peddling.

"That's absolutely fantastic," Jeffries said, an edge of excitement to his toff accent. "You make it sound so exciting. I can't wait to test drive one of those beauties."

"I do have to offer one note of caution, however," Jackie said, letting hesitation enter his words.

"And what's that?"

"For a self-drive contract of this type, we will have to levy a significant surcharge. The insurance alone will be—"

"Money's no object, old boy," Jeffries butted in. "After all, it's our big day, and I'm only getting married the one time."

You think?

"Exactly, Mr Jeffries."

Jackie smiled. Another punter hooked.

"Can I arrange a test drive for today? This afternoon perhaps?"

How keen is that?

"That's not a problem, Mr Jeffries. I'll take you out myself."

"That would be marvellous. I'm really looking forward to meeting you," Jeffries gushed. "I can be there for a quarter past two, if that's okay? And if I like what I see, we can agree the numbers today. I can also lay down a significant deposit."

Too right you will.

He'd hooked a big fish and couldn't wait to stuff it into the keep net.

"It would be helpful, for the insurance, if you could send me a photo of your driving licence ahead of your arrival."

"Of course, Mr Bentley. Of course," Jeffries said without faltering.

Bugger was so keen it hurt.

Jackie grinned at Marco, who'd been earwigging the whole conversation. The big lug winked and shot a double thumbs up.

"Two-fifteen it is," Jackie said. "I'll see you then."

Jeffries ended the call with a cheery, "*Ciao*, Mr Bentley."

Ciao? What? He's Italian now?

Jackie dropped the phone into its cradle and rubbed his hands together.

"Lovely stuff."

"Plonker didn't even ask for a multicar discount," Marco said, shaking his big, rock of a head. "Daft bugger's got more money than sense."

"Don't mock the clients, Marco. They pay your wages."

Marco snorted. "As though you need the money."

"Fair enough, but I ain't runnin' a charity. Geezers like Jeffries help to keep this place tickin' over."

"Assuming he's kosher."

"Why wouldn't he be?"

"Could be a timewaster out for a free drive in a Raptor. For the jollies."

"But we'll see his drivin' licence." Jackie wagged his head from side to side. "And you're gonna check him out, okay?"

"Okay."

"And if he is yankin' my chain, I'll let you loose on the bugger."

Marco gave one of his wolfish smiles and showed off his sharp, white teeth.

"Thanks, boss. I haven't had a decent workout for days."

He leaned back, threw his feet on the coffee table, and reached for the day's tabloid.

"Talkin' 'bout a workout," Jackie said, "how's Logan doin'?"

Marco shook out the paper and scrunched up his face.

"He's got a handful of broken fingers, and the doctor says he might lose the sight in his left eye. Someone gave him a good going over."

Jackie picked up a ballpoint and twiddled it between his fingers.

"Any ideas who done it?"

"Not really, boss. Logan's under sedation. A bit confused. Said something about three geezers attacking him. Told him they were from something called the 'Uplands Road Neighbourhood Watch'. Accusing him of being a paedo after they saw him taking pics of the Fabien twins for you."

Jackie squeezed the ballpoint so hard it snapped in half. He threw the broken pieces into the bin on the floor beside his desk.

"So," he said, "what the fuck are you sittin' there for? Take a couple of the guys and go give them Neighbourhood Watch plonkers a seein' to."

Marco dropped the paper to the table, lowered his feet to the carpet, and leaned forwards.

"That's the trouble, boss," he said. "There's no such thing as the 'Uplands Road Neighbourhood Watch'. I tried checking them out. It doesn't exist. Either Logan heard them wrong, or he's lying."

Jackie frowned. "Why would he lie?"

Marco flared his nostrils and sniffed.

"You know Logan, boss. Dylan's knock-off steroids probably make him think he's hard when he's softer than butter. He probably picked on someone who fought back, and he doesn't want to admit it out of embarrassment."

Jackie sighed. Why did he surround himself with morons?

"Why the fuck didn't you beat the truth outta him?"

The big minder snorted.

"Bloody hell, boss. Logan's lying in a hospital bed surrounded by patients and medical staff. I could hardly work him over there and then, could I? It'll have to wait until he's discharged." The big Italian scrunched up his face again. "Might be a while, though. Like I said, Logan's in a real mess."

Jackie let his shoulders drop. He leaned back in his chair, and stared at the rust-stained ceiling.

"Yeah," he said, working his way through a heavy sigh. "You're right. You did good. But do me a favour, eh?"

"What's that, boss?"

"Don't talk about Dylan's little side hustle. The lad still thinks I don't know nothin' about it."

Marco hiked an eyebrow.

"You haven't spoken to him yet?"

"Nah," Jackie said. "I'm cuttin' the boy some slack."

The eyebrow dropped and formed a frown with the other.

"Why?"

"It's good for him to spread his wings."

"You reckon?"

"By the time I reached Dylan's age, I'd already been drummed out of the army for misappropriation of stores. The second they let me out the Glasshouse I set up my first 'business enterprise'. Truth is, I'm pleased the lad's finally showin' some entrepreneurial spirit."

"But he's taking unnecessary risks."

"What risks?"

"Storing the gear in the workshop for a start."

Jackie took his turn to snort. "This is Jackie Bentley's place. Safer'n a bank. Ain't nobody's got the balls to turn this place over."

"If you say so, boss." Marco reached up and stroked his chin thoughtfully, building up to something.

"C'mon, Marco. Spit it out."

He shook his head. "Nah, boss. It's nothing."

"Out with it, Marco. Do as you're told."

The big lump took a breath and let it out in a sigh.

"Ronnie Sutton might think Dylan's trying to muscle in on his turf. And you know what Ronnie's like. Quick to take umbrage."

Jackie scoffed.

"'Umbrage'? You been readin' the dictionary again?"

Marco shrugged and added a grin.

"Anyway, how's Ronnie gonna find out about Dylan's business. It's too small potatoes to show up on his radar."

Marco tilted his head. Pursed his lips.

"Dylan's working with mouthy idiots like Baz Aldrich. It isn't going to end well. Trust me, boss. Ronnie Sutton will find out at some stage."

Jackie thought things over for a sec, then shook his head.

"Nah. Me and Ronnie Sutton's got ourselves an understandin'. If he tried movin' on my boy, he knows I'd fuck him and his gang over good and proper."

Marco tilted his head, unconvinced. He took a breath. Looked like he wanted to say something but held off.

"C'mon, Marco. Let's have it."

"You don't think …?" He shook his head. "No. No. Forget it."

"Forget what?" Jackie growled.

"Logan's kicking," Marco said after a momentary pause.

"What about it?"

"You don't think it could be a warning from Ronnie?"

Jackie thought for a moment before shaking his head.

"Nah," he said. "Not a chance. Ronnie Sutton knows better'n that. If there were a problem, the bugger'd talk to me first. Ronnie'd give me a chance to sort out my affairs before riskin' all-out war."

Marco nodded. "Fair enough, boss. If you say so."

"I do say so. We cool on this, Marco?"

Marco up-nodded. "You know we are, boss."

"Good."

Marco turned his blue eyes on Jackie.

"You want my advice?"

"Not if you're tellin' me to step on Dylan's toes."

"Nah, boss. Wouldn't dream of it. It's just that, for what it's worth … I reckon the lad could do with some solid help."

"What sort of 'solid help'?"

"Like a minder of his own."

Jackie thought about it for a while.

Yeah, that's good idea.

Marco weren't just a hard nut with a pretty face.

"You got any specific minder in mind?" He laughed at his clever play on words.

"My sister's boy, Vinny's looking for work."

"Vinny? Do I know him?"

"No, boss. He's just graduated from university in London."

Jackie pushed his head forwards and stuck out his chin.

"A smart kid?"

"Smart enough," Marco said, a cheesy smile cracking his face. "Got himself a degree in computer science."

"So, your cousin Vinny's a geek?"

"Sort of, but he's also a boxer. Represented his college in the ring. Middleweight. Fast hands and a decent left jab. Can take a punch, too."

"Why don't he turn pro?"

"And take punches to the head for a living?" Marco scoffed, shook his head again. "Not a chance. He's smarter than that. Anyway, he isn't quite good enough to turn pro."

"I'll think about it."

Marco raked his fingers through his long hair, leaned back in his chair, and reached for the paper again.

"Go grab yourself a ciggie," Jackie ordered. "And tell Dylan I want a word with him on your way past."

Jackie had one hard and fast rule. He wouldn't allow smoking in the building. Too many fire hazards in the place and he'd seen what fire could do to a garage during his stint in the army.

The one thing that terrified him was being burned alive. One of his army mates had gone up in flames. Jackie shuddered. Couldn't help himself. Watching the flesh bubble and melt away from Digger Cartwright's bones had turned Jackie's stomach. Scared him half to death. Not that he'd admit it to anyone. Couldn't show anyone that much weakness. Jackie valued his "hard man" rep too much.

Never one to miss an opportunity for a fag break, Marco jumped to his feet.

"Sure thing, boss," he said, already turning towards the door. "Want something from the food van?"

"Yeah," Jackie answered. "Get me a cheese and ham panini. And get summat for Dylan while you're at it. Here."

Jackie pulled the wallet from his trouser pocket, tugged out a fifty, and held it up.

Marco snatched the note from Jackie's hand and said, "Thanks, boss."

"Don't forget the change."

"'Course not, boss."

"I ain't made of money."

"Yes, you are, boss."

Marco laughed and ducked out the door.

Jackie returned the smile, sat back, and tried to work out the best way to handle Dylan.

Chapter Forty-One

Wednesday 7th July - Dylan Bentley

Eccleshall Way, Stafford, Staffordshire, England

Dylan made a deliberately poor job of cleaning the oil and the bloodstains. Do a good job and he'd be lumbered with it for the foreseeable future. Not likely. He stood still, leaned on his mop. Strained his ears, trying to hear what Dad and Marco were rabbiting on about in the office. Couldn't make out a thing. They insisted on talking too quietly.

Bugger it.

The careful plans had blown up in his face. He'd over-slept and arrived too late to erase the CCTV film of his and Baz's nighttime entry. And then Tony Epps had done his header into the inspection pit and the filth had locked the place down for a day and a night. Marco had been through the surveillance footage to save Dad from some awkward police questioning. At any moment, Dylan expected a summons from Dad, demanding to know what the fuck he and Baz had been up to.

Fuck's sake.

Funny thing, though. Dad hadn't said anything about it yet. Perhaps Marco hadn't scrolled through the whole backlog. After all, he'd been in a rush to protect Dad—which was the whole point of him being on the payroll. Maybe he hadn't seen the pics of him and Baz. Maybe Dylan was still in the clear. He could always hope. But he did need to erase the footage, sharpish.

Upstairs, Marco strode out of the office. Stared at Dylan for a bit. Then he stomped along the balcony and down the staircase, boots squeaking the whole way. Still eyeing Dylan, the hard bugger hit the floor and marched straight up to him. Stood real close, too. Threatening.

"Jackie wants a word," he said, looking Dylan in the eye as though he was more than just a hired lackey.

Arrogant prick.

Dylan averted his gaze. Truth was, Marco scared the living shit out of him.

"About what?" Dylan asked.

Marco's deep blue eyes shining out of a swarthy face could be so damned intimidating. Dylan swallowed. Studied the oil stain, which looked pretty much the same as it had done before he'd attacked it with the sand and detergent. Only difference being the streaks of oil-darkened sand still lying where he hadn't swept it up properly.

"No idea," the arrogant Italian said. "You'll have to go upstairs and find out."

Bugger looked down on Dylan even though they were more or less the same height. How'd he manage that?

"Yeah," Dylan mumbled. "Guess I will."

"I'm doing a sarnie run. What d'you fancy?" Marco said, managing to make it sound like a challenge.

"Cheese and bacon roll," Dylan answered and added, "Please."

Dad liked him to show manners to the staff.

"Coming right up."

Marco tipped a finger to his forehead and nodded. As he headed off, making a wide detour of the pit, he pointed back to the patch of oil and said, "Missed a bit."

Dylan would have given anything to tell the prick to "fuck off". Thought better of it. After all, Marco was Dad's friend as well as his minder. And there was no telling what the meathead might do.

Dylan lowered the mop into the pit, leaned it against the corner. Headed for the stairs. By the time he reached the landing at the top, his heart pounded, and he struggled to regulate his breathing.

Nerves had set in. Why did everything seem so fucking scary all of a sudden? He pushed into the office.

Dad sat behind his grey, steel desk, looking self-important, and serious.

Oh God. He knows. He fucking knows.

"Sit," Dad snarled, pointing to the chair on the other side of the desk.

Dylan took his seat, trying, and failing, to meet Dad's harsh stare.

"What's up, Dad?"

"Two things, son."

Two?

Dad stopped talking and dropped into his silent routine. Scary. Always liked the sound of silence.

Dylan's mouth dried.

"Yes, Dad?" he asked, pleased he didn't croak.

"You got summat to tell me," he said.

Not a question, a statement. An accusation.

"I have?"

If Dad wanted a confession, he wouldn't get one. Never volunteer information. Dad had been telling him that ever since he was little. The saying, "Don't volunteer for nothing", became words to live by.

Dad looked at him. Said nothing.

"What about?" Dylan said, desperate to break another extended silence.

"Don't try playin' me, son. We're talkin' 'bout what you hid in Storeroom Five the other night."

Shit. He does know. Fucking Marco.

Dylan swallowed.

"Oh, that," he said.

"Yeah, that."

Dad's eyes drilled into Dylan's. Hard as nails. Scary as fuck.

Dylan shot a look over his shoulder at the surveillance camera right over the door.

"You sure it's okay to talk here, Dad?"

"Don't worry 'bout the camera, son. I turned that one off at the server."

"You did?"

"Yeah."

You mean Marco did.

Dad could barely operate the TV at home let alone the CCTV kit.

"So," Dad said, leaning closer and dropping his hands on the desk, "what's in the storeroom?"

"I-I didn't think you'd mind, Dad," Dylan said, wincing. "It's only a bit of gear."

"What sort of gear?"

Time for the truth.

"Steroids," he said. "Anabolic steroids. I'm selling it to some of the guys down the gym."

And a few other places.

"Steroids? You're not takin' that shit, are you?"

Dylan shook his head.

"Nah, not me, Dad," he lied. "That stuff's for mugs. I'm just flogging it. Making good money, too."

"How much?"

"Fifty quid a vial."

Dad nodded, eyes wide. Seemingly impressed.

"How much does it cost you?"

"Tenner a shot," Dylan said, smiling, proud of the markup.

"Plus the cost of transportation."

Uh-oh. What's he banging on about?

"Yeah, good point. That's another couple o' quid," Dylan said, plucking the number out of the air.

"So," Dad said, rolling his eyes towards the ceiling, in calculation mode. "That's fifty for a twelve quid outlay. … Not a bad markup. A smidge over four hundred percent." He'd worked out the maths in his head. Impressive.

Dylan let his smile grow.

"Yeah. Easy money. It's really good stuff, too. Medical grade. The punters are lining up to buy it."

Dad lowered his eyes to fix his gaze onto Dylan again. Made him squirm like a sample under a microscope.

"There's summat you've forgotten."

"What's that?"

Here it comes.

"Storage costs."

Bloody knew it.

"What?"

"You heard me, son. Storage costs." He lobbed out an evil grin. "Fiver a vial."

"What?" Dylan repeated. "You're kidding, right?"

Dad nodded. Pursed his lips.

"Business is business. You gotta include all the costs or you can't work out the true profits." Jackie frowned and snapped his fingers. "Bugger it. I forgot 'bout the security element. After all, you're usin' my premises, which are under my protection. I mean, the CCTV alone cost me a mint to buy and install. I reckon that's worth another fiver. So, let's call it a tenner a vial, shall we?"

"Fuck's sake, Dad. After I split with Baz, it'll hardly be worth my time."

"That's the true cost of business, son. Suck it up."

"But—"

Dad's face buckled, and he roared with laughter. Deep, grating laughter.

"What?"

"I'm kiddin', son," he said, through another roar. "Oh dear, the look on your face. Priceless."

"You're kidding?"

"'Course I am, boy. You think I'm the sort of bugger who'd stiff his own son?"

"Well, I—"

"Careful what you say next, lad," Dad spluttered, blinking tears from his eyes. "I can always change my mind, you know."

"But you are kidding, right? You're not charging me for storage?"

Still smiling, Dad leaned back in his chair and let the laughter fade.

"No, lad. You get yourself a pass. I'm happy to help a buddin' entrepreneur."

Dylan smiled in relief. "Thanks, Dad. You're a real diamond."

Dad wiped the tears from his eyes with the heels of his hands.

"Too bloody right I am, son."

"A real diamond," Dylan repeated and added, "I love you, Dad," for good measure.

"Fuck's sake, boy," Dad snarked. "Don't go getting' all soft on me. I hate all that touchy feely bollocks. You know that."

"Sorry, Dad."

Dylan hated it, too. But it seemed the right time to make the effort.

"Now, being serious for a bit," Dad said, crowding the desk, "there's one thing you gotta promise me."

Dylan frowned.

"What's that, Dad?"

"Don't go nowhere near Ronnie Sutton's turf." Dad's brown eyes darkened and his mouth hardened. He'd rarely been more serious. Deadly serious.

"'Course not, Dad. His users don't want steroids. Wouldn't know what to do with it. Couldn't afford it, neither."

Like he'd be stupid enough to risk messing with Ronnie Sutton's business.

Dad relaxed. Pulled away from the desk. Leaned against the back of his chair.

"Okay, son," he said. "That only leaves the other thing."

Fuck. Now what?

"What other thing?"

"The dashcam."

Jesus.

Dylan's heart shuddered.

"The dashcam?"

"Yeah, the dashboard camera from the Raptor you bent," Dad said, speaking slowly and all but spelling it out. "You thought I'd forgotten 'bout it, didn't you."

Yeah. Too right I did.

Dad stared, unblinking. The recent laughter nothing but a distant memory—gone in little more than a heartbeat.

"I-I—"

"Stop pissin' me about, son. What d'you do with it?"

Say something, Dylan. Lie.

Unable to maintain eye contact, Dylan looked at his hands. They shook. Bugger it. Why couldn't he man up? Why did he have to be such a fucking wuss? Such a dick?

"I-I ... destroyed it, Dad."

"How?" Dad asked, probing. Still not blinking.

Dylan picked at the dirt stuck under his fingernails from cleaning out the pit.

Lie, Dylan. You can do it.

"With a hammer. I-In the garage at home."

Dad chewed on his lower lip, nodding. Deep in thought, he finally started blinking again.

"What did you do with the broken bits?"

Dylan cocked his head, looked at Dad, blinked a few times.

"I-I ... threw them in the bin."

"What bin?"

Shit. What bin? What bloody bin?

"Er ... the metal bin in the garage."

Dad slammed the flat of his hand on the desktop. The crack rifled through the metal-and-glass office and stung Dylan's ears.

"Don't lie to me, you little shit. I checked all the bins last night before they was emptied. Didn't see no broken dashcam parts."

Dylan blinked and waited for the ringing in his ears to fade. Dad had to be lying. Like he ever checked the bins. Left all that sort of shit to Doreen and Reg. Trouble was, Dylan didn't have the stones to contradict Dad on it.

Fuck.

"You've gotta be the worst liar in the world, son," Dad growled, the anger simmering close to the surface. "Now tell me. Where's that fuckin' dashcam?"

Been a while since Dad had shown such quiet rage. Scary. Just like when Mum buggered off. Dylan shuddered. Preferred an immediate blowout. Would've been over quicker.

"I-It's safe, Dad," he answered, finally telling the truth.

He'd never lose the dashcam. Watching the clip gave him such a rush. A real turn-on.

"That's not what I asked, boy," Dad said, his voice still a deep growl, but slightly softer. "Where is it?"

"It's in the Raptor. Locked in the glove compartment."

Dad rested his forearms on the armrests of his chair. Formed fists. Made his knuckles crack.

Jesus. How he hated that sound.

"I bloody told you to destroy it."

"I-I couldn't, Dad. Please don't make me—"

"Why not? The evidence on that camera's enough to put you inside for years. Why keep hold of it, you numpty?"

Dylan gulped. Time for the whole truth. No matter how bad it sounded.

"Sorry, Dad," he said, keeping his eyes lowered. "I know it sounds weird, but I … I get a real kick out of watching it."

He looked up. Taking the risk.

"Fuckin' hell, son," Dad said, slowly shaking his head. "What am I gonna do with you?"

"It's safe, Dad. Please don't take it away from me. I'm keeping it safe. Honest."

"In the glove compartment of the fuckin' Raptor? Are you insane? How safe is that? What if the cops come callin' again?"

"That's the clever part, Dad," Dylan said, leaning forwards, smiling, eager to please. "The filth have already been all over it. They didn't find nothing. They're hardly going to impound it again. They wouldn't be allowed to."

"Don't be so stupid, son. The filth are all over us—all over me. They'll do anythin' to take me down. They're jealous on account of me being so rich. They only need one little excuse and they'll be all over us both like a rash. You can't keep the dashcam—"

"But, Dad."

Dad held up his hand. "No, son, hear me out. You can't keep the dashcam in the Raptor. It ain't secure enough. Best to store it in the safe."

He nodded to the heavy, metal box on the floor in the corner of the office. The big, metal box with the combination dial and the thick, steel handle on the front door, and the dusty, box files stacked on the top.

Dylan's heart raced.

"You mean I can keep it, Dad. Really?"

Dad shot him a twisted smile and nodded.

"If you have to."

"I do, Dad," Dylan said. "I really do. You won't believe how important it is to me."

Dad's shoulders dropped and he nodded. "I get it, son."

What's that?

"You do?"

"Yeah. You remind me of me."

"Really?"

"Yeah. A chip off the ol' block." Dad sniffed and turned it into a proper, full-blown smile. "You know that military dagger in the display cabinet at home?"

"The one you bought from an antique shop?"

Dad allowed his smile to fade. He lifted his gaze to the ceiling behind Dylan and stared into the middle distance. Accessing a memory.

"I lied about that, son."

"No shit."

"That dagger was issued to me in the army, and I stole it."

"As a memento?"

Dad snorted. Lowered his eyes. Fixed them on Dylan.

"You could say that, son. You see, I used that dagger to gut my first towelhead. An insurgent. Watched the bearded fucker's eyes bulge and the blood spew from his mouth as I ripped out his innards. Stabbed him five times through the belly." He paused and nodded. "Felt his warm blood all over this hand." He held up his right hand and added, "Happy days."

"Bloody hell, Dad!" Dylan said, unable to think of anything more profound.

"Yeah," Dad said. "Love that ol' dagger, me. Brings the memories to life, it does. That's how I know what the dashcam means to you, son. Like I said, you're a chip off the ol' block."

"Is that why you keep Mum's wedding ring in the box on your bedside table?"

"Don't go there, son," Dad snapped with an air of finality.

"Sorry, Dad. But she deserved it."

"I said, don't go there!"

"Okay, okay. Enough said. So you'll let me keep it in the safe?"

"On two conditions."

"Yeah?"

"First." Dad held up his hand and stuck up his index finger. "Promise me you won't go makin' a habit out of runnin' cars off the road. You got lucky this time, and the cops look for patterns. Don't give 'em none. You might not get so lucky next time.

"Okay, Dad. I promise. And second?"

He extended the middle finger and pressed it against the first.

"Second," he said, "never make a copy of the recordin'. If I know you—and I do—you'll wanna drop it onto your phone. Well don't. It's way too dangerous. It'll end up on the cloud thing, and that ain't safe. Promise?"

Dylan didn't hesitate.

"Yes. I promise."

At that stage, he'd have agreed to anything.

"And never take the dashcam out of the office unless you check it with me first."

"That's three things, Dad."

"Yeah, I know. So, are you gonna promise me?"

Dad's brown eyes locked onto Dylan's.

"Yes, Dad. I promise."

What else can I do?

The old man dropped his hand to the arm of his chair and relaxed. Deal done.

"Okay," he said. "Go get it, then."

"What? The dashcam?"

"Of course the shittin' dashcam! What else we been talkin' 'bout?"

"Oh, okay."

Dylan jumped to his feet and stood there. Looked down at his old man. Dad returned his stare.

"What you waitin' for?"

"Are you gonna give me the combination to the safe?"

"Not a chance."

"Go on, Dad. Please. That way, I won't have to keep asking you whenever I want to look at the film."

"Like I said. Not a chance."

"Even if I promise not to take any of the cash?"

"What cash?"

"The cash you say you've got locked away in the safe."

Again, Dad smiled. He was doing a lot of smiling all of a sudden.

"Jesus, Dylan. You're so bloody gullible. I don't got no cash in the safe."

"So why tell everyone there's money … no, never mind. It's not important. So, do I get the combination?"

Dad sighed. "Yeah, yeah. Okay. It's the year your mother buggered off. You remember?"

"'Course I remember. Twenty—"

The wicket door screeched open, and Dad raised a finger to his lips for silence. "Don't say it out loud, son. Let's keep this 'tween you and me, eh?"

Dylan frowned. "Don't you trust Marco?"

Dad grunted.

"Only people in this world you can trust is family," he said, lowering his voice to a whisper. "It's you and me 'gainst the world, son. Remember that. Okay?"

Dylan nodded.

Why not?

"Go on then," the old man said. "Go get the dashcam."

"Oh, right."

Dylan turned and headed for the door.

"Then get back here for lunch. Marco's bringin' grub."

Dylan turned right at the door, hurried along the balcony, and crossed Marco on the staircase, smelling of ciggies and holding a brown, paper bag in his right fist.

"Cheese and bacon roll, right?" the gorilla asked, holding up the bag, but not stopping.

"Yeah," Dylan grunted. "Be right there."

"Get it while it's hot."

"Yeah. 'Kay."

Somehow, Marco didn't look so intimidating since Dylan knew Dad didn't trust him with the combination. Sharing secrets with Dad made him feel good. Top of the world.

Dylan hurried down the rest of the staircase, marched alongside the gruesome inspection pit, and ducked through the wicket door. Blinking in the harsh light, he stood, eyes closed. Face lifted to the harsh sun, soaking up some of its warmth. Bloody workshop was always cold and damp, even in the height of summer. After a few moments of sun worship, he crossed to the parking bays and unlocked the Raptor. Climbed inside. Keyed the glove compartment, dropped the flap, and dug around. The black plastic felt sleek in his hand, its contents dangerous and sexy as fuck. Unable to resist, he scoured his mirrors for onlookers before pressing the power button. The dashcam scrolled through its boot up routine. Dylan keyed in the password, and it opened on the last-viewed item. It seemed to take forever. He watched the short clip from start to finish. The crumps, the squeal of tyres, the result as visceral as the first time. He shuddered again at the final shunt. Glowed with the joy, the power. The sense of euphoria washed over him.

Christ alive, he nearly came in his cargo pants.

Sweating—not only from the heat in the cab—he powered down the dashcam and climbed out of the Raptor. A glint of silver caught his eye in the seat track. He reached in, grabbed it. Held it up to the light. An earring dangled from his fingertips. One of Chardonnay's. The stupid cow must have dropped it. How come the filth had missed it? Dozy fuckers.

Shit.

DNA on it would have linked Dylan and Dad to the hit-and-run death.

He smiled. The luck was still running with him.

He dropped the earring into his pocket alongside the dashcam, slammed the door closed, and hurried back to his cheese and bacon roll. Wouldn't want to keep Dad waiting.

After a very satisfying lunch, Dylan wiped bacon grease from his lips with a paper napkin and rolled it into a tight ball. Threw it into the paper bag with the rest of the rubbish and tossed it. Hit the rim and bounced in.

Dad was still working his way through the panini—nearly done. Marco sat in his usual spot, listening to another of Dad's boring war stories as though he could give a damn, when all he really wanted to do was head outside for an after-lunch ciggie. Stupid fuckwit. Why let yourself get hooked on smoking? Just by looking at the big fucker, Dylan could tell he was wrapped up tighter than a drum in need of his fix.

The phone on Dad's desk rang. Dad snatched it up.

"Bentley," he said and listened for a second. "Ah, Mr

Jeffries. Turn left at the carpet showroom and you'll see us straight ahead. When you get here, park in one of the customer bays on the left. I'll be right with you."

"Did he send the copy of his driving licence?" Marco asked.

"Dunno," Dad said, after hanging up the phone. "Check the inbox." He pointed towards Tracy's office in the adjoining room.

Marco grunted as he levered his bulk out of the chair and sloped out of the room.

"Okay, son," Dad whispered, holding out his hand. "Pass it over."

Dylan thought about playing dumb, but what good would that do? He stretched out a leg and dug the dashcam from his trouser pocket. The earring came out with it and dropped to the floor.

"What's that?" Dad asked.

"One of Chardonnay's earrings. I found it in the Raptor. I was going to bin it later."

Dad beckoned with his fingers.

"Nah, don't do that. Pass it over," he said. "I'll keep it with the dashcam. It'll be my next memento."

"Whatever turns you on, Dad," Dylan said, grinning.

He scooped the earring from the floor and handed it and the dashcam across.

"Boss?" Marco called from Tracy's office.

"Yeah?"

"Jeffries' driving licence is clean. No endorsements. Want me to scope out his finances?"

"'Course. Do the full background check and arrange insurance cover for the test drive."

"Okay, boss."

Dad swivelled his chair to face the safe, dialled in the

four-digit combination. Yanked the handle a quarter turn clockwise. Tugged open the door and revealed … nothing but a shelf in the middle, and two spaces filled with papers. No blocks of cash. No weapons. No jewellery. Nothing.

Dylan didn't bother hiding his disappointment.

Dad shifted some of the papers on the shelf to one side, made room for the dashcam and the earring, and dropped them in. Slammed the door shut and spun the dial.

"There you go, son," he said, smiling. "Safe as houses."

Dad stood, arched his back in a stretch, and grabbed the jacket from the back of his chair.

"You finished the cleanin'?"

Dylan scratched his chin. Looked away.

"Yeah, yeah. All done."

"You sure? I'm gonna check."

"Okay, okay," Dylan said, jumping to his feet and standing next to Dad. "I'm on it. Bloody slavedriver."

Smiling, Dad slapped him on the shoulder.

"Can't pull the wool over these eyes, son." He leaned closer and lowered his voice. "Don't you come sneakin' in here when I'm out with the punter. My advice? Ration yourself with the dashcam. The buzz is gonna last longer that way."

"'Kay, Dad. You know best."

"Always, son," he said, speaking up. "Always."

They headed out. Dad stopped at the inner office door. Poked his head through the opening.

"Found anythin'?"

"Guy runs an investment house in the city, boss. Megabucks. Looks kosher so far."

"Keep lookin'. I'll go do some schmoozin'. Give the rich bugger the drive of his life."

Dylan followed Dad out onto the balcony. They stared

down at the inspection pit. Hardly looked as though he'd done anything to it.

"Fuck's sake, son. Call that clean?"

A car horn blared twice.

"That'll be the punter," Dad said. "Look lively, son."

Chapter Forty-Two

Eccleshall Way, Stafford, Staffordshire, England

Kaine climbed down from the recently muddied Raptor, grinning inanely and playing the overexcited idiot to the fullest.

"That was fantastic," he gushed. "What a rush."

Jackie Bentley slid out of the passenger side, dropped to the ground, and met Kaine at the front of the pickup.

"The guys will go ape over it," Kaine added. "The girls, too. But I think they'll probably prefer the go-cart track. We could organise races."

"I did say you'd love it, Mr Jeffries," Bentley said, nodding. Keen for a sale.

"You did indeed." Kaine nodded. "You own the farm, you say?"

Bentley smiled proudly.

"And the workshop. Lock, stock, and barrel. It's all mine."

"Wonderful."

Kaine took in the workshop. It looked far worse in the daylight than it had in the middle of the night. Streaks of rust ran down the corrugated-metal walls where the guttering had leaked for decades, and the paint was faded and peeling. A real mess. Almost dilapidated.

He shot Bentley a sideways glance.

"I don't suppose you'd be interested in an investment?"

Bentley dropped his smile.

"What?"

"Cards on the table, Mr Bentley. I represent a consortium of venture capitalists. We're always looking to expand our portfolio in the events industry, and your company would dovetail nicely with our other endeavours."

Bentley crossed his arms and firmed his jaw.

"Not interested."

"With our support, you could move to the next level. I mean, an upgrade of your customer-facing hub would help you to attract a greater number of both high-net-worth individuals and corporate clients." Kaine broke out what he considered to be his most ingratiating smile. "I'm talking blue-chip companies with deep, promotions pockets, Mr Bentley."

Bentley shook his head.

"I ain't bitin'. As for the 'customer-facin' hub' of the business"—he waved his arm in an arc over the rusted-streaked workshop—"I got a team of builders booked in for the end of next month. The place will be completely refurbished by the start of next season."

"That's a shame, Mr Bentley," Kaine said. "But you can't blame a man for trying."

Bentley curled his upper lip.

"Hmm," he grunted.

"When I see a potential investment opportunity, I have to go with my gut. Strike while the iron's hot."

Kaine kept the clichés flowing.

Bentley backed away and cast his eyes over the motor Kaine had rocked up in—an Aston Martin Vantage, 4.0L V8, with specialist numberplates, AJ 1000. One of Connor Blake's dodgy buddies in the trade had provided it as a special rush order, and Corky had doctored the paperwork overnight. It looked the part and suited Jeffries' role as "venture capitalist slash petrol head".

"Like I said, *Jeffries*. I ain't lookin' for investors."

"That's a shame, Mr Bentley," Kaine said, feigning sadness. "A real shame."

"When's the wedding?" Bentley demanded.

"Sorry?"

"You heard me. When's your wedding?"

"Ah, yes," Kaine said, shuffling backwards and lowering his gaze to his feet, "the wedding. Well … I'm afraid … I have a little confession to make." He looked up again, braving the expected wrath.

Bentley's eyes narrowed and his expression darkened.

"You what?" he growled.

Kaine backed away.

"Yes … I-I'm not getting married at all. In fact, Martha and I celebrated our tenth wedding anniversary last month."

"You what?" Bentley repeated, his voice deep and threatening. He edged closer to Kaine.

"Yes, we dined at the Savoy. A wonderful evening. But … please." Kaine held open his hands, keeping them close to his chest, a defensive posture that indicated fear. "Forgive the subterfuge."

"Subterfuge?" Bentley said, one step down from a shout. "What the fuck d'you mean, 'subterfuge'?"

Kaine swallowed, keeping his arms up.

"It means a trick … a ploy … a ruse."

"I know what subterfuge means, fuckwit," Bentley spat out.

"Really, Mr Bentley," Kaine said, allowing a tremor to bleed into his words. "There really is no need for such language. If you'll let me explain …"

Bentley formed fists, ground his teeth, and teetered on the brink of an explosion. Exactly the reaction Kaine expected.

"Go on then," Bentley growled. "Explain yourself."

"It's just that … before making an approach to a … potential investee—especially for customer-facing enterprises—I like to see how they operate. It's part of my … due diligence. You see, it's very important for us to see the person *behind* the enterprise. To be completely honest with you, Mr Bentley, I was delighted with what I saw. Which is why I'm making this formal offer. My partners and I would be prepared to offer you a significant sum for a thirty-percent share in your business." He smiled, arched a conspiratorial eyebrow, and repeated, "A *significant* sum."

Bentley loosened his fists and tilted back his head.

"How significant?"

"Five hundred thousand pounds," Kaine announced,

lifting both eyebrows and allowing his chest to swell with pride.

"Half a mil? A poxy half mil for one third of my hire business?" Bentley laughed. "Are you fuckin' insane?"

"Mr Bentley," Kaine sputtered. "I really don't think—"

"You value my business at one and a half million quid? What is this? A fuckin' wind up?"

Kaine frowned and shook his head rapidly.

"No, Mr Bentley. My accountants suggest that our valuation is more than reasonable for an enterprise of this scale."

"My fuckin' hire fleet is worth more than a million on its own, you piece of shit."

"Really, Mr Bentley. There's no call for that language."

"Bugger off out of it, you fuckin' timewaster," he shouted, pointing at the open gates.

"Timewaster, Mr Bentley?" Kaine said, tugging the creases out of his jacket. "I don't know what you mean."

"Two fuckin' hours I wasted on you, you fuckwit. That's two hours of my life I ain't gonna get back. Go on"—he waved the back of his hand towards the gates again—"bugger off. I've had more than enough of your bull—"

"I'm really sorry you see it that way, Mr Bentley. I'm prepared to compensate you for your time." He reached into his trouser pocket and retrieved his bulging wallet. "Will twenty pounds cover it?"

Bentley roared, lurched forwards, grabbed Kaine's jacket lapels, and jerked him close. Really close. Their faces ended up mere centimetres apart. Bentley's hot breath warmed Kaine's cheeks.

Naughty naughty, Kaine.

He'd gone too far.

"Listen to me, you jumped-up, little shit," Bentley hissed. A fine spray of spittle dampened Kaine's chin. "Two hours of my time's worth more than you've got in that fuckin' wallet. Next time you do your due-fuckin'-diligence, look into your mark's background proper. I'm a fuckin' multi-millionaire you dummy, and my business ain't for sale. Not to you. Not to nobody. Get it? If you think you can swan in here and waste my time for small change, you can—"

"Mr Bentley, please," Kaine whined, weakly trying to prise Bentley's fists from his lapels. "Y-You're hurting me."

"Fuck you!"

Bentley shoved Kaine away and released his grip. Kaine staggered back, stumbled, and all but fell on his rump.

"That's common assault, that is," he whimpered. "I'll … I'll call the police."

"Fuck the police. How you gonna prove assault? There ain't nobody here but you and me!"

Bentley stomped two steps closer.

Kaine scampered away and headed for the safety of the Aston Martin.

"Fuckin' timewaster," Bentley roared. "Show your snivellin' face 'round here again, and I'll tear your arms off and beat you to death with the bloody stumps!"

Not the most original threat Kaine had ever heard.

He'd seen enough. More than enough.

Kaine ripped the key fob from his trouser pocket, pressed the button, and dived behind the wheel. He fired up the engine, revelled once again in its throaty roar, and wound down the passenger window.

"You are out of control, Bentley," Kaine wailed. "Not fit for civilised company. Y-You'll be hearing from my solicitor."

Bentley advanced another pace.

"Fuck your solicitor!"

Kaine sniffed, made his chin tremble, and flapped the paddle to engage first gear. He stamped on the throttle and the car took off, its traction control preventing a rear-wheel slide.

———

STILL SMILING at his antics thirty minutes later, Kaine pulled into the nearest layby and killed the engine. The sun shone through the Aston's gleaming windscreen and reflected his upbeat mood. He gave himself a moment's pause. Mike would have approved of his approach, aimed at protecting the twins. Kaine nodded to himself. Mike was gone, but his memory and his implicit approval lived on.

"Such japes," he muttered to the bearded idiot grinning in the rear-view mirror.

Kaine inhaled the luxurious smell of leather and sighed. Such a shame, but the Vantage had to go. Although drop-dead gorgeous and built to drool over, no one could exactly call the powerful, silver beauty subtle. Hardly the runabout to choose if he wanted to coast below the radar. It had turned too many heads just during the drive through the outskirts of Stafford. Pity though, it was comfortable and drove like an absolute dream.

The phone vibrated in his pocket. He dragged it out, read the caller ID, and accepted the video call. Instantly, Corky smiled at him from the small screen.

"Whatcha, Mr K. Corky sees you've stopped in a layby. Recovered from your mauling yet?" He chuckled and double hitched one of his bushy eyebrows.

"You were watching?"

"Yeah. From Bentley's CCTV. Corky reckons you pegged him just right."

"Thanks, Control."

"What d'you make of him?"

Kaine propped the mobile on the steering wheel and took a moment to think about his response.

"After spending the better part of two hours with the man, I could do with a long, hot shower."

"That bad, huh?"

"Worse."

Corky grinned. "What happened?"

Kaine blew out his cheeks.

Where to start.

"During the test drive—on Bentley's private green lane —I played the clueless 'hooray'. Crunched the gears a couple of times. Drove too fast and kept taking the wrong line into and out of the corners. At one stage, on an easy, downhill right-hander, I came dangerously close to rolling the Raptor."

"And how did Bentley take it?"

"Didn't bat an eye. Totally unfazed. In fact, he seemed to relish the danger. And given his overreaction just now, I'd class him as a latent psychopath. I don't think he's the sort who'd have any problem having the twins hurt if he thought it suited his purposes. In fact, I wouldn't be surprised if he decided to take on the job himself, for the pure enjoyment of it. He's a danger right enough. A genuine threat to the Fabiens."

Corky dropped his natural smile and fixed a serious expression to his round face.

"Bentley needs dealing with," Kaine added. "The only question is, how."

"Corky might be able to help with that, Mr K." He

pushed an index finger into the air, looked to his left, and nodded. "Frodo's setting up a little film show for you. Just a sec."

Moments later, Corky's image dropped from the phone's screen to be replaced by a paused video, showing Jackie and Dylan Bentley sitting across the desk from each other in the workshop's main office. It looked down on the scene, showing the camera as being high up on the wall above the office door. The video started running.

"—leaves the other thing," Jackie Bentley said.

"What other thing?" Dylan asked, frowning.

"The dashcam."

"The dashcam?"

"Yeah, the dashboard camera from the Raptor you bent," Bentley said, speaking slowly. "You thought I'd forgotten ..."

Kaine watched the interchange, engrossed. He paid particular attention to Bentley's revelation about the dagger. Kaine had known plenty of marines who kept mementos, but idolising the weapon used in his first kill stood out as pretty sick.

The scene ended with Dylan leaving the office to retrieve the dashcam.

"One thing's puzzling me," Kaine said as Corky faded back into shot.

"Only one?"

Kaine frowned.

"One thing related to the film show."

"Which is?" Corky asked, eyes wide.

"Why was Jackie happy to talk so openly with the CCTV camera running?"

Corky chuckled.

"Oh that," he said, and his smile widened. "Bentley had

Marco pause the recording, but thanks to the dongle, Corky and Frodo have full control. Frodo overrode Marco's command. Sneaky, eh?"

"Sneaky indeed. Is there anything else?" Kaine asked.

"Yep, there's plenty, Mr K. Frodo's edited out the part where they're eating. It's not a pretty sight. Want to see it all?"

"Yes, please."

The office scene returned, this time including Marco. Well-built, tanned, unmarked face, he looked capable of handling himself in a ruckus. The ringing desk phone interrupted a one-way chat, with Bentley holding the floor, and after giving Jeffries directions, Bentley sent Marco to the outer office to complete the admin. Then he turned to Dylan and pushed out his hand.

"Okay, son," he said. "Pass it over."

As Dylan pulled the dashcam from his pocket, something silver twinkled as it fell to the floor.

"What's that?" Bentley demanded.

"One of Chardonnay's earrings. I found it in the Raptor. I was going to bin it later."

"Nah, don't do that. Pass it over," Bentley said.

Kaine studied the rest of the scene carefully, but Bentley's right shoulder hid the dial when he opened the safe."

The video clip froze after Bentley slammed the safe door shut.

"Damn it," Kaine said. "I couldn't see the combination."

Corky recited the four numbers from memory, beaming with pride.

"How did you know the year Dylan's mother disappeared?" Kaine asked.

"Frodo found it during his deep dive. Jackie spread the

word around that she'd run off with her tennis pro. Never seen again. Either of them. Suspicious or what?"

"Yep. Suspicious alright." Kaine nodded.

"And Dylan mentioned the wedding ring. Another memento, you reckon?" Corky asked.

"Could be."

"And for 'memento', Corky means 'trophy'. You know that, don't you, Mr K?"

"I do, Corky," Kaine said. "I do."

"So, Whatcha planning to do about it?"

"First," Kaine said, "I'm going to 'liberate' that dashcam and confirm it shows what we think it shows."

Corky scowled. "Dylan running the Fabiens off the road?"

"Exactly."

"And then?"

"I imagine DI Fellows will find a use for it. Don't you?"

Corky's chuckle gave Kaine his answer.

"What about the earring?" Corky asked.

"I'll leave that where it is. The dashcam clip together with the CCTV footage we've just watched ought to give Fellows all the ammunition he needs to tear the Bentleys' lives apart."

"Should do, Mr K," Corky announced.

In the background of the call, Frodo repeated Corky's words twice. Kaine smiled.

"And," Corky continued, "maybe the cops will turn up something on the missing wife and her tennis pro."

"You never know," Kaine said.

"Especially if Corky and Frodo give 'em a steer or two."

"I'm sure it'll help." Kaine nodded. "Can you and Frodo bundle all the CCTV footage into a handy, little package to send to the police when I'm ready?"

"Frodo's already on that. Corky's gonna mail it to you the second it's ready to go."

A spotless, cherry-red WV Golf GTI rumbled into the layby and pulled up close behind Kaine in the Aston. The shaggy-haired boy racer in the driving seat took in the glorious machine, all but salivating. He lifted a mobile phone to his eye, took a pic, and stuck up a thumb. Kaine responded in kind.

"Things are getting crowded here, Control. I'd better return the Aston and swap it for something less eye-catching."

"See you later, Mr K. Stay safe."

"Always, Control."

Kaine fired up the Vantage, shot the boy racer another thumbs-up, and rolled the car slowly away. He half-expected the kid to challenge him to a drag race, but he simply sat and looked in adoration at Kaine's sedate departure.

Chapter Forty-Three

Wednesday 7th July - Evening

The Abbey Park Hotel, Stafford, Staffordshire, England

After spending the rest of the afternoon and early evening helping Toby Fabien settle back into his own home—and introducing him and the twins to Nigel and their twenty-four-hour "support" team—Kaine took his chance to relax. He sat on his hotel bed, propped up by three fat pillows, with the phone raised, reviewing the heavily edited video package Corky had sent through. As he watched, he made notes onto a pad.

. . .

16:35:12. Workshop interior. View from first camera cluster of upstairs balcony.

Jackie and Marco leave main office, step through fire door. Cameras don't cover external fire escape platform. No eyes, no ears.

16:41:08. Workshop forecourt. External shot of car park. Gates open.

Bentley throws arm around Dylan. They chat quietly. System doesn't pick up conversation.

16:43:01. Workshop forecourt. External shot of car park. Gates open.

Dylan removes boiler suit, rolls it under arm. Climbs into wet Raptor. Drives through roller shutters. Parks inside workshop between other Raptors.

16:43:23. Workshop forecourt. External shot of car park. Gates open.

Bentley meets Marco at side of building. They speak quietly. Bentley mostly talks. Marco climbs into black Porsche Cayman. Drives past Bentley, sounds two-tone horn. Picks up speed. Storms through open gates. Bentley heads into workshop.

16:47:53. Workshop interior. View from first camera cluster.

Bentley waits for Dylan to get out of Raptor.

"We're done here, son," Bentley says, loud enough to be heard. "Let's go home."

Dylan winces, shakes head.

"I need the loo, Dad. You go on ahead."

"Nah, that's okay," Bentley answers. "I'll wait."

"Better not," Dylan says, face contorting. "Could be a while. Last night's prawn curry must have been on the turn. I've had the shits all fucking day."

Bentley laughs. Pats bulging stomach.

"You poor, delicate, little flower, I had the same curry, and there's bugger all wrong with my guts."

"Yeah," Dylan says. "Thanks for the sympathy."

"Make sure you flush, and don't forget to wash yer hands!" Bentley taunts.

"Bugger off."

Bentley musses Dylan's hair. Dylan shies away, spins, rushes to staircase.

"Lock up properly after you," Bentley shouts. Dylan reaches staircase and grabs handrail.

"Yeah, yeah. Okay,"

"Better hurry, son," Bentley says, still laughing. "You wouldn't want to mess your shorts."

"Fuck off, Dad … Oh shit."

Holding stomach and bending, Dylan climbs the staircase fast. Races along balcony, bursts open toilet door, and slams it behind him.

KAINE SNEERED.

"Such a shame," he muttered. "Couldn't have happened to a more deserving arsehole."

Pun intended.

16:49:31. Workshop interior. View from second camera cluster.

Bentley climbs into black Raptor. Starts engine, reverses past inspection pit. Drives out.

16:49:52. Workshop forecourt. External shot of car park. Gates open.

Bentley roars away, melting more rubber than Marco.

. . .

KAINE SCOWLED and shook his head in disgust.

Bentley had just demonstrated to the world that he actually did have money to burn.

16:51:12. Workshop interior. View from second camera cluster, upstairs balcony. Rear wall.

Toilet door opens. Dylan pokes head through gap. Takes furtive look around. Retraces steps along balcony to main office.

"HELLO THERE. What are you up to, Dylan?" Kaine said, as if he didn't already suspect. He clenched his teeth and waited.

16:52:16. Workshop interior. View from office camera.

Dylan drops into Jackie's chair. Turns to face safe. Dials in combination, cranks open door. Retrieves dashcam. Smiling, Dylan rushes to toilet.

16:58:08. Workshop interior. View from second camera cluster, upstairs balcony. Rear wall.

Dylan reappears. Looks slightly flushed but smiling. Not an upset stomach.

KAINE GROUND his teeth and glared at the insufferable, grinning fool.

You sick bastard.

16:58:16. Workshop interior. View from office camera.

Dylan replaces dashcam inside safe. Slams safe door. Spins dial. Opens desk drawer. Takes key. Unlocks wall unit with two rows of keys on hooks. Selects one key. Exits office.

17:00:02 Workshop interior. View from first camera cluster, upstairs balcony, rear wall.

Dylan strolls to Storeroom #5. Keys door. Disappears to collect "merchandise". Whistling, Dylan skips down stairs, climbs into same Raptor used to run Fabiens off road. Fires up engine.

17:03:32. Workshop interior. View from second camera cluster. Full panorama from end wall towards exit.

Dylan reverses Raptor past the pit. Turns. Drives through opening. Stops. Exits Raptor. Turns off workshop lights. Hits button on outside wall. Roller doors close.

17:08:11. Workshop forecourt. External shot of car park. Gates closed and padlocked.

AFTER STARING at the final shot for a few moments, Kaine opened Corky's CCTV app and selected the live overview —split screen, nine internal images. Nothing had changed. The workshop remained dark and empty apart from the two angled rows of stretch limos and Raptors. The time-stamp showed 21:52.

Kaine sat up, placed his bare feet on the thick, pile carpet, and unplugged the earpiece from its charger. He settled the warm device into his left ear and pressed it once.

"Alpha One to Control, come in. Over."

"Whatcha, Mr K. How you diddling?"

"Good to go, Control. Thanks for the package. Over."

"You is welcome, Mr K."

"Do you have a location for the targets? Over."

"They're at home in Brocton. At least their phones are. Marco's

with 'em. He arrived an hour ago with a couple of mates. Bruisers, they look like."

"Any idea what they're doing? Over."

"Looks like they're watching a movie in Bentley's home cinema. Want Frodo to find out what's showing?"

"No, thanks, Control. Just let me know if anything changes. Over."

"Will do, Mr K. When you heading out?"

"Right now. I want that dashcam before it goes walkabout. Over."

"It ain't my place to ask, but are you sure you want to go in alone?"

"Thanks for the concern, Control, but I wouldn't trust Target One as far as I could dropkick the sick arsehole. After I've secured the dashcam and sent it to the Boys in Blue, I'll decide how to punish Target Two. I'm not letting the bastard get away with threatening the twins. Over."

"Corky hears you, Mr K. Good luck with it."

"Thanks, Control. Alpha One, out."

Kaine tapped the earpiece into silence and dressed for yet another overnight incursion.

Chapter Forty-Four

Wednesday 7th July - Evening

Eccleshall Way, Stafford, Staffordshire, England

Kaine arrived at the scene of his tightrope dance with death in a low-mileage Range Rover Discovery that Cough had bought—along with two others—for the duration of a mission he'd irreverently labelled "Daddy Daycare".

Kaine took in the area as he drove slowly past the workshop. The car park stood out dark and deserted, the double gates padlocked, and the roller shutters down. He carried on to the end of the access road, turned around, and parked half a mile away in the visitors car park of a carpet distribution centre. Then he strolled the long way around to his original observation point and hid in the deep shadows cast by a row of heavy bins. At no point along his route did any cars pass him, nor did he encounter any pedestrians. The place appeared deserted. He settled in for the long haul.

———

MIDNIGHT CAME AND WENT. Heavy clouds rolled in from the southwest to darken an already leaden sky, but a warm breeze kept the temperature comfortable. Once again, Kaine stood alone.

He waited another ten minutes before tapping the earpiece.

"Alpha One to Control. Come in. Over."

"*Corky's hearing you, Mr K.*"

"Any change with the targets? Over."

"*No movement on the phones, Mr K. They're still in Brocton. Corky's gonna let you know if there's any change.*"

"Do you have eyes on the workshop? Over."

"*Corky's got it covered. Nothing happening inside or out. You is good to go.*"

"Thanks, Control. I'll keep the comms open. Over."

Kaine stood and pressed his back against the wall, still hugging the shadows. A gusty breeze swirled through the deserted area, picking up dead leaves and dry litter, and temporarily depositing the debris in dark corners ready to move it again later.

Leaving the sanctuary of the darkness, he darted across the road, heading for the gap the wily, old fox had shown him. He reached the overgrown scrub at the side of the building and dropped to all fours in search of the break in the fencing. At one point, he worried that the break had been sealed, but he found the opening two metres further in than he'd been searching.

Kaine lay prone and, leading with the small backpack,

he wormed his way through the restricted opening and headed straight to the fire escape. As he climbed to the first-floor landing, the rusted metalwork made the same creaking groans as before. He kneeled at the landing and listened. Traffic rumbled along the nearby ring road. Blue lights flashed in the distance, travelling east to west—an ambulance or a police car racing without sirens. Nothing for Kaine to worry about.

The microwire tools gave him the same access to the workshop as before. He stepped inside and pulled the door tight behind him. The quiet clunk echoed through the cavernous interior. Cold, dank air filled his nostrils. He stood tall, relaxed. With Corky in control of the CCTV system, he had no need to crouch or wait. He marched towards the balcony, turned right, and entered the main office as though he had every right to be there.

"Alpha One to Control," he said, whispering out of habit, "can you see me? Over."

"*Clear as day. You is good to go.*"

Kaine crossed to the desk and dropped to one knee in front of the safe. In the dim light, he struggled to make out the numbers on the dial. He pulled a penlight from his jacket pocket and played the pencil beam over the face of the safe. He set the wheel to "0" and dialled in the combination. The clicks boomed through the office. He grasped the vertical handle, cranked it to the left, and tugged. The door opened easily, releasing to a vacuum-sealed pop.

Kaine searched inside and soon found what he was looking for.

"Gotcha!"

Smiling, he held the dashcam up to the CCTV camera.

"*Nice one, Mr K. What about the earring?*"

"I'll leave it where it is. It's covered in the target's DNA. Not even DI Fellows can mess that—"

"*Bugger!*" Corky shouted. *"Get out of there, Mr K. Get out now!"*

The angry thunder of powerful, diesel engines filled the air.

Kaine took off. Dived through the office door.

Gates crashed open. Scraped concrete. Metal clattered into metal. Engines raced. Tyres squealed.

Out onto the balcony. Turn left. Straight ahead, the fire door stood in his way.

Outside, car doors opened and slammed shut. Footsteps crunched on gravel. Voices, male voices, roared. Angry. Braying. Howling. Men psyching themselves up for battle.

Kaine leaned against the slam bar. It gave. The fire door cracked open. Jarred to a stop. The gap no more than three centimetres. Cool air chilled Kaine's sweaty face. He slammed his shoulder against the door. It didn't budge. He tried again. Metal clanked against metal. It rattled.

A chain!

The fire door … locked. How?

Fuck.

Breathing hard, sweating harder, Kaine spun, retraced his steps to the balcony. Grabbed the handrail. Looked down.

The wicket door shot open, crashed against the roller shutter. A dark figure, Marco, climbed over the high threshold and sidestepped to the right. Two more figures followed, moving to Marco's left, fanning out in a line. Each carried something long and heavy, tapping the free end in their empty hands. They aimed for threatening but looked stupid. Marco reached out to his right and snapped a switch. The fluorescent strip lights flickered. Held. It flooded the workshop with a harsh, white, eye-searing light. Kaine squinted, momentarily dazzled.

"Come on!" Marco roared. "Where are you, you bastard?"

"We're gonna fuck you over!" the third man yelled, his voice deep, angry.

The middle one, large head covered in a black beanie, kept quiet. He searched the area with a pair of piercing, blue eyes and sneered.

Keeping in a line, the three men punched further into the workshop.

Behind them, two more figures climbed through the opening. Jackie and Dylan Bentley. The hard-nut father and his sick son. Dylan, looking nervous, stood close to and slightly behind Bentley, seeking the protection of his father's squat bulk. Bentley canted his head upwards, looking to the balcony. He beamed in triumph.

"Well now, look who we've found," Bentley jeered. "Jeffries! I knew you was a wrong 'un. I fuckin' knew it!"

Kaine looked down from the balcony.

Crap. How are you getting out of this one?

Earlier That Day

Chapter Forty-Five

Wednesday 7th July - Jackson Bentley

Eccleshall Way, Stafford, Staffordshire, England

Jackie Bentley stood and watched the silver Aston Martin race through the gates. The idiot, Jeffries, mounted the kerb in his hurry to leave. Wouldn't have done his nearside rims much good. The fucker couldn't drive worth a damn.

"Jumped-up little prick!" Jackie shouted through a scowl he slowly turned into a grin.

That showed the arsehole.

He hadn't enjoyed himself so much since he'd turned Chardonnay into roadkill. Jackie clapped some non-existent dirt from his hands, turned his back on the dickhead in the fancy Aston Martin, and strode, shoulders forced back proudly, into the workshop.

"Dylan," he called, marching towards the lad who still hadn't cleaned up the blood and oil properly. As expected.

"Yeah?"

"Set up the pressure washer. The Raptor's filthy."

"Aw, Dad."

"Here."

Jackie lobbed him the keys. Dylan snapped out a hand, fumbled the catch, and the keys fell to the floor centimetres away from the edge of the pit—boy never could catch nothing but a cold. He bent to scoop them up.

"And don't forget to use the chamois. I want it polished to a shine."

"Do I have to, Dad? Can't it wait 'til Chalky gets here in the morning?"

"Do it now. Before the mud bakes hard in this heat. It's worth a twenty."

"Make it fifty and it's a deal," Dylan said. "She's bloody filthy. It'll take ages."

The cocky little git smiled as he made the counter-offer.

"Yeah, okay. Fifty it is," Jackie said, unable to refuse the idiot boy anything. "You'd better make a proper job of it, though. Else you'll get bugger all."

"Yeah. Okay, Dad."

Dylan lowered the stiff broom into the pit and strolled towards the shutters and the sunshine. Jackie shook his head. Another fifty quid gone, but who cared? Plenty more where that came from. He jogged up the stairs. As he reached the balcony, Marco stepped out of the office. He held a hand up to his chest and shook his head.

What now?

Jackie stopped and waited for an explanation. Marco tilted his head to indicate the fire door and brushed past him on the way.

"Better come with me, boss," he whispered, keeping his back turned to the cameras and barely moving his lips.

"What's up?" Jackie asked, but Marco kept heading for the fire exit.

"You need to see something," he muttered.

"What?" Jackie whispered.

Marco ignored him, pressed the slam bar on the fire door, and pushed through to the outside. He held the door open for Jackie and waited.

Jackie followed Marco into the open and spun to face the big minder.

"What the fuck?" Jackie asked, raising his voice. "Who do you think—"

Marco held a finger to his lips, released the fire door and allowed it to close slowly and hold on the latch. He turned to face the woods, gripped the rusted handrail with both fists, and stood, staring into the treetop canopy. Jackie shuffled over to the handrail and adopted the same position.

"What the fuck?" he repeated, speaking more quietly.

"Sorry, boss," Marco whispered, "but we can't speak inside. It's not safe."

"Not safe? What the shittin' hell are you talkin' about?"

Marco released the handrail and dug into his pocket. He removed his phone and tapped the screen into life. It opened to a video showing the dedicated, CCTV monitor open on its desk in the outer office and running in split-screen mode. Nine tiny squares in three rows of three.

"What's this?"

"Look at camera six," Marco said in his deep, Brummie drawl.

"What about it?"

"It's out of alignment."

Jackie studied the picture in the middle-right portion of

the multi-screen. Couldn't see nothing wrong with it. The tiny picture centred on the concrete steps dropping into the near end of the inspection pit.

"Don't know how I missed it when scanning the film of Tony doing his swan dive. Had other things on my mind at the time. My mistake. Sorry, boss."

Jackie looked closer and sniffed. "Can't see nothin' wrong with it."

"Hang on a sec. Watch."

Marco's hand appeared on the video. His index finger touched the middle-right section of the server's monitor, and the image expanded to fill the phone's screen.

"The shot's slightly out of alignment," Marco announced. "For definite. Not by much, but enough to notice when you're looking hard."

"You sure?"

"Certain," Marco said, nodding. "The picture's slightly lower than it should be."

Jackie still couldn't see it, but he trusted Marco's judgement. The big guy had set the system up and knew it inside and out.

"How'd it happen?" Jackie asked. "You reckon it could be the pigeons?"

Marco curled his upper lip and shook his head.

"No. It's definitely not a bird strike."

"How can you tell for sure?" Jackie asked. He stared hard at the minder, still not understanding what all the fuss was about.

"Wait," he said. "I took this from inside the office. It's not the best shot, but I didn't want to make what I was doing obvious."

He swiped the phone's screen to the right and another

image appeared. This one showed a still of one of the CCTV camera groups taken from below.

"Which camera's that?" Jackie asked, leaning closer, narrowing his eyes for focus.

"The one that took the video of you and Tony arguing. Do you see it?"

Jackie examined the image carefully. Shook his head.

"See what?"

Marco spread his fingers over the screen and enlarged the shot enough to zoom in on the back of the camera he was talking about. A small, white box dangled out of its rear end.

Bloody hell.

"What the fuck's that?"

"I reckon it's a dongle."

"A what?"

"A dongle," Marco answered. "It allows someone to access the cameras via the internet. Whoever attached it must have nudged the camera out of alignment."

"You mean some bastard's spyin' on me?"

Marco looked uncomfortable and nodded.

"Fuck," Jackie said.

"Yeah," Marco agreed. "Fuck."

Jackie stared at the screen for a few moments longer, then glared at Marco.

"Since when?"

"Not sure," Marco said, shaking his head.

"Why not? Can't you work it out?"

"I could do, easy enough." Marco tilted his head to one side. "But if I start taking an undue interest in the system, whoever's spying on us would know he's been sussed." He scratched his chin. "I wanted to clue you in first."

"Yeah, gotcha," Jackie said. "Well spotted." He clapped Marco on the shoulder.

"Thanks, boss."

"Any idea who planted it? The filth?"

"Could be, I suppose. But"—he twisted his mouth—"I doubt it."

"Why not?"

Marco held up the phone and pointed to the dongle thingy.

"I did a little online research. Tried to find something that would plug into those specific cameras. Couldn't find anything. In short, you can't buy a dongle like that off the shelf. I reckon someone built that thing … bespoke."

"Yeah?"

Marco nodded. "Yeah. It's expensive and way too sophisticated for the cops. This has to be a private job."

Jackie stopped for a moment to absorb the implications.

Nah. It couldn't be the filth. If the cops planted the dongle, they'd have raided the workshop the moment they'd heard Jackie and Dylan talking about the dashcam. But that didn't happen. They were safe. Jackie'd paused the surveillance in the office. Unless …

Oh shit!

"Are you tellin' me whoever planted that thing has full control of the system? Like, they can switch the cameras on and off and shit?"

Marco lifted a shoulder in a shrug.

"Yeah. That's exactly what I'm telling you."

Jackie's blood ran cold. He desperately tried to remember exactly what he and Dylan had said. His mind blanked. But whatever they'd said in the recording, with a good brief, they could probably explain it away. It wouldn't be worth bugger all without the dashcam itself and the explosive footage it contained.

Either way, if it was the filth, they'd have called already, and they'd have brought a dirty, great, big search warrant along with them. Nah. Not the filth. The cops wouldn't have waited. Had to be someone else.

"Ronnie, you reckon?" Jackie asked.

"Dunno, boss." Marco shrugged and glanced into the distance where sunlight reflecting from the windscreen of a truck on the nearby ring road sparkled through the trees. "Could be, though."

Fuck it.

"Who else would have the nerve?" Jackie asked.

Marco sighed.

"Can't think of anyone."

"But me and Ronnie ain't rivals no more. Not after I stepped away from the leisure business and gave him free run of the county. How fuckin' dare he?"

"I'm not saying it's Ronnie Sutton for definite, boss, but he's been pissed ever since you won the big money. Jealousy's a bitch, and like you said, he's probably the only one with the balls to have a go."

"What a bastard. If it is Ronnie, what's he after?" Jackie asked.

Marco broke eye contact. He swiped and tapped the screen, then dropped the phone into his pocket.

"Don't be shy. What d'you reckon?"

"Wouldn't want to upset you, boss."

"Spit it out, man. I won't bite."

The big Italian turned to face Jackie. He stepped back a pace, moving out of range.

"I can think of two reasons, boss."

"C'mon then, Marco. Hit me with 'em."

"You keep telling people how you don't trust the banks. And you keep flashing the cash."

Jackie jerked back his head and grinned.

"If you've got it … flaunt it."

"But you did start the rumour about the cash you keep in the safe. You and I both know there's no money in there, but Ronnie doesn't. Maybe he wants to put one over on you. I wouldn't put it past the bugger. He's greedy enough."

Too right he is.

"And the other reason?"

Again with the hesitation.

"C'mon, Marco. Lay it on me."

"You aren't going to like it, boss."

"I'm gonna like it even less if I have to ask again."

"Dylan's side hustle."

"The 'roids?"

Marco nodded. "You sure he hasn't started treading on Ronnie's toes?"

"You're kiddin', right?" Jackie scoffed. "The boy's only movin' a few vials of the stuff. It's strictly small time. It ain't enough to put Ronnie's nose outta joint."

"Like I said, boss. Ronnie's the jealous type. Greedy, too."

Jackie had another thought. One that meshed with Jackie's growing theory.

"You know what?" he said.

"What?"

"Maybe you were right about Ronnie bein' behind the attack on Logan. Maybe the stupid fuckwit's makin' a move on me after all."

"Makes sense, boss," Marco said. "Want me to contact him? Arrange a meet? Nip this thing in the—"

"What? You want me to go cap in hand to Ronnie

Sutton and ask for peace talks after he's turned over one of my men, broken into my gaff, and planted that bug? Well fuck that for a—"

"It may have nothing to do with Ronnie, boss," Marco said, holding up his hands. "Why don't I just put out some gentle feelers?"

What's he playin' at?

Jackie didn't like the way Marco was trying to lead the direction of movement. It didn't sit right. It was as though he were trying to take control. Who was the boss here?

What's his fuckin' game?

"Maybe," Jackie said, looking Marco dead in the eye. "I'll think about it."

"Okay, boss. In the meantime, do you want me to close the CCTV system down and get hold of a cherry picker to remove the dongle?"

Jackie held up a hand to give himself time to think. After a few moments, he smiled and shook his head.

"Nah. Don't do that," he said, breaking out a smile. "I got a better idea."

"Yeah?"

"Leave it runnin'. Let Ronnie—"

"If it is Ronnie."

There he goes again with the doubt.

Who else had reason to plant the bloody dongle?

"Yeah. If it is Ronnie. Let him think we don't got a clue 'bout the bug."

"Good idea, boss. Then what?"

"Contact the boys. Tell 'em to be at my place tonight."

"What time?"

"Eight o'clock sharp. Tell 'em to come dressed and tooled up for an overnighter."

"You got it, boss." Marco reached for his mobile again. "I'll call Mo from out here. Tell him to sort it."

"You do that," Jackie growled. "Meanwhile, I'll go have a word with Dylan. Tip him the nod." He reached for the fire door.

"Careful about what you tell him, boss. You know what he's like."

What the fuck?

Who the fuck was Marco to tell Jackie what to do? The bugger were getting way too big for his size thirteens.

"No. Marco. Do tell!" Jackie scowled. "What exactly is my boy like?"

Marco raised his hands in a show of respect. Too little, too late.

"Sorry, boss. I didn't mean anything by it. It's just that Dylan can have a bit of a short fuse. I wouldn't want him to do anything …"

"What? Stupid?"

"Well, no, but …" Marco winced, finally realising how far he'd strayed out of line.

Yeah. He has a point, though.

Jackie dialled back his anger a couple of notches. He'd started overreacting. Seeing spies where there weren't none. Marco was only trying to help, and Dylan could be a little … hasty.

Marco dialled and put the phone to his ear.

"Mo?" he said, keeping his voice low. "Get a hold of Shelly. The boss wants—"

Jackie pulled open the fire door, marched through the landing, and trudged down the stairs, all the time trying not to glance up at the spy in the sky. Ronnie Sutton didn't know who he were messing with.

He hurried down the stairs and stomped past the

inspection pit that still didn't look anywhere near clean enough. At some stage, he'd have one of the guys go over it again. Do it proper. Dylan couldn't get nothing right. Stupid lump.

But he's my *stupid lump.*

He reached the roller shutters and made it out into the warm, afternoon sun.

"Dylan!" Jackie called, standing back out of range of the pressure spray.

For once the lad had done a half-decent job of removing the thick, red mud from the Raptor but had succeeded in covering himself with filthy backwash. Good job he'd climbed into a boiler suit.

"Dylan," Jackie roared for a second time.

Dylan released the trigger, lowered the nozzle, and spun to face him.

"Come here, son," he said. "Leave that for now. We need to talk."

Chapter Forty-Six

Thursday 8th July - Night

Eccleshall Way, Stafford, Staffordshire, England

Shit.

Kaine's mouth dried. He'd blown it. With the fire door chained up tight behind him and the only other exit blocked by a row of thugs, things didn't look good.

"Whatcha doing working for Ronnie Sutton, Jeffries?"

Who?

"Ronnie Sutton?" Kaine called down. "Sorry. I've never heard of him."

"Liar!" Dylan screamed.

Kaine looked around for an escape route. Found nothing obvious.

"Keep him talking, Mr K. Corky's workin' on something."

"Roger that, Control," Kaine muttered.

The three men who were lined up in front of Bentley and Dylan—all dressed in black, all six footers and beefy—stopped tapping their weapons to listen.

"What?" Bentley shouted. "What you say?"

Kaine released his grip on the handrail and stood up straighter.

"I said, I've never heard of a Ronnie Callan."

"It's *Sutton*, moron," Bentley roared. "Ronnie Sutton. And don't you give me no more o' that bullshit."

Kaine held out his hands and grinned. "It's the truth."

"You lyin' piece of shit. Get down here!"

Kaine flipped the grin into a quizzical frown. "Why on earth would I want to do that?"

Bentley bared his teeth in a wolfish smile.

"So we can have a quiet, little chat. Shoutin' hurts my throat." He laughed.

Behind Bentley, Dylan stood taller, puffed out his chest, and added a nervous chuckle.

"Not my problem," Kaine said. "I'm happy where I am."

"*Not long now, Mr K,*" Corky said over the clack of finger-tips rippling over a keyboard.

Whatever Corky had in mind, he needed to be bloody quick.

"You know you've just broken the law," Kaine said, conversationally. "I should call the police."

Bentley cut his laugh short.

"What's that, you arsehole?" he snarled, his face turning red. "You break into my place and threaten *me* with the filth!"

"You put a chain on the fire door. I'm pretty sure that's

430

breaking all sorts of health and safety regulations. Tut, tut. Shame on you!"

"Shelly," Bentley said, "you hear that?"

The third man turned towards Bentley.

"Yeah," Shelly answered, nodding, "I heard him, boss."

"The fucker's threatenin' to call the filth on you."

"Yeah, he is."

"You worried?"

"Nah, boss," Shelly answered. "Won't take me long to remove the chain when we've done the fucker over. By the time the pigs arrive, everything'll be cool."

"But he'll be way past worrying about it," Beanie said, and added high-pitched laughter to the rest. It sounded false.

Bentley tapped Marco's shoulder.

"Get up there and drag the arsehole down here by his bollocks. Don't take all night about it, neither."

Marco nodded. "We're on it, boss."

"Just a minute, Marco," Kaine said, holding up his right hand like a policemen stopping traffic. "Before you do anything rash, listen to me."

If Marco was surprised Kaine knew his name, he didn't show it.

"Up yours, Jeffries," he shouted.

Marco started walking but stopped when Kaine dug a hand into his pocket and pulled out the dashcam. The other two, Beanie and Shelly, hadn't moved.

"Do you know what this is, Marco?" he asked, brandishing the dashcam. "What about you two?" He pointed to Beanie and Shelly in turn. "Any ideas?"

"Looks like a dashcam to me," Bentley announced, sneering.

"Yep," Dylan agreed, finding his voice again. "It's a

dashcam alright." He stood up even straighter, confidence flowing through him. Hardly the reaction Kaine expected.

"Wonder what's on it?" Kaine asked, directing the question at Marco and the other hired hands.

"You gonna tell us, I suppose," Marco said.

"It shows Dylan running a car off the road and causing the death of a woman called Melissa Fabien."

Marco frowned, turned to face Bentley. "That true, boss?"

Bentley shook his head.

"No way," Dylan shouted.

"The only thing on that one is of you drivin' the green lanes near my farm!" Bentley gloated.

"Why keep it in the safe, then?"

"To draw you out, fuckwit," Dylan shouted even louder. "Go on, check it out. We'll wait. The password's 'Jackie5'. Capital J and the number five." His grin stretched wide.

Kaine powered up the dashcam, thumbed in the password, and watched the first clip.

Bugger.

He switched the dashcam off and, without thinking, dropped it into his pocket.

"So," Kaine said, nodding and understanding his mistake, "you swapped dashcams with the one from the Raptor you were cleaning."

"Yeah," Dylan shouted. "That's right. Gotcha!"

Yep. You've got me there.

"Clever," Kaine said, still nodding. "I didn't see that coming."

"Moron!" Dylan added.

Damn it.

"Where's the original?"

"I destroyed it!"

Now who's lying?

"Don't be stupid, Dylan. It's still around somewhere. It's too precious to you. Later, I'll ask you where you hid it. And you'll be only too pleased to tell me. Won't you, you sick, little boy."

"Fuck off!" Dylan screamed. "Fuck off! Go get him, Marco. Go on! Kill the fucker."

"What's he talking about, boss?" Marco asked, still not moving.

Kaine answered for Bentley.

"I'm talking about how Dylan likes to jerk off to the clip of him running the Fabiens' Toyota off the road and killing an innocent woman, Marco. And by helping him, he's making you all culpable. You're open to charges of perverting the course of justice. You're all going down for a long, long time." Kaine paused for breath and pointed at the goon standing in the middle. "You understand me, Beanie-boy? You're going to prison."

"Only if you live to tell the tale, fucker!" Bentley snarled.

"Boss?" Beanie asked. "What's going on?"

"Do as you're told, Mo!" Bentley roared. "Go get him."

"But …"

Bentley reached inside his jacket and pulled out a handgun—a ten or fifteen shot Beretta APX Compact.

Bloody hell.

Kaine hadn't seen that coming either.

"Do as you're fuckin' told, arsehole!"

Kaine dived backwards into the depths of the balcony, expecting to feel the bullet before hearing the shot. Nothing. He rolled onto his front and scrambled forwards, keeping low.

Bentley—wide-eyed and fully absorbed with his disobedient hireling—racked the slide and pointed the Beretta at Beanie.

"Don't you fuckin' *dare* question me!"

Crap.

Things had just become a whole lot more serious. Five thugs armed with bats and knives was bad enough, but one with a Beretta?

"Control," Kaine whispered. "Any time you're ready. Over."

"One sec … Got it."

A key clicked.

All the lights cut out.

Darkness fell. Total, utter blackness. Inside and out.

An explosion—a bulbous, orange flash. The Beretta. One shot. It echoed through the workshop. The retort rang in Kaine's ears.

"The lights," Dylan said. "What happened to the fucking lights?"

"Power cut?" someone snapped. Marco?

"I'm hit!" a man screamed. "I'm fucking hit! You bastard. You shot me!"

"Where?" another asked. Definitely Bentley.

"My arm. I'm fucking bleeding."

"Shelly," Marco called. "How bad?"

"Dunno," Shelly wailed. "Can't fucking see nothing. God, it hurts. I-I think it's broken. My fucking arm's broken!"

Kaine smiled. Maybe things weren't so bad after all. One down, and only three to go—including Bentley with at least fourteen more shots. He didn't include Dylan. The kid's eyes alone called him out as a coward. Under any sort of pressure, he would melt like butter in a hot skillet.

"Sorry, Shelly," Bentley called. "I'll see you right. Just shut your fuckin' wailin'."

"But you shot me!" Shelly sobbed. "Fuck ... it hurts."

"It were an accident. The lights ... Fuck. Nobody move."

Kaine reversed deeper into the platform and spun through one-eighty degrees. Working from memory, he pictured the layout. Somewhere close by, on his right, he'd find the ladder up to the roof of the office and storage units. He reached out, sweeping with his outstretched arms. Fingertips brushed the fire door. Sliding the fingers upwards, his hand found the slam bar and followed it further to the right. He located the twenty-five-centimetre gap between the workshop's corrugated, rear wall and the smooth back of the pod where they stood proud of the eaves.

"Everybody down!" Bentley roared. "On the floor. Now."

Kaine dropped flat, predicting Bentley's next move.

Three flashes. Three cracks. Bullets hit metal, ricocheted, screamed away. One slammed into the fire door well above Kaine's head and dropped to the platform centimetres from his left hand. Its heat warmed Kaine's fingers.

Eleven shots left.

"*What's that, Mr K? Sounds like shooting.*" Corky's voice sounded in Kaine's ear. He'd almost forgotten the earpiece.

"Bentley's taking potshots at me in the dark. Over."

"*What? With a gun?*"

What else?

"Yes," Kaine answered, shaking his head in the dark. "With a gun. Over."

"*Nasty. Why ain't you shooting back?*"

"I left my SIG in the car."

Bloody idiot.

"What did you do with the lights? Over."

"Corky took control of the nearest electricity substation. Dropped out all the power for that part of town. Corky figured you could do without the streetlights, too."

Superb.

"Thanks, mate." It sounded woefully inadequate. "How long 'til the lights come back on. Over."

"Not before Corky gives control back to West Midlands Power, and that won't happen until you give Corky the okay." He let loose an encouraging chuckle.

A bright light snapped on in the cavern below. Then another and two more. Bentley and his minions had found a use for their mobiles.

Chapter Forty-Seven

Thursday 8th July - Night

Eccleshall Way, Stafford, Staffordshire, England

Four beams—searchlight-bright—rolled around the building, shooting random, overlapping arcs of light through the blackness. No pattern. No organisation.

Four lights. Five bad guys. One light missing. Shelly's?

One of the beams steadied, locked on Kaine's previous location on the balcony. A second overlapped the first, adding more ferocity to the floodlight. Their combined power created a blind spot behind the pool of brightness. It picked out the rungs of the ladder Kaine was searching for.

"Gone," Bentley shouted. "Fuck."

"Can you see him, Dad? Did you hit him?" Dylan

asked, overly eager, voice pitched high, both terrified and excited.

"How the fuck do I know?"

"Shoot him again, Dad! Go on!"

One of the focussed torch beams dipped. The other held steady. Two more blasts punctuated the short silence. The bullets punched neat holes in the corrugated wall above the fire door, grouped reasonably close together. Half-decent shooting. Their trajectory arced over Kaine's back, but not close enough to cause concern.

Nine left.

Kaine had an idea. A stretch but worth a try.

Nothing to lose.

Kaine rolled onto his side, turning his back to the balcony. He retrieved the dashcam from his pocket and rolled it in his fingers, searching for the power button. Found it. Hugging the device tight to his chest, he held the button down. The power light glowed red between his fingers and the screen lit up his jacket.

Hiding the dashcam in the folds of his jacket, he rolled onto his front. Chin to the treadplates, he snaked closer to the balcony. Its raised, front lip threw a deep line of shadow, hiding Kaine from the figures below.

He leaned to one side and tossed the dashcam to his right. The illuminated screen flashed, spun, and twinkled in a high arc. It cracked into a storeroom door and fell.

"Dad!"

Bentley fired three snapshots. One hit close to the illuminated dashcam. The other two, high and wide to the left, ricocheted off metal and whined away.

Six left.

"You hit him, Dad! You hit him!"

"What?"

Four phone beams focused on the dashcam screen's faint glow, overwhelming it with their searing, combined light.

Someone whimpered, groaned.

"Shut the fuck up, Shelly," Bentley snarled. "Grow a pair!"

"I'm fucking bleeding here!" Shelly wailed.

Kaine reversed deeper into the darkness of the platform. He scrambled to his feet, hugging the corner between fire door and protruding office wall.

"Put pressure on the wound," Marco ordered.

"I-I can't!"

"It'll help."

Kaine reached out, searching blind.

"My arm's broken."

"Tough," Bentley said, showing a total lack of concern. "Shut the fuck up. You're doing my head in!"

Kaine's fingers grasped a cold, metal rung.

The ladder.

"I-I need an … an ambulance."

"Later," Bentley growled. "Quit your bellyachin'!"

"Shit," Marco said. "Boss, this is getting out of—"

"Fuck off! We deal with Jeffries first. Then we take care of Shelly!"

Kaine found the lowest rung with his foot. He climbed the ladder in near-silence, the only sound the swish of material sliding over sweaty skin.

"Let's go get him!" Bentley called. "Dylan, stay here with Shelly. Lock the wicket door."

"Er, yeah," Dylan answered. "Right. I-I got you." Relief flooded his words.

Nine rungs up the ladder, the suspended, cubicle roof stretched out into the darkness. Into oblivion. A narrow gap between outer and inner wall to his left, and an open chasm falling away to his right. Kaine crawled forwards, onto the reinforced walkway, disturbing years of accumulated dust. He held his breath, desperate not to sneeze. Slowly, he stood, reaching up at the same time, searching for the sloping roof. His hand located the cold metal of a truss.

The third roof truss. The truss before the one that held the CCTV cluster. No way would he go out there again. Not a chance.

Below, rubber-soled boots scuffed and scraped along concrete. Three of the lights clustered together near the far end of the inspection pit.

Whispers and low voices reached Kaine's ears. Bentley issued hushed instructions.

The beams lowered, played on the floor, lighting the way. Three moved as one. Crowding, hurrying closer. Heading for the staircase. Avoiding obstacles. They moved between the row of stretch limos and the elongated inspection pit.

Dylan's light remained close to the roller shutters, the beam climbed from the floor at his feet and reached the handle of the wicket door. He keyed the lock on the door and dropped the key into his right trouser pocket. Kaine took careful note. Almost as an afterthought, Dylan pointed the light at the fallen Shelly who sat, leaning against the shutters, curled into a ball. Feet flat on the floor, knees up, rocking. The blood-soaked right arm cradled in his left, pressed tight into his chest. His pale, bloodless face was creased in pain. Tears ran down his cheeks, catching the torchlight.

With Dylan an obvious coward and Shelly out of commission, the odds had slid in Kaine's favour, but not by much. The Beretta trumped all, reducing his chances of survival. Kaine dropped to one knee. His left hand nudged something—a plastic container. Its liquid contents gurgled and sloshed thickly against the container's inner walls.

"Jeffries. Oh Jeffries!" Bentley sang out, his tone mocking. "We're comin' for you, arsehole. You're goin' down."

"C'mon!" Marco roared.

"Yeah," Mo added.

Metal struck metal. The clang rang out loud through the open space. A second clang. A third. More. Rhythmic. Speeding up. Aggressive.

Kaine risked a peek over the edge of the flat, office roof.

Marco and Mo repeatedly struck the inspection pit's guard rail with their weapons—a crowbar and a tyre lever —in another ineffective and ludicrous attempt at intimidation. Maybe they needed to psych themselves up.

Pitiful.

Kaine pulled back from the edge of the cubicle and picked up the plastic container. He unscrewed the top and sniffed the contents. Burned. Dirty. Pungent.

Used motor oil.

He smiled.

Nice one.

It would do well enough.

Still kneeling, he replaced the top and lay the five-litre container on its side, making sure it slightly overlapped the edge of the cubicle. He loosened the top enough to let the used oil seep out without glugging. The backwash from the phone lights showed the viscous, black liquid seep from the lid, pool on the walkway, and flow slowly down the cubicle's end wall. Too slowly. He loosened the top another quarter turn and increased the flow rate. Better. It wouldn't take long to reach the balcony and puddle across the worn treadplate.

Satisfied, Kaine squirmed backwards into the blackness.

"Enough!" Bentley yelled.

The clanking stopped and the echoes faded.

"Let's go."

The lights started moving again, drawing ever closer to the staircase.

Too soon. The oil needed more time to puddle on the treadplate.

In the rippling darkness cast by the moving lights, an outline near his nose solidified into a large, rectangular box. Kaine reached out. The box, cardboard, moved easily. Not enough mass. Beside it stood a second box. Smaller than the first but much heavier. He nudged it—fifteen kilos, maybe more—and opened the interlocked flaps. He felt inside. Cans of something. He pulled one from the box. Shook it gently. The ball-bearing agitator rattled. A can of spray paint. He replaced the can and picked up the box. The damp cardboard flexed under his grip. He stood and crouched, ducking when his head brushed the sloping roof.

With the collapsing box heavy in his hands, he stepped closer to the edge, keeping well clear of the oil container. Restricted by the slope of the roof, and unable to free his arms or aim the soggy box, Kaine trusted luck. He swung, released the box at the end of the arc, and stepped back into the shadows.

An upturned face, eyes wide. Marco.

The box sailed through the air. Caught the handrail. Exploded in a heavy shower of part-used spray cans.

"Look out!" Marco yelled, diving into the protection of the overhead balcony.

Mo yelped, threw up an arm, and lurched backwards. He collided with the guardrail protecting the inspection pit, bounced clear, and took a spray can to the top of the head which dislodged the beanie. He fell on his arse. Three more cans slammed into his chest. Bounced off. Clattered around him. Some hit the floor, others fell into the pit. One exploded in a spray of pillar-box-red paint. The broken, cardboard box floated down to land on the luckless Mo, who lay in a heap, hatless, bleeding from a gash to the forehead.

"Bastard!" the deep-voiced Mo howled, slamming the collapsed box away and picking himself up off the floor. "Cowardly, fucking bastard. I'm gonna rip your fucking head off, arsehole!"

Bentley, on the other side of the pit and well clear of the paint-can bombardment, roared. Raised his gun arm.

Kaine dived to the walkway. Lay flat. Covered his head with his hands.

Bentley fired, again and again.

Six unaimed snapshots rained through the loft space. Bullets drilled through roof panels, cardboard boxes, metal walls. A ricochet plugged into the wooden platform close to Kaine's face. Stinging pain pierced his forehead. Splinters. Blood ran into his eye.

Close. Too bloody close.

Empty. Bentley had emptied the Beretta.

Ringing silence spread up from below.

Kaine reached up to his forehead, found the splinters. He tugged the largest one free. Left the rest for later.

Clicks. A metallic slide and another click. The familiar sound of a magazine being replaced, and a semi-automatic handgun being cocked.

The clear sounds of Bentley reloading.

Damn it.

Still prone, Kaine edged forwards and looked down.

"Bastard!" Mo bellowed. "Fucking bastard!" He dabbed his forehead with his fingers—they came away bloodied.

"I saw him lob the box," Marco called from his hiding place under the balcony. "He's in the roof space."

"Get up there," Bentley shouted, raising the Beretta and lining it up with the torchlight, taking a much more careful aim. "I'll keep the fucker's head down."

Bentley's phone light flooded the area above Kaine's back, holding steady, pinning him down.

Kaine swiped the blood from his eye with the back of his hand. The wound stung like hell, but it didn't seem serious. Not too deep. The blood had already stopped flowing.

A shot boomed. The bullet buried itself inside a cardboard box to Kaine's left. The box started hissing. More cans of spray paint. A second gunshot blasted another hole in the roof well above Kaine's head. By the time Bentley had finished, the roof would leak like a colander. A third shot followed the second, hit the girder, and whined off into the distance.

Below Kaine, two men yelled. The first reached the staircase ahead of the other and stamped his way up, breathing heavily. The second followed a few paces behind. Metal clanked on metal as steel tools connected with handrails.

Kaine flattened himself onto the walkway, spun through a quarter turn to face the fire escape and the next threat. He squirmed closer to the eaves and the gap between sloping roof and pod. He poked his head out far enough to see the platform. The waving torch beams glistened on the thin pool of oil.

Mo reached the top of the stairs first. Leaning forwards, he planted his boot on the oil-soaked tread plate. The boot shot out from under him. He yelled and pitched headlong, arms outstretched. The crown of his head slammed into the sharp corner of the cubicle. Bone smashed into metal, the noise sickening. Mo slumped, face first, into the dirty oil. Stopped moving.

Kaine grinned. Another one down. Two contenders left. And Dylan.

Marco hit the top step. Panting, he stopped, craned his head to look up. Rage distorted his darkly shadowed face.

Kaine smirked down at him. Winked.

"Fucking arsehole!"

"Language, Marco," Kaine chided. "What would your mother say?"

Two more gunshots broke into Kaine's taunt. The bullets hit high, three metres behind Kaine's latest hiding place. One drilled through the roof. The other two buried themselves into the stored rubbish.

"Boss!" Marco roared, locking his dark eyes with Kaine. "Stop firing. I'm too close. Leave the bastard to me!"

"Okay!" Bentley shouted. "Make your move."

Marco stepped over the oil puddle and his mate. He swung the crowbar high. Kaine squirmed backwards. The crowbar smashed against the roof truss above Kaine's head. Rang out loud.

Marco grunted, swore.

"Ouch," Kaine jeered. "I bet that hurt."

"Fuck you, arsehole!"

Marco jumped up, thrust the crowbar out, using it like a spear. It fell short. Well short. Kaine shot out a hand and grasped for the bar. Missed. He pulled his hand away and wriggled deeper into the gloom.

"What happened?" Bentley called. "Where's Mo?"

Marco retracted the bar.

"Damn it, Marco. Speak to me."

Marco grunted. "Jeffries spread oil over the landing. Mo fell. He's hurt."

"Bad?"

"Yeah. Pretty bad. He's not moving."

Kaine crawled back into the light.

"Such a shame," he crowed, stretching out another smile.

"I'm gonna kill you!" Marco said. Ice-cold venom chilled his voice.

Kaine beckoned with his fingers. "Come get me, big guy."

"You piece of—"

"Where the fuck's Jeffries?" Bentley shouted.

"Hiding in the eaves. Arsehole's looking down at me. Smirking."

"Go get him then! What the fuck you waitin' for?"

Marco turned to face the balcony, grabbed hold of the handrail, and leaned out.

"I don't wanna get shot."

"Good thinking, Marco," Kaine shouted loud enough for Bentley to hear. "Your boss couldn't hit the side of a bus if he was sitting inside it." He rattled out a contemptuous laugh.

Two more gunshots drowned out Kaine's laughter. Both missed high and wide. Kaine stopped laughing and gritted his teeth.

What a bloody idiot.

Such a balls-up. He should be armed.

If he'd brought his SIG, the little disturbance would already be over. Bentley had it coming. Anyone who threatened children deserved no mercy. Bentley had earned a heavy boot to the back of the neck. Dylan, too. And anyone who helped them. Marco and Mo included. And Shelly.

"See what I mean?" Kaine said. "He's bloody hopeless."

Bentley responded to Kaine's latest taunt with two more

rapid shots. They struck closer to home, but still missed on the high side. He'd moved further away. Changed his firing position.

"Boss!" Marco called. "Stop shooting and let me deal with this bastard."

"Okay, okay. But leave enough of him for me to question."

"Not fucking likely," Marco muttered.

Marco pushed off the handrail and played his torch over Mo's crumpled frame. Kaine winced at the sight. Mo looked in a bad way. Blood flowed from a serious laceration to the top of his head, and he lay deathly still. Kaine couldn't see any chest movement.

Marco smashed the crowbar into the handrail, checked Mo's carotid artery for a pulse, and rolled him into the recovery position. Mo groaned. Alive. A surprise. Marco climbed over his comatose buddy and raised the torch. He stared up at Kaine, glowering.

Kaine bared his teeth in a snarl.

This'll be interesting.

Chapter Forty-Eight

Thursday 8th July - Marco Gallo

Eccleshall Way, Stafford, Staffordshire, England

Jeffries, you bastard.

Barely able to control his rage, Marco stared at the mess on the floor and slammed the crowbar on the handrail. It crashed into the metal, ringing out loud and angry. The shockwave vibrated through his hand and thumped into his wrist.

Shit. Stop doing that, you idiot.

How had everything got so royally fucked? After he'd told Jackie about the dongle, the plan had been so bloody simple. Watch the warehouse, wait for some bugger to show up, lock them in, and beat the crap out of them to find out who was behind it. When had it become so shitting complicated with guns and dashcams, and that thing with Dylan? What kind of sick fuck gets his rocks off over killing an old lady?

Jesus fucking Christ.

He reached down and gently pressed his fingers to Mo's throat, stunned to find a pulse. Faint, but a pulse just the same.

Thank fuck.

He threw Jackie a thumbs up and rolled Mo onto his side to pull his face out of the oil. As he settled, Mo let out a quiet groan.

Keeping clear of the spill, Marco stepped over Mo and into the relative darkness of the fire exit. He shone the torchlight up into the eaves and caught the sparkle in Jeffries' eyes and the whiteness of teeth bared in a vicious smile. Bloody hell. The bugger was enjoying himself.

Mad bastard.

"I'm coming for you, arsehole," Marco snarled.

"And I'm waiting," the arsehole chuckled.

Jeffries winked and slithered out of sight. A coward, hiding in the darkness. But the arsehole would pay for hurting Mo. By Christ would he pay. And the hell with saving him for the boss.

"You're mine, arsehole," he muttered. "All mine."

Leading with the torch, Marco reached for the ladder with the hand holding the crowbar. Bloody awkward. He could only grip the rung with his thumb and index finger. The crowbar clanked against the metal and the rung grazed his knuckles, but he couldn't drop it. The crowbar would come in handy.

He dropped back to the floor.

"Boss?" he shouted.

"Yeah?"

"Shine your torch up here, will you? I need the light."

Jackie arced his beam around and up, illuminating the area above the ladder. The light juddered in Jackie's hand. No doubt about it. He was as livid as Marco. Too bloody right.

"Okay?"

"Yeah. Thanks, boss."

Marco dropped the phone, still lit, into his trouser pocket. He wouldn't want to be messing about with it up in the loft with a madman nearby.

C'mon, Marco. Let's do this!

With the crowbar held high above his head, Marco grabbed a rung and climbed quickly. Three steps.

Near the top, he swung the crowbar hard and fast. Left-right-left. Hit a steel stanchion on the return left arc. The heavy contact jarred his hand again.

Bloody hell.

It stung like shit.

Keeping his head down, he climbed another rung and hesitated. He straightened his legs and popped his head over the office roof, preparing to duck back down if Jeffries' boot flew towards his face.

Nothing.

He jabbed the crowbar straight out ahead, swung it to the left in a tighter arc. It slammed into a cardboard box. The box caved in easily. Empty.

Still no sign of Jeffries.

With two more rungs climbed at the crouch, Marco stepped out onto the walkway. He stood, bent at the waist and knees to keep from banging his head on the sloping roof. He paused. Held his breath. Listened. Heard only silence.

"See him?" Jackie called.

Marco held out an arm and flapped his hand for quiet, risking a bollocking later. Jackie Bentley didn't like taking instructions from employees.

Still crouching, Marco dug a hand into his pocket and pulled out his lit phone. Averting his eyes to avoid blinding himself with the bloody thing, he pointed the beam down at where he'd last seen Jeffries. Found nothing but an empty and dusty floorspace.

"Well?" Jackie roared.

"He's gone, boss."

"What d'you mean 'gone'? He can't be fuckin' gone. There's only one way down from there, and he ain't used the fuckin' ladder!"

"He'll be hiding down the far end. Hang on."

Marco played the torchlight along the empty walkway which stretched out into the black distance. To the left lay piles of mismatched rubbish, crammed into the eaves. To the right, the edge of the cabin rooftops, and then nothing. Not so much as a safety rail. Nothing to stop a plunge to the concrete floor but the balcony. Marco swallowed.

The left. Focus on the left.

Jeffries was up ahead somewhere. Couldn't be anywhere else.

"Hey there, Jeffries," Marco called, his tone mocking. "Come out, come out wherever you are."

Marco held his breath, waiting for a reply he knew would never arrive.

Fuck you, arsehole.

He advanced slowly, waving the crowbar ahead of him like a sword. Marco reached the second roof truss. Stopped. Stared ahead and to the left. Shone his light into the shadows. He counted to five before stepping over the horizontal crossbar and ducking through a gap between a pair of diagonal, cross braces. His torch lit a stack of cardboard boxes, four rows wide, three tall. The top right box sported two bullet holes drilled low into its front face. A creamy, white slime pooled at its base, running down the lower boxes to puddle on the floor beneath. Marco sniffed. Identified the sharp tang of car polish. Another spillage. More mess to clean up. Not Marco, though. Marco didn't do cleaning. Marco was management.

He raked the torch along, edging ahead, sliding his feet to minimise the chance of tripping. Leading with his right foot and dragging his left. Open mouthed. Barely breathing. Barely blinking.

Beyond the tower of boxes, a dark gap, as the junk dropped back behind the leaking stack of polish.

Marco took a breath, darted ahead, swinging out and around. The crowbar connected with a stack of rusted jerrycans. They scattered, clattering to the pod's roof, the torchlight picking out the drab, green paint. Still no sign of Jeffries. One jerrycan rattled out into the walkway, blocking Marco's progress. Growling, he booted it out of the way. It hit the next truss—the one holding the CCTV cameras and the dongle—bounced right, and skimmed towards the edge.

"Watch out!" Marco yelled.

The jerrycan flew over the side of the pod and disappeared. A moment later, a hollow bang announced the jerrycan connected with the balcony below. It clattered to a stop.

Marco edged closer, wrapped his arm around a cross brace, and leaned out.

"You okay, boss?"

Jackie looked up from behind his torchlight, gun arm raised, taking aim.

Bugger looked like he was going to shoot at Marco.

What the hell?

"Yeah, yeah," Jackie yelled, waving the Beretta to his right. Egging Marco onwards. "It's all cool. Keep at it."

"Go get him, Marco!" Dylan shouted, as though Marco would take a blind bit of notice of anything that shit-for-brains said.

If Marco hadn't wanted to stomp Jeffries into a bloody pulp for what he did to Mo, and for taunting him, he'd have been on his toes by now. Things were taking too long. Why all the shooting hadn't brought the filth down on them already was nothing short of miraculous. Every local within earshot of the workshop had to be stone deaf. Either that, or they'd mistaken gunshots for fireworks.

Morons.

He leaned back in from the edge, ducked through the cross braces, and regained his balance on the other side. Right foot leading, back bent to avoid grazing his head on the roof, he scanned the next bay with the torchlight. Used tyres filled the space—all bald, some so worn they showed canvas—stacked in neat towers that stretched to the roof. No room for Jeffries there.

Marco stalked forwards, the crowbar raised as high as it would go, held ready to strike, scraping the roof panels.

"Look out!" Jackie roared. "Behind you!"

Marco spun.

Jesus, what the—

An open hand shot out of the dark, lit by Jackie's torch. A straight thrust. The heel of the hand drove into Marco's chin, snapping his head up and back, smashing it into the roof. Stars sparkled behind Marco's eyes.

The crowbar fell from his hand. Clattered to the wooden walkway at his feet. Marco blinked and shook his head, momentarily stunned.

Something brushed past him, slammed into his right hip. Marco staggered outwards. Threw his arms wide. Regained his balance.

Jackie fired three times.

The first bullet missed. The second snicked the front of Marco's jacket and drilled into the wall of tyres to his right. The third zipped past the tip of his nose. So close, he felt its heat.

What the fuck?

Marco dived flat to the walkway. Kissed the wooden boards. His heart hammered inside a tight chest.

You bastard. You stupid, arrogant bastard.

Jeffries was right. For all his bluster, Jackie couldn't shoot worth a damn.

Chapter Forty-Nine

Thursday 8th July - Jackson Bentley

Eccleshall Way, Stafford, Staffordshire, England

Close to the safety barrier on the far side of the inspection pit, Jackie watched the action play out in complete safety. Keeping one eye on Marco, the other on the loft space ahead of him, praying for Jeffries to show himself. Whatever happened, he'd take the shot. No fucking hesitation. Even if Marco was in the line of fire. It didn't matter. In war, people got hurt. Even the good guys. Friendly fire. Thems were the breaks.

Up in the loft space, Marco swung the crowbar at a pile of jerrycans. The stack collapsed into a messy heap. One spun out onto the walkway. Marco snarled, kicked out. The jerrycan clattered against something metal and flew off the roof.

"Watch out!" Marco yelped.

The jerrycan clanged into the balcony and jammed up against a vertical post.

Marco grabbed a steel strut and leaned out.

"You okay, boss?"

"Yeah, yeah," Jackie answered, twitching the Beretta to the right in encouragement. "It's all cool. Keep at it."

"Go get him, Marco!" Dylan shouted from near the roller shutters.

Jackie glanced towards the lad, smiled, and gave him a nod of approval.

That's my boy.

For all his faults, Dylan was still a Bentley. Jackie's son and heir. He'd be good. Just so long as he kept out the fucking way.

Marco pulled himself back in from the edge, climbed through the opening in the roof truss and entered the bay stuffed full of bald tyres. He shuffled forwards, crowbar raised high, making enough noise to wake the fucking dead.

Get on with it, man.

Jeffries weren't in that bay. No room for the fucker.

"He's bloody useless," Jackie muttered loud enough for Dylan and Shelly to hear.

Sod Shelly, though. Didn't matter if he heard it. The plonker was just as useless. Didn't count worth a damn.

"Who is?" Dylan asked.

"Marco. Stompin' around up there like a fuckin' rookie."

"Are you going up there, Dad?"

"Might do, son," he said. "Might well do."

But why keep a dog …?

Leading with his torch, Jackie shifted his gaze to the right, ahead of Marco. Peering into the next bay. Searching for …

Movement.

A shadow exploded out of the darkness.

The darkness *behind* Marco.

What the fuck?

"Look out!" Jackie roared. "Behind you!"

Marco twisted. Slow. Too fucking slow.

A lightning-fast blur of movement.

Marco's head snapped up and back, slamming into a roof brace. The crowbar fell from his hand and thumped into the floor.

Jackie swung the Beretta and pulled the trigger, three times. Three snapshots on the move, just like on the army firing range.

Marco staggered, dropped to the floor like a stone. Lay still.

Shit.

"Marco!" Jackie called. "Marco!"

No response. Nothing but silence. A worrying stillness echoed through the workshop.

"Marco!"

A moment later, the big guy stirred.

"B-Boss?"

Marco raised a hand to rub the back of his head.

"You okay, Marco?"

Marco turned. Looked down. Scowled.

"Boss?" he said. "What the fuck? You shot me."

"Don't be stupid."

"You fucking shot me!"

"No, I shot at Jeffries," Jackie called. "He were right behind you. I nearly had him."

He'd missed. How could he have bloody missed? Didn't make sense.

The lucky arsehole.

So many shots. So many misses.

"You bastard!" Marco recovered enough to yell. "You could have fucking killed me!"

What? How the fuck dare he?

"Bugger off," Jackie shouted. "You were safe enough. I'm a bloody good shot."

Marco pushed himself up onto one knee, touched the front of his jacket, then climbed to his feet. He muttered something Jackie couldn't quite make out. It included a shit load of swearing.

Well, fuck you.

"Where's Jeffries?" Jackie demanded.

No reply.

"Marco," Jackie growled. "Answer me, damn it."

"What?" Marco asked, still rubbing his head, and sounding distracted.

"Where'd the fucker go?"

"Dunno," Marco answered. Again, he lowered a hand to his jacket and shone his torch over it. "You fucking … shot me!"

Grow a pair, dickhead.

"How'd he get behind you?" Jackie asked.

"What? I … dunno."

What the hell do you know? Useless fucker.

While Marco pulled his shit together, Jackie shone his torch back along the walkway towards the fire escape. Nothing. The fucker, Jeffries, was a ghost. He swept the torch the other way. Shone it ahead of Marco. One of the shadows moved. It showed a white face.

Jackie raised his gun arm, took aim. Fired three times. The Beretta's slide shot back. Clicked. Empty.

Fuck it.

The shadow sagged. Fell.

"I hit him," Jackie roared. "I fuckin' hit him!"

Chapter Fifty

Thursday 8th July - Night

Eccleshall Way, Stafford, Staffordshire, England

Kaine stared down at the platform from his hiding place in the eaves.

Marco stepped over Mo and the puddle of oil and shone the torchlight up into the eaves. Kaine narrowed his eyes and grinned at the big, angry lump.

"I'm coming for you, arsehole," Marco snarled, looking up, teeth gritted.

"And I'm waiting," Kaine answered, adding a cheery wink.

Time to go.

He wriggled backwards, keeping low—out of the sightlines.

"You're mine, arsehole," Marco mumbled. "All mine."

Good luck with that, mate.

Kaine shuddered in anticipation of what came next, but with an armed Bentley out in the open and a rabid, crowbar-swinging Marco so close, he had no choice. A frontal attack was out of the question. Suicide. He'd be too exposed. Time to play it canny.

Kaine slithered around the empty, cardboard box, negotiated the second roof truss, and tucked into the shadow of the eaves, staying beneath the line of fire. A ricochet might reach him from where Bentley took aim, but not a direct shot—the low angle wouldn't allow it. If Bentley had taken the high ground on the opposite balcony, things would have been different. From there, he'd have had an easy shot. A rookie move that worked in Kaine's favour.

Quickly, Kaine shrugged off his backpack, peeled out of his jacket, and stuffed them into a small gap behind a stack of boxes that reeked of car wax.

In the dark, he reached out and down, feeling for the gap.

Bugger.

It seemed a hell of a lot narrower than it did when he'd checked it out earlier—before he knew he be required to use it.

No choice. Here goes.

Kaine rolled onto his front, stretched out as flat as possible in the cramped angle of the eaves, and lowered his right leg into the void, searching for a foothold as he went. His inner thigh scraped the cubicle roof's jagged edge. His trousers caught. He added more weight and tore the cloth free, scraping the inside of his right leg in the process. The cut seeped blood. Not enough to bother him, but enough to sting. He took more care with the left leg, stretching it out and over the lip and brushing the heel of his boot down a gully in the corrugation. Then, legs dangling into nothingness, rough lip digging into his hips, he wriggled out and away until his backside scraped against the workshop's ridged, outer skin. The forty-five-degree slope of the roof made it tricky to generate much leverage with his arms but by pressing up with his elbows and rotating his hips, gravity took over and he slipped deeper into the opening. Belly, chest, and shoulders dropped into the gap. The thin, leather gloves protected his fingers from the sharp edge.

"Boss?" Marco yelled.

"Yeah?" Bentley answered, his voice distant, but loud enough to hear clearly and identify his location. The fool still hadn't claimed the higher ground.

"Shine your torch up here, will you? I need the light."

To Kaine's right, a shaky torch beam raked over the roof and down the wall. It lit the area around the fire escape to his left and eight metres away.

Kaine lowered himself deeper into the dirty, cobweb-filled cavity. He shuddered. Cramped spaces weren't his favourite. His nose rubbed against the flat, office wall, and the back of his head brushed the dusty, corrugated, outer wall. The vertical ridges pressed into his back with each deep breath.

Kaine forced himself to take slow, shallow breaths. It took effort. The next part was worse.

Do it, Kaine.

He exhaled, collapsed his ribcage, and slipped deeper into the cavity, holding tight with his fingertips. He searched with his feet.

Finally.

The heel of his right boot caught one of the horizontal ribs onto which the wall panels were bolted. It made a decent foothold and eased the pressure on his hands and arms.

With boot heels hooked over the steel rib, knees splayed and pressed into the pod wall, and head a few centimetres below the cubicle's lip, Kaine dangled like a spider in its web. He waited, breathing slowly, quietly. Hoping.

Above, the torchlight crawled back up the wall, jagged right, and lit up the loft space Kaine had recently vacated.

"Okay?"

Bentley's voice. Bentley's torchlight.

"Yeah. Thanks, boss."

Marco's torchlight fluttered, then cut out. The ladder creaked under his weight. He'd started his climb. Moments later, he grunted, and three heavy whooshes ended in the deafening ring of the crowbar cracking into a steel brace over Kaine's head. A muttered curse followed another grunt. More creaking as the walkway boards deflected under Marco's heavy weight. Another swish and the cardboard box above and to Kaine's left imploded under the weight of a solid blow.

Marco's strained breathing rasped loud in the silence. Smoking would do that to a person.

"See him?" Bentley shouted.

Marco didn't respond. A second light added to the first. Marco's torch.

"Well?" Jackie called.

"He's gone, boss."

"What d'you mean 'gone'? He can't be fuckin' gone. There's only one way down from there, and he ain't used the fuckin' ladder!"

"He'll be hiding down the far end," Marco called. "Hang on."

The new light tracked off to Kaine's left, deeper into the loft space. Marco pulled in a long, slow, grating breath.

"Hey there, Jeffries," he taunted. "Come out, come out wherever you are."

Despite the discomfort of his position, sandwiched between two sheets of immovable steel, Kaine stretched out a tight smile.

The torch beams moved further to Kaine's left, leaving the area above his head in deep blackness.

It wouldn't take Marco long to reach the far end of the loft and find it empty. After that, he and Bentley would soon work out where Kaine had gone. To be caught in the narrow void would be the end of him. He had two choices. Drop down or climb up and out. Dropping down would expose him to the Beretta. Up. His only real option.

Move. Now!

Kaine straightened his legs and pulled himself upwards until his eyes drew level with the office roof.

The torch beams lit the loft space far to his left, one slightly ahead of the other, leaving the area directly ahead dark and clear. Kaine reversed his grip on the roof, pressed his forearms onto the dirt-ingrained panel, and heaved and wriggled his way out of the gap. He scrambled up onto his hands and knees, stretching the grazed, inner thigh. His left hand touched something wet—the car polish. He swiped his fingers dry on his T-shirt.

Away to the left, Marco shone his light beyond the tower of boxes. After a short pause, he dashed ahead, swinging.

Marco's flailing crowbar scattered a pile of metal cans— jerrycans. One shot into the walkway. Marco snarled. Kicked out. The errant jerrycan bounced off a roof brace and out into the darkness.

"Watch out!" Marco yelped.

A clank. The jerrycan hit the balcony and rattled to a stop.

Marco darted forwards, hugged a cross brace, and stretched out.

"You okay, boss?"

"Yeah, yeah," Bentley answered. "It's all cool. Keep at it."

"Go get him, Marco!" Dylan shouted.

Marco stared hard over the balcony, strong jaw jutting. Clearly he was unimpressed with the kid's instruction. He pulled himself through the roof truss. Both torch beams focused on the bay ahead of Marco, leaving Kaine in total darkness. He climbed to his feet, crouched, and closed the gap on the minder.

Marco, crowbar raised, made ready to strike.

"Look out!" Bentley shouted. "Behind you!"

Marco turned.

Kaine leaped up and threw his whole bodyweight behind an opened-fisted, straight right. The heel of his hand drove into the point of Marco's chin. A solid, crunching blow. Marco jerked upright. The back of his head slammed into a roof panel. The crowbar clattered to the walkway. Kaine brushed past the big minder, kicked out at the crowbar on the way past. Missed.

Three gunshots roared.

Kaine dived headlong to the walkway, slid to the wooden flooring, rolled to his knees. Kept going.

Marco dropped.

"Marco!" Bentley shouted. "Marco!"

Kaine slithered to the side and hid behind another stack of tyres that smelled of dirty, old rubber.

Marco lay flat on his face, unmoving. Silent. Feet towards Kaine.

"Marco!" Bentley repeated.

Marco twitched.

"B-Boss?" he mumbled. His hand came up and fingers felt the back of his head.

"You okay, Marco?" Bentley asked, showing a little concern.

Marco turned his head.

"Boss?" he slurred. "What the fuck? You shot me."

"Don't be stupid," Bentley snapped.

"You fucking shot me!"

"No, I shot at Jeffries. He were right behind you. I nearly had him."

"You bastard!" Marco shouted, recovering impossibly quickly. "You could have fucking killed me!"

By God, the man could take a punch. Kaine had landed what should have been a stunning blow, but Marco had all but shaken it off. Kaine's troubles deepened. Bentley had three shots left. Kaine had been counting, and Bentley had been wasteful. What were the chances of him having another spare mag? Impossible to know one way or another. But Kaine had landed in a mess. Things couldn't get much worse.

"Bugger off," Jackie roared. "You were safe enough. I'm a bloody good shot."

Bentley was delusional as well as inept. Kaine reassessed the situation. He still had a chance. If he could make Bentley empty the Beretta, and if he didn't have another mag. If … if … if.

Marco staggered to his feet, swayed, and straightened. Still holding his head, he turned to face Bentley, showing Kaine his broad back.

Kaine measured the gap between them. Less than four metres. He could close it in seconds and barge Marco over the edge before he or Bentley could react. A chance. A slim one, but a chance.

"Fuck this shit," Marco muttered. "I don't earn enough to put up with this bullshit. No way. No fucking way."

Kaine hesitated.

Damn it.

Marco was nothing but a paid hand. Did he deserve to die?

"Where's Jeffries?" Bentley shouted.

Marco shrugged. Didn't respond.

"Marco. Answer me, damn it."

The minder looked up, showing his profile to Kaine.

"What?"

"Where'd the fucker go?"

"Dunno," Marco answered, his voice hesitant. He tugged his phone out of his jacket and shone the light on it. Saw something. "You fucking ... shot me!"

"How'd he get behind you?" Jackie asked.

"What?" Marco shrugged, shook his head. "I ... dunno."

Jackie growled in frustration. He used his torch beam to light up the fire escape. Someone groaned. Mo? Another fast recovery?

Kaine braced his foot against the tyres.

Now or never.

Marco's shoulders slumped.

"I've had enough of this shit," he said, again lifting his free hand to his head.

Bentley's torch returned. It tracked past Marco towards Kaine. Lit him up. Kaine paused for a microsecond, then dropped, and flattened himself into the walkway.

Bentley fired three times. Two bullets smacked into the tyres fractionally above Kaine's head. The third hit metal, ricocheted, and tore a white-hot lance of flame through his left buttock. The muscle burned like liquid flame.

Shit!

"I hit him," Jackie howled. "I fuckin' hit him!"

Shot in the backside.

How embarrassing!

Kaine ground his teeth. Sweat popped out on his brow.

The wound stung like hell. Warm blood ran down the outside of his hip. It felt bad. How serious, how debilitating, he wouldn't know until he tried standing.

Kaine blinked stinging tears from his eyes.

Bright side. Think of a bright side.

No more shooting.

Cautiously, Kaine raised his head. Risked a quick peek.

How many shots?

Fifteen? Surely, fifteen.

Below him, across the open space on the far side of the inspection pit, the Beretta—pushed out in front of the torch beam—pointed up. It trembled in Bentley's fist. The man couldn't hold the weapon steady with one hand. No wonder he kept missing. Apart from the last bloody shot. One lucky shot. Unlucky for Kaine.

Damn it.

The Beretta's slide had locked open. Empty.

Kaine managed a wry smile through the pain.

Bentley stared up at him, mouth open, eyes wide. He shook himself free of his momentary stupor and turned to Marco.

"Kill him, Marco," Bentley howled. "Finish him off!"

"Yeah," Dylan screeched. "Do him, Marco."

Marco turned slowly towards Kaine. He pulled the hand away from his head. The fingertips came away bloody. His shoulders straightened.

Chapter Fifty-One

Eccleshall Way, Stafford, Staffordshire, England

Assessing his options and finding precious few, Kaine pushed up off the walkway and stood. He favoured his left leg but tried not to show it. The bullet wound thumped fire with each heartbeat. Blood seeped through the gash, soaked his trouser leg, and trickled down the back of his thigh. It pooled behind his knee, hidden. He took up a southpaw stance, angling his left side away from Marco, and smiled through the pulsing agony.

Marco stood at over six feet tall and was built like a side of beef. And the man could take a punch. He'd proved that well enough already.

To defeat a man with the power of Marco, Kaine would

have to be at his best, but he didn't fancy his chances. Not with an untested injury. He straightened, shook out his gloved hands. Waited.

"Do him, Marco," Dylan repeated, his voice squeaking. "Fuck him over."

The kid deserted his post by the injured Shelly and scurried over to his father who'd lowered the Beretta without reloading it. Definitely out of ammo.

Good news. Kaine needed it.

Marco stood as tall as he could in the cramped conditions, swiped the blood from his fingers on the leg of his trousers, and rubbed his bruised chin.

"You pack a hell of a punch, Jeffries," he said. "For a little guy."

He spoke quietly. So quietly, Kaine doubted Bentley or Dylan could hear what he said.

Deliberate?

Kaine rested his left hand on the tyre stack and eased the weight from his damaged leg. He tilted his head to the side and sniffed.

"Nah," he said, slightly above a whisper, "that was a gentle tap to draw your attention. There's worse to come if you want it."

Marco took half a pace closer and stopped.

"Who are you?"

"You know who I am," Kaine answered. "Arnold Jeffries at your service." Without taking his eyes from this opponent, he bowed his head.

Marco narrowed his eyes.

"Are you working for Ronnie Sutton?"

Kaine sighed. "You already asked me that."

"So? Are you?"

"Before tonight, I'd never heard of anyone called Ronnie Sutton."

"Don't give me that bollocks," Marco muttered.

Kaine winced as he moved, and another surge of pain drove through his injury. Blood ran down to his calf.

"I'm not a liar," he said, teeth gritted.

Except when it suits me.

"Who else would put you up to planting the dongle?" Marco jerked his thumb over his shoulder in the direction of the cluster of CCTV cameras.

Kaine shook his head.

"No," he said. "That was all my idea. Well, me and a very special friend of mine."

"*Thanks for them kind words, Mr K,*" Corky said through the earpiece.

Kaine said nothing. Corky wouldn't expect a response.

"Who's that then?" Marco demanded, voice still low.

"You don't need to know. Let's just keep this between ourselves, eh?"

"Why are you spying on us?"

Kaine levered himself away from the tyres.

"The Fabiens are under my protection."

Marco arched an eyebrow. "Who?"

Kaine held up a hand. "Don't give me that guff, Marco. You know who I'm talking about. I'm here for the dashcam."

"What bloody dashcam?"

"The one that proves Dylan ran the Toyota off the road and killed Melissa Fabien." Kaine paused for effect before adding, "That dashcam."

"You're joking."

Kaine shook his head. "I don't joke about murder."

"But it's evidence."

"I know."

"If the police get hold of it—"

"They will. That's what I'm here for."

"Jesus wept," the minder gasped and shot a glance at Bentley and his idiot son. "Why the hell wouldn't they destroy it?"

"I've already told you what Dylan does with the dashcam footage," Kaine said and studied the big man's reaction. It was a picture.

"You weren't lying? What a sick fuck," Marco said, his upper lip twisting in disgust. "I always knew he was a nut job."

"So's his father."

Marco dipped his head.

"Yes," he said. "Agreed."

"And I think he's killed to protect his son."

"Who?"

"A young woman called Charlotte Smith, Dylan's girl-friend. He ran her down."

"Christ," Marco said. "The hit and run on Hope Way?"

Kaine nodded.

"Can you prove it?"

"I think so. There's a keepsake in the office safe. And we have a recording. From the CCTV."

"Jackie kept some evidence?"

Again, Kaine nodded.

"For the same reason they didn't destroy the dashcam."

"Fuck," Marco gasped.

"Yes, exactly. And by helping them you're making your-self an accessory after the fact. Mo and Shelly, too."

"We are, huh?"

"What the fuck you waitin' for, Marco?" Bentley screamed. "Kill him!"

Marco half-turned towards his boss and held up a hand, but kept an eye on Kaine.

"Shut your mouth you piece of shit," he said, his deep voice low, almost calm. "I don't work for you anymore."

"What?" Bentley yelled. "What the fu—"

"You heard me," Marco said, speaking up. "I don't work for you anymore. I've resigned."

"Are you insane?"

Kaine lowered his arms but not his guard. He eased more weight off his left leg, staggered, righted himself. The periphery of his vision greyed. His mouth dried. Sweat soaked his face, arms, and body. He dropped his left hand to the wound and squeezed hard, adding as much pressure as he could stand. He couldn't afford to lose so much blood.

"You shot me, you bastard," Marco shouted down to Bentley, venting his anger. "Look!"

He slapped a hand to his chest and shone his torch over the front of his dark jacket. A thin, black scorch mark ran across the left breast. A few millimetres deeper and the bullet would have drilled into his heart. He'd been lucky. A damn sight luckier than Kaine.

"You're a bloody lunatic," Marco added.

Bentley stepped closer to the inspection pit's guard rail, fuming.

"Nobody walks out on Jackie Bentley," he raged. "You're a dead man! I'll put a contract out on you. A contract, you hear me? You're a dead man."

Smiling, Marco faced Kaine again, ignoring Bentley's continuing rant.

"So," Kaine said, "what now?"

Marco fingered the rip to his jacket and fixed Kaine with an appraising gaze.

"Do we have a problem," he asked, waving a hand in the air between them. "You and I?"

Kaine shook his head. "Not as far as I'm concerned. Just as long as you leave. And leave now."

Bentley's former minder snorted.

"I'm going."

"Good." Kaine waited.

"If it's okay with you," Marco said, "I'll be taking Mo and Shelly to the hospital. They need medical treatment."

"Good idea. You do that."

"Now Jackie's out of ammo, I imagine you can deal with them on your own?"

Kaine lifted his chin.

"I imagine so."

We'll see.

Stretching his hand up to use the roof as a guide, Marco backed a couple of steps further away, then stopped.

"I could take you apart, you know?" he said, with absolute confidence. "You wouldn't stand a chance against me."

Another shaft of pain wracked through Kaine's backside.

No doubt at all about that. Not now.

Kaine stared back, stone faced.

"Possibly," he answered. "We'll never know … unless you hang around a little longer."

Marco grinned.

"No, no," he said, hands raised in surrender. "I'm going."

"You want Corky to turn the lights back on yet, Mr K?"

"No, thanks, Control. Better not. Over." Kaine winked at Marco.

"Okay. Let me know when you need them."

"What was that?" Marco asked.

"I'm making sure the lights stay off."

Again, Marco arched an eyebrow.

"The power cut," he said. "That was down to you?"

Kaine didn't feel the need to reply.

"I thought it must be. Bloody hell, man," Marco gasped. "Who are you?"

"Watch your step on the ladder," Kaine said, ignoring the question. "I wouldn't want you to slip and fall in the dark."

Marco nodded, gave up the interrogation, turned about face, and headed for the end of the suspended cubicle. He shone his torch along the floor and ducked lower than strictly necessary to avoid cracking his head on the roof again.

Kaine picked up the fallen crowbar and followed at a distance, moving slowly to minimise the limp. He hid the crowbar behind his right leg and stopped a few metres from the end of the walkway, giving Marco plenty of room to descend the ladder without feeling crowded.

The former minder stepped off the bottom rung and shone the torch on a bleary-eyed, bloody-faced, and oil-smeared Mo, who had recovered enough to sit up and lean against the toilet wall. He looked up at Marco in confusion. Vomit mixed with oil stained the front of his jacket.

"C'mon, Mo," Marco said. "Let's get you to hospital."

Mo blinked and held up an arm.

Marco stepped over the patch of oil and helped the injured man to stand. He draped Mo's arm over his shoulders and half-caried, half-dragged the heavily concussed man down the staircase.

Across the way, Bentley stuffed the Beretta into his jacket pocket, pointed his torch at the advancing pair, and grabbed the inspection pit's guard rail. The action left Kaine in total darkness.

"Marco," Bentley said. "We can sort this. Help me do Jeffries, and I'll double your wages."

"Bugger off," Marco said, grunting under Mo's almost-dead weight. "We're out of here. You've fucking lost it." He tapped two fingers to his temple and stopped in front of his former employer and his weakling of a son.

"Key," Marco said, talking to Dylan.

He held out his hand.

"What?" Dylan asked.

"The key to the door," Marco said. "Give it."

"Dad?" Dylan asked, looking sideways at his father.

Bentley stared over his shoulder. "Don't you dare."

Marco propped Mo against the guard rail. The concussed man sagged when Marco released his arm, but he stayed upright.

"Don't make me come around there and take it from you, boy." Marco's deep-throated growl rumbled through the garage. "Throw it to me. Now!"

"Dad?" Dylan repeated, his voice quaking.

Jackie hesitated, then relented.

"Lob 'em over."

Dylan reached inside his trouser pocket, pulled out the keys, and underhanded them across the inspection pit.

Marco snatched the keys out of the air.

"Good decision, boy."

"You'll pay for this, arsehole," Bentley snarled. "You'll pay."

Marco ignored the hollow threat, ducked his head under Mo's arm, and they made their slow progress towards the exit.

Shelly, his injured arm held tight to his chest with his

other hand, leaned heavily against the roller shutters, waiting.

Using the standoff as a distraction, and keeping his left leg straight and immobile, Kaine worked his way to the edge of the cubicle's roof. To descend the ladder with the crowbar, Kaine had to release the wound. The blood flow increased. It ran down his leg, collected in the heel of his boot, and squelched each time he moved. He reached the balcony, swapped the crowbar into his left hand, and pressed it against the bullet wound.

Marco and Mo reached their mate, paused long enough for Marco to unlock the wicket door, and the trio left without a backwards glance.

Bentley and his son hadn't moved from their spot by the guard rail.

"*Is you alright, Mr K? You is looking a bit wobbly.*"

"I've been … shot, Control. Over."

"*Damn. How serious?*"

"Pretty bad. Over."

"*Bugger. Hang on in there, Mr K. Help's on its way. Delta Team will be with you inside five minutes.*"

"Tell them to come straight in. And would you mind … asking them to hurry, please? Over."

"*Will do, Mr K.*"

With backup on its way and a wounded leg, Kaine needed as much time as he could win.

Bentley and Dylan swung their torches away from the wicket door and onto the balcony. Both beams shone bright, lighting Kaine up, clear as day. He twisted slightly to show them his right side, stepped over the oil spill, and eased out onto the balcony in front of the toilet cubicle. Pressing the crowbar harder against the wound, he grabbed the guardrail with his blood-free right hand.

"It's just the three of us left, Jeffries," Bentley said.

"For now," Kaine responded.

His words sounded muffled, thick in his ears. He tightened his grip on the guardrail, holding himself up. Slick with blood, the crowbar slid through his grasp. The hooked end caught on his wrist, held. Teeth gritted, he clamped the wound closed with his bloody fingers.

Bentley sneered. "Whatcha mean by that?"

"The police are on their way," Kaine answered.

"Bullshit!" Dylan squealed.

"They'll be here any minute."

"Bullshit."

"You just said that," Kaine said. "No need to repeat yourself, son."

"You piece of shit," Bentley said, a sneer forming on his square face. "You think you can break into my place and pull this crap?"

"Yeah, right," Dylan crowed.

Kaine's vision dimmed, and his lips started to tingle.

Damn it. Too soon.

The way Kaine felt, he wouldn't be able to put up any kind of defence. He had to hold them off a little longer. Or separate them … Or draw them closer.

"Dylan Bentley," he called out, "you are under arrest for the unlawful killing of Melissa Fabien. … Anything you say will be … will be …"

Kaine's left leg gave way. Collapsed beneath him.

Chapter Fifty-Two

Thursday 8th July - Jackson Bentley

Eccleshall Way, Stafford, Staffordshire, England

Jackie wanted to pound Jeffries into the middle of next week. He'd had more than enough of the smarmy, little git's bullshit.

"You piece of shit," he jeered. "You think you can break into my place and pull this crap?"

"Yeah, right," Dylan said at his side.

Good lad. Nice one.

Always at his side. Reliable. The only person in the world Jackie could really trust.

Jeffries stood on the balcony, looking … what? Smug. No, something else. Weird. With one hand on the railing, he swayed slightly. Didn't look right.

What the fuck?

His face was sweaty. Pale.

"Dylan Bentley," Jeffries said, slow and forceful, "you are under arrest for the unlawful killing of Melissa Fabien."

Fuck this.

Time to end the bullshit. Jackie let go of the guard rail.

"Anything you say will be … will be …"

Jeffries dropped. He fell backwards. Like he'd been poleaxed.

Bloody hell.

The fucker slammed into the office wall and crumpled slowly to the balcony floor. His right leg bent. Knee raised to his chest. The left leg pushed straight out in front. The foot poked through a gap in the railing and dangled in the air.

What the hell?

"Fuck," Dylan said, moving close enough to breathe down Jackie's neck. "Look, Dad." He nudged Jackie's shoulder.

"I can see him, son."

"No, Dad. Look!"

He jabbed a finger out and up, and focused his torchlight on Jeffries' outstretched foot. Something glistened on his ankle. Something wet and red.

Blood.

"He's bleeding, Dad," Dylan yelled. "Bleeding!"

Yes!

"I knew I'd shot the fucker," Jackie called, thrilled. "I bloody knew it!"

Dylan moved behind Jackie, making for the end of the pit. Jackie shot out a hand, grabbed his forearm, tugged him back.

"Let me have him, Dad," Dylan pleaded, trying to rip his arm free. "Let me kick his head in. Please?"

"No," Jackie said, definite. "That bugger's all mine. You can have what's left."

"Aw, Dad. Please."

Dylan pushed out his lower lip like he used to do as a little kid. Back then, it was cute. As an adult, not so much. Made him look like a spoiled brat. He'd have to learn to control himself. Still, he had time. He was only young.

Jackie released his grip on Dylan's arm and held up a finger for silence.

"Enough," he said. "My house, my rules. Wait here 'til I call you over. Keep the light on him."

Dylan lowered his head, and his shoulders slumped.

"Leave some of him for me, Dad."

"I will, son." Jackie nodded, smiling. "Promise."

He turned and, keeping well clear of the inspection pit, hurried towards the staircase, excitement mounting. He couldn't wait to smash the bugger into bloody pulp. He raced up the stairs, taking them two at a time.

"Watch out for the oil, Dad," Dylan shouted.

Jackie stopped three from the top.

"Thanks, son."

Watching Jeffries the whole way, Jackie took the last few treads slowly, stepped over the glistening oil, and made it onto the dry part of the balcony without a problem.

Jackie took one pace closer and stood over Jeffries, staring down at the man who'd caused him so much hassle. He sneered.

The arsehole hadn't moved since he'd dropped.

He sat, leaning against the office wall, head slumped, chin on his chest. His right, gloved hand lay in his lap, empty and unmoving. The left hand was hidden beneath his extended leg. The side of the left trouser leg was dark red with blood. Saturated. So much blood. Bastard lay so still, it didn't look like he was breathing.

Bugger it.

Too bloody late.

"I think the bugger's already dead," he called out.

"Kick him, Dad," Dylan yelled. "Make sure. Kick him in the head."

Jackie turned his sneer into a grin. When had his son become such a sick puppy? Such a chip off the old block.

"Okay, son," Jackie said, smiling. "This is just for you."

"Excellent." Dylan laughed. "Pity I can't film it with the torchlight on."

"Watch and learn, son," Jackie crowed. "Watch and learn."

Jeffries slumped to his right. Groaned.

"Will you look at that," Jackie shouted in delight. "Arsehole's still alive."

"Kick him, Dad. Boot the fucker in the face."

Jackie grabbed the handrail, planted his left foot firmly, and raised his right in preparation to drive the heel of his boot into Jeffries' bearded face.

This is so much fun.

Jeffries' long, left arm swung up and out. Long. Abnormally long.

Fuck!

The crowbar crunched into Jackie's left leg. Smashed through skin and bone. An agony of pain shot through his whole body. An electric shock. His leg turned to jelly.

Jackie shrieked. Fell backwards.

Chapter Fifty-Three

Thursday 8th July - Night

Eccleshall Way, Stafford, Staffordshire, England

Kaine shifted his weight to free his left arm. He added a groan for good measure. Lifted his chin a fraction. Glanced up through half-closed lids.

Bentley's silhouette stood out sharp in the halo of light cast by Dylan's phone. Bentley's torchlight played over Kaine's lower half, focusing on his blood-soaked leg.

Wait.

"Will you look at that," Bentley shouted. "Arsehole's still alive."

"Kick him, Dad," Dylan screamed. "Boot the fucker in the face."

Wait.

Bentley grasped the balcony's handrail and raised his foot. A maniacal grin appeared on his underlit face.

Now!

Kaine lunged. He swung the crowbar hard and fast, throwing his whole weight behind the blow. Metal smashed into the shin of Bentley's standing leg. The trouser leg crumpled. Tibia and fibula shattered and collapsed beneath him.

Bentley screamed and fell, arms flailing, thrashing the air.

"Dad!"

Bentley slammed into the balcony floor, hit the oil, and slithered backwards. He tumble-rolled down the staircase. The hideous, wet crunch of his head slamming into one cast-iron step after another might have turned Kaine's stomach—if he gave a damn.

"Dad!' Dylan cried. "Oh Jesus."

Bentley came to an abrupt stop at the foot of the staircase, head cranked awkwardly on the dirty, concrete floor. His left foot, rotated to the right at an unnatural angle, had hooked itself between the last two open treads. Blood had already started soaking through the trouser leg. So much blood, he might have ruptured an artery. On the balcony, Bentley's phone lay on its face, its beam illuminating the roof panel directly above it.

Dylan stared at his father for a beat, then turned his head to look up at Kaine. His mouth gaped. Terror filled his eyes.

The world stood still for a moment as the memory of Bentley's crunching, flailing tumble down the staircase weighed heavy in the chilly, dust-filled air.

Seconds later, Dylan screamed. He spun and took off in a mad, scrambling dash, lurching towards the roller shutters. His wildly swinging torch beam sliced a ragged dance through the darkness.

Kaine released the blood-soaked crowbar. It thunked into the tread plate and the chisel end bounced into the oil. He reached out, grabbed the middle rail, and tried to haul himself upright. The world shifted sideways from the head-rush. He slumped back down, and another shaft of pain tore through his backside.

Crap.

Dylan reached the open wicket door, dived through, and disappeared into the night.

"Bugger," Kaine muttered. "There goes the dashcam."

Kaine had no chance of chasing the coward. Not in his weakened state.

"Nice one, Mr K. Corky liked it. What about the lights? Does you want Corky to turn them back on now?"

"Yes, please, Control. Over."

"Be right with you."

Kaine made to swallow but couldn't. His dry mouth wouldn't allow it. He tried to think.

What next?

Priority task—stop the bleeding.

Kaine leaned away from the office wall, tore off his T-shirt, and wadded it into a tight ball. He pressed it into the wound and sat down on it hard, adding as much weight as he could endure. He'd created a makeshift, compression bandage. Useful, but not a permanent solution. It would only work for as long as he stayed put and kept the pressure on.

Kaine pulled in a deep breath, released it slowly, and waited for his head to clear. He leaned back against the cold, metal, pod wall. Shivered.

What a God-awful mess.

"Ready, Mr K?"

Kaine shaded his eyes as the main strip lights flickered, caught, and shone dazzling bright. Cautiously, Kaine opened his eyes again, but kept them narrowed.

Bentley groaned and lifted his bruised and battered head. His shoulders moved and his left leg twitched. He screamed. His head cracked onto the concrete and the scream cut short in the blessed release of oblivion.

Too good for you, arsehole.

"Thanks for that, Control. Over."

"You is welcome, Mr K. How's you doing?"

"I think I've stopped the bleeding, but I'm immobile."

And bloody freezing.

"Could do with a little assistance. Over."

He hugged himself, fighting to retain some warmth.

"Ah, now. Corky can help you with that one, Mr K. Yes, indeedie. … And here they is right now."

Outside, scuffling footsteps broke through the quiet.

"No! Please, don't," Dylan wailed, his voice high-pitched. Pleading.

"Get in there, you piece of crap!" A familiar voice boomed through the air.

Kaine smiled in recognition.

Good timing.

The wicket door slammed open. Dylan staggered over the threshold and into the light, propelled by Cough's heavy thump to the back. Dylan skurried further into the work-shop and, blinking under the bright lights, shaded his eyes. He looked straight ahead and stared at his father's unmoving form. A bruise had started darkening the kid's right eye, and a fresh cut decorated his lower lip. It didn't bleed much.

Cough stepped through the opening, grasped Dylan by

the shoulder, and spun him around. The kid tripped over his own feet and dropped to the floor.

Stefan followed Cough inside and closed the door. He searched the workshop with a fast-raking sweep of his eyes, spotted Kaine on the balcony, and raced towards him.

"Get up," Cough roared.

Kaine had rarely heard the normally calm and genial Cough so angry.

"P-Please don't hurt me," Dylan squealed, cowering on his knees.

"Not so brave now, are you, you little bastard. You're not terrorising an old man and his family now, are you. Get up!"

He reached down, grabbed a fistful of Dylan's hair, and tugged him from his knees. Dylan's hands flew up to his head, trying to break Cough's hold, and he squealed the whole way to his feet. Cough released his grip and wiggled his fingers. A tuft of dark hair floated to the floor.

Openly bawling, Dylan backed away until Cough's raised finger stopped him in his tracks. Mouth wide open, Dylan threw his hands up to his chest and clasped them together as if in prayer.

"Stay right there," Cough ordered.

"Wh-Who are you?"

"Shut your mouth."

Dylan clamped his jaws together and stood, shaking.

Stefan reached the staircase, skirted around the comatose Bentley without so much as a sideways glance, and raced up the steps. Before Kaine had time to warn him, Stefan stepped carefully over the oil spill and dropped to his knees in front of him.

"Well spotted," Kaine whispered.

"Boss?"

"The oil. Well spotted."

"Oh, that," Stefan said, shaking his head. He tugged off his backpack and placed it on the floor between them. "Corky gave us access to the CCTV feed. We've been watching you all the way here. Nasty, little boobytrap that, boss. Loved it."

Grinning, Stefan unclipped the top flap of the backpack and pulled out a bottle of water. He broke the seal and handed it across.

Kaine swallowed half its contents in three long and satisfying glugs.

"Thanks, Stefan."

"Where is it, boss?"

"What?"

"The bullet wound."

"My ... er ... the back of my left thigh," Kaine said, trying to keep a straight face. "High up."

"You were shot in the arse?" Stefan made a valiant effort but couldn't help snorting. "Nasty."

He removed a large, compression bandage from the backpack and tore off the paper wrapper. He leaned over and took a peek. Winced.

"Ouch. That's a load of blood on your pants. You made a good job with the T-shirt, though. I'll leave it in place and wrap this"—he held up the bandage—"over the top. Ready?"

Kaine nodded.

"Go for it, lad. We can't hang around here forever."

"This is going to hurt, boss."

No kidding.

Kaine gritted his teeth and closed his eyes.

Chapter Fifty-Four

Thursday 8th July - Peter Coughlin

Eccleshall Way, Stafford, Staffordshire, England

"Stay right there," Cough said, right hand raised in threat.

Dylan Bentley trembled. Tears flowed down his cheeks. The arsehole looked powerful enough but had all the backbone of a jellyfish.

"Wh-Who are you?"

"Shut your mouth!" Cough snapped.

Dylan sniffled and gripped his hands tight to his chest, trying to stop them shaking. He leaned forwards and mumbled, "But I haven't done any—"

Cough stepped closer, clenched his hand into a fist.

"One more word … just one," he growled.

"What do you want with me?" Dylan whimpered. "I've

done nothing to you. I-It's my Dad you want. Not me. Look"—he jerked his head towards the back of the garage —"he's over there. Let me go. I haven't done anything wrong."

"Melissa Fabien," Cough said.

Dylan blanched. Snapped his mouth closed. His knees buckled, trembled.

"That shut you up, didn't it," Cough sneered. "You little bastard."

After spending time with Toby and the twins, Cough wanted nothing more than to smash seven bells of crap out of the kid, but the boss wouldn't have wanted that. Sometimes, he could be too damn soft.

Up on the balcony, Stefan—the team's best first-aider in the doc's absence—leaned close to the boss, busily wrapping a heavy-duty bandage around his hip. The boss, his face creased in pain, endured Stefan's ministrations in stoic silence. As expected.

"How's it going?" Cough called up.

"He'll live," Stefan answered, head down, deep in concentration.

"How long you gonna be?"

"Nearly done."

Dylan tried to edge away. Cough faced him.

"Where d'you think you're going, dickhead?"

Dylan shook his head. "N-Nowhere."

"Too bloody right."

Cough stepped around and to the side so he could take in both Dylan and the balcony above the staircase without losing sight of either.

Eventually, Stefan nodded. Done. He held out his hand and helped the boss to stand.

Shirtless and pale, unsteady on his feet, the boss grabbed

the handrail for support. Stefan had strapped the heavy bandage high on his left leg and wrapped it tight around his hips.

Dylan snorted.

"What?" Cough demanded.

"Looks like he's wearing a nappy."

"Shut your stupid mouth."

Cough threw out a hand and clapped the idiot around the back of his head.

"Ow. But it does."

Cough had to agree, but unlike the stupid kid, he would never say so out loud. He valued the captain's friendship too much.

The boss leaned close to Stefan and spoke quietly. Stefan nodded and moved around the corner of the office unit, out of sight.

What's he up to?

"With me, you," Cough said.

He grabbed Dylan's heavily muscled arm and dragged him further into the workshop, closer to the far end of the inspection pit.

Seconds later, Stefan climbed a ladder bolted to the end wall of the suspended units. He stepped into the loft space and, crouching low, made his way along what looked like a gangway running in front of some randomly stacked piles of rubbish. Once through the first roof truss, he stopped, ducked into the darkness of the eaves, and reappeared clutching a small backpack and a dark jacket.

Cough smiled. He understood Stefan's task. They couldn't leave physical evidence behind. Blood spillage wouldn't matter too much, though. Corky had taken care of the DNA issue when he'd doctored the biometric data in every team member's military dossier.

Stefan retraced his steps to the edge of the unit and turned about-face. He descended the ladder and reemerged on the balcony. Leaning over the oil spill, he handed the jacket to the boss, who dressed quickly and zipped it up to the throat. Leaning against a metal wall without a top would have chilled him to the bone. Never mind the blood loss. Cough shivered in sympathy.

Rather you than me.

Stefan bent to collect his backpack, slung it over his shoulder, and offered his arm to the boss, who shook his head.

"No, thanks," he said. "I can manage."

"What about this?" Stefan asked, pointing to the upturned phone on the floor near his feet. Its torchlight illuminated the roof space above Stefan's head.

"Leave it there," he answered. "Bentley can use it to call an ambulance. When he wakes. ... If he wakes."

"How's he gonna reach it?"

The boss shrugged. "That's his problem. Let's go."

Together, they descended the stairs. The captain took the steps one at a time. He kept his left leg stiff and straight, and leaned heavily on the banister's handrail.

When they reached the bottom, the captain paused over Dylan's old man. He looked down for a moment, shook his head, turned, and limped towards them. Stefan stayed close, watching the boss the whole way, making ready to catch him if he stumbled.

Chapter Fifty-Five

Thursday 8th July - Pre-Dawn

Eccleshall Way, Stafford, Staffordshire, England

Kaine, trying to ignore his throbbing backside, stared down at the comatose Bentley. His chest rose and fell, the breathing shallow. Still alive, but only just.

He studied Bentley's bruised and battered face and took in the elevated and deformed leg. Blood soaked his trousers and dripped to the concrete below. The small section of exposed shin below the twisted break had already started to turn grey. A sure sign of restricted blood flow to the foot. Without rapid medical attention, he'd likely lose his leg below the knee. Assuming he survived at all.

Tough.

It served the bugger right.

Kaine could generate no pity for a thug who would threaten children to pressure an injured, old man. None at all.

Bentley deserved a special place in hell.

He turned away from the bloodied wreck and hobbled towards Cough and his wretched captive. Dylan stood, head lowered, shoulders slumped, hands still clasped tight to his chest.

Stefan stayed close alongside Kaine, fussing over him like an old, mother hen. A good lad. Reliable. Still a mother hen.

By the time they closed on Cough and Dylan, Kaine had started to fade. Sweat formed under his arms and ran down his back.

He stopped in front of Dylan and waited. The kid's head remained lowered, the chin tucked into his chest.

"Look at me, son."

Slowly, Dylan lifted his chin. Fear glowed in a pair of dark brown eyes that refused to meet Kaine's hostile glare. Dylan blinked. Tears ran down his cheeks and his nose dribbled. He sniffled.

"Dashcam," Kaine said, speaking quietly, barely above a whisper.

Dylan frowned.

"Huh?"

"The dashcam. Where is it?"

Dylan shook his head.

"I-I don't know what you're—"

Kaine slapped the kid's tear-streaked face. A hard, stinging, humiliating blow. The resounding crack rang out loud and sharp. Dylan staggered sideways. Cough caught him. Stopped him falling into the pit. Held him upright. Dylan snivelled and raised a hand to his reddening cheek. A stain darkened the crotch of his jeans.

Oh dear.

"Don't make me ask you again, son."

Kaine held out his left hand, keeping his right primed and ready to deliver another slap.

"Okay, okay," Dylan whimpered through a sniffle. "B-But please d-don't hit me again."

He dug a fist into his jacket pocket. He fished around, plucked out the dashcam, and placed it in Kaine's outstretched hand.

"That wasn't too difficult, was it?"

Dylan sniffed, shook his head, and lowered his eyes. He said nothing.

Kaine turned to Stefan and passed him the device.

"Confirm it's the right one," Kaine said. "And for God's sake, please don't delete anything."

Stefan grinned and shook his head. Like most youngsters, he knew his way around tech and was almost as proficient as Connor Blake. Nowhere near as good as Corky, though. No one knew their way around tech like Corky … except maybe Frodo … and Sabrina.

"And if it's not the real one?" Cough asked.

"Someone else will have to beat the location out of him. I don't have the energy."

"Can I do it?" Cough implored. "Please."

He glared at Dylan.

"Of course," Kaine said, "but there's no need to beg."

"I-It's real," Dylan said, finding his voice again. "I-I p-promise."

"I do hope it isn't," Cough said, deepening his glare.

Dylan hesitated a moment before raising his hand as though he were in a classroom.

"C-Can I ask a question?"

He cowered in anticipation of another slap.

Kaine nodded. "Ask away. I don't have to answer."

"Wh-What are you … going to do with it?"

Kaine edged closer to the guard rail and, after leaning against it, he found the strength to smile.

"I imagine the police might find a use for it."

"No!" Dylan squeaked, taking half a pace forwards. "You can't. Please don't. Let me buy it back. Please. Twenty thousand … pounds."

"Er, boss?" Stefan said, holding up the dashcam and pointing the screen towards Kaine. "This is the real one. And it's worth more than twenty grand to that little sod. A hell of a lot more."

"Fifty," Dylan shouted. "No. One hundred. One hundred thousand pounds."

Kaine appraised Dylan as though considering the offer.

"Where are you going to get that kind of money?"

"D-Dad's got it. You know … h-he's a millionaire."

"You think he's going to stump up a hundred grand after you ran out on him? After you left him to bleed to death?" Kaine asked.

"N-no … I-I didn't leave him," Dylan cried. "I-I didn't."

"You ran away," Cough jeered.

"I-I was going for help," Dylan said, looking down at his feet, not at all convincing.

"You've got a phone," Kaine said. "Why not use it as something other than a torch?"

"Battery's dead," Dylan mumbled, eyes still lowered.

Cough punched him in the back.

"Liar. Hand it over."

"I-I can't. I-I dropped it when you jumped me."

"You've got an answer for everything." Kaine flapped his hand at the kid. "Go on. Off you trot."

"Huh?"

"Go take care of your father."

"I-I …"

Cough punched him in the back again, this time to help him on his way. Dylan stumbled and kept heading for the staircase. When he reached the far end of the inspection pit, he stopped and turned to face them.

"What about the dashcam?" he cried.

Cough made a move towards him, and he shuffled back, getting perilously close to the edge of the pit.

"Leave him, Sergeant," Kaine muttered. "Time to go."

Cough relaxed and nodded.

"Can't leave here fast enough for me," he said. "Shitty bloody place."

"I couldn't agree more."

Cough glanced up at the balcony and shook his head.

"You had us worried," he said.

"Sorry?"

"When you collapsed up there," Cough said. "We thought you were … well, you know."

Kaine shrugged. "I couldn't think of anything better at the time."

"You collapsed on purpose?" Stefan blurted out, incredulous.

"Yep," Kaine answered, then winced. "Well, sort of. To be honest, I didn't fancy climbing down the stairs and taking them both on at the same time. I needed to separate them."

"And if they'd both climbed the stairs?" Cough asked.

Again, Kaine shrugged.

"Calculated risk," he said. "I figured Bentley would

want the honour of taking me out all on his own. And you've seen how brave Dylan is."

Cough snorted. Stefan nodded.

"In any event," Kaine added, fighting to keep his eyes open, "it's a little cramped up there. They'd only have had enough space to tag-team me. One at a time, I could take them."

Probably.

Cough glanced up at the balcony again and tilted his head in appraisal.

"Suppose so," he agreed. "But you took a hell of a chance."

"Worked out okay in the end." Kaine tweaked his shoulder in a half-shrug.

"Corky's got something to say. Can you hear this, Mr K? You too, Team Delta."

Cough and Stefan shared a glance. They'd picked up the message, too.

"Go ahead, Control. We're reading you. Over," Kaine said.

"Corky thought you might like to know that, despite what Dylan just said, Jackie B ain't a millionaire no more. In fact, the bloke's dead broke." His chuckle rang out loud down the comms line.

Cough grinned. As did Stefan.

"Can you repeat that, Control? Over."

"You heard correct, Mr K," he said, between gasps of laughter. *"Corky set Frodo the task yesterday afternoon."* He paused for a moment before adding, *"The little guy's just finished clearing out all Jackie B's bank accounts together with his investment portfolio. Like Corky just said. Jackie B ain't a millionaire no more. In fact, the guy don't have a bean."*

The news, along with Corky's continuing laughter did as

much to improve Kaine's mood as Cough and Stefan's timely arrival.

"Nicely done, Control. You too, Frodo. Brilliant, in fact. You think of everything. Thanks. Alpha One, out."

Kaine gathered what remained of his strength and pushed himself away from the guard rail. He nodded to Cough.

"I've had enough of this place. Let's go."

"We're with you, boss."

Kaine turned to Stefan and smiled.

"Not you, Stefan," he said. "I've a special mission for you ... should you ... choose to accept it."

Chapter Fifty-Six

Thursday 8th July - Riley Fellows

Eccleshall Way, Stafford, Staffordshire, England

DI Fellows stared up at the workshop roof, counting the bullet holes.

As SIO for the Fabien investigation, he'd been notified the moment Bentley's name had been mentioned during the emergency call. Even though he lived twenty miles further away, he'd arrived at the same time as the ambulance.

The early-dawn light shone through each bullet hole, making the count easier than it had been when he'd first arrived. He counted five holes in the thin, steel roof panels above the loft area, and several more in the storage bays.

Matt Skarrats had beaten Fellows in. He'd taken control

of the crime scene, set up the perimeter, and organised the uniforms. He'd also called in the forensics unit, which had yet to arrive.

"What the hell's happened here?" he asked Skarrats, who stood at his side, looking up at the damage.

He'd rarely seen the DS so lost for words.

"Looks like a bloody gun battle," Fellows added.

"Those holes weren't there on Tuesday," Skarrats said, his lips forming a grim smile. "I'd have noticed."

"I should bloody well hope so, Sergeant. You wouldn't be much of a detective if they'd got past you. What does Dylan say?"

Skarrats shook his head.

"Claims not to know anything about it. Says he found his father lying at the foot of the staircase, unconscious, and with a smashed leg. That's when he called the ambulance."

"Do you believe him?"

Skarrats snorted. "Do I, bollocks. Young bugger's lying through his whitened teeth."

"Yeah," Fellows said. "You can tell he's lying, because …" He paused long enough for Skarrats to add the requisite tagline to the familiar joke.

The DS obliged with a smiling, "…because his lips are moving."

"Exactly. How'd he know Jackie was here overnight?"

"No idea. The bugger ended up giving me the silent treatment."

Fellows sighed. "It figures."

"Did you see the kid, guv?"

"Not close up. Why?"

"He's got a bruised cheek and a cut lip. Bugger's been in a fight. D'you reckon he pushed Jackie down those stairs?"

Fellows thought for a moment before shrugging. "Who knows? Might have done, I suppose."

"Can we arrest him for it? On suspicion?"

"To further our enquiries?" Fellows asked. "Yeah, why not. Go for it."

"Bloody hell!" The ambulance paramedic jumped up and backed away from her patient. Her partner did the same. "Inspector!" she called, pointing down at the comatose Jackie Bentley. "Gun!"

Fuck!

"Stay back," Fellows shouted unnecessarily as both paramedics had kept going until they'd cleared the immediate danger area. "Matt, call for a firearms unit, now."

He should have called in the ARU the minute he'd seen the bullet holes. What the hell was he thinking?

"I'm on it, guv."

As Skarrats dragged a phone from his pocket to call it in, Fellows hurried to face the staircase.

"Where is it?"

The lead paramedic jabbed a finger towards her patient. The muzzle of a matt-black, semi-automatic handgun poked out from beneath him, pointing at the rear wall, under the staircase. Safe for the moment.

"I opened his jacket to check his vitals. That fell out."

"Leave it with me," Fellows said. "I've been on a course."

He winked and added a smile, trying to put the woman at ease. It didn't seem to be working.

"Hurry, please," she said, her voice firm. "He needs urgent treatment."

"Can I move him?"

She hesitated and opened her hands. "If you have to."

"I do."

"Please go carefully."

"Of course."

What else am I going to do?

Fellows pulled on a pair of gloves and kneeled beside the patient. He leaned over and locked the muzzle in place with his left hand, ensuring the gun remained pointed towards the staircase. Then he tugged Jackie clear, fully exposed the gun—a Beretta—and grabbed its grip, keeping his fingers well away from the trigger. He released Jackie and stood, pointing the Beretta well away from anything important.

Skarrats approached but kept a safe distance.

"Firearms unit can't get here for half an hour, guv."

"Okay," Fellows said, wincing. "I've got this."

He removed the mag and cleared the weapon the way the instructors had drilled into him on every firearms course he'd ever attended. The gun reeked of burned gun oil and spent gunpowder.

It answered some of his earlier questions related to the bullet holes in the roof.

"Gun's empty," he told Skarrats and the paramedics.

"Is it safe to approach?" she asked.

"Not yet," he answered. "We need to search him. He might have other weapons."

"Can you do it quickly, please. He's in a bad way."

Fellows stepped back and nodded to Skarrats, who patted Jackie down, quickly and efficiently, keeping well away from the mangled leg.

"He's clear, guv."

Fellows nodded to the paramedics.

"He's all yours."

FORTY MINUTES LATER, the ambulance pulled out through the workshop doors, blue lights flashing, sirens off. A patrol car with two uniformed officers followed them to the hospital. The officers, a sergeant and a constable, would collect Bentley's clothing for evidence and guard the prisoner until he regained consciousness and was capable of being charged with the unauthorised possession of a firearm. The charge carried a minimum sentence of five years. The resulting penalty would be much more severe if they discovered he'd actually shot anyone.

Let's see him buy his way out of that.

Fellows allowed himself a grim smile. They were finally getting somewhere with the case against the Bentleys.

Jackie had seemed almost dead when they loaded him into the back of the bus. White-faced, barely breathing through his oxygen mask, he'd lost a shedload of blood. The puddle of thickening claret spread at the foot of the staircase looked like something Fellows would expect to see on the floor of an abattoir.

After Fellows had dealt with the Beretta, the paramedics loosely bandaged Jackie's leg and hooked him up to a bag of clear fluid. Then the Air Ambulance doctor and emergency paramedic dropped in—literally—and took over. With a generous degree of grunting and straining, the doctor and his oppo twisted Jackie's foot back into general alignment with the rest of his leg and set it in traction for the short trip to hospital. Jackie, unconscious and dosed up to the eyeballs with ketamine, didn't move a muscle throughout the whole procedure.

As the doctor and his team worked on Jackie, a spare paramedic gave Dylan the once over and pronounced him fit and healthy. Fellows ordered Skarrats to arrest him for assault on his father—a holding charge—and take him to the station for booking. It took two burly officers to cuff a vocal and non-compliant Dylan and stuff him into the back of a secure police van. Fellows and Skarrats stood back and watched the unseemly performance in quiet amusement.

Skarrats took his leave, saying, "I'm going to enjoy charging that arsehole."

When the ambulance's blue lights had faded into the distance, Fellows vacated the workshop and called for the waiting forensics team to do their stuff inside. The lead technician—dressed head to foot in a hooded, paper suit, facemask, booties, and gloves—waved her team into action. Each knew their role and was keen to start work after what would have been a frustrating wait.

Outside the workshop looking in, Fellows finally had a chance to breathe. While the medics worked to save Jackie's life, Fellows had walked the interior, taking care to avoid contaminating any evidence. Interestingly, someone else had bled all over the balcony. If they could identify the victim, they might be able to add attempted murder to Jackie's growing list of charges.

Wouldn't that be nice.

Time to report progress to his DCI. Reluctantly, Fellows pulled out his phone.

Where to start?

"Sir?" A woman called to him from a distance.

Fellows turned to face a female officer he recognised but couldn't name. A young PC, trim figure, pretty face, searching, brown eyes, and dark hair. Very nice.

"Yes, Constable ...?"

"Jensen, sir," she answered, tentative. She stayed on the far side of the crime scene tape.

"Yes, Jensen?" He strode forwards and stopped in front of her, the crime scene tape between them. "What is it?"

"Sorry to disturb you, sir. But"—she held up a clear, plastic bag—"a man, a civilian, asked me to give you this. He said you've been looking for it."

The bag contained a small, black object instantly recognisable as a dashcam.

Bloody hell.

Fellows' heart rate jumped.

The dashcam?

"Hold it right there, Jensen."

She looked alarmed but stood still while Fellows tugged on a fresh pair of gloves.

"Okay," he said, hardly daring to breathe in his excitement. "I'm ready. Pass it across."

Fellows snatched the plastic bag from her outstretched hand and removed the dashcam. He paused for a moment's anticipation before pressing the power button. The home screen lit up. He hit run on the queued clip and watched the sixty-second file with mounting excitement.

"Yes!" he blurted out, unable to stop himself. "Gotcha!"

"Sir?" Jensen asked, confusion showing on her attractive face.

"You say a man gave you this?"

She nodded. "Yes, sir."

"What man?" he snapped, searching the expanse of car park behind her.

Jensen pointed off to her left.

"Over there, sir," she said, frowning. "I asked him to wait."

The area she pointed to, near a row of three overfilled dumpsters, stood empty.

"He's gone, sir."

"I can see that, Jensen," Fellows said, trying not to snap. "Describe him."

She hesitated.

"Come on, Jensen. It's an easy enough question. What did he look like?"

Jensen blinked and shook her head as though trying to drag the memory out of the darkness and into the light.

"Er, about your height, sir. Mid- to late-twenties. Brown hair. Brown eyes. Broad-shouldered. No distinguishing features. He was pleasant and smiled as he gave me the package. I didn't get the sense that he was a threat, sir."

"Exactly what did he say?"

Jensen's frown deepened.

"Er, something like, 'Would you mind giving this to Inspector Fellows, please? He's been searching for it.'"

"That's it?" Fellows asked. "He definitely used my name?"

"Yes, sir."

Fellows nodded. "Thank you, Jensen. Are you on nights?"

"No, sir. Earlies."

He nodded. "Good. Make yourself available this afternoon before you go off duty."

She stiffened and looked upset. "Did I do something wrong, sir?"

"No, Jensen," he said. "Not at all." He pointed up to the CCTV cameras attached to the workshop's roof. "I'll need you to go through the footage and point out the man to me. I'd rather like to identify him."

And shake his hand.

Her shoulders relaxed and the frown melted away. She really was a good-looking woman.

"Thank you, Constable Jensen."

"The dashcam, sir," she said. "Is it important?"

"Yes, Jensen. It is."

Unable to stop himself smiling, Fellows turned away and reached for his phone again. This time, he had no hesitation in calling his DCI. No hesitation at all. He finally had something positive to report.

Chapter Fifty-Seven

Thursday 8th July - Early Morning

Location Unknown

A vague passage of time. Heart racing. Breathing shallow.

The constant growl of an engine and vibration of movement.

The hum of tyres on tarmac married to the irregular crump of rubber digging into potholes and rolling over road cracks.

Pain pulsed through … everywhere. Hip, leg, back, head. Buttock.

The leather seats cocooned him in comfort. Kaine floated in a world that rolled and swayed. Rocking him to sleep. To unconsciousness.

Distant voices. Natural and electronic. An urgent tele-phoned conversation.

Why the urgency?

On his left, lights glared and faded behind closed lids. Vehicles roared past. Disappeared into the night.

Something jogged his shoulder. A familiar voice reached to him from the foggy distance.

"Try to keep awake, boss." Cough talking. Soothing. Worried.

"Not long now."

Kaine tried to answer. Failed.

"Forty minutes." Cough spoke again. "Stay with me …"

———

BREATH HELD, Kaine swam through the cold, dark waters, reaching towards the light. Up, up, up. Arms and legs … reluctant to obey his instructions. Cold. So damned cold.

"Ten minutes …"

———

THE WORLD BUMPED AND SWAYED. Rolled downhill. Into the abyss.

"We're here, sir." Cough again.

Why wouldn't he let him sleep?

Movement stopped. The engine cut. Silence.

Above his head, movement. Car door opened. Cold air rushed around his face. Tried opening his eyes but the lids were made of lead. Heavy and immoveable.

"Everything's ready." Different voice. Deep. Dele Hunter.

Hands reached under his arms. Pulled. He slid out … over the soft leather, into the cold. Onto a firm board.

"Take him straight through. The doc's already prepped."

———

"RYAN?"

A voice. Soft. Warm. Familiar. Comforting.

"Can you hear me?"

Lara.

"Y-Yeah," he said, voice thick.

"I've got you, Ryan. You're going to be okay."

What happened to the sea?

He lay on his right side. Unable to move. Unable to turn his head. The comforting darkness returned. Somewhere in the distance, a pendulum clock ticked. Eventually, the ticking faded … to silence.

Chapter Fifty-Eight

Thursday 8th July - Afternoon

Mike's Farm, Long Buckby, Northants, England

Kaine opened tired eyes to a vision of loveliness. Unfortunately, this particular vision of loveliness wore a deep scowl and held her arms folded tight across her chest. Aggressive, defensive, and totally stunning. The sunshine pouring through the sickbay window backlit her auburn hair in a red-and-gold halo.

He licked dry lips with a glasspaper tongue.

"Water?" he croaked, playing for time.

Lara softened her scowl and unfurled her arms. She reached for a glass and held it out. He grabbed it with a shaking hand, sucked on the straw, and enjoyed the caress of the cold liquid bathing his throat.

"Thanks."

She took the glass and set it on the bedside table. The frown returned in all its angry glory.

Kaine braced himself for the onslaught.

"Is that what you consider taking care?" she demanded, jabbing an index finger at his hip. His rump.

"Sorry, love?" he asked, in forced innocence.

"Getting shot in the backside is taking care of yourself, is it?" she said, her delivery clipped.

"Ah, yes. That." Kaine grimaced, swallowed. "Can't we say I was shot in the upper thigh?"

She shook her head.

"The bullet ripped through the outer facia of your left *gluteus maximus*, not the upper thigh."

"But the upper thigh sounds better. Far less embarra—"

"You're a bloody idiot," she snapped.

He opened his eyes wide, feigning surprise.

"I am?"

"You could have been killed. You nearly bled to death."

No kidding.

"But I wasn't killed, love," he answered and showed her a timid smile. "You saved me."

Colour darkened her throat and climbed into her face.

"Going in alone and unarmed was asking for trouble. What's wrong with you? You're never usually so … so rash."

Reluctantly, he nodded. She had a valid point.

"Okay, I'll admit it. Leaving my SIG in the car was a mistake, but—"

"Why?"

He frowned.

"Why didn't I take the SIG?"

"Yes!"

Kaine twisted in the bed. The movement caused a fiery

pain to shoot through his arse cheek and radiate down his left leg and up into his kidney. The meds had started to wear off, but he wasn't about to ask his favourite medic for a top-up dose. At least not until she'd finished hauling him over the coals. And he'd let her. She had every right to be angry. After all, he was angry enough with himself.

He *had* been a bloody idiot.

Again, he grimaced.

"Didn't think I needed the SIG," he answered weakly. "I had no reason to think Jackie Bentley knew about the dongle, and there were no weapons warnings in his police file. I thought it would be safe. A quick in and out, smash and grab."

Lara's face crumpled.

"Ryan ..." Her eyes filled. "I've just lost Mike, and I nearly lost you."

Her words struck like a slap to the face.

"I'm sorry, love. I really am."

He held open his arms. She hesitated for a moment before accepting his offer and falling into a hug. Her added weight depressed the mattress, jogged him, and another lance of red-hot flame shot through his "upper thigh". He stiffened and ground his teeth against the pain.

"Sorry," she said, lifting her head and trying to ease away.

He held her tight.

"No, don't go, love."

"But I'm hurting you!"

"It's nothing." He smiled and kissed the top of her head. "I'll trade a little pain for a 'Lara hug' any day of the week."

She relaxed back into his arms. Her breath warmed his neck and eased his ache.

"I haven't forgiven you yet," she said.

"I know, and I am sorry. Won't happen again."

Again, she pulled away and left a cold spot on his chest.

"You could have been killed."

He nodded. "You already said that."

"And I'll say it again and again." Her eyes glistened, close to tears. "I nearly lost you."

"I know, I know. Next time, I'll be better prepped. I will take my SIG."

At the very least.

She stood and looked down at him.

"Make sure you do."

He gritted his teeth and used his arms to lever himself higher up the bed. The bed in Mike's sickbay … but no … he couldn't think of it like that, not after …

He returned his focus to the present—to Lara. "I promise." He crossed his heart in confirmation.

"I'll hold you to that."

"To be honest, Bentley got lucky. The bullet that hit me —in the thigh—was a ricochet."

"It did the same damage."

Kaine shook his head.

"Not necessarily. Some of the velocity was lost after it struck the steel bracing. It could have been a lot worse."

And probably should have been.

"Brilliant," she scoffed. "You still were taking too much of a risk."

Again, Kaine shook his head.

"Nah. Bentley was a terrible shot. The man couldn't hit the side of a bus—"

"—if he was sitting inside it!"

Bloody hell.

"Ah," he said. "You were listening?"

"I heard every damn word you said. You were taunting them. Talk about tempting fate." The scowl returned. "Have you developed a death wish?"

"No, love. That was calculated to make Bentley angry. To goad him into shooting wild and emptying his gun. Worked, too."

Almost.

"It was horrible. Listening to what you were saying but not knowing what was happening and not being able to do anything to help."

She paused for breath. Kaine tried to think of something to say to placate her but came up blank.

"Then ... when I heard you say you'd been shot," she said, starting up again and looking away. "I was frantic."

"I know what it's like, love. I've been there. Listening to an op go south when you're safe at base, miles away from the action. It's one of the worst things about active service. Bloody horrible. I am sorry."

"I know. And I hear you."

"But I'm trained for action. Decades of experience. You're still so new to this and again, I hate the fact that I've dragged you into my world. For that alone, I will never forgive—"

"Oh get over yourself, Ryan," she said, flicking her hand against his upper arm and catching him with her fingernail. "I'm here now, and I know what I'm doing."

"Ow. That hurts. Is a doctor allowed to hit her patients?"

"When they annoy her, yes. And I'm no doctor. So watch what you're saying."

He raised a hand in apology.

"So," he said, "I was a bit out of it this morning. Can't

remember much about what happened after Cough and Stefan fed me into the car. Care to fill in the blanks?"

Nodding, she edged closer.

"While Stefan delivered your message to DI Fellows, Cough brought you home in double-quick time. It took him just over an hour. It was a wonder he wasn't pulled over by the police. But it did give me a chance to prep for surgery."

"Surgery? Not a simple sew-up job, then?"

Lara shook her head. "You'd lost a lot of blood. Went into hypovolaemic shock." She blanched. "That's why you passed out. If not for Hunter, we might have lost you."

Kaine frowned. No wonder Lara had been so upset. He didn't realise how serious it had been.

"What did Hunter do?"

"He's a universal donor. The only one available with O negative blood apart from me—and I could hardly donate before operating on you. He donated a litre of whole blood. Fortunately, as backup, I had a couple of bags of saline in the fridge for the horses."

"What? You gave me horse medicine?"

She sighed.

"For your information, Ryan Liam Kaine, there's absolutely no difference between saline for human or animal use. None whatsoever."

"Oh," he said, nodding. "That's good news. At least it means I won't start neighing." He shot her a sheepish grin.

Lara closed her eyes and shook her head slowly.

"Oh dear."

"Sorry."

"Don't keep apologising. It'll start wearing pretty thin."

"Okay. Sorry, love."

Kaine arched an eyebrow and felt the resistance of a

sticking plaster. He raised a hand to his forehead and reached for the bandage.

"Don't touch," Lara ordered. "I removed a few splinters. Had to stitch one gash. Leave it alone."

He withdrew the hand.

"You're the boss."

"Yes I am."

Lara rewarded him with a smile that lifted his mood beyond all reason.

"You won't get any argument from me on that score," he said, unable to stifle a yawn as a wave of fatigue washed over him.

Lara leaned closer, did something to the IV line attached to the saline drip sticking into the back of his hand, and tugged the creases out of his bedding.

"Thanks, Doc," he said, sinking back into the pillows. "Would you send Hunter in? I'd like to thank him."

"No can do. Hunter's resting."

Kaine blinked his eyes open, tried to sit, but the ache flared again, and he flopped back down. Sweat formed on his stitched brow. It stung.

"What's wrong? Is he okay?"

"Didn't you hear me? I said he donated a litre of blood this morning. That's twice the recommended limit. I've sent him to his bed with a packet of sweet biscuits and a gallon of water—and with orders to rest until dinner tonight."

Struggling to keep his eyes open, Kaine tried to smile. Failed.

"Will you thank him for me?"

"I already have."

He nodded.

"Thanks. Where's Cough?"

"Don't worry about—"

"Where is he?"

"As soon as he knew you were going to be okay, he returned to Stafford. The twins needed collecting from school."

"Good man, Cough. ... Stefan, too."

"Now get some rest. I'll send one of the guys in with some broth in a couple of hours."

"No need. Give me an hour or two and I'll be up and about."

Lara shook her head in defiance.

"Not a chance, Buster. You have three days' bed rest ahead of you."

"What?"

"Doctor's orders."

"But you've just ... told me you're ... no doctor."

Outside the window a deep baritone sang, "And did the boss, get shot in the arse? Crawling through Bentley's workshop scene!" to the tune of *Jerusalem*. The singer broke off mid-verse and let out a cackle of laughter.

Lara opened the window and shooed the culprit away.

Smiling, Kaine closed his eyes and eased back against the pillows.

Chapter Fifty-Nine

Sunday 11th July - Tobias Fabien

Coppenhall Mews, Coppenhall, Staffordshire, England

Toby rolled his wheelchair closer to the window for a better view. He twisted his hips, trying to ease the cramp in his aching leg. No matter what he did, he just couldn't get comfortable. Still, being at home was a distinct step up from festering in the hospital bed with all its incumbent noise and disturbances. The view was a distinct improvement, too.

Children's happy laughter lifted his mood further and drew his attention to the back garden. He smiled as he took in the sun-washed scene playing out on the freshly mown lawn—mown courtesy of the attentive and helpful Stefan.

The twins chased Emma around the quarter acre of

trimmed grass, playing tag. Where the lass found the energy to run around the garden, two days after her seventeen-hour flight from Harare, was anyone's guess, but she positively glowed with vitality. Seven years Melissa's junior, the family resemblance was astonishing—and unintentionally painful.

Melissa.

Toby drove the sharp hurt into the background and focused on the joy outside.

Having grown to know her via video calls, the twins had welcomed their great aunt as though she were a familiar and long-lost friend. They'd taken to their protectors, too. Stefan, in particular. They treated him more like a favourite uncle than a security guard. They seemed happy. And long may it last.

Mr Coughlin, on the other hand, was polite rather than friendly. Strictly professional. He seemed less comfortable around the twins than Stefan. Probably less familiar with children. As for Connor, Toby had no idea how he'd interact with the twins. Connor covered the nightshift and only appeared after the twins had put themselves to bed.

Toby tensed as Rupert, chasing a fleeter-footed Olivia, took a tumble, barrel rolled, and jumped straight to his feet. He turned to face Stefan, a proud smile on his normally serious face.

"See that, Stefan? See that?" he shouted, beaming with pride. "I did it! Just like you taught me."

Stefan—sitting on a patio chair, watching—smiled and threw the lad a thumbs-up.

"Excellent. And no grazed knees, either."

"You can't catch me, Rupert," Olivia called, from behind the heavy, oak tree at the bottom of the garden.

"Yes, I can," Rupert yelled and took off after her.

Toby hadn't seen him so boisterous in ages. He'd shaken off his long-term lethargy and, at least for the moment, seemed more like his old self. The Rupert from before the disaster. Melissa, bless her kind heart, would have been delighted.

Rupert reached the oak, darted to the left, then the right, and tagged Olivia as she emerged from behind its gnarled bark.

"Tag! Tag!" he squealed.

Toby blinked away a happy tear. He felt stronger than at any time since the crash, although he still had a long way to go. It would be weeks, maybe months, before he could walk again, but walk he would. And without crutches or a stick. Determination and the memory of a promise he'd made himself and Melissa would see him recover. He'd work his socks off. He'd rehab himself into a full recovery even if it killed him.

My darling Melissa. My dear girl.

After the courtesy phone call from Fellows that morning, Toby could finally see a future for them all. A future without Jackson Bentley's intimidation. Without his threat to hurt the twins.

Yesterday, Mr Jeffries had assured Toby that he'd neutralised the threat posed by the Bentleys, but Toby hadn't dared to believe him. Jeffries' assurances seemed too optimistic, unbelievable, but Fellows' phone call had confirmed it.

He could finally move on. Plan Melissa's funeral service.

Melissa and Toby had talked about it briefly when they'd approached retirement age. Having lost her faith years earlier, well before Robert and Helen passed away, Melissa had made it known that she wanted a humanist funeral. They'd even gone so far as to discuss the music they'd play at the service. Uplifting, happy songs that would generate a singalong, a celebration of a life lived to the fullest. Never one to talk about such things, Toby had changed the subject. But now, he'd give everything for a chance to talk to Melissa about anything … anything at all.

A knock on the door drew Toby out of his musings.

"Yes?"

The door opened and a smiling Nigel walked into the room carrying a tray. He had a folded newspaper tucked under his arm.

"Morning, Toby," he said. "Time for your meds. And I thought you'd like a nice cuppa with the local news."

"Thanks, Nigel."

He set the tray down on the occasional table next to Toby and handed him his tablet.

"The online local news," he said, his smile widening. "I think you'll like the lead story. It'll help the medicine go down."

Toby raised an index finger.

"Nigel," he said, "don't you dare burst into song."

The live-in nurse kept smiling. "Wouldn't dream of it, Toby. But read the lead story. You're going to find it … restorative."

"Thank you."

With Nigel standing over him expectantly, Toby tapped the tablet's screen into life and read the banner headline.

Local Man Charged with Murder and Possession of a Firearm. Son Charged with Serious Traffic Offences.

TOBY GLANCED up at Nigel and nodded.

"Restorative indeed," he said and continued reading, barely able to make out the small print through tears of anger and relief.

"LOCAL CELEBRITY, JACKSON 'JACKIE' Bentley, 54, has been charged with a number of serious offences, including the murder of Charlotte Smith, who died in a hit-and-run incident on Hope Way. Bentley, who lost his leg in a bizarre, overnight accident three days ago when he fell down a staircase, has also been charged with possession of a firearm and with assisting an offender.

"Detective Inspector Riley Fellows, Senior Investigating Officer in the case, made the following statement ..."

TOBY READ through to the end of the article that continued over the page.

"IN AN EXTRAORDINARY ADDITION to the story, Bentley's son, Dylan, 21, has been arrested and charged with causing death by dangerous driving when, it is alleged, he deliberately ran a family car off Doom Lane, on Saturday 26th June. The collision resulted in the unfortunate death of ..."

UNABLE TO FINISH THE ARTICLE, Toby lowered the tablet to the side table, face down.

"Unfortunate!" Toby snapped. "'Unfortunate', they say. Bloody rag."

"Easy, Toby," Nigel soothed. "I'm just about to take your blood pressure."

"How dare they call it 'unfortunate'. Murder's what it was. Murder. Plain and simple."

Nigel scooped up the tablet.

"I know it's upsetting, Toby. But I thought you needed to see it."

"Bentley's likely to get off," Toby said, a sense of pessimism overwhelming him. "Both of them."

"What makes you say that?"

"He's a multi-millionaire. They're never sent down. They always get away with it."

"Ah, now," Nigel said, his smile returning, "I didn't tell you the best part, did I?"

"No, Nigel," Toby answered. "You didn't."

"Well, it's like this. Apparently, all Jackson Bentley's money has disappeared. It's a total mystery. No one has any idea how it happened, but Mr Jeffries was telling me that rumours suggest it might have something to do with a man called Ronnie Sutton ..."

By the time Nigel had finished delivering the revelation, Toby's mood had improved so much he couldn't help smiling.

Chapter Sixty

Thursday 15th to Sunday 18th July

Election Night and Afterwards

BBC1: Election Special. Thursday 15th July. 21:56.
"Welcome to the BBC's Election Night Special," the smartly dressed presenter announced. *"With only minutes to go before we are permitted to announce our exit poll results, excitement is rising …"*

ITV1: Election Live, The Results. Thursday 15th July. 22:53.
"Although we are predicting a change of government, the numbers are extremely tight. With a three percent polling error, all results are still possible. Let's cross to Sunderland City Hall, where Daniella Simic is at the count. Houghton and Sunderland south are widely tipped to be

the first constituency to declare a result. Daniella? Can you tell us what's …"

Sky News, General Election Live. Friday 16th July. 05:48.
"With a few dozen results still to be announced, we are now confident that the former leader of the opposition, Sir Kelvin Grant-Smith, will be in charge of the largest political party when all the results are in. Whether he will have a working majority is still too close to call. Our Chief Political Correspondent, George Hadrian is at party headquarters with the latest …"

BBC1, Morning News. Friday 16th July. 09:15.
"Well, after a long, long night of drama, we still don't know who will form the next government. For the second time in three decades, the country wakes to a hung parliament. Sir Kelvin Grant-Smith, leader of the largest single party is expected to make an announcement shortly. Meanwhile, Deputy Prime Minister in the previous government, Richard 'Dickie' Farnsworth, has already admitted defeat in an emotionally charged concession speech in the early hours of the morning. We can now go live to our special correspondent …"

Chronicle & Echo Online, Northants, Sunday 18th July.
"More than one hundred and twenty mourners gathered at The Memorial Hall, Long Buckby, yesterday to celebrate the life of Michael Procter, 74, who passed away peacefully in his sleep on Saturday 3rd July following a long battle with illness.
"Chief Petty Officer Procter served with distinction in the Royal Navy for more than thirty years before retiring to his dairy farm more than fifteen years ago. He is survived by his great-niece, Ms Loren Verger, a veterinary surgeon, who said, "Mike was a gentleman who will be remembered for his wit, his charm, and his bravery in the face of …"

The END.

About the Author

#1 International Best-seller with *Ryan Kaine: On the Run*, Kerry was born in Dublin. He currently lives with Margaret in a bungalow in Nottinghamshire. He has three children and four grandchildren.

Kerry earned a first-class honours degree in Human Biology and has a PhD in Sport and Exercise Sciences. A former scientific advisor to the Office of the Deputy Prime Minister, he helped UK emergency first responders prepare for chemical attacks in the wake of 9/11. He is also a former furniture designer/maker.

kerryjdonovan.com